ENTER THE EDGAR RICE BURROUGHS UNIVERSE™

A century before the term "crossover" became a buzzword in popular culture, Edgar Rice Burroughs created the first expansive, fully cohesive literary universe. Coexisting in this vast cosmos was a pantheon of immortal heroes and heroines—Tarzan of the Apes®, Jane Porter®, John Carter®, Dejah Thoris®, Carson Napier™, and David Innes™ being only the best known among them. In Burroughs' 80-plus novels, their epic adventures transported them to the strange and exotic worlds of Barsoom®, Amtor™, Pellucidar®, Caspak™, and Va-nah™, as well as the lost civilizations of Earth and even realms Beyond the Farthest Star™. Now the Edgar Rice Burroughs Universe expands in an all-new series of canonical novels written by today's talented authors!

THE LAND THAT TIME FORGOT®

FORTRESS PRIMEVAL

EDGAR RICE BURROUGHS®

THE LAND THAT TIME FORGOT®

100 YEARS IN PRINT

50 YEARS ON FILM

1924 ◇ 2024

EDGAR RICE BURROUGHS UNIVERSE™

The Edgar Rice Burroughs Universe is the interconnected and cohesive literary cosmos created by the Master of Adventure and continued in new canonical works authorized by Edgar Rice Burroughs, Inc., the corporation based in Tarzana, California, that was founded by Burroughs in 1923. Unravel the mysteries and explore the wonders of the Edgar Rice Burroughs Universe alongside the pantheon of heroes and heroines that inhabit it in both classic tales of adventure penned by Burroughs and brand-new epics from today's talented authors.

TARZAN® SERIES

Tarzan of the Apes
The Return of Tarzan
The Beasts of Tarzan
The Son of Tarzan
Tarzan and the Jewels of Opar
Jungle Tales of Tarzan
Tarzan the Untamed
Tarzan the Terrible
Tarzan and the Golden Lion
Tarzan and the Ant Men
Tarzan, Lord of the Jungle
Tarzan and the Lost Empire
Tarzan at the Earth's Core
Tarzan the Invincible
Tarzan Triumphant
Tarzan and the City of Gold
Tarzan and the Lion Man
Tarzan and the Leopard Men
Tarzan's Quest
Tarzan and the Forbidden City
Tarzan the Magnificent
Tarzan and "The Foreign Legion"
Tarzan and the Madman
Tarzan and the Castaways
Tarzan and the Tarzan Twins
Tarzan: The Lost Adventure (with Joe R. Lansdale)

BARSOOM® SERIES

A Princess of Mars
The Gods of Mars
The Warlord of Mars
Thuvia, Maid of Mars
The Chessmen of Mars
The Master Mind of Mars
A Fighting Man of Mars
Swords of Mars
Synthetic Men of Mars
Llana of Gathol
John Carter of Mars

PELLUCIDAR® SERIES

At the Earth's Core
Pellucidar
Tanar of Pellucidar
Tarzan at the Earth's Core
Back to the Stone Age
Land of Terror
Savage Pellucidar

AMTOR™ SERIES

Pirates of Venus
Lost on Venus
Carson of Venus
Escape on Venus
The Wizard of Venus

ERB UNIVERSE™

EDGARRICEBURROUGHS.COM

EDGAR RICE BURROUGHS UNIVERSE™

THE LAND THAT TIME FORGOT®

FORTRESS PRIMEVAL

MIKE WOLFER

Includes the bonus novelette

WEIRD WORLDS™
VOYAGE INTO TERROR

EDGAR RICE BURROUGHS, INC.
Publishers

TARZANA   CALIFORNIA

THE LAND THAT TIME FORGOT: FORTRESS PRIMEVAL

© 2025 Edgar Rice Burroughs, Inc.

WEIRD WORLDS: VOYAGE INTO TERROR

© 2025 Edgar Rice Burroughs, Inc.

Cover art by Daren Bader © 2025 Edgar Rice Burroughs, Inc.
Map of Caprona and The Favonia and The Favonia Cargo Crawler
illustrations by Mike Wolfer © 2025 Edgar Rice Burroughs, Inc.

ERB Universe Creative Director: Christopher Paul Carey

Special thanks to Julio Arellano, Daren Bader, Kathleen Bonnaud, John Burroughs, Win Scott Eckert, Janet Mann, James Sullos, Jess Terrell, Cathy Wilbanks, Charlotte Wilbanks, Mike Wolfer, and Bill Wormstedt for their valuable assistance in producing this book.

First paperback edition

Published by Edgar Rice Burroughs, Inc.
Tarzana, California
EdgarRiceBurroughs.com

ISBN-13: 978-1-945462-76-4

- 9 8 7 6 5 4 3 2 1 -

CONTENTS

Il Continente Insulare di Caprona

Band-lu

Kro-lu

Galu

Sto-lu

Isola di Oo-oh

Kro-lu

Bo-lu

Grande Mare Interno

Alu

Band-lu

Sto-lu

Oceano Sud Pacifico

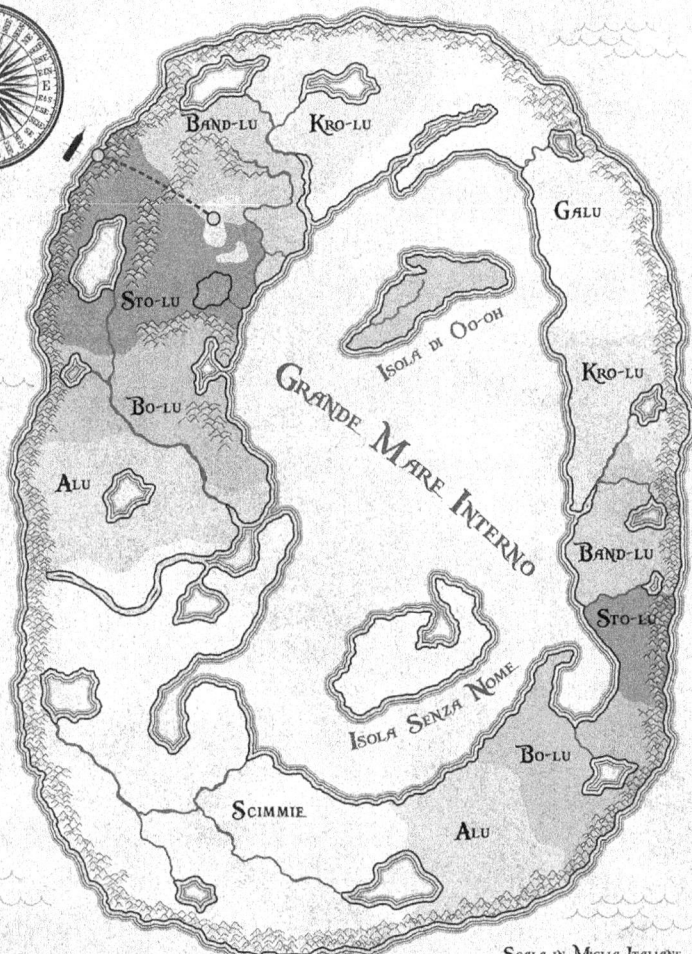

Isola Senza Nome

Bo-lu

Scimmie

Alu

Isola - 130 miglia X 180 miglia

Lago - 60 miglia X 120 miglia

Scala in Miglia Italiane.

10 20 30

THE LAND THAT TIME FORGOT ®

FORTRESS PRIMEVAL

PROLOGUE

THE HAUNTING SONG OF THE SOUTH PACIFIC whistled through the rigging above the deck of the *Pegaso* as the galleon's mainsail billowed full with the ocean's icy breath. As the majestic ship plied across the brine at a fair clip, the captain looked east to the towering gray walls of the continent around which his vessel had circumnavigated for the past eight days. The golden brushstrokes of dawn painted the vault of heaven, and past the undulating waves behind the ship, the somber charcoal silhouette of the island bisected the far horizon, where ocean met sky.

The dark landmass watched the departing seafarers in mute arrogance. Its secrets had been preserved.

By the helmsman's order, the crew secured the halyards, as tacking of the mainsail was unnecessary. The prevailing winds that belched forth from the granite walls of the landmass inexplicably radiated from the newly christened isle of Caprona and were more than sufficient to propel the galleon on a direct course toward the open sea. One of fanciful imagination might postulate that the singular intent of the continent was to repel any who might venture toward its forbidding palisade.

The wind that flowed outward from the dour granite facade of Caprona was not the only curiosity the crew had observed that defied the principles of nautical science. Over three weeks past, the *Pegaso* had sailed east-southeast after weighing anchor in Tahiti and bound for the Strait of Magellan. The vessel enjoyed calm seas before encountering a heavy fog on the twelfth day. What followed were forty hours of cleaving an atmospheric shroud, throughout which the navigational astronomer discerned unusual deviations in the magnetic compass. To facilitate the correction of its inaccuracy, the device was dismantled, cleaned, and lubricated, but the effort did not yield a satisfying result. Barely visible through the swirling gloom, the sun validated the direction of true north, yet the compass needle adamantly pointed toward what the astronomer knew to be east-southeast.

At last, the vessel sheared through the cloying mist that draped heavily upon the water. To the astonishment of the *Pegaso*'s crew, a mere half mile before them the foot of the lofty cliffs of an undiscovered continent stretched across the horizon.

After eight days of abject vexation, Captain Enzio Caproni leaned against the taffrail at the ship's stern as the *Pegaso* departed from Caprona. He lowered his glass. There was no more to see now than during the past week, nothing but the island, roughly a hundred and fifty miles in diameter, mile upon mile of unremarkable, towering rock. The tantalizing secrets of Caprona's topography—if the island possessed any secrets—were concealed atop what appeared to be a great, flat plateau at least a thousand feet above sea level. At the ship's fore, the cutwater of the *Pegaso* cleaved through the waves dotted by pale chunks of floating ice while the triangular wake behind the vessel quickly dissipated, as if Neptune himself were eager to erase all evidence of the vessel's passing.

Immediately upon the island's discovery and by order of Captain Caproni, the helmsman had brought the ship to within a stone's throw of the rock wall. Sounding performed by the seamen revealed no shelf on which to weigh anchor at the base of the lichen-spotted cliffs. A gig with a small crew was launched to inspect the foundation of the continent, but no adequate beach that might accept a landing party could be located. By all appearances, the precipitous wall extended vertically from the very floor of the ocean, penetrated the foam, and rose into the clear skies above.

Over the following week, the *Pegaso* cruised the island's perimeter twice, and a full accounting of Caprona's shoreline was charted. As days passed without sighting a break in the formidable wall, the piqued curiosities of the captain and his crew curdled into frustration. Any natural riches that might await on the elevated plateau would remain undiscovered.

Mixed feelings welled within Enzio Caproni as he savored one last look at the unknown land. The discovery of the mysterious isle had upended the entire trajectory of his exploratory mission. The charted course of the *Pegaso* was to follow in reverse the oceanic route blazed by Captain James Cook during his first Pacific voyage. Only recently and upon the conclusion of Cook's third voyage, the ship of the renowned English explorer returned to its home port in October 1780 after the murder of its celebrated captain in the Sandwich Islands. At that time, Caproni was amid preparations for an expedition of his own and cast off from the isle of Sicily on March 9th of the following year, intent on extending trade proposals—or at the very least, cordial introductions—to the colonies of New South Wales, Nova Zeelandia, the Sandwich Islands, and ultimately Alta California.

The discovery of Caprona had changed everything. The continuation of the voyage to the proposed ports of call was now of far less value than an immediate return to Sicily to officialize the immense island's discovery before Sir John Acton and King Ferdinand III. Captain Enzio Caproni had no way of knowing that his dreams of grandeur, of his name being recorded in the annals of history, would never materialize.

As the *Pegaso* dipped slightly to port, Caproni gripped the taffrail and instinctively leaned away from the roll. It was then that, for the briefest of moments as his attention was full upon maintaining his balance, he thought he spied a dark shape rise above the gray foundation of Caprona. The island was receding from clear view, making it difficult to determine what he saw, but as quickly as he noticed the thing, it dropped from sight. It could not have been a bird, as at the ship's current distance from the isle something that small would not be discernible.

Captain Caproni reckoned that what he had seen must have been at least as big as a man, or possibly larger, if he had truly seen anything at all.

1
THE EVE OF EMBARKMENT

MARINA CAPRONI HELD HER FACE SKYWARD, her skin warmed by the midmorning sun. She breathed deep the salty sea air and opened her eyes to the lofty masts of the *Redenzione* poking at the white clouds that drifted lazily over the isle of Sicily. Indeed, the galleon was majestic, but Marina had never been overly enamored of seagoing vessels.

Her ambivalence toward nautical conveyances was unusual, as several generations of Sicilians considered her family name synonymous with the shipping industry. The hearts of sailors were helpless to the romantic stirrings that rolling waves engendered within them, but Marina did not so eagerly embrace the charms of the open sea. With her own eyes, she had seen what calamities could befall those seduced by the siren call of adventure upon the water. She had seen how easily a seaman's dreams of glory could be crushed by men of power and influence, like the dreams of her revered grandfather, Captain Enzio Caproni. For that matter, Marina did not even care for the taste of fish, broiled, fried, or otherwise.

Yet, there she stood, dockside to the galleon on which she would depart the following morning for a voyage into the unknown.

Like minnows in a raised trawling net, deckhands flitted about the stately ship in pre-embarkment activity. Among the masts, sinewy, half-clothed men tied lines and replaced worn roping and tackles, and the mainsail and jibs were inspected luff to leech one last time to ensure their integrity. The arduous task of scraping the hull of barnacles was completed and the

1

fresh pitch applied the past week to the seams between the deck planks had dried thoroughly. Only minor preparations and the completion of the loading of supplies needed the crew's attention before they enjoyed one final night of pre-voyage revelry.

Ocean-bound sailors regularly gathered in the seaside taverns of Palermo on eves of departure, but the crew of the *Redenzione* was prohibited from leaving the dock that night. By the captain's order, the men could imbibe to their hearts' content aboard the vessel, but venturing into the village of their births was strictly forbidden. Because of the recent rash of scarlet fever reported in the seaport, the captain would allow none of his crew to mingle with locals for fear of encouraging the disease to accompany them on their journey.

Every man knew his role, and each performed his tasks diligently in the rising morning heat. That did not prevent them from snatching an occasional glance at the striking young woman who watched them work, the woman who—they were informed—would make the voyage with them. However, each crewman knew not to let his gaze upon the woman linger too long, as undue attention to her would not sit well with the protective instincts of the ship's captain. Every sailor appreciates a pretty face, but the crewmen aboard the *Redenzione* considered their promised wages much more attractive than "the Rose of Palermo," as some privately called Marina.

The appellation bestowed upon her was neither insult nor disrespect. Although they were born to different castes, Marina Caproni and the boys of the village had played and grown up together, and most of the young men of Palermo looked upon her as a sister, regardless of their fantasies of asking for her hand in marriage. None dared tempt fate, however, as they all remembered how Marina had rendered Giovanni Pellegrino unconscious with a single punch to his face after he made a most ungentlemanly advance upon her during the Feast of Saint Rosalia a few years past. Attending to the stitching of the mainsail, Giovanni sheepishly waved down to Marina and smiled. His missing front tooth was a daily reminder that the temper of Marina Caproni was not to be tested.

Marina would not consider herself a mere passenger on the impending voyage, and even though she had reservations about the objective of the excursion, she had offered her assistance to the crew and captain in every way possible. She stroked the neck of the horse that had pulled her wagon down onto the wharf, then rounded to the back of the cart and began to unload the crates she had delivered. The tart aroma of freshly picked lemons and oranges from the sprawling groves surrounding Palermo swirled about her as she neatly stacked the crates to one side of the gangway that crossed the water to the *Redenzione*. Immediately, two burly deckhands began transferring the wooden cases below the ship's deck, where the citrus fruits were stowed in the hold alongside substantial stores of salted beef, cheeses, the ingredients for ship's biscuits, and other victuals, all in quantities sufficient to feed the crew for an extended period at sea.

The young woman seemed unconcerned with the by-product of her labor. She wiped her dirty hands upon her front, lifted the hem of her dress and petticoat, and crawled into the back of the wagon to retrieve the last item to be delivered. Exercising unusual gentleness, she hefted the wicker container by its leather handles and carried it to the end of the gangway. There, she opened the basket and released four rather large cats that scampered down the short stairwell to the deck of the galleon. Within seconds, all four felines had disappeared through the companionway. The rodents in the deepest recesses of the cargo hold would not be happy about this latest development.

"Get away from my ship!" a youthful but commanding voice rang out, but just as promptly, the author of the utterance laughed heartily. "Everyone knows that women bring nothing but bad luck to sailors!"

"As do captains who are barely old enough to tie their own bootlaces," Marina shouted, not even deigning to raise one of her dark eyebrows as she shot the sarcastic response over her shoulder. She did not need to turn to identify her verbal assailant, as she had been entertaining the voice of her younger brother since his birth.

Fausto Caproni motioned frantically and Marina joined him on the quay. "Keep your voice down!" he whispered harshly. "The last thing we need is for you to tarnish my reputation among the crew."

"Oh. A reputation. I wasn't aware you had earned one," Marina responded teasingly, after which she hugged her brother and gave him a warm smile. Fausto reciprocated, punctuating his cordial welcome by calling her a foul name. Marina called him something far saltier, and together they laughed.

Marina paused thoughtfully, eyeing Fausto from head to toe. "That's new," she said, tipping her nose toward her brother's hat.

"What's new? Oh. That," he concluded.

"That and everything under it," she noted dryly. Marina ran her fingers over one of the bright red plumes adorning the bicorne that sat upon her brother's unruly black locks. As a doting seamstress would inspect the dress of a countess during a fitting, she tugged at the wide scalloped collar that lay over Fausto's crimson short coat and vest. She narrowed her eyes and continued quite pointedly. "Silk. How much did that cost?"

Fausto knew his sister was not requesting an answer; she was demanding one. In situations like this, he did what he always did. He took a conversational side step.

"You're always so concerned about money," he said in an even and indifferent tone. "I've taken care of everything. Everything is paid for. You know how hard I've worked to raise the funds for this voyage," he added. "You know what this means to me, to our family name. The least you can do is allow the ship's captain a new traveling wardrobe."

Marina nodded in acquiescence. The journey upon which they would embark at the next dawn was a lifelong dream of Fausto's. He had followed in the footsteps of his father, and his father before that. Fausto had worked with extreme diligence his entire life, and now, at twenty-five years of age, he was at last competent to captain a ship far beyond the Mediterranean, where he had previously honed his nautical skills under the tutelage of their father. Had his parents not both succumbed during the cholera outbreak that ravaged Sicily two years past, they would surely have beamed in approval of Fausto's ambition. In truth, Marina was proud of her brother, but always did she cleverly rein the charging horses of his enthusiasm with cautious reason. Fausto was not reckless, but he did overlook minute details that screamed for attention, or so Marina believed. But that was beside the point; she had questions. And she wanted answers.

"*Everything* is paid for?" Marina asked directly. Fausto's pause told her all she needed to know. "Fausto," she said quietly, more from disappointment than scorn. Her gaze took in the totality of the ship as the sailors labored arduously upon its deck. "You do have enough to pay the crew, correct?"

Fausto walked to the rear of the wagon and sat on its bed. He patted the wood to his side and, with a sigh, Marina joined him.

The siblings had discussed Fausto's plan at great length over the years. At the end of each conversation, wherein Fausto adamantly swore he could rediscover the fabled lost continent of Caprona, Marina could not say that she believed the veracity of the fantastic tale she and her brother had heard throughout their childhood. Composed of mere speculative scenarios based on the remembrances of his grandfather, Fausto's whimsical theories were about to be tested. The captain's duty of ensuring the security of fifty-three crewmen—and also, at her insistence, his sister—weighed heavily upon the young Sicilian, but within him burned the faculty of youthful conviction. He would succeed, and before the end of summer, they would stand atop Caprona's plateau and claim the land in the name of the Kingdom of the Two Sicilies, an act of which Captain Enzio Caproni had dreamed fifty-five years prior upon discovering the island continent in September 1781.

But Fausto knew that before celebrating his glorious, pre-destined achievement, he must be truthful with his sister. As she sat at his side, he raised his hands to chest level and softly requested, "Don't hit me." The fiery, raven-haired young woman scowled. "Marina, promise not to hit me," he repeated.

She rolled her eyes and crossed her arms. That was as close to a confirmation that she would not strike him as Fausto could hope to receive.

"I've worked my fingers to the bone," he began, "and why? Because throughout our entire lives, and before we were even born, people have laughed at Grandfather, at his story. They say he was a liar. Or crazy. You know how that disturbed Father, but even he never knew the truth for certain. So, we're doing it. We're going to find Caprona. That's why," he reminded her, "the *Pegaso* has been rechristened the *Redenzione*."

Redemption.

Marina turned her full attention to her brother,. Fausto recognized the look in her eyes that urged him to get to his point. "You want to know about the money," he continued. "The sale of Father's smaller boats—which we both agreed to—barely covered the expenses of refurbishing the *Pegaso* and paying the crew's salaries for their work thus far."

"Then where did you get the money to pay for the construction of . . . *that*," Marina said, motioning toward the odd, canvas-covered object that lay perpendicular across the deck of the *Redenzione* just past midships. It was a large thing, long and rectangular, its edges jutting twelve feet past the port and starboard bulwarks. Its shape was roughly that of a small ship, but the object was one-quarter the length of the galleon, with a long tarp securely tied around it to preserve the integrity of its mystery.

"That took a bit of creativity," Fausto admitted, before revealing a facet of his plan that he had kept a closely guarded secret, not even shared with his sister. "You know the monastery, the one at Monte Gibilmesi?" Marina nodded, obviously intrigued by this unexpected turn in her brother's explanation. He continued: "When I used to haul deliveries from the port to the monastery, I learned a lot about what goes on there. If you think that behind its walls live cloistered monks who recite prayers all day long, you would be wrong. The majority up there are rich men who have fallen into varying degrees of trouble with the law. Rich men in debt. Rich men who owe taxes. Rich men whose wives mysteriously died, after which they hastily found sanctuary by joining the monkhood. Behind those walls, the law cannot touch any of them. Despite what you might expect of monks, they are still rich. Now, I happen to know there are two factions within the monastery, constantly at odds with one another. Last summer, I arranged a meeting with one of those factions and explained that I was exploring private funding for a seagoing expedition. In return for their financial backing, I promised that during the voyage I would investigate the securing of certain—shall we say—peculiar and exotic commodities."

Marina's eyes burned with fury. "Fausto . . . you didn't . . ."

"And I will not, Marina. I would *never* do that. I only said I would 'investigate' the possibility. I made no promise to actually deliver. Now . . . here is where it gets more interesting. I made my proposal, but when the other faction within the monastery heard about it—by 'accident'—they would not be outdone and matched the offer made by their brothers. The combined donations of the two factions paid for the new construction," he revealed, "but still, there's not enough left to cover the crew's wages for the duration of the voyage."

Marina frowned and repositioned herself. "Aren't we

supposed to weigh anchor tomorrow morning? How in the world can you . . ."

"So," Fausto interrupted, "I've had to make even more creative arrangements."

"What arrangements and with whom?" she asked sharply.

Fausto took a deep breath and exhaled through puckered lips. "You promised not to hit me," he reminded her.

"I did no such thing." Marina was livid. "Tell me what you've done, Fausto."

He had but to speak a name for Marina to comprehend his plan. "Maria Christina," he said resolutely.

Years ago, when the Caproni siblings were children, one of their frequent playmates was a little girl named Maria Christina. All three were quite fond of one another, and they shared many joyful remembrances of chasing each other through the streets of Palermo, lazing in the orange orchards on sunny summer days, and fishing from the pier at the Caproni shipyard. As they matured, and through a string of calculated social engagements, Maria Christina eventually found herself betrothed to King Ferdinand VII of Spain. Upon her husband's death in 1833, however, Maria Christina of the Two Sicilies was enthroned as Queen Regent of Spain, overseeing the rule of the kingdom, as her daughter—the rightful heir to the throne of the Spanish Empire—was still but a child.

"After the *Redenzione* sets sail tomorrow morning," Fausto explained, "our first port of call will be Valencia. From there, it is a day's travel overland to Madrid, where I have been granted an audience with the Queen Regent. Our childhood friend," he added, to emphasize his point. "Then, depending on the outcome of my conversation with Maria Christina, the *Redenzione* will either sail through the Strait of Gibraltar and into history, or I will be right back here in a few days, sitting on this dock, dreaming of what might have been."

"This is very important, Fausto," she said, her voice adopting the tone of a patient teacher speaking to a child. He held in esteem both her shrewdly analytical mind and her unbiased opinions, as she was right more often than not and Fausto had learned to pay the strictest attention to her words when she spoke to him thus.

"Did you tell the Spaniards about Caprona?" she asked with a bluntness that barely concealed what might have been panic.

Fausto smiled. "I'm not stupid, Marina. I did not tell them," he assured her. "I've not breathed a word about it to any of the crew, either. Like I said, I'm concerned about my reputation. All anyone knows is our general sailing route and that I'm seeking to establish import and export partners across the South Seas. But nothing about Caprona. If I inform the crew of the true intent of this voyage and we find nothing . . . No. I'm not that stupid."

"I would hope not," Marina replied. "But you've said nothing to the Spaniards?"

The young captain furrowed his brow. "No," he emphatically spat.

"Good," she replied. "After everything Sicily endured when we were under the rule of the Spaniards . . ." She paused and shifted to another thought. "Whatever the result of your meeting in Madrid, we must always remember the sword of a colonialist is as bloody as that of a conqueror."

The following morning, Marina's words reverberated in Fausto's recollection as the *Redenzione* weighed anchor and began its voyage west toward Spain.

2

THE NEGOTIATION

FAUSTO AND MARINA CAPRONI marveled at the intricate painting that adorned the ceiling of the *saleta oficial* adjoining the royal throne room within the Palacio Real de Madrid. Above their heads, cherubs and saints lounged among the clouds and bestowed their blessings upon those within the expansive parlor. The Queen Regent's meeting chamber within the Spanish Royal Palace was opulent, the walls of crimson adorned with enormous gold-framed portraits of the figureheads of the House of Bourbon. Spain's former monarchs were immortalized in oils, and the austerity evoked by their unblinking gazes was tacitly affirmed by the halberd-bearing guards stationed at each entrance to the chamber. After all, Spain was currently in the throes of a civil war and the Queen Regent would be protected at all costs.

Beneath a chandelier of ostentatious proportions, Queen Regent Maria Christina greeted her childhood friends with warm embraces. It had been years since the Sicilian natives had seen one another, and the passage of time had touched them all favorably. They smiled and laughed, and marveled at how each had physically matured since their days of making mud pies under the watch of the soldiers of Maria Christina's father, King Francesco I of the Two Sicilies.

As the three rekindled their childhood friendship amid giggles and exuberance, the elbow of Marina discreetly found Fausto's ribs. "I beg your pardon, Your Grace," he sputtered after the prodding of his sister, who alerted him that a prolonged informality of his demeanor would be indelicate, if not outwardly rude. "I'm so taken by your beauty that my manners have failed me," he offered apologetically.

The Queen Regent laughed. "I would be disappointed if you were not still the same boy I knew years ago, Fausto Nefasto," she said. It had been years since anyone had called him by the pet name, bestowed upon him by Maria Christina in her younger days. Because of Fausto's propensity for always finding himself in trouble of one kind or another, she had tacked the rhyming word "nefarious" to his first name. To his chagrin, the jest was exceedingly accurate, and he eventually accepted it as a badge of honor.

Maria Christina turned her attention to the diminutive white-haired elder who accompanied the Capronis. Fausto introduced Leonardo Ricci, who removed his hat and bowed deeply, then knelt as he kissed the hand of the Queen Regent.

"And what is your role aboard the *Redenzione, il signore*?" she asked.

"I am the ship's astronomer," Ricci explained with pride. "I served the great Captain Enzio Caproni; his son, Captain Marco Caproni; and now his son, Captain Fausto Caproni."

The Queen Regent beamed at Fausto. "Such an experienced navigator will surely keep you out of trouble, I trust," she said with a smile, before turning to the heart of matters. "As you know, the throne is endangered by the Carlists, so I would like to apologize in advance if our reunion is cut short by pressing matters of state. Captain Caproni, your letter requested an audience with me to propose a unique trade opportunity. Tell me more about it." Maria Christina motioned for them to sit at the gilded marble table at the room's center.

Fausto composed himself, intertwined his fingers, and rested his hands upon the tabletop. During his teenage years, he had worked as a fish peddler along the seafront of Palermo, and now, in his proposal to the Queen Regent, he employed every ounce of the shrewd salesmanship he had learned in his youth. The success of the voyage—in truth, the very voyage itself—would hinge upon it.

Maria Christina sat patiently as she absorbed the deluge of words pouring out of Fausto, who extolled the virtues of himself, the *Redenzione*, and the astronomer, Leonardo Ricci. The Queen Regent smiled knowingly upon hearing the elder's credentials recounted. Fausto had paraded the venerable astronomer before her to lend prestige to his offer. The young captain was not an experienced orator, a seasoned negotiator, or a diplomat, but no one could deny that his proposal illuminated great potential value to the Spanish Empire.

After several minutes, Maria Christina cordially halted Fausto's speech to reassemble the puzzle pieces he had laid before her into a smaller, more coherent picture. "This is all quite intriguing," the Queen Regent admitted, before adding, "but one must understand we are a country at war with ourselves. Resources must be cautiously allocated in defense of the throne. What you propose is the enlistment of Spanish soldiers . . ."

Fausto stopped Maria Christina abruptly. "You misunderstand, Your Grace. I do not need soldiers. I simply need money."

Marina rolled her eyes at Fausto's unrefined admission. However, there was no other way for her brother to express his intent, for it was the truth.

"Yes, I need money, to pay the wages of my crew for the duration of our voyage," he stated fearlessly. "But what I extend to the Kingdom of Spain is the possibility of riches that would—perhaps within a matter of only months—overshadow what paltry sum you provide to me. Very simply, the *Redenzione* will explore the islands of the South Pacific Ocean in search of ideal ports as yet uncharted, and with luck, lands for which there are no petitions of ownership. Once found," Fausto continued, "those locations will be claimed in the name of the Kingdom of the Two Sicilies, under written agreement affixed with your royal seal that Spain will be granted preeminent annexation rights from my kingdom, along with equal and undisputed access to all suitable ports."

Marina furtively glanced in the direction of Ricci, who sat with arms folded and a smile upon his lips, barely visible beneath his bushy white mustache. Her elder was just as impressed with Fausto's words as she was. At that moment, Marina felt immense pride in her younger brother. *Perhaps he does know what he is doing*, she thought.

The room grew uncomfortably silent as the Queen Regent digested Fausto's offer. Marina would have been lying if she professed not to have been sweating from nervous anticipation, as all about her Spain's former monarchs seemed to glare down in judgment from their richly adorned frames.

As they awaited a response from the Queen Regent, Marina recalled the heated conversation she had with Fausto on their short voyage across the Mediterranean, from Palermo to Valencia. As they stood upon the quarterdeck, Marina had asked one pointed question of her brother: "Why did you not first secure a deal with Maria Christina through courier before putting the entire crew through their paces, preparing the ship for an extended voyage, buying all of the supplies for that voyage, and even asking these men to say farewell to their families . . . All without knowing if we would ever make it past Valencia?"

"You're never happy unless you're belittling me, are you, Marina?" he had shot back loudly, unconcerned that the crew might hear. "Why didn't I do things the way you suggested? Because it's not your expedition! I'm the captain, not you! I *know* I'll get the money and I *know* we'll find Caprona.

"You wouldn't understand," he had added, bringing his anger down to a low simmer. "We were both teased our whole lives for having a 'crazy' grandfather, but you're not a man. You could ignore the taunts, but I could not. I have to prove myself, every day. It was expected of me to captain a ship, and now I do. And I'm also expected to be crazy, like everyone thinks of our grandfather. I have to prove that I'm *not* crazy, Marina. You have no idea what it's like, every day, trying to live up to everyone's expectations while also fighting to prove wrong all of your detractors."

Marina knew her brother well and understood that his emphatic outburst sprang not from any resentment he held toward her, but from uncertainty, fear, and the burden of responsibility with which he had saddled himself. She had seen this kind of behavior from Fausto innumerable times in her life, and knowing its roots, she had learned to ignore it. What she could not ignore were the next words he uttered.

"Besides," he had added, "you're just a woman. No one expects anything from you, other than to be a wife and to bear children, neither of which you've accomplished, by the way."

Her brother's venomous barb had shocked the young Sicilian woman. Her question to him subsumed no malice, and her only intent was to assist him in cataloging the various aspects of the voyage into a cohesive and logical master plan. When necessary, she would suggest adjustments to the scheme already set in motion to steer it toward more favorable results. But this personal attack upon her— an embarrassing and juvenile outburst—had been absolutely without merit.

Fausto might have had self-induced turmoil boiling inside of him, but Marina's glare would have chilled anyone to the core. "I see. I'm *'just* a woman,'" she had growled. "You don't know how lucky you are to be a man. But one day you'll grow up. I *know* you will," she had said, parroting his earlier words. "Maybe then you'll appreciate which of us is most unfairly judged. Until then, you'll remain exactly what you are now . . . not a brave sea captain but a frightened little boy."

Marina stormed off, caring not one iota how deeply her words had injured her brother.

Now the voice of Fausto jostled Marina from her

uncomfortable reverie. "Your Grace," Fausto offered, "with Spain's loss of Alta California to Mexico, this could be an opportunity to expand the empire while you serve as Queen Regent. Think of that." His appeal to the reputational vanity of Maria Christina was transparent but did not fall on deaf ears.

The ruler meditated on the facts before her. At length, her voice broke the silence of the chamber. "It will be done," she proclaimed, "but not without a few minor concessions."

For another three-quarters of an hour, Marina and Leonardo Ricci sat patiently as Fausto continued his negotiations with Maria Christina. It was not a comfortable wait; sunlight streaming through the east windows had crept toward the table around which they sat until it ultimately shone directly upon the visitors. It was not just the rising temperature of the chamber that most vexed Marina and Ricci; rather, it was the contractual request made by the Queen Regent that caused them the most discomfort. Fausto pushed on stalwartly until, at length, a full agreement was struck with terms favorable to both parties.

"What do you think?" Marina whispered to Ricci as Maria Christina and a complement of guards accompanied the visitors to their carriage at the palace portico.

Ricci adjusted his hat to protect his bald pate from the midday sun and smiled beneath his walrus-like mustache. "It is only one additional passenger on our voyage, and his inclusion is at the Queen Regent's request. That follows logic. Spain is making a monetary investment in this voyage, so proper oversight must be exercised. However," the wizened astronomer added, "when the survival of the crew rests upon the integrity of a ship's sails, one must beware of moths. You understand me, Marina?"

"I do," she said firmly. Marina turned and smiled at her brother, who escorted the Queen Regent five paces behind her. Under one arm, Fausto carried a tightly scrolled parchment, belted by a length of blue silk ribbon. He returned his sister's smile and tauntingly mouthed the words, "I told you." Fausto had secured exactly that which had brought him to Madrid.

"You've grown into quite a handsome man," the young widow commented, tightening her grip upon Fausto's elbow as they strolled. The newly minted captain might have been idealistic, but he was not naive, and the flirtatious compliment did not appear to weaken his resolve. "You said yourself that the Kingdom of the Two Sicilies has not endorsed or funded or even knows about your impending voyage," Maria Christina continued. "Are you certain that you would preclude the *Redenzione* from sailing under the colors of the Spanish flag?"

Of the many things Fausto's father had taught him, diplomacy was not one of them. Marco Caproni was at all times direct, even to the point of abrasiveness, but one could not say that he ever uttered a word of dishonesty. His son had absorbed this trait from his father, but he had learned to temper the boorishness of uncomfortable truth by instilling diversionary tactics into tenuous conversations, thus allowing him to answer questions without actually answering them. He did just that with Maria Christina, but this was more than that; what he said next was uncharacteristically guileful in light of Fausto's agreeable behavior throughout the morning's visit.

"You say you have but two children, Your Grace?"

Maria Christina's eyes widened involuntarily. It was a simple inquiry, save for the inclusion of the word "but." Three letters changed the entire context of Fausto's remark.

Fausto was not proud of what he had just done. It was immediately apparent that his royal host had been struck by the underlying—yet unspoken—implication of his question, one whose underpinning was decidedly personal for the Queen Regent. Further utterance was unnecessary.

Fausto had just revealed that he knew Maria Christina's darkest secret.

Only three months after the death of her husband, Ferdinand VII, Maria Christina had secretly married a sergeant of her Royal Guard in December of 1833. A public scandal would have erupted had it been revealed that the mother of two and the widow of the country's revered king had been courted and married in such a short period. Rumors of a romantic entanglement that predated the expiration of the monarch would surely have spread like wildfire had the truth of her covert marriage been exposed.

But far worse than the possibility of ribald gossip were the dark murmurings of political manipulation that were already circulating through the austere halls of Madrid's royal palace. In what the King's inner circle casually dismissed as incorrupt happenstance, Ferdinand VII had enacted the Pragmatic Sanction in 1830, allowing the crown to be passed for the first time to a female heir upon his death. This act prevented Ferdinand's brother, Carlos, from ascending to the throne after the King's demise, and amid cries of illegality, Carlos and the loyal Carlists had for years attempted to overthrow the rule of Queen Isabella, the young daughter of Queen Regent Maria Christina. Any public recognition of Maria Christina's new marriage would dilute her power and precipitate the deposition of the young monarch and her mother, the Queen Regent.

As is all too commonplace among the elite, the aristocracy of Spain guarded Maria Christina's secret in a desperate attempt to remain in power. Compounding the endeavor to keep the marriage undisclosed was the existence of two daughters the Queen Regent had birthed to her new husband, Agustin Fernando Muñoz. The children were never overtly acknowledged by any among the court in legitimate conversation; they were dutifully attended to and, if necessary, identified as nieces of Maria Christina upon inquiry. Still, uncomfortable truths do have a stubborn propensity to rise to the crest of gossip.

Somehow, Fausto Caproni had learned of the Queen Regent's secret espousal and children. Although the young captain made no overt threat to expose the confidential matter, Maria Christina surely recognized that her childhood friend had just issued a resolute denouement to their mutual arbitration. Her silence assured Fausto that she would not proceed with further overtures of negotiation.

Unflustered, the Queen Regent bade farewell to her three guests, and Maria Christina chuckled apathetically as the Sicilians' carriage departed the Palacio Real de Madrid on its journey back to Valencia and the waiting *Redenzione*.

3
ON THE HIGH SEAS

THE CALLS OF THE GULLS searching for their dawn repast echoed across the still Mediterranean waters. There was an odd quality to the air that morning, a heaviness imposed by the thick blanket of fog that lay across the port of Valencia and swirled among the seagoing vessels docked along the quayside. Among the ships was the magnificent *Redenzione*, awaiting the loosing of ropes that moored it to shore, and the captain's order to weigh anchor on its voyage into history. Although the crew was of sound temperament and eager for departure, one final order of business arranged by Captain Caproni on the previous afternoon would need to be addressed. Very few on the ship's deck knew exactly what that deal entailed.

Santos Ignacio was one of a mere handful among the crew who knew the intimate details of that contract. He stood at the *Redenzione*'s bulwark and anxiously watched the morning's activity upon the dock. Immediately upon the captain's return to the *Redenzione* the evening before, Santos was informed of Fausto's arrangement with the Spaniards. The contract drawn with Queen Regent Maria Christina did not sit well with the quartermaster, but despite his misgivings, Santos had dedicated himself to the Caproni family and would follow Fausto's commands to a word. That did not mean he would blindly obey Fausto, a man fifteen years his junior; rather, Santos would tap his vast seafaring experience and do all in his power to steer the young captain toward the soundest judgments. Just as he had faithfully served Captain Marco Caproni, so too would Santos Ignacio serve Caproni's son.

Marina glanced toward Santos as she, Fausto, and a complement of crewmen traversed the gangway and assembled on the fog-shrouded dock. The Sicilian woman's face bore a mien of neutrality as her eyes connected with the steely blue gaze of the quartermaster. The look exchanged between the two confirmed their mutual agreement on the matters of the morning, the details of which Marina had shared the night before with *Señor Santos*, as she respectfully addressed him.

Just after sundown of the previous day, Marina, Santos, and Leonardo Ricci conferred in private while Fausto was belowdecks, attending to the rearrangement of the ship's cargo to accommodate additional supplies to be delivered to the *Redenzione* the next morning. During their meeting, the three agreed to support the captain's decisions, although each had misgivings about Fausto's contract with the Spaniards. Ocean voyages were fragile affairs. If the entire crew displayed nothing less than an obsequious support of the ship's captain, even a mundane voyage could be doomed to failure. Thus, the three agreed they would not taint the minds of their fellow seamen with their apprehension. The unease of Marina, quartermaster Santos Ignacio, and astronomer Leonardo Ricci would remain confidential; however, the three agreed to exercise vigilance against any sign that their fears were not just paranoid delusions.

Fausto's customary smirk of self-confidence widened as the distant clatter of horses' hooves drew nearer, ushering the arrival of a black carriage bearing royal markings. It crept through the morning gloom and came to rest before Fausto and the assembled crewmen. Marina shot a final glance at Santos, who watched from the bulwark with intense scrutiny. She turned her attention to the Spanish dignitary who marched toward her and her brother.

"I am Colonel Don Carlos de Valdez, of the Royal Guard of Queen Regent Maria Christina," the Spaniard announced. Draped in the finery of his station, Valdez wore a white coat adorned with golden accents and epaulets, pale blue trousers with a wide stripe of yellow-gold fabric running the length of the outer seams, and a tall, black hat whose brim nearly concealed his eyes. A sheathed rapier depended from his left hip. Although gunpowder muskets and flintlock pistols had become standard weapons among Spain's military forces, there was nothing more reliable than cold steel in the hand of an expert swordsman. By design, the officer's uniform exuded an air of authority that could not be denied, even by the skeptical Marina.

The young ship's captain seemed similarly impressed. "Colonel, I am Captain Fausto Caproni, and this is my sister, Marina," he said with a tip of his hat.

If Fausto had hoped to impress the Spaniard, his effort was lost on Valdez, who was distracted by matters disassociated with business. "I am pleased to make your acquaintance, *Signora*," he said, his voice oozing with barely concealed lasciviousness. "And yours as well, Captain," he added as he leaned forward to respectfully kiss the back of Marina's hand.

Ever cognizant of Marina's fiery disposition, Fausto quickly redirected the conversation. "It is my honor to have you along on our journey, one that will surely be a most lucrative endeavor," he said pridefully.

The colonel collected himself and ran gloved fingers over his black mustache and goatee. "The weight of a man's purse matters little to a soldier," Valdez flippantly remarked. "The worth of a military man is measured in honor and devotion to Queen and country. As such, I will do all in my power to ensure your voyage is safe, and you may count on my complete devotion to duty."

The siblings glanced over the broad shoulders of the colonel as the sound of hoofbeats again clapped through the fog. From behind the swirling veil appeared a long wagon drawn by a team of horses, which was reined to a halt behind Colonel Valdez.

"What is this?" Marina asked suspiciously.

The colonel motioned to the wagon and the eight uniformed and armed soldiers it carried. By his command, the troops disembarked and assembled into two regimented rows behind their superior.

"I don't understand," Fausto announced. "Why are they here, Colonel?"

"They're going with us," Valdez declared.

Marina instantly bristled at the thought. "With all due respect, Colonel Valdez, this was not part of the agreement with the Queen Regent."

"And how would you know, little flower?" he responded condescendingly. "Were you present at the negotiation?"

"Yes, she was," Fausto interjected, abruptly halting his response. Marina knew Fausto had learned from their father, and even more so from Quartermaster Ignacio, that a cool head must always prevail. Methodical and casual responses to unforeseen developments were always most tactful. Given the protracted voyage that lay ahead of them, Marina was heartened as Fausto resumed. "What is your intent, Colonel?" Fausto asked with calm detachment.

With sincerity, Valdez explained that Queen Regent Maria Christina had assigned to him the duty of serving as the official envoy of the court on the voyage of the *Redenzione*. However, because of the colonel's prominence, his safety must be ensured. Thus, he had handpicked a contingent of soldiers to accompany him, but he explained with utmost assurance that each man had mastered combat skills, and each was an expert marksman. In addition, three of his soldiers had served in the Spanish Marine Infantry. Valdez assured Captain Caproni that the combined experience of the Spaniards would enhance the capabilities of the *Redenzione*'s cannoneers, and their addition to the ranks of the crew would in no way impact the voyage or stores, as the Spaniards had arrived with wooden cases of food and provisions.

Fausto looked to Marina, who glared back at him. He turned his eyes to Santos Ignacio behind the bulwark and received a similar unspoken response. But the die had been cast and the adventure of which he had dreamed his whole life lay tantalizingly before him.

"Then I welcome you and your men aboard the *Redenzione*, Colonel," Fausto graciously acceded.

At their captain's bidding, the quayside sailors began unloading the many wooden cases from the wagon's bed and carrying them into the cargo hold of the ship. These included the soldiers' chests of personal belongings, which were delivered to the cabin belowdecks that would serve as the Spaniards' living quarters for the duration of the voyage.

About an hour later, the sailing master hailed the wheelman to position the rudder hard to starboard as the raised mizzen sail caught the cool morning breeze, and after executing a textbook tact turn, the majestic *Redenzione* was underway. Atop the forecastle, the salty breath of the Mediterranean tossed Marina's black locks. Beside her, Fausto stood silently as the siblings gazed past the bow to the wide open sea before them.

"This will be a historic adventure," he said. To Marina's ears, the statement rang more of self-reassurance than optimism.

Marina smiled at her brother, then wrapped an arm around his shoulder to pull him to her. "Despite how I pick at you, I trust you, Fausto," she said proudly.

She turned to look down toward Santos Ignacio, who was conferring with Leonardo Ricci on the main deck. The two men appeared to be contemplating the large canvas-wrapped object that straddled the ship's width and was securely roped in place across the deck. The quartermaster noticed Marina's gaze, and with a wink assured her that should she still harbor any misgivings about the voyage, he would be watching her back, along with the back of her headstrong and idealistic brother. The gesture was just what she needed at that moment, as so many unknowns lay before the entire crew.

Above the frothy wake, the gray cloud of seabirds abandoned its pursuit of the *Redenzione* and glided back toward the dock, leaving the ship to cleave the deep blue expanse of destiny.

Marina Caproni had never partaken of a sea voyage of such protracted duration. Although she was loath to admit it to Fausto, Marina spent the *Redenzione's* first week at sea in quite an indelicate fashion, alone in the captain's quarters where she slept. Within three days, however, she had happily gained her sea legs, and—much to her relief—her digestive balance eventually grew accustomed to the rolling of the elegant ship upon the waves.

As oceanic expeditions go, the voyage of the *Redenzione* was relatively tranquil and uneventful, at least while traversing the open water. Upon the third day, Fausto Caproni's ship made port in Santa Cruz on Tenerife, and after an overnight stay that was not without incident, the *Redenzione* began a long trek skirting the western coast of the African continent. Following thirty days at sea, the proud ship anchored at the Cape of Good Hope to take on fresh water and fruit. Colonel Valdez and his soldiers enjoyed liberty on shore, as did select members of the crew. The reputation of Captain Caproni's charges remained unblemished during their shore leave, unlike that of the Spaniards.

During the *Redenzione's* sojourns at both Santa Cruz and the Cape of Good Hope, Colonel Valdez insisted his men dress in full regalia while ashore. As representatives of the Spanish Empire, the colonel and his men would accept nothing less than full respect from the residents of the port towns. That attitude was justifiable at Tenerife, as the Canary Islands had been under Spanish rule for over three centuries. However, concerned sailors reported to Captain Caproni that three of Valdez's soldiers had engaged in a brawl with several of the island's native Gaunches at a port tavern. Decades had passed since Spain conquered the island and assimilated Tenerife's culture and people into its own. That did not mean that resentment of oppression did not still simmer within the hearts of the Gaunches. Harsh tavern rum gave that hatred full throat. Thus, on only the third night of the voyage and well past midnight, Santos and his men had returned to the safety of the *Redenzione*, leaving behind five beaten and bloodied natives.

Things had gone even more poorly at the Cape of Good Hope. There, Colonel Valdez and his men strode into a dockside tavern in a display that was nothing less than arrogant. As the night wore on, a scuffle abetted by inebriation resulted in the disappearance of a Dutch trader after some manner of disagreement with the Spaniards around a backroom roulette table. The following morning, a local constable visited the ship and questioned the colonel about the missing Dutchman, but he took no action, as there was no evidence of a crime. The *Redenzione* quietly and hastily set sail as a creeping unease settled within the stomachs of Fausto and Marina Caproni. Neither could ignore the dubious reputation of their military passengers, nor would they for the duration of the voyage.

Thirty-four days had passed since the *Redenzione* departed the Cape of Good Hope, and Leonardo Ricci calculated that the Australian coast would be in sight by the following day. After sailing from the tip of Africa, the voyagers had benefitted from "The Roaring Forties," the strong easterly winds that hastened the passage of vessels across the southern Indian Ocean. True to Ricci's astrological prediction, the tan hues of the continent, which until recent years was known as New Holland, came into view along the eastern horizon upon the rise of the morning sun.

On deck, the chill dawn breeze whistled through the rigging as the seamen tended the canvas sails. Deep within the bowels of the *Redenzione*, Marina pulled open the heavy bulkhead door. With her oil lamp held high, she entered the cargo hold to begin her usual morning search for her four special friends. It was not so much in response to their names being called out but simply the sound of Marina's voice that spurred the felines to happily spring from their hiding places. The quartet eagerly bestowed their affection upon her at every given opportunity, but Marina did wonder if that behavior was indicative of the felines' adoration of her or because she daily brought them fresh water and dried and ground fish to supplement the spoils of their mouse hunts. Within seconds, Mezzanote, Stivali, and Poca were circling her feet and singing to her in their little cat voices, but Sovrano, the largest of the four, had yet to appear. It was unusual that he did not greet her, since the big orange ruffian had the heartiest appetite among the clowder.

The whereabouts of the fourth cat were soon revealed, as a loud thump, a feline squeal, and cursing in the Spanish tongue erupted from the recesses of the tightly packed cargo hold. Marina rushed down the center aisle to the back of the chamber, which was brightly lit by several lanterns. She rounded a corner composed of stacked wooden crates to find two of the *Redenzione*'s sailors on their hands and knees, inspecting the inner hull for signs of water leakage, and an angry Spanish soldier, still cursing and his rapier drawn. It was Sergeant Lago, one of the least likable members of the Spanish contingent. The source of his rage was immediately apparent as he thrust his blade between two crates in an attempt to skewer the large orange cat. The animal moved like quicksilver and bolted around the far side of the cargo containers, past Marina's feet, and into the darkness behind her. The angry Spaniard turned to give pursuit.

"Stop that right now!" Marina screamed. She read in his expression that he had not expected anyone to question the actions of a Spanish soldier, least of all a woman. "How dare you!" she added, her cheeks flushed with anger.

On the ship's flooring, the pair of sailors laughed to themselves as they pretended to focus on their work. This only further enraged the soldier, who grabbed one of the men by the arm and roughly pushed him onto his back. The sailor looked up at Sergeant Lago and grinned. "What are you going to do now? Kick me?"

"And miss, like you did with that cat?" added the other sailor. Together, the two seamen laughed, unintimidated by the soldier's violent temper.

"I don't know what transpired before I got here," Marina growled, "but those cats are my charges, here by order of Captain Caproni. If you so much as harm a whisker on any of them . . ."

The sailor whom Lago had assaulted righted himself and chuckled, pointing a finger at the fuming soldier. "He nearly tripped over the cat, took a wild kick at it, and struck a crate instead. So much for Spanish marksmanship." The sailor laughed, revealing a missing front tooth.

Marina smiled at Giovanni Pellegrino and regretted altering his smile several years ago. He was a good man, if uncultured, but she was comforted knowing that should she ever face peril, Giovanni would vigorously defend her. However, Marina was about to show all those assembled in the musty cargo hold that she was quite capable of defending herself.

Infuriated, Sergeant Lago advanced upon Marina with fire in his eyes and his sword held out menacingly at waist level. "I don't care if you are the captain's sister," he spat, "you will show me the proper respect."

But the young Sicilian woman would not be intimidated. To the surprise of all who witnessed it, Marina's hands shot toward Lago's sword arm. With one fluid motion, she pressed his elbow inward with one hand and twisted his grip on the sword hilt counterclockwise with the other. With a yelp of pain, the soldier could do nothing but watch the unnatural rotation of his forearm. The surprising action forced Lago to release his hold on the rapier, which Marina deftly recovered, its tip pointed directly at the soldier's chest. He had been disarmed in the blink of an eye, and the young woman's unbroken glare informed him that if she willed it, he would be dead.

The two sailors were now on their feet, and Marina threw the rapier down the darkened aisle in the direction of the bulkhead. "Do not cross my path again, Sergeant Lago," she hissed. "And if any of the ship's cats go missing, I'm going to come for you. Do you understand?"

Without a word and deeply humiliated, the Spaniard brushed roughly past Marina and retrieved his sword from the floor planks. Lago coughed as he stomped up the creaking wooden stairs leading to the upper decks and at length, the sound of the angry soldier's heavy footfalls was swallowed by the dank bowels of the ship.

Giovanni bowed deeply to Marina in acknowledgment of the incredibly entertaining show she had just performed. *"Bravisima, signora!"* he exclaimed, laughing.

Unfazed by the incident, Marina adjusted her sleeves and cuffs and tested the fullness of her dress at her hips. "Do you know why he was down here?" she calmly asked Giovanni.

"He was inspecting those," the sailor responded, throwing a thumb over his shoulder. Behind him were multiple large crates wrapped in burlap that the Spaniards had loaded into the hull.

"What is it?" Marina inquired.

"Gunpowder, mostly, from what I hear," Giovanni explained. "You'd think they were planning on going to war."

The other sailor spoke warily. "I don't like it. One stray spark and the whole ship will go up," he cautioned.

The trio was suddenly unbalanced as the *Redenzione* took an abrupt turn to starboard, proceeded by the sound of an explosion that reverberated through the cargo hold and emanated from one of the decks above. There was no mistaking it; one of the ship's cannons had been fired!

4
DEADLY WATERS

MARINA RUSHED THROUGH THE BULKHEAD, followed by the two sailors, and the three sprinted up the stairs to the gun deck. There, they were met by a scene of frantic activity. The smell of sulfur hung heavily in the chamber. The gun master was shouting to his crew, who cleared gunpowder residue from the barrel of one of the massive iron cannons. Through the raised hatches, other crew members anxiously watched something transpiring on the open water.

"What is it?" Marina shouted to the gun master.

"Pirates, or privateers," the man shouted back, before returning his attention to the ship's defenses. His men worked diligently, and within what seemed mere seconds to Marina, the crew had reloaded the cannon barrel with gunpowder, inserted the munition, sealed the barrel with wadding, and run out the muzzle through the open hatch. The same process was being performed on two other massive guns, sitting patiently in their carriages, and primed to deal death to the enemy.

"Are we being fired upon?" Giovanni excitedly asked.

The gun master replied with steel in his voice. "We didn't give them the opportunity," he shouted, before instructing the gun crew, "Prepare to fire!"

Marina covered her ears as she rushed from the chamber and felt the percussion of the shot in her very bones. She flew up the stairway, then burst through the companionway to the open quarterdeck. There she found Fausto in full command of his ship. In two heartbeats—between fearing for her life and flashes of panic—Marina glimpsed Fausto's true soul. Before her stood not the man-child, not the pesky little brother pulling her hair, not the insecure boy practicing a fabricated clearness of vision. Marina's eyes beheld a genuine man of action. But as she rushed toward him and he turned to her, his face told another story. His voice rang out in words of command but his visage was racked with fear.

"Get below!" Fausto shouted to his sister. "Go!"

"I will not!" she yelled, as her dark eyes spied their attacker.

It was a three-masted galleon, much smaller than the *Redenzione*, but much faster than the grand vessel. The pirate ship had sped from the east, concealed by the brilliant morning sun on the horizon. The vessel had turned sharply to fall into the wake of the *Redenzione*, where its captain surely hoped to disable the larger ship's rudder with cannon fire. Quartermaster Santos Ignacio immediately recognized the tactic and stealthily fed his concerns to the young captain, along with a course of action. Fausto seized upon Santos' recommendation, and rather than try to outrace the pirates, the *Redenzione* turned to expose to the aggressor not only its flank but the row of heavy iron guns behind its starboard hatches.

A low rumble erupted from the pirate vessel. A cannon had been fired, but luck was with the *Redenzione*. The ball passed above the deck and splashed harmlessly into the water on the ship's port. Captain Caproni's gun crew replied in kind with a shot of their own, but a rising swell beneath the Sicilian ship spoiled their aim and the ball flew too high.

"Captain!" shouted Colonel Valdez as he rushed onto the quarterdeck and pointed wildly to something out at sea. "On our port side!"

Four ship lengths distant, a second pirate vessel was approaching. Marina watched in horror as the new arrival began a slow arc to allow it to bring its guns to bear on the *Redenzione*.

They were now trapped between two aggressors.

Fausto made a Herculean effort to conceal his alarm as he shouted to the Spanish officer. "You said some of your men have naval experience . . ." He did not have to finish his sentence. Colonel Valdez saluted the captain and sprang into action by gathering his men and rushing them below to the gun deck. There, the Spaniards took up the cannons on the ship's port and began priming them for firing at the attackers.

"Regardless of the outcome," the burly gun master shouted to Valdez, "I salute you!"

A starboard cannon barked again, shaking the entire room. For this shot, the gun crew had succeeded in predicting the rise and fall of the waves, holding the linstock to the touch hole only at the precise moment, as there would be a delay between the ignition of the gunpowder and the ball's expulsion from the barrel. The crew's calculation was impeccable, and the projectile struck dead-on. But they had not fired an ordinary ball. Instead, the crew had loaded the gun with a chain shot. The two linked balls rocketed through the attacker's rigging and struck the ship's main mast, the swinging, chained projectiles splintering the upper boom. With a thunderous report, the mainsail and the weighty timber that had held it aloft crashed to the deck of the marauder.

The Spanish soldiers had been working feverishly and the fruit of their effort could not have been borne soon enough. By making several unsuccessful shots at the *Redenzione*, the second pirate vessel had calculated the range to strike the galleon. A direct hit would be achievable within seconds.

On deck, Fausto again yelled to his sister. "Marina! Please! Get belowdecks! It's not safe up here!"

"It's no safer down there, Fausto," she yelled back in response. "Besides, who's going to keep you out of trouble?" Under different circumstances, her jest would not have rung so hollow.

Fausto looked to port as a plume of smoke erupted from one of the second raider's hatches. Instinctively, he leaped at Marina. The two hit hard against the rough deck planks a fraction of a second before grapeshot shredded the taffrail against which they had been standing.

Again, Fausto yelled, but his words were unintelligible as three of the *Redenzione*'s port cannons fired at once. Colonel Valdez's boasts about his soldiers' wartime prowess were not exaggerated. One ball hit the keel of the second raider just above the water line; another smashed a great hole at the level of the gun deck; the third struck the poop deck just above the captain's chamber, sending a shower of splintered wood into the air. The midships shot must have caused chaos within the confines of the gun deck and upon its stores of gunpowder. Within seconds, a fiery explosion erupted from the pirate ship, throwing shredded planks and debris into the fathomless depths.

With one of the pirate vessels afire and the other crippled without a mainsail, the *Redenzione*'s crew took to the sheets and the majestic galleon pulled away from its attackers, leaving them to their fates far from the distant shore.

Fausto helped his sister to her feet. He gripped both of her shoulders at arm's length to examine her. "Are you hurt?" he sputtered. "Were you hit?"

Although shaken to her core by the near-death experience, Marina collected herself in the blink of an eye and reciprocated Fausto's concern. To their relief, both siblings came through the attack without a scratch. Likewise, after a quick survey, it was determined that none of the crew—nor the Spaniards who helped defend the ship—had suffered injury.

With a smile, Marina retrieved Fausto's bicorne from the deck and placed it over her brother's black curls. "I see that I'll need to teach you how to care for an expensive hat," she teased. Their laughter dissipated in the midsea winds as the *Redenzione* cut through the waters toward the Australian coast.

5
DISCOVERY

F OR ANOTHER TWENTY DAYS, the *Redenzione* rode the winds south and east around the great Australian continent. The ship's encounter with—and subsequent disabling of—the pirate vessels three weeks prior must have sent an adequate message to other cutthroats in the region, as they suffered no further molestation by sea raiders. At length, the penultimate segment of the voyage concluded with the Sicilian vessel docking at Port Jackson on the eastern shore of the massive continent. That this was the last stopover before the hopeful discovery of the expedition's secret destination was known only to Fausto, Marina, Santos Ignacio, and Leonardo Ricci; all others on board, including Colonel Valdez and his men, held the belief that the *Redenzione* would sail on to explore ports around the entire Pacific perimeter. With luck on Fausto's side, such would not be the case.

The crew replenished the ship's stores of victuals and fresh water at Port Jackson, and the welcomed shore leave included no ill behavior by the Spaniards. The *Redenzione* soon weighed anchor and pursued an easterly course. Upon the fourth day out of Port Jackson, the galleon encountered a squall that roared from the northwest, but the experienced crew easily mastered the rough seas. Only clear skies lay ahead for the subsequent week.

After one hundred and nineteen days upon the water, Marina had adjusted marvelously to life at sea and was as sure-footed upon the ship's rolling deck as any of the four mousers she had brought along on the voyage. She had also grown accustomed to seeing Fausto in a new light, as a ship's captain, but she still held some nervousness regarding her brother's ability to lead others. To Marina's chagrin, her intuition whispered that Fausto continued to exhibit a subservient reliance on the advice of others, primarily that of quartermaster Santos Ignacio. However, young Captain Caproni was learning and was slowly—if not surely—following a path that might someday lead to complete self-assurance and decisive leadership. That they had made it at least this far on their voyage was a testament to Fausto's ambition.

As was a common sight aboard the *Redenzione*, Mezzanote and Sovrano scampered in pursuit of Marina as she approached the portal to the captain's chamber. Wherever she went, one or more of her feline charges would follow her loyally. Anyone who knew Marina Caproni would tell you that for some reason, animals absolutely adored her.

She skillfully balanced the silver platter in one hand while reaching for the door handle of the quarters she shared with her brother. She had long since grown weary of Fausto's reminders that he, as the captain, and she, as the captain's sister, should avail themselves of every convenience that their stations afforded them. One of those entitlements was the ever-present service of the cabin boys, but Marina was adamant that she would never conduct herself as one superior to those who served her brother. If she desired a meal, she would trot down to the galley and fetch it herself.

"Lunch is served, Captain," Marina announced cheerily as she pushed the chamber door closed with the heel of her boot after Mezzanote and Sovrano slunk into the room and disappeared under one of the beds. Expecting her brother to be alone, Marina was surprised to find him in the company of Leonardo Ricci, Quartermaster Ignacio, and Colonel Valdez. It was not unusual for Fausto to conduct meetings within the private chamber he shared with his sister, but this was the first time Marina was aware the Spanish military man had been welcomed to the inner sanctum. It was readily apparent that Valdez was the impetus for the unexpected gathering.

Brilliant midday sunlight streamed through the lead-sealed windowpanes and across the men seated at the dark oak dining table. Only Colonel Valdez stood, hovering over the shoulder of the elderly astronomer and the maps spread on the table before him.

The colonel was in midstatement. "The course of Captain Cook's voyages in this area were here, here, and here," he said sternly. "According to what my men have observed, our present course appears to be thus." He tapped on the topmost map, the point indicated being farther south and much farther east of the traditional routes. "Cook thoroughly charted this area on his second voyage, and he found nothing but open seas. Why, then, are we here?" The Spaniard's accusatory tone could not be mistaken.

Marina was uncertain what had transpired before her entrance to the chamber, but she reckoned that her countrymen might benefit from a moment of disruption in which to collect their thoughts. Purposely, she knocked a wooden cup from the tray she carried. It clattered loudly on the floorboards.

"I'll speak no further in the presence of a clumsy serving wench," Valdez snarled.

Fausto's face flushed. "I'll warn you but once, Colonel. Mind your tone," he said measuredly, his voice dropping in pitch.

"And I will warn you but once of the same, Captain Caproni."

Throughout the voyage, an uneasy tension existed between the Sicilians and the Spaniards. Extended periods on the water tend to bring out the best in some, while in others it inflames only the worst of human behaviors. In this case, the long years of poverty and distress the Sicilians had endured under cruel Spanish rule were beginning to manifest as short tempers directed at the soldiers. Left unchecked, that form of emotional imbalance could evolve into impulsive violence.

Instinctively, Marina looked to the quartermaster, whose cool head she had come to admire and trust. Santos sat silently with his arms crossed over his chest. His gaze had no focus as if he were in deep contemplation. Marina had always sensed something hidden beneath the seaman's customarily placid exterior. He possessed an unspoken confidence, as well as a quick wit and diplomatic poise that could defuse any volatile situation. Words were his weapons, and he wielded them in elegant strokes. Marina anxiously awaited a response from Santos—any response.

Much to her disappointment, Señor Santos said nothing. But upon closer inspection, Marina discerned that while his arms were casually crossed before his lower chest, both hands of Santos Ignacio were inconspicuously clenched in fists.

Leonardo Ricci noticed as well and quickly spoke out. "Please, gentlemen," he offered peaceably. "Let me put your mind at ease, Colonel." The old astronomer wiped his hand across the map to flatten it, then adjusted his spectacles and placed a shaky finger upon the parchment. "See here . . . we have indeed veered slightly southward. That was entirely intentional, as my atmospheric observations and the surface water temperature indicated we were on course to intersect with a midsea storm. We are simply circumnavigating the danger," the old man explained, looping his finger over the surface of the map, "before resuming the route of Captain Cook." Leonardo Ricci removed his spectacles, intertwined his fingers before him on the table, and smiled curtly at Valdez. "Have you any other concerns, Colonel?" he asked.

Valdez placed his hat upon his head and methodically slipped on the gloves that had hung over his forearm during the discussion. "I have no other concerns," he replied sharply. "As of now."

As Valdez exited the chamber, Marina called out to him in a light, singsong tone of utter sincerity. "Colonel, would you be interested in a midday meal?"

The Spanish officer paused at the doorframe. The conversation had been tense, but the query of the captain's sister rang with notes of reconciliation, if not an unspoken willingness of the woman to serve him. Colonel Valdez surveyed Marina's beauty from head to foot and back again. "I am a bit hungry," he admitted, smoothing his mustache with his fingers.

"Then hurry down to the galley," she imparted mockingly. "There's usually quite a line of sailors that forms this time each day."

Without a word, Valdez slammed the door behind him.

After the sound of the Spaniard's retreating stomps dissipated, Fausto laughed. "You are a wonderful liar, my friend," he said, patting the elderly astronomer on the shoulder. "And you," Fausto directed at Marina, "you know just how to twist a knife."

"Why thank you, Captain," Marina laughed. "Mother taught me many valuable skills far beyond the gentle arts of sewing and cooking."

Ricci once again balanced his eyeglasses on the bridge of his nose and perused the unscrolled nautical chart. "Since we are all gathered and the maps are right here, we do have something to discuss, just among the four of us. According to my calculations, we are very nearly at the general location where Captain Enzio Caproni got his first glimpse of Caprona."

Marina and Fausto looked at each other with excited smiles. Over the years, Marina's attitude about the existence of the continent had been one of cautious optimism, but now she could not help but thrill at the prospect of encountering the fabled land. For her entire life, she had heard the tales told by her grandfather and father, all repeated religiously by Fausto. Those stories might at last be validated. However, Marina had to prepare mentally for a less triumphant outcome, and she hoped with all her heart that should they find nothing, the disappointment would not crush the spirit of her younger sibling. Fausto had invested a great deal into the voyage, both emotionally and financially. For his sake, Marina secretly prayed that the hand of divinity would intercede in their search for the legendary isle.

Santos lifted the apron draped over the silver tray Marina had delivered to the captain's table and removed a biscuit from beneath. "I want to be honest with everyone," the quarter-master said between chews, then turned his attention to Fausto, and to Marina, who had taken a seat near the windows. "As you know, I greatly respected your father. During my years of service to him, we talked many times about Caprona. Your father was a man of the sea and a man of great intelligence. But never did he propose an expedition such as this. Had he done so, I would have happily followed him. But he never did. I think I know the reason that was so. He had witnessed what had happened to his father when the court of public opinion declared him a charlatan. Nearly all the people he loved and respected had abandoned Captain Enzio Caproni, including those who had faithfully served him for decades. His reputation—and his life—was destroyed by Caprona."

The old astronomer withdrew a gold compass from his pocket and inspected it. "There is truth to that observation, Santos, but other factors led to my dear friend's downfall. Enzio was an outspoken critic of the government of the time. He felt the people of Sicily were overburdened by taxes. It was the truth, but the government officially censured and ostracized him for his political beliefs. His sensational report of an unknown continent only compounded his problems. I know. I was there." Ricci squinted at the compass and put a finger to his lips. He rose from his seat and shuffled over to the chamber windows overlooking the vastness of the South Pacific.

"True," Santos responded, "and you were also aboard the *Pegaso* when Enzio supposedly discovered Caprona."

Ricci continued to examine the compass in the sunlight. "Not supposedly, my son. He *did* discover Caprona." Form-ulating mental calculations that had no relation to the topic at hand, the old man looked out to the sea behind the ship, pointed at the horizon, thought to himself, and then turned to raise a finger toward the front of the cabin. Again, he consulted the compass. Marina had always been impressed with Leonardo Ricci's ability to divide his attention between two subjects at once, while meticulously absorbing himself in both. But whatever it was he was mentally calculating, she did not know.

Santos continued his thought, respectfully sidestepping the old astronomer's conversational idiosyncrasies. "The point I would like to make," Santos explained, "is that at some point, questions will be asked if we sail without a definitive direction. Further, if we find nothing, how long do we continue to sail in circles? The Spaniards already suspect that something is amiss. Soon enough, Colonel Valdez will become harsher in his demand for answers."

But Ricci was still lost in thought. He looked about the room, again glanced out of the windows, and again looked to the front of the cabin. He consulted his compass a final time before breaking his silence.

"We'll not have to be concerned with a bit of any of that," the astronomer assured his companions with a sly smile. "Come with me to the deck."

Within minutes, the four stood upon the forecastle at the bow of the *Redenzione*, their eyes upon the great oceanic expanse before them. The first observation to strike Marina was the relative calm of the waters; there were no swells, and no whitecaps embellished the tops of the waves. All was eerily still, which was highly unusual that far out at sea. The sun was still visible, but its glow was dulled by a mist that undulated above the waves. The fog, in itself, was intriguing. Leonardo explained that the atmospherics favorable for the creation of fog were the temperature of the air far exceeding that of the cold water beneath it, a condition not to be found in the Pacific's southernmost waters. The air was cold and the wind sporadic, causing the sails to deflate and sway listlessly from their masts, providing just enough propulsion to ensure the galleon's forward momentum. Even the Sicilian flag, proudly adorning the tip of the foremast, had ceased its dance and produced barely a flutter.

"You see? It is exactly as the *Pegaso* experienced," Ricci excitedly announced, passing the compass to the ship's captain. Fausto looked at the device and confirmed the astronomer's finding: Despite the position of the sun, the compass needle indeed pointed to the direction that was clearly not north. Astoundingly, some unknown phenomenon had abrogated the preeminent pull of the Earth's magnetic pole.

The deckhands had also noticed the strange calm of the waters, but Fausto did not want to create undue curiosity among them by displaying his unbridled joy at the compass' revelation. He returned the navigational instrument to the astronomer and calmly asked, "What next, then?"

"We follow the compass needle," Ricci said with a smile, "and we see where it leads us." The *Redenzione* continued its slow trek through the mist.

Fausto, Marina, Santos, and Leonardo stood anxiously at the bow for the better part of the next hour. Few words were exchanged between them, as they were all scanning the waters before the galleon for some sign of the phantom continent. But there was nothing to see, just calm waters lightly rolling beneath the white mist that obscured the horizon on all sides of the vessel. Above them, the sky was a pale gray.

Then, something happened, something so minuscule and unobtrusive that everyone except Marina Caproni overlooked it. For the briefest of moments, an odd sensation washed over her. It was indescribable, but she could favorably compare it to having two large conch shells pressed against both of her ears. It was as if she were being confined within a lead box or held underwater; such was how she would describe the brief hollowness of her range of hearing, also accompanied by a high-pitched ringing. As quickly as the sensation overtook her, it disappeared. But as she looked at the others on the forecastle, they had obviously experienced a similar sensation but paid it no mind. Fausto's brow was creased, and he placed one forefinger in each ear and wiggled them. His features softened as he immediately dismissed the slight auditory anomaly, but Marina had seen his action.

"You felt that, too," she said, as a statement of fact.

Fausto's eyes widened and he raised one eyebrow. His sister had experienced the same fleeting sensation as had he. "What was that?" he asked.

"Captain!" Santos Ignacio intoned with barely contained astonishment. "Ahead of us!"

The *Redenzione* cruised through the waters, now inexplicably free of the blanket of mist. It was as if the fog had been drawn into the heavens in the blink of an eye. Overhead, the sky was now clear, its hue of the richest blue, the waters randomly punctuated by broken slabs of pale white ice that had not, as yet, been observed on the voyage.

Marina's breath caught in her throat and she gripped the sleeve of her brother's coat. "Fausto . . ." she whispered. "We've found it."

Had Marina been seated in Milan's Teatro alla Scala as the symphony orchestra reached its crescendo, any emotion she could have experienced there would have paled in comparison to the soul-shaking amazement that overtook her senses when she looked upon the towering cliffs of Caprona. Not a half mile distant, the dark granite rose to the sky from the level of the sea and stretched across the horizon. Fausto was silent, in complete awe of the majestic lost continent, a sentiment shared by Marina, Santos Ignacio, Leonardo Ricci, and every sailor upon the deck.

The presence of that which could only have been sculpted by the hands of God Himself humbled all on board. Even taking into account the mist through which they had sailed, there was no logical explanation for how such an enormous landmass could have gone unobserved by the lookouts far in advance of the ship's arrival at the foot of the island continent.

An electric euphoria surged through the four onlookers. Dispensing with the stony pretense of measured emotion,

Marina threw her arms around her brother, but no words could express what she truly felt. Seeing the young Sicilian woman's reaction, Santos burst into laughter and repeated Marina's words. "We've found it!" he exclaimed, lifting the young woman into the air as she moved to hug him. At that, all three converged on the frail astronomer, showering him with their appreciation, for it was through Leonardo Ricci's navigational expertise that Caprona had at last been rediscovered.

Gathered at the bulwarks of the *Redenzione*, the crewmen and Spanish soldiers watched the exuberant display intently. They had been assessing the actions of the captain and quartermaster to discern the meaning of the unexpected landmass before the ship, but when they saw the exhilaration of Caproni and Ignacio, they followed suit with their own cheers. What land had been discovered they did not know, but they could not help but be moved in the moment.

"I think an explanation is in order," uttered Colonel Valdez, who now stood behind the captain and his trusted advisors on the forecastle.

Fausto adjusted his hat, knocked askew by the round of hugs that had been exchanged. "An explanation you shall receive, Colonel! Gather your men on the quarterdeck and all will be revealed."

6
THE ASCENT

BENEATH THE BRILLIANT SUN and azure skies, the crew of the *Redenzione* assembled on deck. As they awaited the commencement of Captain Caproni's proclamation, all eyes wandered over the towering rock cliffs of the strange continent. The galleon had drawn to within three hundred feet of the continent's lichen-splashed foundation, whose sea-level face was ringed by a thirty-foot band of multitudinous barnacles. All on board could only guess what wonders lay at the crest of that grand plateau.

Fausto Caproni stood at the taffrail of the forecastle, facing the anxious crewmen below. To his right was Leonardo Ricci; to his left stood Santos Ignacio. On the quarterdeck below, Marina had positioned herself at the forefront of the sailors. As she surveyed those behind her, the smile left her lips when she observed a visibly anxious Colonel Valdez speaking to his men in their native language. Marina's mother had always urged her to trust her intuition, a practice she had followed up to—and including—that very minute. The Spaniards bore watching, her instincts told her.

Upon the shrill call of the bosun's whistle, the crew's full attention shifted to their captain.

"Before I answer the question that all of you are burning to have answered," Fausto began, "I want to commend every man on board for his dedication to duty on this expedition. To each of you, I extend my sincere gratitude and—although I know your sights are set on the wages you will collect upon our return to Palermo—please accept my indebtedness for the hard work that has led us to this historic day.

"Yes, it *is* a historic day," Fausto continued pridefully. "The *Redenzione* now cruises the coastal waters surrounding the lost continent of Caprona."

As one, the crew gasped in astonishment at their captain's pronouncement. At one time or other in their lives, each man had heard the fable attributed to Captain Enzio Caproni, but none believed the tale's veracity.

"That is correct. *Caprona*," Fausto said. "My grandfather, Captain Enzio Caproni, discovered this land in the year 1781. Unfortunately, he never returned, nor could he convince anyone in the King's court that the continent truly existed. Today, we *have* returned. Today, our very presence transforms the myth into fact. Today, we shall at last claim Caprona for the Kingdom of the Two Sicilies!"

Murmurs swirled around Marina, but the well-founded questions about how the impossibly sheer cliffs could be scaled would soon be answered. Fausto motioned to a handful of sailors on deck, and by his command, they pulled loose the ropes to unveil the large object lashed across the midsection of the ship.

The crew gathered around the strange construction. When considered in its entirety, it was not remarkable. In fact, it was unremarkable. The great oblong box was composed of hundreds of bamboo poles lashed tightly together, with a flat top and inward-sloping bottom side in the fashion of a ship's hull. At its fore, a prow was formed from the convergence of its two sides, and its aft was rounded and approximated that of a seagoing vessel. By all appearances, the object that Captain Caproni had kept jealously guarded was nothing more than a bamboo schooner, sixty feet in length.

No masts were affixed to its recessed deck, however. Aside from the raised gunwale and a hatch to access the vessel's interior, the only outstanding feature of the deck was two cylindrical vats, four feet in height and three in width, whose interiors were lined with a coating of glass. The two odd barrels were securely fastened to the deck, one fore and one aft. The crewmen considered the odd boat, most notably the unusual constructs that jutted two from port and two from starboard. At the ends of the four stabilizing arms were attached round, vertical frames of bamboo. Mounted to flywheels at the center of the frames were four-bladed screw propellers similar to those created by Bohemian inventor Joseph Ludwig Franz Ressel, only now coming into common use as propulsion devices for small ships.

It was the first time Marina had seen the completed vessel, and her reaction to its unveiling was lukewarm. It was beyond her reasoning how Fausto could have spent the gracious donations of the monks of Monte Gibilmesi on such an unimpressive and odd contraption.

The excited voice of her brother shook Marina from the gray haze of her misgivings. Fausto was approaching her; he bore a smile and chatted excitedly with Colonel Valdez, who marched at the captain's side. As they drew nearer, it became apparent to Marina that Valdez was peppering Fausto with questions of a most suspicious nature.

"This was your plan, was it not?" Valdez pointedly asked the young captain. "It was not by accident that we have come to these exact coordinates, was it, Captain Caproni?"

Fausto's response was aloof. "What difference does it make? We have rediscovered Caprona." He placed a hand on the shoulder epaulet of the military man. "As per our agreement, both of our countries will benefit greatly. How we got here matters not, does it? We're here," he said. Fausto gestured toward the mysterious island with a wide sweep of his hand. "And now we explore and uncover all of Caprona's hidden treasures."

If Marina's practical nature had fur, it would have stood on end at his proclamation. As was always her inclination, she immediately moved to tamp the fire of Fausto's exuberance, out of an abundance of caution. "Surely we'll circle the continent first to survey its exterior," Marina offered, "and perhaps find the most ideal location for a landing party to . . ."

"There's no need," Fausto curtly interrupted his sister. "According to Grandfather's account, and that of Leonardo Ricci, the entire continent is just like that," he said, pointing to the towering gray rocks. "Why waste a week cruising the perimeter when we can reach the top by the morning?"

Valdez had questions of his own. "How do you propose we do that, Captain Caproni?" he asked sarcastically, then he pointed to the bamboo ship. "And what role could this little schooner possibly play? Can it fly?"

"Yes, Colonel Valdez," Fausto beamed. "It can. Come! I'll show you!" Fausto ushered Marina, Valdez, and a contingent of curious crewmen to the odd vessel lying across the midriff of the *Redenzione*.

Throughout the following afternoon and night, Captain Fausto Caproni guided small groups of sailors through unfamiliar paces, separate from their daily onboard duties. Few of the men were convinced that the captain's plan was not a madman's folly, but follow his instructions they did, to the letter. The crewmen worked in shifts, and when each group was discharged, they joined the celebratory festivities on deck. Flowing wine piqued already-heightened curiosities as they beheld the odd contraption that took shape before them.

Guided by their captain, the sailors fed two gigantic bolts of rubber-coated silk from belowdecks, and the material was suspended by harnesses above the two iron vats on the deck of the bamboo vessel. The yards of silk were then enveloped by two huge sheets of rope netting, later secured along all sides of the vessel's bulwarks. Next, large, corked glass bottles were retrieved from the ship's stores, and the sulfuric acid they contained was gingerly poured into the small ship's two top deck vats until each was nearly half full. Scoops of iron filings transported in wooden casks were then poured into the corrosive liquid, their dissolution resulting in the production of hydrogen gas that was fed into the enormous silk envelopes.

By daybreak, and in the blue shadow of the lost continent, two great balloons had inflated to their fullest extent and swayed hypnotically in the early morning breeze above the unusual bamboo schooner. As those on deck at that early hour gazed upon the sight, the intangible call of adventure plucked at every heart. Their captain was not mad; in truth, the incredible vessel he had constructed pointed to an ingenuity previously unsuspected. The new level of respect the crew had for Fausto Caproni was clear. However, their admiration of the young captain did not translate into a foolhardy willingness to ride the strange vessel into the air, as was the obvious intent of its construction.

Santos Ignacio turned to listen to the murmured misgivings among the crew. At his side, the captain gave his quartermaster a knowing smirk and shrugged. There was nothing to be said. Silver could only be spent if one made it home alive to collect it, and it would be callous for Fausto to begrudge his loyal crew for wishing to remain sea-bound.

"I'll be honest with you, Fausto," Santos confided, "I'm still unconvinced that it will work."

The young captain laughed. "We have yet to see it fly, so you might be proven correct." Santos' playful punch to Fausto's shoulder told the captain all he needed to know about the ulterior motive beneath the quartermaster's comment. Wasn't it always the way of Santos Ignacio to tell him he could not possibly accomplish a task, thereby spurring him to expend the additional effort to succeed at all costs?

"A sky cutter," Santos mused, pointing to the odd vessel. "Who could have imagined such a thing?"

"He stands before you," Fausto replied with pride, his arms held wide. "But it needs a name. Yes. Yes. I'll name it *Pegaso II*," he said proudly, "to honor both my grandfather and the original name of this ship that has delivered us to the very foot of Caprona."

With the raising of his finger, Fausto Caproni signaled to the boatswain, who rang the quarterdeck bell, alerting all hands. Within minutes, the entire crew, including Colonel Valdez and the Spanish military contingent, had gathered around the bamboo ship on the deck of the *Redenzione*. Just then, a sudden gust of wind drew the dual balloons to port, and had it not been for the ropes that securely moored the sky cutter to the deck, the craft very well could have departed unmanned. It was clear to all that the fundamental concept behind the vessel's construction was sound.

It was time to put that concept to the ultimate test.

Fausto climbed the rope ladder to the deck of the *Pegaso II*. Without a word, Santos Ignacio, Leonardo Ricci, and twelve hearty crewmen advanced toward the craft. Fausto beckoned toward the crowd with an outstretched hand. "Colonel Valdez, if you will accompany us."

The assembled seamen parted as Valdez passed, followed closely by six of his men, all bearing rifles, rapiers, and halberds. It took no stretch of the imagination to recognize that the Spaniards were prepared for battle, should one arise.

Santos Ignacio turned to the approaching soldiers, and though his eyes burned like coals, his voice was smooth and dismissive. "What is this?" he asked.

Colonel Valdez's tone was aggressive, but he tempered his response with cold logic. "For the safety of all those who are about to embark on this journey, my men will accompany us."

"I'm sorry, Colonel," Fausto said, "but that is impossible. The sky cutter can only lift so much weight, and as my own men are needed to—"

"Captain Caproni," the Spaniard harshly interjected, "my men will accompany us. They will take the places of six of your men. Spanish soldiers are quite intelligent, and can easily master whatever duties you have assigned to your sailors."

Leonardo Ricci was wary of the unwelcome offer. "What do

you expect to find up there, Colonel? Carlists?" the elderly astronomer chided. "Good sir, it's a big rock. We are planting a flag is all."

Colonel Valdez would not be swayed. "I will remind you that this voyage was made possible under the auspices of Queen Regent Maria Christina and the Spanish Empire. As such, I must fulfill my duty to ensure that no ill befalls a single member of this expedition. Since we do not know what might lie at the top of the plateau, I must insist, Captain Caproni, that there be no further objection to the security we offer you and your crew."

Marina stepped forward from where she had been standing among the men. Fausto flinched noticeably when he considered her clothing. Gone were Marina's fashionable dress, vest, and shoes, now replaced by dark blue men's pants and a buttoned white blouse, over which she wore one of Fausto's spare long coats. Black boots that her brother recognized as his protected her legs from the knees down. A rapier that hung from the belt around her waist completed her wardrobe.

She adjusted the bicorne upon her head. "I'm going, too," Marina declared, in no uncertain terms.

All hope of a simple ascent to the top of the precipice was now dashed due to multiple conflicts of personality and desire. Santos climbed the rope ladder to privately consult with Fausto. "You did make a deal, Fausto," the quartermaster reminded the young Caproni.

"With the Spaniards. Not with my sister," Fausto reminded him.

Santos seemed to consider the situation for a few moments, then offered his advice. "I understand their wariness," he explained of the Spaniards. "They were deceived once already, were they not?" Fausto conceded with a nod, and Santos gave him a reassuring pat on the shoulder. "We'll watch them closely. As for Marina," he said, watching Fausto's sister scamper up the rope ladder with the deftness of a seasoned sailor, "I think she can take care of herself."

It was decided that seven of the *Redenzione*'s volunteers would stay on deck, while the balance of their number boarded the sky cutter. The crew hoisted meager supplies to the deck of the *Pegaso II*, including additional stores of sulfuric acid and casks of iron filings to ensure the craft could remain aloft for an extended period if necessary. The bamboo craft's passengers would be Fausto, Marina, Santos, Leonardo Ricci, and four Sicilians, along with Colonel Valdez and six of his men.

Marina marveled at the great silk balloons that hovered overhead, held at bay by netting and the pull of the *Redenzione* to which the sky cutter was bound. The huge white balloons yearned to break free; to fly; to chart a wild course into the unknown, unrestrained by convention and inherent expectation. She laughed to herself. In that moment of anticipation of an experience unlike anything she had ever understood, she contemplated how she was not unlike a balloon. It was a sobering moment of clarity, but there was no time to appreciate the realization.

"Loose the mooring lines!" Fausto commanded. At their captain's order, the crew hands on the deck of the *Pegaso II* slipped the looped ropes from the vessel's bollards, and nearly immediately the fantastic vehicle lifted from the ship's deck.

The bamboo rods of which the ship was composed creaked as it rose into the air and Marina instinctively gripped the hand of her brother who stood at her side. Below, Giovanni Pellegrino smiled and waved to her. When it had come time to determine which of the sky cutter crew would return to the *Redenzione*, Giovanni had volunteered to let Marina assume his position on the flight. His action stemmed not from cowardice, but from compassion. He knew how Marina yearned for adventure, and no man on board understood the fiery young woman's burning desire to chase fate better than Giovanni. Marina had thanked him for his sacrifice with a hug before he descended from the sky cutter to the deck below. "Take care of my cats!" she yelled down to him. He held up a thumb in acknowledgment.

Up the craft rose, past the ship's masts, cleared of the stays that tied them together. With no roping overhead to prevent its ascent, the sky cutter floated ever higher.

"It might be better if you don't look down," Fausto warned Marina. Still, she was intent on experiencing every possible thrill on what would surely be only a short trip to embed the Sicilian flag into the peak of Caprona's foundation. Once clear of the ship, the craft and the balloons that held it aloft began to rotate in the wind, and the fore of the *Pegaso II* began a slow spin to face away from the rocks.

"Port side, bow and stern! Slow and steady, twenty rotations!" Captain Caproni called to Santos Ignacio, who knelt by the hatch that led belowdecks.

The quartermaster cupped a hand to his mouth and repeated the order into the hatchway. Within the belly of the vessel, four of the crew and a quartet of Spaniards were seated on benches. Each pair of men held in their grip an iron crankshaft attached to sets of toothed gears, tightly girdled by roller chains that fed through small ports on the ship's hull. Upon hearing the captain's instruction relayed by Santos, the four men on the vessel's port side began cranking the shafts. The chains grew taut, and the rotational aspect of their motion gave locomotion to the dual screw propellers within their frames on the outside of the ship. Slowly, the incredible flying machine rotated clockwise to face the massive granite foundation of Caprona, only fifty feet from the bow.

Fausto turned to Marina, and the two laughed in relief now that the ship's course had been righted. No words were exchanged between them, as Marina knew it was in her brother's best interest not to yell out, "I cannot believe that this insane contraption really works!"

Upward the *Pegaso II* rose, still within the chill shadow of the rock wall. Colonel Valdez watched Fausto closely as if impressed by his command of the vessel. Had they attempted to scale the sheer cliff, the effort would surely have taken weeks, if not months, and would have been an immensely treacherous undertaking. But now, only minutes after the flying machine had left the deck of the *Redenzione*, they were only fifty feet below the pinnacle of the plateau.

"We're nearly there!" Fausto called out. At the ship's current altitude, the air was quite cold, but the bitter wind did not spur the chill that Marina knew must be running up the spines of the entire crew. They were experiencing the thrill of wild expectation. After nearly sixty years, Caprona was about to be conquered at last or so believed the intrepid explorers aboard the *Pegaso II*.

The hydrogen-filled bladders above the sky cutter began to glow a radiant white as they rose above the lip of the rock wall and emerged from the cloak of shadow. The radiance of the dawn sun crept down the rope netting and halyards as the vessel continued its ascent, until finally the luminous rays bathed the deck of the ship and warmed Marina and her companions. Fausto's eyes grew wide with wonder; in them she could see that his dream had at last been realized. The *Pegaso II* had surmounted the formidable obstacle that had kept Caprona's secrets. None aboard the sky cutter could have prepared for the fantastic sight they now beheld.

"Fausto," Marina sputtered, "Caprona is not a plateau!"

7
TERROR IN THE SKIES

THE SKY CUTTER HOVERED hundreds of feet above sea level over the rim of Caprona's impregnable wall, and the sight that greeted Marina and her fellow passengers left them breathless. Before them lay not a vast rocky plain, as Fausto and his countrymen had expected; rather, the flat, stony ridge extended inward several hundred feet from the outer perimeter of the continent before plunging into an immense canyon beyond imagining.

From the vantage point of the *Pegaso II*, the geological structure of the colossal island was akin to a wide, stout volcanic mountain, the interior of which had collapsed, with only the outer conical conformation remaining. Unlike a volcanic crater, however, the landmass and its bowl-like interior were nearly a hundred and fifty miles in diameter, with the most distant edge of the towering halo of rock indiscernible.

The crew of the sky cutter was silent, as words could not possibly convey the shocking sight of the unexpected and breathtaking natural disposition of the lost continent.

"All ahead, gently," Fausto commanded to the operators of the ship's propellers. Within moments, the sky cutter had glided past the interior edge of the rock wall to hang suspended over the inward-sloping precipice. There, they viewed mile upon mile of descending mountainous terrain that fell toward the interior of Caprona hundreds of feet below. Beyond the highland were thickly wooded forests of towering pines that contained a blanket of thick moisture suspended above the central interior of the continent. The current altitude and position of the *Pegaso II* made it impossible for the ship's crew to peer through the misty veil. What lay beneath the atmospheric haze was a tantalizing puzzle.

"It's astonishing," Santos whispered.

"Let's go down," Fausto responded.

Marina's exuberant, "Let's!" summarized the unspoken desire of every man on board.

The fantastic airship continued its swaying crawl across the sky and soon approached the forested highlands. Fausto ordered the venting of small amounts of hydrogen gas from the envelopes to effect a gradual descent into the layer of mist that concealed the interior of the continent. The air was still quite crisp, but as the altitude of the sky cutter decreased and it dropped through the layer of clouds, the crew was met by a noticeable warming of the atmosphere.

The *Pegaso II* floated ever downward, and once beneath the high-level mist, the totality of the continent of Caprona lay before them. It was a vista of unimaginable and primal beauty. A proliferation of dense jungles lay interspersed with wide grassy pastures and lowlands, with some areas appearing desertlike. Veins of volcanic rock wove across the terrain in other areas and ridges and canyons of sedimentary rock rose in the distance. The full extent of the land was so far-reaching it could not be calculated upon its initial revelation. Yet, the most distinguishing feature of Caprona's interior was an enormous central lake—vast enough that it might be classified as a sea—around which the fantastic array of topography was arranged.

Marina intently scanned the jungle. Between the sky cutter and the ground hundreds of feet below, the air was filled with life, as indistinguishable species of birds soared and flitted with abandon.

"Down there!" Santos excitedly shouted. Marina and Fausto rushed to the quartermaster's side as he leaned over the starboard bulwark. "In the jungle. There!"

"What do you see?" Marina asked excitedly.

Santos paused to collect himself. "It was . . . I don't know. I saw something. An animal, I suppose."

"What kind of animal?" Fausto inquired.

"I don't know," Santos admitted. "But it was something big."

The ominous admission snapped Marina from a euphoria energized by adrenaline. The words of Santos were sobering. The thrill she had been experiencing had quashed any consideration that danger might lurk within the lush green that splashed the interior of the secret world they had just discovered.

With her full attention locked on the swampy jungle far below, Marina did not see the approach of a flock of small flying animals that streamed toward the sky cutter.

"Watch yourselves!" Colonel Valdez called out as the airborne creatures flew over the deck of the bamboo vessel and weaved between the startled crew members. Like an undulating wave of brightly colored leaves upon the wind, the hawk-sized animals flew with curious intent, but so speedy was their passage that Marina could not determine just what manner of birds they were.

Clearly annoyed by the unbidden appearance of the bothersome fowl, Sergeant Lago lashed out with his rapier as the last of the flock darted past him. As luck would have it, his thrust struck one of the creatures and killed it instantly. The winged animal tumbled across the bamboo flooring and lay still before the wide-eyed crew.

"Astounding," Leonardo Ricci said, marveling at the deceased animal as he lifted it by one wing. What the crew had initially believed to be birds were revealed to be something different altogether. The animal was not feathered at all; its ocher skin was smooth and leathery, like that of a shorn ewe. The membranous wings paralleled those of a bat, but the creature's most remarkable trait was its distinct resemblance to a lizard. The tail and neck were both elongated, while the head was dominated by large snakelike eyes and a long, pointed beak, the interior surface of the jaws lined with needle-sharp teeth. Though no larger than a small hawk, it was nightmarish, nonetheless.

"What in Heaven's name is it?" Marina asked as she peered over the shoulder of the elderly astronomer.

Leonardo's attention was transfixed on the odd animal. "My dear," he said, adjusting his spectacles, "never in my life have I beheld anything of its like." Santos and Colonel Valdez both concurred.

Fausto was also fascinated by the animal of indeterminate genus, but he would not be distracted from his duty to his charges. He kept careful watch over the envelopes while surveying the terrain below the flying ship and monitoring the craft's gradual descent. A shift in the wind nudged the prow to starboard, but the propeller operators quickly righted the ship's course toward a large and flat open plain. Fausto determined it would be an ideal location to set the sky cutter down.

Herds of animals, perhaps antelope or deer, could now be seen on the plain ahead. None aboard the *Pegaso II* could positively identify the fauna from the ship's current height; their efforts were further frustrated by the scattering of the herds that disappeared into the abundant verdure as the ship drew near.

Before the sky cutter could land upon the plain, it must first clear the tops of the towering jungle trees whose heights reached well over a hundred feet. What occurred next brought into question whether the ship would make a safe landing at all.

A jolt of fear shot through Marina when the piercing shriek rang out. She spun, as did the others on deck, to view the author of the hideous sound: It was a flying creature that hovered on leathery wings off the port side of the sky cutter. The wingspan of the enormous beast was nearly equal to the airship's length, and although the beast was similar in form to the tiny creature that had fallen to the sword of Sergeant Lago, this creature appeared exponentially fiercer. The thing must have been a cousin of the smaller creatures, the only distinctions being that it did not have a tail, and it bore a fin—equal in length to its bill—protruding from the back of its head. Its size alone made it formidable, but when the strange giant thrust wide its bony beak and let out another terrifying screech, Marina imagined the hideous teeth could easily tear a human in half.

All but one of the aeronauts on the ship's port side fell away from the bulwark. Sergeant Lago stood resolutely as he swiftly tamped the wadding into the barrel of his rifle with the ramrod. The intent of the great beast was as yet undetermined, but its deafening roars insinuated a most certain motive. Lago was not intimidated and gazed down the musket barrel at the hideous face. But before he could pull the trigger, his aim was spoiled as the rifle was sharply pulled away from his intended target.

"You idiot!" exclaimed Santos, attempting to wrestle the musket from the Spaniard, who resisted with all his might. "That's hydrogen gas in those balloons! One stray spark and we're all dead!" Santos yelled angrily. Despite the dire warning, the soldier was intent on reestablishing control of his weapon and killing the flying terror.

There was not a glimmer of intelligence in the eyes of the creature, but it seemed to Marina that the dragon—for that is how it appeared to her—would take full advantage of the scuffle. Its mighty wings thrust downward and the beast ascended above the sky cutter. As those on deck watched helplessly, the creature pumped its diminutive hind legs, attempting to claw at what it must have perceived as a flying enemy. Fausto's face elongated in horror as one of the taloned appendages raked across the rubber-coated envelope at the aft of the ship, slicing a yard-long gash across the face of the balloon.

Almost immediately, the balance of the sky cutter shifted as the gas holding the rear of the ship aloft escaped its enclosure.

A throaty yell escaped Marina's brother as he warned her and the others to drop to their stomachs to prevent them from sliding toward the depending end of the *Pegaso II.*

"All propellers double-time!" Fausto shouted belowdecks to the crew. He had clearly reasoned that only a sudden increase in the ship's forward momentum would prevent it from colliding with the jungle treetops. His hope was borne out. Seconds before the underside of the ship's aft would have scraped against the jungle canopy due to its decreasing altitude, the sky cutter cleared the trees and limped toward the green plain ahead.

The second the deck began its rearward tilt, Santos released his grip on Lago's musket and rushed to the side of Leonardo. Marina perceived the move as an instinctive effort to protect the man who had always acted as Santos' surrogate father. Moreover, the elderly astronomer was the most learned of them all, and Santos would have believed him to be an asset of the utmost value to the expedition. With one arm around Leonardo, Santos pressed both himself and his charge against the deck as close as possible to the ship's prow. Had he secured himself and his elder below the central vats, they would have been exposed to splashed sulfuric acid should the containers empty themselves.

Small animals hidden within the meadow scattered in all directions as the ship rushed on, its altitude decreasing in equal measure to its forward advancement. Because of its sudden burst of speed, the sky cutter was now traveling far too fast to effect a soft landing. The ship's hull grazed the deep ground cover for several dozen yards before scraping against the ground, splintering its underside. Plant matter, sod, and flying insects filled the air as the sky cutter plowed through the field before at last coming to a sudden stop one hundred feet from where it first touched down.

The abruptness of the ceasing of forward momentum was jarring, and Marina saw Sergeant Lago and Sergeant Molina flung from the fore of the ship and into the deep stalks beyond.

In a blink, they disappeared from view, as the depth of the wheat-like plants exceeded that of a man's height and reached halfway up the sides of the grounded flying machine.

Marina heard her brother cry out her name in fear for her safety, but she had managed to gain a secure position, clinging tightly to the restraining ropes that held together the bamboo flooring toward midships.

Marina yelled out, "The dragon! Where is it?" The unexpectedness of the crash had temporarily superseded the fear of the beast that initiated their current predicament, but the threat of the flying terror came once more to the fore of concern. All on board scanned the skies as best they could, but their efforts were in vain as the enormous balloons swaying overhead obstructed their view.

Fausto made an immediate assessment of his crew, including those belowdecks. Although the hull had ruptured and shattered bamboo had been thrown about the cabin, the four seamen at the propeller mechanisms were uninjured. Colonel Santos also reported that his men belowdecks were unharmed, but the fates of Sergeants Lago and Molina were unknown. The Spanish leader rushed to the bulwark and called out to the missing soldiers, but there was no response from the impenetrable field of stalks surrounding the ship.

As Santos helped Leonardo to regain his footing, Marina and Fausto rushed up the gradual slant of the ship's deck.

Concern was etched on the face of her brother. "Are you hurt, Signore Ricci?" he asked.

The old man smiled and brushed the front of his coat. "If you knew of some of the adventures your grandfather and I had together, you would understand why he called me his 'good luck charm.'" Although Leonardo made light of the incident, Marina could see that the old man was covertly favoring his left arm. He had been injured, she surmised, but he would maintain an air of vitality so that he would not be perceived as a liability.

Just then, two of the deckhands cried out. From above, the

rapidly deflating balloon and the tangle of rope netting that once restrained it fell like a shroud over the rear of the ship. At the sight, Marina felt a sickening hollowness in the pit of her stomach as her mind rushed to a disturbing conclusion: With the ship irreparably damaged and one of the balloons destroyed, they might forever become the prisoners of Caprona.

Santos Ignacio must have sensed the need for Fausto to affirm order among the flustered crew. "What do you recommend, Captain Caproni?" he asked.

But as Marina looked at her brother, her heart sank. There was no air of authority about Fausto, and from the furtive movement of his eyes, she knew that he was experiencing a complete lack of faith in himself. It was a look she had seen many times in her life, but now was not the time for him to falter, particularly not before the contingent of foreign soldiers.

"Captain?" Santos gently prodded. He would not want to verbalize his own recommendations in front of the men, as that would undermine faith in their captain. Captain Fausto Caproni must speak for himself, but Marina's fear grew as each second passed without a response. Those fears were compounded when she noticed the Spaniards quietly talking among themselves.

"It's back!" screamed one of the Sicilian crew. All eyes shot skyward as the shadow of the flying beast that had downed the sky cutter fell over the craft. The shrieks of the creature were deafening as it reached down with its hind legs and attempted to snatch one of the crewmen from the deck. Two of the sailors, Puccini and Trimboli, had slid to the aft of the sky cutter during the crash and were now scrambling away in panic from the monstrous attacker. To their good fortune, both reached the lower-deck hatch and disappeared into the hull before the beast's outstretched claws could snare either of them.

Fausto's body became a protective shield as he assisted Leonardo in descending the ladder to the ship's interior, but his selfless action also made him a tempting target for the flying creature. The monster eyed him hungrily.

As the Spanish soldiers loaded their muskets, Marina cried out, "What do we do?" The response was one she could never have expected.

Santos had read the beast's intent, and without hesitation the normally sedate quartermaster sprang into action. Marina watched in astonishment as Santos leaped amidships, crouched, and slid on the soles of his boots down the entire length of the bamboo deck directly beneath the hovering monster.

Whether the act was foolhardy or courageous, Marina could not decide. Fausto had always maintained that Señor Santos was not simply a staid naval administrator. That observation was gleaned during the fencing exercises the quartermaster had provided to Fausto since he was ten years old. Marina had never witnessed those exercises, nor had she observed Santos Ignacio in any situation other than that of a mundane bent. In Marina's eyes, Señor Santos had always been a man who was most comfortable with a glass of wine in hand and a ledger book before him. Now, he was something altogether different.

Like a graceful ice skater upon a frozen pond, Santos flew under the talons of the flying monster, and in the blink of an eye, he slid to a stop at the lower end of the sky cutter. With a cool deftness that Marina could only admire, he scooped up a Spanish halberd that had been dropped during the crash near the ship's rear bulwark. Gripping the long-handled axe by its end, he began slashing at the taloned feet that sought to drag him to his doom.

The blade of the halberd found its mark, drawing blood from the calf of the creature. The airborne attacker shrieked in pain, but the wound only further enraged the beast. At the low end of the ship's deck, Santos was alone, facing a monster ripped from a nightmare.

Just then, three simultaneous reports filled the air. A Spanish musket ball struck the weaving creature in the thigh, but the other two shots seemed to pass through its leathery wings harmlessly. Santos took advantage of the distraction provided by the soldiers and thrust upward with the halberd. The pike mounted at the end of the weapon penetrated the side of the screaming creature's chest, but the monster's wings did not cease flapping.

"Marina! Get belowdecks!" Fausto yelled to his sister as he stood transfixed by the bloody confrontation.

Marina's eyes widened as she screamed the name of the heroic quartermaster, but it was too late. Like lightning, the claws of the flying creature lashed out and dug deeply into the shoulders of Santos' heavy coat, lifting the man into the air like a child's doll. He swung the halberd wildly, but the long-handled weapon was of little use at such close range.

Marina's scream was unintelligible as she helplessly watched the wildly flapping dragon lift Santos Ignacio into the sky and over the jungle treetops that ringed the field. In an instant, a man she had known most of her life and the intellectual mentor to her brother was gone. In utter despair, Marina and Fausto both dropped to their knees on the deck of the *Pegaso II*.

Colonel Valdez's primary focus was locating the two soldiers pitched from the front of the craft during the crash. He shouted an order to Alonso and Montes, and the men obediently descended the ladder to begin their search on the ground fifteen feet below.

Marina watched as the soldiers, exercising an abundance of caution, loaded their rifles and readied themselves to fire. They pointed their weapons toward the wall of vegetation that surrounded them. The field was not as it had appeared from the sky; the plants bore throngs of vibrant green leaves, more akin to corn stalks whose stems were more than an inch in circumference. Growing tightly together, the plants would make passage through the field arduous.

"Lago! Where are you?" called Montes.

"Molina! Are you hurt?" Alonso yelled.

Save for the incessant songs of insects, only silence was returned. Cautiously, the pair moved away from the sky cutter and into the field. Marina watched from afar as, only moments later, Alonso parted the stalks to reveal Lago, crouched close to the ground. He appeared to be unhurt, but upon sight of his retrievers, Lago quickly put a finger to his lips to indicate that stealth was in order. Alonso raised a hand to Montes, though it was unclear to Marina if he even knew why they should halt. But the reason soon became apparent to all.

It was a low and rumbling sound but none of the soldiers could be certain from where it originated. There was a sharp staccato rhythm to it, as when the segments of a chain grind against a wood portal when a ship's anchor is hauled in. Still silent, Lago drew the attention of Montes and Alonso and pointed through the stalks. Twenty feet away, the barest glimpse of Molina's deep blue jacket and white trousers was visible through the foliage. It appeared that he, too, was standing stark still. The rumble seemed to circle them, but just what the sound was none could say. All three soldiers slowly raised their muskets into firing positions and waited.

Molina's scream ripped through the field as a phantom agent violently shook the stalks around him. From her vantage on the deck, Marina could not see what was happening or what had attacked him, but his guttural shrieks of terror were cut short within seconds.

On the deck of the sky cutter, Valdez must have heard the terrified outburst, for Marina could see him lean anxiously over the bulwark. He called to his men, but none responded. Now at their Colonel's side, two of his sergeants, Garza and Ortega, held their rifles ready, but no target—nor the soldiers among the stalks—could be seen.

The constitutions of the three soldiers on the ground had been tempered on the battlefield, but they fled in fear of the unseen killer. Marina caught a glimpse of something behind them crouching upon the body of Molina, but now another attacker was plowing through the stalks toward them as they ran. Luck was with them; they managed to reach the sky cutter before they fell to whatever it was that now roared furiously. Climbing the ladder to the deck would expose them to the creature's assault. Instead, they frantically pushed through a horizontal gap in the cracked bamboo hull of the ship. The last to make it to safety was Lago, who turned his head before sliding through the jagged hole. Marina and the others on the deck gazed down from above in utter astonishment at what they beheld.

The beast charged through the stalks. It was a massive four-legged thing, whose back and shoulders reached the height of a man's. Short tan fur covered its powerfully muscled body, and it had a huge round head with short ears and a black nose. Its eyes blazed golden yellow, its pupils like black slits. But the mouth of the creature was its most terrifying feature. The thing roared in anger as it charged, its lips curled back to fully expose the long, saber-like upper fangs, each of which was at least two feet in length. Similar animals were known to prowl the mangrove swamps of India, but no known tiger of this size and ferocity had ever been recorded.

Gasping for breath, Lago took to coughing as he squeezed through the crack in the hull just as a shot rang out from the deck above. Ortega's musket shot slapped wetly into the upper shoulder of the saber-toothed beast. The attacker leaped back to thrash wildly on the ground in furious anger and pain, but before another shot could be fired, it bounded into the curtain of stalks that surrounded the ship and disappeared.

Marina was still numb from the shock of seeing Señor Santos carried away to face a hideous fate. Likewise, Fausto was sickened to his very soul by the loss of his quartermaster, his friend. In their grief, the siblings watched almost enviously as Colonel Valdez, apparently unfazed, coolly assessed the calamity. This was a man of action, whose cold, calculating military mind dismissed the loss of two men to focus on the greater needs of the survivors and the securing of the site of the crash. After taking count of his men, Valdez instructed four soldiers to take posts at aft, stern, port, and starboard.

The colonel was apparently as indifferent to the young Caproni's standing as ship's captain as he was to the situation. "Don't you worry, Captain," Valdez sneered. "I have everything under control."

The sarcasm was stinging, but Fausto, despite being rattled by the events that had unfolded, would not let the insinuation go unanswered. "I appreciate your dedication to the duty for which you have been tasked, Colonel," came his cold reply. "I am fortunate to have you in my service, so that I may fulfill my duties to my crew."

"Indeed," Valdez said with a sneer before adjusting his tone to one of detached professionalism. "What are your orders, Captain Caproni?"

To Marina's relief, both men eased their hostile posturing in favor of the practicalities of the moment. Faced with such dire circumstances, there was no other logical course to pursue. Thus, the Sicilians and Spaniards buried their apprehensions toward one another and moved forward with the daunting task now before them: the repair of the sky cutter and their return to the *Redenzione*. But there was one important task yet to be performed.

Captain Caproni whispered to the sailor, Collazo, who climbed belowdecks and returned bearing a long pole and a length of folded fabric. Fausto smiled at Marina and Leonardo, who joined them on the deck.

"I'll be right back," he told his sister. The young captain proceeded to climb down to the ground below, and under the watchful eyes of the Spanish soldiers, he firmly embedded the pole into the soil. From the top of the wooden mast hung the flag of the Kingdom of the Two Sicilies. Marina breathed a sigh of relief when her brother climbed back up to the deck of the damaged craft.

Fausto stole a glance at Marina, smiling weakly in what must have been an attempt to rally his confidence after the sacrifice of his great friend, Santos Ignacio. "Now," he said, "let us plan a course of action."

8
INTO THE UNKNOWN

T HE MORNING SUN HAD SINCE BURNED OFF the misty haze
that had blanketed the interior of Caprona, and now all
within the walls of the crater-like continent basked beneath
a heavenly expanse of crystal blue sky. Marina removed the
heavy long coat and hat she had borrowed from Fausto. She
was not the only one to experience discomfort from the unexpected heat of Caprona. Before the *Pegaso II* launched from
the deck of the *Redenzione*, the crew had donned cold-weather
apparel, a decision reached from the observation of ice bobbing
in the waters around the ship. At sea level, the air was quite
chill; it was a fair assumption that the summit of a plateaued
continent must be frigid. To their surprise, the atmosphere
within the bosom of the encompassing cliffs bordered on the
clime of the tropics. Heavy clothing was not only no longer
necessary; it was now a debilitating hindrance.

Although she was still distrustful of the motives of the
Spaniards, Marina was comforted when she heard casual words
and an encouraging exchange of ideas between Fausto and
Colonel Valdez. Between them, the two leaders compared
ideas about how to escape their current predicament. They
decided repairing the damaged balloon would be their secondary objective; the first would be to secure a source of fresh
water and food should they be forced to endure an extended
tenure within the unchartered land. To aid in that effort and
ensure their safety, a perimeter of clear ground would need
to be established around the sky cutter to defend the ship and

its crew from roving predators. They would accomplish this by using halberds to cut back the tall stalks and embedding torches in the ground at a radius of thirty feet from the grounded vessel, far enough away to prevent the ignition of any residual hydrogen gas from the undamaged balloon.

Returning the sky cutter to airworthiness would be a daunting task. The lowest extremity of the ship needed repair. The hull's structural integrity was unnecessary for flight, but it would be vital if the sky cutter made a sea landing upon returning to the *Redenzione*. They could dismantle parts of the ship's deck to reuse the bamboo to patch the hole in the ship's hull, but a preferable solution would be to search for similar rigid stalks in the jungle that loomed at the periphery of the field. If the damaged balloon were sewn together tightly enough, it could sufficiently contain hydrogen, but the probability of the leakage of gas would endanger all aboard the vessel and greatly reduce the ship's airworthiness. Leonardo Ricci assured Fausto and Valdez that painting the repaired tear with rubber diluted by a small amount of sulfuric acid would be the wisest measure to ensure a successful return voyage to the *Redenzione*. By happenstance, several bottles of sulfuric acid lay secured below the deck. It would be another matter entirely to find trees of the proper species from beneath whose bark they could extract the pale liquid rubber.

With the sun now at its zenith, Fausto ordered an exploratory party composed of half the passengers of the *Pegaso II* to prepare itself for departure. Fausto would lead the group, accompanied by Trimboli and Collazo. Colonel Valdez conferred with his men and decided that Sergeant Lago and Sergeant Ortega would travel with the Sicilians to ensure their safety as they searched for food, water, and materials to repair the ship. One other person would make the dangerous trek, and although it was Fausto's initial instinct to object, he knew better than to stifle the ambitions of his headstrong sister. Marina was going with him, whether he liked it or not.

Marina watched as the Spaniards conferred among themselves

one last time on the ground beside the downed sky cutter. Curiosity about the intent behind Colonel Valdez's words burned within her, for how could it not? The Spanish commander would speak a few sentences, after which his men would conspicuously turn their heads to look upon the Sicilians before returning their attention to their leader. Fausto was busying himself with instructions to his men, so he failed to notice the odd behavior of the Spaniards, but the keen eyes of Marina were ever alert, and she made a mental note of what she witnessed. If the brave Santos Ignacio were still alive, he could have translated the conversations of the military men, as he was of Spanish descent. Tears welled in Marina's eyes at the mere thought of Señor Santos; he was a kind man, an intelligent man, and he had not deserved such a hideous fate. She took a deep breath and buried her grief. The heroic quartermaster would have wanted it that way.

And so, the group set out through the thick stalks and toward the closest copse of trees. On the deck of the *Pegaso II*, the elderly Leonardo wagged a finger in the air. "Do not forget to bring back fruit, but do not eat any of it until I inspect it!"

"We won't forget, Signore," Fausto replied with a smile, and the band of explorers disappeared into the deep brush.

Marina was relieved that she wore the knee-high boots she had borrowed from her brother, which protected her calves against the sharp blades of the verdant shoots that proliferated throughout the field. Even so, passage was laborious, but at least she was able to maneuver through the stalks without bloodying her legs. Each member was equipped with some form of weapon; the Sicilians all bore rapiers, while Lago and Ortega carried rifles and halberds. Fausto had taken the lead and employed the razor-edged steel of Ortega's halberd to clear a discernible path across the field.

The location of fresh water was of utmost importance, but transporting it back to the ship was still a puzzle to be solved. If fruits with suitable rinds were discovered, perhaps they could be hollowed out and their husks used as crude canteens, but all of that remained to be seen. First, the group must locate water, preferably from a flowing stream. The waters of Caprona's vast interior sea were likely unpotable, and it lay far more distant than the nearby jungle, rolling hills, and mountains that rose to the lip of the crater miles behind them. However, if no streams could be found, an expedition to the massive body of water would need to be mounted.

As they moved, they tried to keep all noise and talking to a minimum. If the tigers they had seen earlier were still in the vicinity, they did not want to alert them to the presence of a meandering meal. Likewise, all in the party took turns periodically glancing skyward, but the only flying creatures to be seen were much smaller than the monster that carried away Santos Ignacio. Marina noted that while some of the flying animals were large and distinctly reptilian, with some species even bearing brightly colored feathers, others were much smaller and appeared no different from the birds that darted through the lemon groves of Palermo.

Palermo. Never in her life had Marina been so far from home. The thought was at once terrifying and thrilling. While adventures such as this had always been woven into the fabric of the men of the Caproni family, it was not so for the women. At the outset of the voyage, Marina had felt an immense pride in being the first woman in her lineage to have ventured beyond the Mediterranean. But more than that, she felt a debt of gratitude to Fausto, Santos, and Leonardo for accepting her as an equal member of the crew. Fausto had taken a bit of persuading, but still, Marina appreciated her brother's confidence in her mettle.

However, things were now different. Now, after the horrifying deaths of Santos Ignacio and Molina, all Marina could think about was returning to the safety of the *Redenzione*, sailing back to Palermo, and never again stepping foot upon this hideous landscape. There was nothing on Caprona for her; there was nothing there for any of them, except death.

At half the distance to the edge of the jungle, the group paused when they heard rustling among the stalks nearby. Marina's fear that the tigers had crept upon them was allayed when she spied several small animals wandering through the tall grass no more than ten feet away. She tapped the arm of Fausto and pointed to the animals. Upon closer inspection, the extraordinary nature of the creatures became apparent. The largest of the animals stood only two feet tall at the shoulder, and the creatures' mottled, furred frames recalled those of full-size horses, only remarkably miniaturized. Their noses were broader and their legs stouter than those of conventional horses and most notable were their feet, which sported toes rather than conventional hooves. The animals grazed upon the light green sprouts that covered the field, but when Lago whispered to his companion, the tiny horses bounded into the stalks amid a chorus of high-pitched whinnies.

As the band ventured farther from the sky cutter, more of Caprona's natural wildlife revealed itself. Insects were abundant in the field; some species were recognizable, while others were unknown to them, or simply much larger than any they had ever encountered. One of the sailors, Trimboli, pointed to the rolling green hills to the east. The explorers were much too far away to make a concrete identification, but a herd of hardy animals bearing large antlers meandered over the distant hummock. At least their party would not go hungry during their sojourn on the lost continent.

Marina walked to the head of the group and positioned herself beside her brother, casually guiding him out of earshot from the others. She spoke quietly to him. "We've been lucky so far," she whispered.

Fausto gave her a reassuring smile as he employed the halberd to widen the passage between an imposing cluster of stalks. Once past the grouping of plants before them, it would only be a short distance to the wall of green that delineated the perimeter of the jungle.

Marina continued her thought. "Do you think Leonardo is safe back there?" she asked.

"I don't think it matters much where any of us are," Fausto admitted bluntly. "But you're not speaking about being safe from animals."

"You know I'm not," Marina said, in a hushed tone.

Over the past few months, Fausto's sister had steadily fed him her distrust of the Spaniards. The siblings had quarreled on the topic, but never in the presence of others. As the weeks at sea turned to months, Marina had abandoned speaking overtly of her unease; instead of voicing concerns, she simply glared at Fausto when she disagreed with the words or behavior of the soldiers. For Fausto, Marina's unrelenting warnings became like an old song repeated much too frequently, to the point of its eventual dismissal. She knew he was convinced he held the upper hand over Colonel Valdez and his men, but with his primary advisor killed, Fausto was very much alone in his decision-making. Despite her love for her brother, Marina could not help but feel that the lives of the entire crew rested in the hands of a well-meaning but inept captain. That she doubted her brother caused her immeasurable hurt, but she kept those feelings bottled inside of her and continued to hope for the best.

Fausto used the sole of his boot to push aside a stubborn stalk he had loosened with the halberd, then wiped his forehead with the ruffle of his sleeve. The air became increasingly humid as the day progressed and the thought of finding fresh, flowing water was now the primary objective in the explorers' minds. Behind Marina and Fausto, Collazo let out a short whistle. They froze in their tracks at the sound of the sailor's warning. They listened intently, but Collazo's concern of danger was not borne out, and the group resumed their trek toward the looming trees.

The wall of foliage that greeted them was as foreboding as it was immense. Towering palms intertwined with the vast array of tree species, many of which reached over a hundred feet in height, while others exceeded even that. From the overhead branches hung a tangle of vines, ivy, and runners that resembled an airborne tapestry. Similarly, bushes and fern fronds of astounding proportions densely packed the jungle floor.

"It's beautiful," Marina offered respectfully.

The rest of the group remained silent while they absorbed the ramifications of the task before them. As Marina had observed, the jungle was beautiful, but so was the hide of a cobra. What dangers might lie in waiting within the shadowy forest were unknown; however, their parched throats reminded them that death might come for them, regardless of whether they took another step.

"Onward," Fausto commanded.

Rather than traverse the thirty-foot span of low ground vegetation between the tall stalks and the trees, the explorers hesitated and looked at one another. The shadows beckoned to them, but with each step they would move farther from the wreck of the sky cutter and closer to the fearsome unknown. Although no one spoke, Marina knew exactly what caused their collected pause, for she felt it within her own heart. She drew a breath, smiled at Fausto, and cautiously marched toward the trees. Not to be outdone by a woman, the others followed her lead.

Within seconds, Marina and Fausto reached the copious ferns that fenced the denser jungle proper. The siblings pushed aside the dark green foliage to clear a path when a flourish of activity rustled the plants to their right. Before Marina could digest what was transpiring, three small animals darted past her feet and rushed toward the tall stalks from whence the travelers had come. Whatever they were, the creatures moved like lightning, their pale yellow bodies appearing as nothing more than a blur to the startled onlookers. Two of the creatures disappeared between the tall stalks, while the third stopped short as if curious about the beings who had roused them from their hiding place.

"What in the name of God is that?" Sergeant Ortega whispered. He and the others had no name for the animal they looked upon. By all appearances, the thing was some form of lizard with a long slender neck and a tapered, whiplike tail. Unlike lizards found in the Mediterranean, however, this one ran upon its thin hind legs and now stood upright—nearly three feet in height—as it assessed those who looked upon it. The tiny head upon the long neck tilted from side to side with quick, jerking movements.

Trimboli stuttered in amazement. "Is that a lizard? It stands like a man." The others were just as confounded as the sailor, but all were roused from their fixation by Collazo's short whistle. It was another warning, but what threat could the small animal possibly present, Marina wondered? The Sicilians and Spaniards froze in their tracks, unsure how to react or what exactly they were supposed to beware.

Time stood still as an immense jungle cat leaped between the stalks to land atop the screeching lizard. The primal beast had lowered its belly to the ground and lay crouched, its great curved claws instantly killing its much smaller prey. Without acknowledging the human onlookers, the saber-toothed predator grasped the carcass between its jaws, stood, and padded back into the dense brush.

Marina, Fausto, and the others did not hesitate, and as one they frantically plunged into the jungle in the hope of finding safety among the maze of boles, bushes, and ferns.

The monster has been stalking us the whole time, Marina thought. As she ran, the realization of just how close death had pursued them without their knowledge sent a shiver up her spine. Even more chilling was the possibility that the savage cats had intentionally isolated the humans to obstruct their safe return to the sky cutter.

9
GREEN HELL

The panicked travelers' headlong plunge into the jungle growth was not how Marina imagined an organized party should proceed. With no indication that the enormous tigers had followed them, Fausto and his charges eventually curbed their fears into a semblance of composure, and within minutes they ceased their flight to catch their breaths.

Around them, the jungle was alive with sound. Overhead, birds hopped through the dense canopy, their mocking calls reminding all in Fausto's party that they were quite vulnerable to the threats that prowled the sky. *Let them taunt*, Marina thought. At least the tangled canopy overhead would prevent the large airborne predators from swooping down upon them unexpectedly. The thought was of minor consolation, but it was something.

Although the party's course had been directionless, Trimboli assured the others that he had been carefully memorizing their path. The last thing they needed was to become lost within the primeval maze of trees and foliage. Sergeant Lago, as was his wont, objected to Trimboli's recollection of the direction of their travel, but the others paid little heed to the soldier's protestation; if one stated the sky was blue, Lago would insist it was yellow, such was the combative nature of his personality, to the benefit of none.

Fausto wiped a bead of sweat from his forehead and assessed all within sight. Marina watched as he noted the sun's position, barely visible through the jungle's ceiling. From what she could recall of the terrain surrounding the sky cutter's landing point, their best chance for finding water was to travel west. In that direction lay rolling hills at the base of forested highlands, and there, freshwater streams fed by the higher elevations of Caprona might be found. Sergeants Lago and Ortega inspected their muskets and the exploratory party continued their advancement in an orderly fashion.

They had walked for only a short time when they discovered trees bearing large fruits resembling coconuts, similar to those that grow in the tropics. Collazo scaled a tree and cut loose several of the large green fruits. Further inspection revealed a hollow interior beneath the thick rind and fibrous meat that they scraped from the husk. Ants found the fruits delightful, which assured them that the pomes were not poisonous, allaying the concerns of the absent Leonardo Ricci. Six canteens with sturdy vine slings were soon fashioned and now hung from the shoulders of the crew as they continued their march through the dense jungle undergrowth.

Before leaving the relative safety of the downed sky cutter, Fausto and his team received a detailed description of the species of tree that might yield the liquefied rubber that they needed to repair the damaged balloon. All the searchers, including the Spaniards, examined trees and tugged at bark as they passed, but their efforts to find a specimen of the exact stripe for which they hunted yielded no favorable results. The soldiers did not vocalize their unease, but it was clear to Marina that Lago and Ortega were equally eager to uncover a store of natural latex that would precipitate a safe return flight to the waiting *Redenzione*.

They had walked for only a little over an hour, but already stomachs were beginning to protest their emptiness. However, the strangers to Caprona had yet to find fruit they could recognize or identify. Despite the beauty of her surroundings and the thrill of exploring a lost continent, frustration began to mount within Marina, and she was certain that the silence of the others indicated they felt likewise.

As they walked, Marina pointed to various unusual plants along their path, and she and her brother marveled at the striking beauty of Caprona's flora. Whether ferns or flowers, berries on bushes, or the tree boles themselves, much of the plant life of Caprona was of outsized proportions, at least in comparison to those of commonplace plants in the outside world. Here, flowers bloomed larger than a man's head, and the insect pollinators of the land that buzzed among them were much larger than those of Sicily. Several bees the size of falcons had been noted. The travelers exercised extreme caution not to rouse the massive insects from their routines among the huge, vivid flowers that proliferated throughout the jungle.

The members of the party also encountered small, lizard-like creatures such as the ones they had seen at the periphery of the jungle. The odd animals came in various colors and markings, and not one showed a sign of aggression toward the noisy strangers, much to the relief of Fausto's crew. Had they been hostile toward the humans, the sheer number of the loping reptiles could easily have posed a formidable threat, but as it was, they were easily frightened away by the approaching explorers.

Marina could not help but feel an austere reverence for the jungle. It could very well be the case that humans had never before set foot there, and it was very much as if they were trespassers on the private estate of the Almighty. The two sailors independently shared as much with Fausto and Marina, who reciprocated the notion. Notwithstanding a few sparse interactions, the voyagers were unusually quiet throughout their search for water. Each of them would confess that their silence had less to do with alerting whatever predators might be near and more about feeling utterly humbled by the lush, unspoiled beauty of Caprona's interior.

A second hour, then a third, passed since they had ventured beyond the tree line, and the group's failure to find a source of flowing water began to take its toll on Marina's confidence.

Cautiously out of earshot of the others, she shared her reservations with Fausto.

"Let me ask you something," she said. "Just between you and me. Are you scared?"

Fausto blanched at the suggestion. "Scared?" he scoffed. "Of what?" His aloof facade did nothing but stoke her frustration.

"Sometimes I wonder why I bother with you," she growled.

"Well, what do you want me to say, Marina? That I'm terrified we're all going to die here?" Fausto was careful to lower the volume of his voice before uttering his retort. "Listen. We're all stranded here; we're all thirsty. I understand how you feel, but—"

Marina interjected before he could finish his thought. "Do you understand how I feel? Do you really?" she snapped. "I don't think you do. I don't think you ever have."

"What is that supposed to mean, and what does that have to do with anything?" he asked with what seemed genuine innocence.

Marina thought for a moment, recalling the harsh words Fausto had uttered not long after they sailed from Palermo. She remembered them word for word. He had said, "You're just a woman. No one expects anything from you, other than to be a wife and to bear children, neither of which you've accomplished, by the way." Months later, Fausto's comment still stung, and perhaps it was not her brother's current casual disregard of her worries that fueled her anger, but rather the recollection of the cruel assessment of her life he had made months prior.

"Listen, Marina, you need to make up your mind whether or not you trust me," Fausto said. "Your confidence always depends on which way the wind is blowing, and frankly, I don't need that right now. You also don't always have to be right. You know, the problem with you," Fausto sputtered, "is that you always wager everything on what only *you* think is true."

She grabbed his coat sleeve to stop him in his tracks. The others walked past and when the sailors and Spaniards were several yards away, Marina freely voiced her thoughts. "And the problem with you, Fausto," she said, fuming, "is that you will wager everything on something you *know* might not be true at *all*. That's not a gamble. That's foolish and selfish."

"Well, why did you even come on this voyage?" he shouted to her as she stomped away from him.

The outburst caused the other men to halt their progress and look with curiosity in Fausto's direction as Marina marched past them. *"Sisters,"* he muttered as a feeble offer of explanation to the others. Fausto, his crew, and the Spaniards followed Marina's path forward.

The sun was still quite high in the sky when the group paused to rest in a clearing of low grass and moss. The area was devoid of trees in a fifty-foot radius. A large fallen tree provided seating above the ground; considering the size and number of insects and spiders that scurried over the face of Caprona, Marina was more than happy to take a break from shaking curious pests from her boots. Fausto joined her atop the downed tree and diligently surveyed the surrounding curtain of jungle growth.

"I certainly did not expect this heat," he said as he removed his heavy coat.

It was the first time he had attempted to speak to Marina since their earlier altercation, which she now greatly regretted. Although Marina had left her coat back on the sky cutter, she was not the least bit comfortable. She had unbuttoned her blouse to below the clavicle, but it did little to ease the effects of the humid clime. They needed to find water soon.

At one side of the clearing, Sergeants Lago and Ortega conversed in a patch of shade. Marina watched them warily. "Look at that," she said to her brother, bobbing her head toward the Spaniards. Judging from their vigorous hand movements, the soldiers appeared to be engaged in a minor disagreement. "What do you think they're discussing?"

"I don't know," Fausto admitted dismissively, "and I don't care. We need to find water for Signore Ricci. He's old, and he's depending on us." Marina concurred.

Collazo joined the siblings in their quiet observation of the Spaniards. "Do you understand Spanish, Collazo?" Fausto inquired with his eyes still on the soldiers.

"I was about to ask the same of you, Captain," Collazo responded. "Not to cause alarm, but while we were walking, your name, and yours, Signora . . . Sergeant Lago brought them up quite a bit. I don't know if it means anything, but I thought you should know, sir," the sailor said.

"Quiet," Marina whispered. Sergeant Ortega had parted from his countryman and walked toward the Sicilians. A distinct air about him indicated he had something to say, but his conscience kept his lips sealed.

Fausto spoke as if he detected nothing amiss. "How are you and Lago faring, Sergeant?" he asked.

The soldier shot a glance in Lago's direction. The surly Spaniard was attending to sharpening the blade of his halberd. "We're doing well enough, sir," Ortega replied politely. Still, his demeanor indicated he had something unspoken on his mind.

"Have you ever been on an expedition such as this, Sergeant?" Fausto asked.

With good-natured sarcasm, Orgeta responded, "Has anyone?"

Marina gently interjected. "I think Captain Caproni is wondering the same thing as I," she said. "Have you ever been a part of a colonization party? And if you have, what might we expect, and are there any considerations you and Sergeant Lago are taking into advisement that have not been shared with us?"

Fausto stiffened, an act perceived only by Marina. Fausto would have taken a different tack to gather information from the soldier, but Marina saw no point in beating around the bush.

Before giving the Spaniard an opportunity to answer, she continued. "I couldn't help but notice that you and Sergeant Lago seem a bit . . . at odds about something. Is it anything that should concern the rest of us?"

Ortega paused as if to consider his words, or perhaps to decide whether he wanted to speak at all. He glanced at Lago, found him still concentrating on his halberd, and turned his attention back to the Capronis. Marina knew he was about to take them into his confidence. That alone proved to Marina that she had been right all along, that there was something inscrutable about the behavior of Colonel Valdez and his men.

Fausto looked uneasy, as if wary of what underlying cause might be the root of Ortega's hesitation. "What is it, Sergeant?" he whispered.

"You asked what you might expect," Ortega replied in a hushed tone. "When we return to Madrid, you can expect the same expansion of the Spanish Empire as the world witnessed in Hispanola, Mexico, Alta California. Any natives of Caprona will become subjects of the empire."

Ortega's assertion was fundamentally flawed, as the agreement between Fausto and Maria Christina explicitly stated that any lands discovered during the voyage would be claimed in the name of the Kingdom of the Two Sicilies. It did not matter to Marina that the soldier misunderstood the finer details of the agreement; the reminder of what the Sicilians endured under Spanish rule set her blood to boiling.

"Alta California? Look how well that turned out for Spain," Marina said mockingly. "Alta California has been returned to Mexico. The native peoples are once again free."

"But not before years of suffering, Signora," Ortega said darkly. "I was there. I saw it with my own eyes . . ."

"So far there is no indication of people on Caprona," Fausto interjected, "but that is beside the point. Respectfully, everything you have said is irrelevant, Sergeant! The agreement signed by Queen Regent Maria Christina states that Spain

will be granted favored annexation and port rights, not ownership of the land," Fausto explained resolutely. "I have claimed
this continent in the name of the Kingdom of the Two Sicilies.
The Spanish Empire has no authority here."

"And I ask you, Captain Caproni," Ortega voiced in a tone
as cold as steel, "who will know of your discovery if the
Redenzione returns to Europe without you and your Sicilian
crew?"

Marina did not bother to look at her brother, as she could
assume he was similarly flabbergasted by Ortega's nefarious
insinuation. Instead, her focus was on her balled fist. Whether
or not it would be a wise move, she fully intended to follow
through with what her temper urged her to do.

In her wildest imaginings, she could not picture her brother
doing the same, however. Try as she might, Marina could not
recall ever having seen Fausto engage in fisticuffs with another.
Fausto was not the violent type, even when pressed by aggressors. It just wasn't in him, to a fault, in Marina's opinion. She
knew that some called it cowardice.

Marina, however, had no qualms about smashing the face
of someone who dearly asked for it. Just ask Giovanni
Pellegrino.

But before she could act on her impulses, Collazo let out
a short, shrill whistle.

At the periphery of the small clearing, something was
moving through the jungle, shaking the bushes and even the
trees themselves. Several small bipedal lizards sprinted from
the low foliage, darted across the clearing past the fallen tree,
and disappeared into the jungle. Whatever was coming their
way was large and heavy, its thudding footfalls splintering
fallen branches with each step.

"Hide!" Fausto shouted to the others. He and Marina
dropped stealthily to the ground, and Collazo and Ortega
joined them behind the rotting tree husk. At opposite edges
of the jungle, Sergeant Lago and Trimboli quickly and quietly
backed into the bushes to conceal themselves from whatever

animal was making its noisy approach. As the explorers collectively held their breath, the beast revealed itself as it meandered forth from the verdure.

Never had Marina beheld, or even conceived of, such an unusual creature. To say it was large was an understatement; the mass of its body was that of an elephant, but the animal was twice the length of a pachyderm when considering its long tail, the end of which was tipped with a large bony ball twice the size of a wine cask. A thick, leathery skin of light purple covered the beast, and even if the creature intended to devour them, Marina found its color quite fetching. The beast trod across the low jungle brush on four stout legs, and its lumbering gait and the oval, charcoal-colored half-shell upon its back reminded Marina of a turtle. Bony spikes jutted from the shell in all directions and skirted its circumference perpendicular to the ground while decreasing in size as they continued down the flanks of its tail.

Seemingly oblivious to the humans, the great reptilian creature rooted its blunt muzzle across the jungle floor as it meandered closer to the fallen tree behind which the Capronis hid. After only a few anxious seconds, the enormous animal butted the top of its bone-plated head against the side of the trunk. The animal was now snorting heavily, and Marina assumed it had picked up their scent, but the creature's intentions were unknown. The strength of the shelled reptile was considerable; with each thrust of the creature's head, the entire rotting tree shook and threatened to roll atop those who had taken refuge behind it. The dislodging of the tree from its resting place roused insects and small snakes from their dens beneath the decaying husk, all of which crawled and slithered past the feet of the explorers.

Ortega was loading his rifle with practiced precision, but before he could fire a loud report ushered forth from the tree line. Lago had fired upon the beast. The range was only half a dozen yards, but the musket ball appeared to have missed its target. Not a sound ushered from the creature.

With lightning speed, Lago had again loaded his weapon and fired, but the second shot did not miss the giant, nor had the first. The projectiles had indeed hit the beast but had no impact upon its activity, nor had the lead balls injured or distracted the animal to any degree.

While they remained in the clearing, they were vulnerable. Marina and her companions crouched low and crept the length of the ivy-covered trunk to its exposed roots with the intent of dashing to safety among the trees. Trimboli stood among the ferns at the tree line, his hand motions indicating that it was safe for his trapped companions to run. But as Fausto tensed to begin his dash to safety, he paused. An odd, droning sound wavered through the air, but from where it originated he could not determine. The rotting tree shook once again. Marina, Fausto, Ortega, and Collazo fell away from it, as all were certain that, at any second, the massive trunk would roll upon them. However, as the shelled giant retracted its head upon its short neck, the trunk fell back where it had lain.

"We must run, now!" Fausto ordered the others in a hushed tone.

Another musket ball burst forth from Lago's rifle, but the immense beast's uninterrupted snorts indicated the stinging impacts of the shots were the equivalent of harmless insect bites. Fausto gave Marina a nod of assurance. At the tree line, Trimboli waved frantically. Her brother began a crouched trot across the grassy expanse between the fallen tree and the jungle. Gripping his halberd in one hand, Fausto extended his other behind him as he kept his eyes on the trees. "Come, Marina! Quickly!"

"Fausto, wait!" Marina yelled. Through the din created by the shaking of the tree trunk behind which she was hidden, another sound had caught her attention. Something distant, but increasing in volume.

It was only after taking a few steps that Fausto seemed to realize that Trimboli's gestures were intended as a warning.

The authors of the odd, whirring noise wove through the peripheral tree line and floated sluggishly toward the fallen tree and the turtle-like monster at the clearing's center.

Marina stood frozen, a mixture of awe and terror etched on her face, but to her relief, the swarm's flight appeared directionless and not to be focused on her brother. The drone of their transparent wings grew ever louder as they approached the fallen tree, the bright sun over Caprona causing the insects to cast large shadows on the jungle floor below them. Each of the huge wasps was at least the size of her biggest cat, Sovrano, their shiny black bodies devoid of any distinguishing marks save for the bright red terminuses of their abdomens. Marina imagined the sting of such a colossal insect would feel not dissimilar to being impaled by a sculptor's chisel.

Ortega fell forward away from the tree as the turtle creature continued to butt against the opposite side of the barrier. "This is a land of madness!" he shouted. "We should return to the sky cutter!"

"Coward!" Marina shouted angrily, drawing her rapier from its sheath. "Slink back to your conniving commander. The rest of us will complete this mission without your help." She intended to dash from the tree toward Fausto, who had reached safety beside Trimboli among the jungle boles. Marina's impulsive plan was spoiled as suddenly as she conceived it when the deafening, high-pitched buzzing descended upon her.

The flying black terrors hovered angrily over Marina, and several alighted on the rotting bark of the shaking tree. The giant wasps were visibly angered by the presence of the humans but seemed most concerned about crawling down the side of the dead tree toward the rich earth beneath. In the dark soil tilled upward by the rotation of the trunk, Marina spied dozens of sickly white larvae wriggling in the dirt, each nearly the length of her forearm. The fallen tree had provided sanctuary for the adolescent wasps, but the actions of the shelled beast had disrupted the tranquility of their nesting site.

The sword of Collazo joined Marina's and together they swiped through the air at the hovering horrors. "Run to the captain!" the sailor shouted. "I'll hold them off."

Marina's eyes shot to Ortega, half-expecting him to have fled to join Lago at the tree line. Instead, Ortega drew his sword and respectfully bowed his head to her. "I am no coward, my lady," he said proudly. "I have been tasked with the protection of the crew of the *Redenzione*, and at that, I will not fail." With a grim smile, the Spanish soldier reaffirmed his sworn duty.

From each side of the clearing came shouts; Fausto's from the left, Sergeant Lago's from the right. Treading either path would be equally treacherous for Marina, Collazo, and Ortega. The head of the reptilian giant again impacted the tree, nearly pushing it atop the Europeans. At any second they could be crushed, and if they ran, the angry swarm of insects would likely overtake them easily and sting them to death. As it was, they were out of options.

"Marina!" Fausto screamed from the tree line. She looked in her brother's direction, but it was not on her that his attention was focused. Rather, he gazed intently at the tangle of vines and trunks directly behind the shelled creature rooting at the fallen tree at the center of the clearing.

An involuntary gasp of astonishment caught in Marina's throat as she watched a terrifying and much larger titan stride from among the dense jungle growth at the perimeter of the clearing. Caprona, it seemed to her, had every intention of arrogantly displaying the myriad ways it could kill the shipwrecked explorers.

10
LOST ON CAPRONA

THE MASSIVE BEAST TOWERED over the jungle floor. By Marina's reckoning, it must have been at least twenty-five feet in height. She had never seen its like, nor had she ever dreamed that such an immense land animal drew breath anywhere upon the Earth. Yet there it stood, a terrifying lizard-like behemoth similar to the smaller animals they had previously encountered but magnified in size to nightmarish proportions.

Like its much smaller cousins, the creature strode upon two powerful legs, the massive head and torso counterbalanced by a prodigious tail, held aloft and parallel to the ground. Its two arms were feebly small, but clearly, its claws were of little value compared to the beast's enormous jaws filled with ivory fangs. Like the shelled creature that continued to root at the fallen tree, the giant's pale auburn skin was thick and leathery, not scaled like the lizards they most closely resembled. Dark splashes of olive mottled the hide of the horrifying animal. If nature intended for the savage creature to prowl through forests undetected, its innate camouflage was a sinister touch. Marina was sure that this animal, this monster, was designed for the singular intent of killing.

The cowering humans held their breaths and tried to ignore the shaking of the fallen tree that concealed them. Collazo and Ortega had dropped to the ground, but Marina still stood and peered through the thick entanglement of the tree's exposed roots. Despite the terror that filled her heart and the giant wasps that buzzed angrily through the air, she had to keep the newly arrived creature in sight.

"Oh, no," she whispered. What she had seen made her abruptly join the soldier and the sailor on the ground.

"What is it?" Ortega said in a tone that made it clear he wished he did not have to ask. "Does it see us?"

"I don't know," Marina responded, with a tremor in her voice. "But there's not just one. There are three."

At each side of the titan stood two diminutive replicas of the creature, lighter in hue and standing only as tall as the underside of the larger's belly. The smaller variations approximated the height of a man, making them no less deadly. By all appearances, the creatures composed a family, with the elder leading its offspring on a hunting mission. To Marina's surprise, the obvious target of the larger beasts—the shelled monster that still plowed against the fallen tree—seemed not at all concerned about the pack of predators.

Fausto tightly gripped the halberd as the steps of the newly arrived pack brought the monsters closer to the downed tree. Meanwhile, Marina was trapped with Collazo and Ortega. The two soldiers thrust their swords as inconspicuously as possible at the enormous wasps that hovered around them. Only through the intervention of either Fausto or Trimboli might they escape, or perhaps Lago at the far side of the circular clearing would be of some help.

But Marina quickly realized that any hope of Sergeant Lago rescuing them was but a fantasy; upon seeing the arrival of the three monstrous hunters, the Spaniard secured the ramrod along the barrel of his weapon, tightened the strings of the purse that contained his supply of musket balls, and disappeared into the shadows of the jungle.

As if insulted that its presence was ignored, the two-legged giant released a thunderous roar that seemed to shake the very ground. It was a horrifying utterance, a savage, bloodthirsty cry of rage. At last, the shelled monster ceased its prodding of the fallen tree and craned its neck to view the trio of challengers. With lightning swiftness, both smaller predators sprang toward the shelled beast. They snapped their jaws futilely; try as they might, their fangs could not pierce the spiked carapace of their prey. At last, the defender displayed its annoyance at the intrusion by rotating its positioning upon truncated legs and swinging its tail through the air. With a crushing impact, the massive bony ball at the end of the creature's tail struck both smaller attackers in one swing, sending them sprawling to the ground at the feet of their much larger elder.

In the shadow of the fallen tree, Sergeant Ortega stiffened in fear as the high-pitched droning of insect wings filled his ears. One of the huge wasps had landed on his back and clung tenaciously to his uniform coat, steadily scaling toward his head. Before the insect could employ its deadly crimson stinger, Marina dropped her rapier and, without time to consider her own surging terror or safety, grabbed the flying horror with both hands. Touching the thing made her skin crawl, but in one fluid motion, she raised the insect above her head and smashed it to the ground with all her might. The wasp was only slightly injured but was now even more infuriated, thrashing and tumbling about the grass. With a sickening crack, the boot heel of Collazo put an end to the wildly buzzing horror.

"Thank you, Signora," Ortega sputtered. "I—"

"We have to get out of here," Marina interjected. "You were right. This is madness."

Collazo had seen the desertion of Sergeant Lago and quickly informed his companions. No help would be found at that edge of the clearing. "Our only chance now," he cried, "is to . . ."

But the sailor's next words were like the faintest of whispers, drowned out by the furious bellows of the beasts of Caprona.

Now engaged in a roaring match with the elder of its hunters, the shelled monster swung its weighty tail cudgel at the lower legs of its attacker. Somewhere in its dim reptilian brain, the upright beast must have recognized the danger of being struck; thus, it remained a safe distance from its intended prey and scratched its black talons in frustration across the jungle floor.

The two youngsters had other plans. One had spotted Fausto and Trimboli at the tree line, and with a guttural hiss, it began to stalk across the clearing in their direction. The lizard's sibling nimbly leaped upon the fallen tree and found prey much closer to the battle being waged by its parent. The predator loomed so closely over Marina that she could see the black slits of its vertical pupils expand in its golden eyes in anticipation of the kill. Death was upon them.

The monster crouched on its muscular hind legs and prepared to spring from its perch, but the gigantic wasps thwarted its intention. The buzzing black terrors hovered near the head of their enemy, and though the juvenile hunter shrieked warnings at its aggressors, its roars and gnashing of teeth did not intimidate the insects and they pressed their attack.

Marina, Collazo, and Ortega knew their only recourse. The three shot from the natural barricade toward the assumed safety of the jungle beyond. Marina's heartbeat pounded in her ears as she fled. Almost instantly, she regretted dropping her rapier to tear the wasp from the back of Ortega. She had not the opportunity to retrieve the weapon and was now defenseless against the horrors of Caprona.

"Split up!" Ortega shouted as he bolted across the underbrush. "They can't catch all of us!" It was a sobering, if not fatalistic, plan, which assumed that success equated to not all of them dying. But Marina knew the soldier was right, and she, Collazo, and Ortega all chose widely varying escape paths into the dense verdure.

With no immediate thought of her direction of travel, Marina crashed through the ferns and vines and briars. She could not look behind her for fear of seeing a mouthful of reptilian fangs, and she ran as she had never run before. The spindly fingers of jungle undergrowth clawed at her clothing as the boots she had borrowed from her brother carried her down a headlong course with no destination . . .

Fausto's boots . . .

Fausto! She had fled without him! And to where was she running? If she stopped her mad flight to determine her location by glancing up at the sun, one of the beasts would surely rend the flesh from her bones. She had to keep running; she had to live. She had to find water! Marina gripped the only possession on her person, the hollowed-out fruit that would serve as a canteen. Surely, Leonardo Ricci direly needed water by now.

Onward she plunged over uneven ground, gnarled roots, and downed tree limbs. Her heart leaped to her throat—something had grabbed her arm! She pulled back from the unseen assailant and wrenched her left arm across her chest, only to find not an animal gripping her but several vine creepers adorned with thick thorns like the teeth of a shark. Marina would not stop, she could not stop, and the barbs pulled at the fine material of her garments, tearing both the blouse sleeve and her skin. The thorns burned where they had raked her; she had been cut, but there was no time to tend to superficial wounds or scrutinize the damage done to her sleeve.

Marina vividly recalled the day she had purchased the blouse. The sky was exceptionally blue that morning and a cool breeze was blowing in from the Mediterranean. She and her mother had saved enough money to buy some new clothes. Just after lunch—they had eaten roasted peppers stuffed with fresh goat cheese—Marina's mother had noticed the white blouse on a street vendor's cart. It was perfect for the summer, with delicately embroidered frills at the cuffs and collar. And now she had torn it, irreparably. It was ruined. The blouse she had bought on the last happy excursion to Palermo's Ballarò street market before her mother . . .

No. This was not the time to dwell on the past, not the time to dredge up the soul-wrenching helplessness she experienced as she watched her beloved parents succumb to the horrible disease two summers ago. As she ran, Marina recalled the words of Santos Ignacio, a proverb she had once overheard him proclaim to her father: "Only in calm waters can you see the coral reef below the surface. If you cannot see it, you cannot safely navigate past it." Somewhere behind her, where the roars of the hideous titans shook the trees, her brother needed her. Marina buried the panic that threatened to overwhelm her senses—she "calmed the waters"—and resolved to be strong, not only for her own sake but for that of Fausto.

Gathering her courage, Marina ceased her flight, ducked into a thicket of towering ferns, and pressed her back against the trunk of a large palm concealed therein. A sudden shriek filled the air and she dropped to her stomach among the ferns, but to her relief, the cries came not from her human-sized pursuers but from a pair of small, feathered flying lizards that wildly chased one another. The brightly plumed creatures wove through the trees and disappeared, and then all became quiet, save for the sound of Marina's staccato panting. Rising to a crouch, she realized the rich black loam beneath the huge fronds was quite damp. The young Sicilian wiped her muddy hands on the rough tree bark, then examined her soiled palms. Her slender hands were shaking.

At last, her breathing became controlled and she absorbed the entirety of the sounds around her. The trees were filled with exotic chirps and squawks, but the distant roars of the battling beasts had ceased. How the conflict had ended she did not know, but there were no musket shots nor human cries to be heard. With luck, all in her party had escaped. But to where? Marina was chilled by the thought that she was desperately alone, a solitary woman lost in a savage jungle, with no idea where she was or in which direction to find Fausto and the others.

The little speech by Sergeant Ortega about his steadfast devotion now thrust itself to the forefront of her thoughts. Ortega seemed quite sincere about his loyalty to duty and the protection of Fausto and his crew, which included herself.

But it was his delivery of the statement, the tone of his voice . . . there was a distinct implication that the Spanish soldier's sentiment was not shared by his countrymen. If Ortega was to be trusted, then his additional warning that the Sicilians might never return from Caprona while the Spanish claimed the land for themselves took on a more potent relevance.

If Ortega were to be believed, the crew of the *Redenzione* had just as much to fear from their human companions as they did from the nightmarish beasts of Caprona.

The young Sicilian's paramount concerns were locating her companions and assuring the safety of her younger brother, none of which could be accomplished unless she was adequately prepared to weather the harsh environment of the lost island continent. Marina had ignored her torn arm while she was running, but now, in the cool shade of the copse of giant ferns, she pulled at the bloody sleeve of her blouse to inspect the stinging wounds. The gashes inflicted by the jungle thorns across the back of her forearm were not serious, but they were deep enough to require bandaging. Even though her white blouse was already beyond repair, it still pained her to tear loose the entire sleeve at the shoulder seam, for such is the foundation of sentimentality. Caprona's hot clime could have benefitted from the cool breeze of the Mediterranean, to which Marina was so accustomed, but it was only a blouse; she removed the remaining sleeve and felt immediately cooler. She wrapped the clean sleeve around the wounds on her arm and tied it tight enough to prevent the introduction of dirt and bacteria into the cuts, then wadded the bloody and shredded sleeve and discarded it on the ground.

Much as she would have liked to retrieve her lost rapier, Marina concluded that returning to the site of the monstrous battle—and the nest of the giant wasps—would be foolhardy. Instead, she crept stealthily from her hiding place and, detecting no enemies about her, searched for something from which she could construct a weapon. Whatever it would be, it must be lightweight enough not to be a hindrance and useful at keeping adversaries at bay. Caprona would need to provide for her.

Marina searched the jungle floor and examined the trees for anything that could be used as a weapon, but it was while she was casually attending to the bandage on her arm that an idea struck her. It did not take long for her to find an adequate tree branch on the ground that conformed with the required length and weight to suit her needs. She broke off the tapered end of the softwood limb in such a way as to create a pointed spear-end, and then with great care ripped long lengths of thorned vines from the undergrowth. Those she wrapped and tied about the end of the makeshift lance to create a formidable club. Caprona's jungle had "bitten" her, now she would use the island's own "teeth" against the ferocious monsters that prowled its face, should they be foolish enough to challenge her. She laughed at her bravado, but after swinging the makeshift club a few times to test its weight, she felt satisfied with its defensive potential.

"Marina!" a voice cried out. The young woman's heart leaped. It was Collazo!

She could not yet see the sailor, but she was encouraged beyond measure and excitedly pushed forth from the gigantic ferns behind which she had been hiding. Her gaze shot about the surrounding jungle and landed upon her young countryman, moving as quickly as possible through the dense undergrowth.

"Collazo! I'm here!" she yelled, her face alight with relief. If Collazo had escaped the enormous predators as she had, it was highly likely that Fausto, too, was safe. Marina waved her hand above her head to draw the sailor's attention, only thirty feet from her.

The shot rang out just as Collazo's eyes met Marina's. He gripped his chest with a clenched fist as the spark of life instantaneously drained from his face. The sailor, dead on his feet, collapsed forward upon the cool green bosom of Caprona.

With the utter detachment of a huntsman stalking pheasants,

Sergeant Lago reloaded his rifle as he marched toward Collazo's corpse. He kicked the body to verify the sailor's death. Marina took immediate advantage of Lago's distraction and receded quietly into the tall ferns. She prayed that the murderous Spaniard had not seen her, but Collazo had yelled out and she had reciprocated. Had Lago heard her cry? The soldier scanned the surrounding woods. His smile confirmed that he suspected she was very near.

Sergeant Ortega had not lied about Lago, but to where could Marina run to escape her hunter? Even if she could successfully evade the terrors stalking the face of Caprona, returning to the wreck of the *Pegaso II* would yield nothing but the delivery of herself into the den of vipers. It was clear to Marina that she had only one recourse. Fausto and Trimboli were somewhere in that vast jungle, and she must warn them of the soldiers' treachery. As adrenaline surged through her, Marina slid around the bole of the tree within the copse of ferns and bolted into the jungle behind her. But to where she was running, she did not know.

The wonderment Marina experienced upon first seeing Caprona's strange animal life was now dulled to a curt dismissal. As her boots crunched through the jungle's twisted ground cover, unnamed reptiles and mammals hissed and barked at her as she passed, and she gave not one of them the slightest regard. There was no time to marvel at the bizarre species. There was only time to run. Marina was unsure how far she had traveled, but each time she slowed to catch her breath, she could hear the distant approach of another; Lago, damn him, was still in pursuit. Even if she could not find Fausto, she hoped to at least stumble upon the perimeter of the plain on which lay the *Pegaso II*, if only to register her location with relation to where she might find her brother. But the farther she ran, the jungle grew denser. Marina was hopelessly lost and was certain her flight carried her farther into oblivion.

Before Marina realized that the ground beneath her feet

had disappeared, she was already tumbling forward uncontrollably. Her frantic trek had carried her to the edge of a ravine down whose rocky side she now slid. Throughout her progress through the jungle, she had gripped the club tightly, but now she had to release her hold on the weapon to attempt to slow her fall. She lay back, spread her arms, and dug the heels of her boots into the rocky ground, and within seconds succeeded in ending her downward slide.

As the dust around her cleared, Marina quickly got her bearings. She had not fallen far, only fifteen feet from the top edge of the ravine, and she had come to rest upon a mossy ledge. Cautiously, she peered over its edge. Below her, the rock walls dropped precipitously to the black waters of a muddy swamp some thirty feet down. From the water's surface to the ledge upon which she sat, a web of twisted vines and tree roots blanketed the canyon wall and dangled above the steaming marsh. The concentric rings that rippled across the water's surface below revealed the unfortunate location of her club.

A heavy shroud of fear enveloped Marina when she heard the oily voice, only a few feet above her. "You've come a long way to die, *Signora*." Sergeant Lago's mocking words came between ragged breaths. The Spaniard stood proudly, holding his musket across his chest to project an appearance of vigor, but Marina perceived otherwise. Lago's face was unusually flushed, his forehead dotted with perspiration; the chase through the wood had taken an obvious toll on his stamina. Though he had been taxed physically, his well-being did not cross the periphery of his concern. Lago grinned as he tightened his grip on the rifle. His prey was now trapped. There would be no escape for Marina Caproni.

Marina recognized her predicament and the odds of a safe outcome for herself. Perhaps she could escape by dropping into the swamp below . . .

Then, she saw it.

The ripples created by her club striking the dark water were now met and overlapped by other ripples, radiating toward the cliff wall. Something in the water was moving, something ebon and large, its scaled surface glistening in the sun. It glided through the black murk, undulating like a snake, a fearsome creature whose length was at least equal to four times Marina's height. Then, to the creature's right came another; then to the left, two more. Marina watched in horror as the huge reptiles investigated the source of the splash, and displeased that a living thing had not fallen into its realm, each rose on four stout legs and raised its snout from beneath the muck. The terrible reptiles threw wide their massive jaws and emitted nightmarish hisses. Their black eyes had spied her, trapped upon the ledge.

Marina had once seen a similar animal preserved and on display in a museum; it was a crocodile, captured in the waters of the Nile. A crocodile was a fearsome creature in itself, but these variations were much larger, with rougher, scalier hides, and each seemed to have three times the number of teeth as the stuffed specimen she had studied. A few yards above her, Sergeant Lago laughed tauntingly.

She looked to the soldier, her dark eyes filled not with fear or pleading, but with rage. Marina was bloodied, her clothing torn; she was encrusted with mud and dust; her dark hair was mussed and her tanned and porcelain-smooth complexion and hands were smudged with streaks of black soil. But nothing could dampen the fire within her. "Why?" Marina demanded.

The Spaniard again laughed, delighting in the impossible plight of the pretty Sicilian woman. "Why?" he echoed. "Because children are not meant to rule. The ignorant are not meant to rule. The Kingdom of Spain," he crowed, "we were meant to rule. And rule we shall. Caprona will be ours."

Marina edged closer to the precipice. Below her, the tangle of vines extended far beneath the view of Sergeant Lago, but only a few yards below them prowled the monstrous crocodiles.

"Would you prefer a musket ball through your heart, or shall I just give you a little push?" Lago asked fiendishly.

She must save Fausto. She must save Leonardo Ricci. She must do for them what she could not do for Santos Ignacio. With utmost determination and with no shred of fear, Marina flung herself over the side of the ledge and fell below the lip. Within seconds, her pleas for help resounded across the swamp, followed by a loud splash. The monstrous crocodiles lunged through the black water and Marina's terrified screams were mercifully cut short.

11
HUNTERS AND PREY

F AUSTO HAD WATCHED HELPLESSLY as Marina, Collazo, and the Spanish soldier, Sergeant Ortega, bolted from the natural arena dominated by the thundering giants. He knew not if they had seen a prime opportunity to escape from the monstrous reptiles or if their flight was an impulsive last-ditch effort to save their lives, but he was heartened that none of the monsters pursued them as they fled. However, Fausto's hope that his sister might find safety among the trees was dashed in the blink of an eye as the three runners chose widely divergent paths into the dense jungle.

"They did it, Captain!" shouted Trimboli. "They escaped!"

Fausto's response was tinged with dread. "Marina and Collazo should have stayed together."

"Surely the soldiers will find them," Trimboli offered optimistically.

Fausto's demeanor was dour. "That's what I'm afraid of," he said. But before the young captain could clarify his ominous statement, one of the juvenile beasts was upon them.

The creature had eyed them warily from the downed tree where its parent was unsuccessfully engaging the shelled giant and had quietly stalked toward the pair of humans who had been distracted by the flight of their companions. With astonishing speed, the hissing beast leaped to within only six feet of the two men. It lowered its head nearly to the ground, then swiftly craned it upward toward the blue sky, its maw held wide to expose dozens of pearly white fangs, as it expelled a shrill screech throughout the motion. The call was not one of fear or warning; it was a presumptive cry of victory.

Fausto and Trimboli fell away from the creature, but with each of their frantic backsteps, the beast strode forward, pushing them from the edge of the clearing into the jungle. They would not escape, and running from the nimble hunter would avail nothing. Fausto gulped hard. For the sake of Trimboli, there could be only one recourse. He must face death head-on.

"Run, Trimboli!" Fausto shouted. "Find Marina and Collazo and get them back to the sky cutter!"

Upon signing on to the crew of the *Redenzione* months prior, Trimboli had taken a solemn oath. Despite the unprecedented nature of the threat they now faced, Trimboli would never desert his captain. "No, Captain," the sailor said, "without you, we are all lost. Go! I will hold off the beast!"

Trimboli proceeded in a tensed crouch toward the astonishing creature that was his equal in height. He held his rapier in his trembling hand, the blade's point extended far ahead. The creature again lowered its head, its reptilian lips pulled back to reveal a grimace of death. Both men instinctually sensed that their enemy was about to spring upon them, and as one, lunged simultaneously at the hissing beast.

The pretenses imposed by wealth and social standing dissolved in that instant for Fausto and Trimboli. They were not captain and underling, nor were they aristocrat and indigent; they were two proud men sculpted of the same divine clay, and each would willingly die defending the other. Fausto's halberd and Trimboli's sword cut through the air in a flurry of thrusts and brandishes. With a quick jab of the halberd, Fausto connected with the reptile, puncturing the side of its neck. It was a superficial strike, but the creature shrieked in pain and could well have been astonished that the animals it stalked had such formidable offensive capabilities.

The reptile snapped its mighty jaws repeatedly, and the taloned hind legs upon which it stood upright raked across the soft mossy earth. The unrelenting attacks of Fausto and Trimboli had the desired effect; the gigantic lizard could do naught but dodge their blades, leaving it no opening to strike.

"Do we kill it?" Trimboli shouted. His blade slashed across the dwarfish forearm of the beast and it screamed in rage before thrusting forward and snapping its mighty jaws upon Trimboli's withdrawn sword. Fausto jabbed again with the pointed end of the halberd, this time superficially piercing the creature's bony chest. To Trimboli's relief, the savage animal flung wide its jaws and released its hold on his rapier. "Captain!" Trimboli shouted. "What do you command?"

A dozen possible scenarios flashed through the mind of Fausto Caproni and in an instant he landed upon the best course of action. Santos Ignacio—God rest his soul—would have been proud of the novice captain.

"Do not kill it," Fausto instructed Trimboli. The sailor's expression indicated that his captain's order was not one he had expected. Fausto again jabbed the pike toward the hissing monster. "We are the invaders here, are we not? We know nothing of this land, its animals, or its . . ." He paused, not uttering the anticipated word, "people." There could be no human population upon Caprona given the savagery and sheer size of the animals that walked its face.

"We don't know what might result from killing this thing, or how its parent might react," Fausto explained between thrusts of his halberd. "You've seen what blood in the water does to a school of sharks?"

Trimboli nodded in affirmation and slashed again at the beast, which whipped its tail wildly through the air behind it in frustration.

"We'll hold it at bay until it loses interest in us," Fausto explained.

Trimboli added, "Or until it spots something else to eat that doesn't carry a sword."

The question of which outcome was most likely was rendered irrelevant by the earsplitting roar. Fausto looked skyward at the vast green canopy of leaves and fronds just as the massive head of the parental predator came crashing down toward them. Somehow, the massive beast had crept within only a few yards of them while they were engaged with its offspring. The jaws of the terrible lizard were held wide, its glistening white teeth providing a hideous fringe to the sickly pink interior of the mouth. Fausto leaped away from the adult as did the attacker's younger counterpart, but Trimboli was not so fleet-footed.

Fausto watched in horror as the gaping maw of the beast slammed down upon Trimboli where he stood, taking the man's entire body into its mouth and clamping its mighty jaws upon him to prevent his escape. Upward the head ripped, with only the thrashing arms and legs of the screaming sailor still visible. The beast snapped its jaws rapidly, while repeatedly jutting out its nose, as does a common barnyard chicken. Trimboli was being ground between the fangs of the monster. Within seconds, the bloodcurdling screams ceased. Trimboli was no more.

It was all Fausto could do to suppress the urge to retch, but from somewhere inside himself he found the fortitude that would be his salvation. The adult beast was preoccupied with its grisly feast, and the furious roar that preceded its attack had caused its progeny to scramble back into the clearing. Now was Fausto's chance.

Tightly gripping the halberd, Fausto bolted into the jungle, vaulting over fallen limbs and erratically ducking between trees. If the hunters pursued him, they would have been hard pressed to follow his weaving path. To Fausto's relief, such was not the case.

He could not put enough distance between himself and the horrific creatures, so onward he ran until his heart was fit to burst. How long he traveled he did not know, nor did he have the vaguest concept of what direction he ran. All he knew was that the ground was beginning to incline, moderately at first, but now, after a lengthy span of directionless flight, the incline had become far more precipitous. With no large predators in sight, Fausto determined it was safe for him to rest. He dropped to the ground in exhaustion. When he was finally reunited with his sister, she would no doubt tease him for losing his expensive hat somewhere along his panicked trek.

Fausto surveyed the area where he had come to rest. There were far fewer tropical trees here, but a lush carpet of ferns, some almost waist high, still covered the mossy ground. Of particular note were the bright green trunks of some of the trees whose tops resembled fountains of huge petallike leaves in hues of yellow, pink, and mauve, each the length of a man's body. Never had he seen a similar species; in truth, he was unsure whether they were trees at all, as they most closely resembled gigantic flowers. They were gathered in towering clumps, dispersed haphazardly between large plates of smooth gray slate. These plates, stacked one upon the other, rose in elevation until they effected a scalable wall not fifty feet from him. The tiered barrier wove into the surrounding forest and reached a height of at least a hundred feet. He must climb, for at the base of the wall he would be an easy target for predators. Once upon the top of the rocky acclivity, he might more easily spot Marina and their other companions within the jungle, and perhaps he could even spy the plain where rested the *Pegaso II*.

It wasn't until Fausto began his climb that a distant and familiar sound reached his ears. He paused and listened. He had heard it! It was the sound of flowing water!

Excitedly, he returned to the ground and followed the lowest tier of massive slate plates around several bends. At length, he was greeted by a most welcome sight: a majestic waterfall, showering down the face of the dark gray cliff that rose before him. Over centuries, the falling water had chiseled an enormous hole into the slate below to form a natural cistern at least two dozen yards in diameter. The water was clear and the mist from the fall delightfully cool. Fausto noted that the water flowed from the pool to form a wide, rocky river that roared down to the lower elevation of a nearby forest. That was a good sign, as it was likely that others from the doomed *Pegaso II* would find flowing water—if not this very same river—elsewhere on Caprona's landscape.

Much to his relief, the water was crisp and pure, and only after taking several gulps did he realize just how thirsty he had been. Not forgetting the driving factor for their excursion into the jungle, Fausto filled the hollowed-fruit canteen and secured the makeshift cap, tied to the top of the container with leafless vine runners.

Refreshed and reinvigorated, Fausto began his climb to the summit of the slate ridge. In short order, and without incident, his scraped and dirty hands grasped the top of the rocky plateau. There, scratched and sweating but none the worse for wear, Fausto collapsed face down upon soft, green grass and under the unrelenting sun in the blue sky above.

His strenuous climb accomplished, he barely had time to catch his breath before a shadow crept upon him. Fausto bolted upright on his knees and clenched the halberd with both hands, but he was unprepared for the shock that came next. Before him was not a reptilian monster, nor had one of the airborne dragons returned to pluck him from the plateau.

Before him stood a man.

No, it was not just one man, but a group of men, eight in number. Their near nakedness called to mind the tribesmen of Africa of whom he had heard tales, but the skin of these people was of a pigmentation only slightly darker than his own. The men appeared to be approximately his own age, some younger than he but none particularly older. Each bore dark knotted hair and a beard, and in light of the fact that they were naked save for primitive sandals and animal-hide thongs, Fausto could see that each of the men was exquisitely muscled. Over the shoulders of two men was a carrying yoke from which suspended the carcass of an antlered animal resembling an elk. Fausto's initial surprise at being confronted by humans turned to unease as the realization swept over him: All the men carried spears, stone knives, crude axes, or bows. Even if the group was an innocent hunting party, the halberd in his grip felt pitifully inadequate.

Caprona was inhabited by humans. The very concept swept through him with a dizzying impact. In all of Fausto's years of direct engagement in the voyage's preparation, and notwithstanding two decades of dreaming of rediscovering the lost continent, never had he objectively weighed the humanitarian concerns that would be raised were Caprona to host an isolated civilization. How the Kingdom of the Two Sicilies chose to govern those who would fall under its reign once the island was conquered—rather, colonized—had not concerned him. It was always Fausto's belief there must be an entrustment of faith necessary to assuage any misgivings about the methodology employed in bringing civilization to wild lands. Whether these savage men would welcome the generous overtures of the Kingdom of the Two Sicilies was unknown, but the suspicion etched on their stoic faces indicated resistance to colonization might be an issue.

Based on the dress of these people, Fausto concluded they were far removed from the cultural norms of European society, but it would be indelicate if he did not extend to them a formal greeting. He was greatly outnumbered by the tribesmen, who looked none too pleased by his presence and were cautiously beginning to surround him. A few yards behind him was the cliff edge, so an immediate and friendly introduction was vital and just might save his life if the islanders had murder on their minds.

To avoid startling the onlookers, the disheveled young captain rose to his feet slowly. He brushed his hands together and ran his fingers through his unruly black locks in a vain effort to make himself presentable. In the relatively short span of his life, Fausto Caproni had come to appreciate the wisdom of looking smart; doors were graciously held open if one wore the coat of a diplomat, but the rags of a pauper locked and barred them. For the sake of appearances, he was determined to present himself as a confident and influential sea captain; whether a professional demeanor would hold any weight with those who confronted him was unknown. With a smile, he spoke in an unaggressive yet commanding tone.

"Hello. I am Captain Fausto Caproni of the Kingdom of the Two Sicilies, and I come to this land in peace." He extended one hand in friendship, his other tightly gripping the shaft of the halberd lowered at his side.

But when Fausto stepped toward what appeared to be the leader of the band of hunters, the stocky native lifted his axe and angrily shouted. What followed was an outburst of one- and two-syllable words, none of which held any meaning to the young Sicilian. By command of the leader, three of the islanders advanced toward Fausto, their weapons held at the ready. Their intent was palpable. Fausto raised the halberd, gripping it with both hands; if the situation were about to become violent, his enemies would soon learn that he would not go down without a fight. Marina, Leonardo Ricci, and too many others depended on him. He had led his friends to this terrible country and would do everything in his power to shepherd them back to safety.

Just then, one of the men wielding a bone knife broke from the pack and rushed toward Fausto. The warrior was particularly handsome for a savage, with long wavy hair that reached to his muscled chest. Unlike his bearded counter- parts, he had little facial hair, leading Fausto to believe that perhaps this was a junior member of the tribe. Whatever the case, it mattered not, as a child could kill just as effectively as a senile elder.

Before Fausto could sufficiently defend himself, the warrior was upon him, tackling him to the ground. Between their thrashing limbs, Fausto tried to espy the surrounding area; as close as they were to the edge of the precipice, his only avenue of escape would be the open field upon the plateau. As far as his eyes could discern, aside from the river that fed the waterfall, nothing but grassy plains stretched to the horizon where another jungle forest loomed nearly a mile away, with a mountainous region behind that.

The warriors watched the struggle, but none offered to assist the young savage. With his hands on either end of the halberd, Fausto managed to push against his attacker's chest and thrust him away, but the young native fought like a panther and was immediately back upon Fausto, forcing his shoulders to the grass. A hot rush of panic swept over Fausto; his opponent had succeeded in wrapping the fingers of one hand around his throat, the warrior's other hand raised and prepared to plunge the dagger into his chest.

Curiously, the killing blow did not come. Instead, the warrior returned the knife to the sheath at his hip.

Seizing the moment, Fausto desperately kicked upward with one knee and knocked the young warrior forward over his head. Fortune had smiled upon Fausto, as the tumble of the savage carried him over the edge of the rocky precipice. Fausto knew not why what he did next. As the warrior plunged over the edge, Fausto scrambled forward and lunged toward the man in an attempt to save his life, but it was not to be. The tribal leader shouted "Tro-va!" as the scrappy warrior fell awkwardly, striking the collected water a hundred feet below. Fausto's eyes followed the plunge, and he watched as the rapids generated by the massive waterfall whisked away the lifeless body of the warrior.

Fausto had been attacked, and by all appearances, the warrior had intended to kill him. He had to defend himself. No other decision could be made. But why had the powerful savage not thrust the knife into his breast? The mystery was perplexing, but the greater burden for which Fausto was unprepared to shoulder was the knowledge that he had just killed a man.

Rough hands gripped Fausto's shoulders and pulled him away from the edge of the precipice. The halberd was ripped from his grasp, and within minutes his arms were bound before him with crude rope. He had come to Caprona to claim the land; now, he was a helpless prisoner of its savage and mysterious inhabitants.

The natives were quite enraptured by their captive, picking and tugging at Fausto's clothing while they conversed in their indecipherable language. One of the men scrutinized the makeshift canteen, then turned it upside down to empty its contents. The tribesmen laughed, apparently mocking the crude design of the water carrier. Two of the men intently watched the pool and rapids below and informed the others of their observations in a disconsolate tone. Several times they spoke the word "Tro-va," which Fausto assumed was the name of the warrior who had met his end. Although he had contributed to the death of one of their number, Fausto was befuddled that they had not immediately put him to death. Perhaps they were distracted by his odd weapon, which they now examined with great fascination.

The back-and-forth conversation between Fausto's captors ranged from angry words to curious rambling. At times, the leader would angrily raise his voice, point to the sky, and reverently utter "Luata." The disagreement members of the party were having among themselves seemed to go on forever, and it quickly became apparent that the tribesmen were just as fascinated by Fausto as he was by them. *Let them be fascinated*, he thought. *At least it's keeping me alive.*

But fate was about to interject itself upon Fausto's dilemma in two simultaneous ways.

To his good fortune, the natives had not removed his sword; they either did not fear it or had no idea a weapon was sheathed at his flank. Suddenly, the tribesmen tensed and raised their weapons when a chilling shriek filled the air. A "dragon," as Marina had described it, dropped from the sky and circled the party at the cliff's edge. This monster was just as enormous as the beast that had carried away Santos Ignacio, but its skin was a mustard color that faded to white across its chest, stomach, and the underside of its long neck. Spears were raised defensively in preparation for attack, but the winged reptile did nothing more than squawk and circle them before soaring off across the grassy plain.

While the tribe was occupied with the flying threat, Fausto had deftly lifted the hilt of his sword from the scabbard, exposing four inches of the rapier's blade. Against it, he began rapidly rubbing the rope that bound his wrists, and within seconds he snapped his bonds and slid over the edge of the slate cliffside.

Almost immediately the guttural shouts of the tribesmen rained down upon Fausto as he scrambled down the face of the rocky cliff. Each passing second was an eternity of frantic doubt, for one move made too hastily, one sweaty palm against a smooth rock surface, or one misstep of a bootsole would send him crashing to his doom on the rocks below.

The argument between the tribesmen continued, which eased Fausto's mind; the longer they debated their next move, the closer to the base of the cliff he climbed. When he was still twenty feet from the ground, he could stand the suspense no longer and jumped. As soon as he landed, he rolled with the impact, rose quickly, and ran toward the jungle.

To Fausto's chagrin, a glance behind him revealed the worst: The tribesmen were now scaling the wall and descending so rapidly they appeared as limber as the wild macaques of Gibraltar. Within seconds, his savage pursuers were dropping to the ground and giving chase, their angry cries resounding from the stony cliff behind them.

His legs pumping wildly, Fausto plunged through the jungle intent on losing himself within the dense underbrush. Behind him, the echoes of native shouts dogged his heels; three times wooden shafts embedded in trees near him, barely missing him by inches. Down several ravines he slid, up steep jungle slopes he clambered, and he forded three small creeks, but he could not stop. The arrows of the tribesmen could find his back at any second.

Or would they? There was no longer any shouting

behind him. His pursuers had either assumed more stealthy tactics or had given up the chase.

After dashing across an expanse of large ferns, he ducked beneath a verdant canopy and listened intently. Only birdsongs and distant terrifying roars met his ears. He had escaped!

Something caught Fausto's eye across the clearing and beneath a clump of ferns at the base of a nearby tree. It was something white, and as most of Caprona was splashed in vibrant hues of green, the white object was most conspicuous. Cautiously, he traversed the clearing and slid through the ferns to retrieve the object from the muddy soil. His heart leaped to his throat.

It was the sleeve of a white silken blouse, with a delicate frill circling the cuff. Down its length were jagged tears, the edges of which were soaked with blood.

It was the sleeve of Marina's blouse.

Fausto's head began to spin as a lightheadedness overcame him. Every harsh word he had ever spoken to his sister resurfaced in his memory, whether those words were spoken in true or mock anger.

Marina's blood . . .

It could mean only one thing.

Fausto examined the dark soil in the shade of the canopy of fern fronds and looked for anything that might prove his sister was alive or any evidence to indicate that she was . . .

Then he saw it, against the tree behind him. Several muddy handprints were smeared on the tree's bole. The delicate handprints of Marina. She had been there, in the exact place he now stood, and God knows what horror she had faced as she gripped the tree. The swirl of emotions within him became a raging flood. He was alone, thousands of miles from home, stalked by ravenous man-eating reptiles and savage islanders. Those who had followed him on his mad quest were even now at the mercy of Caprona's predatory giants. Santos Ignacio, the man he idolized, and the devoted, good-hearted Trimboli were dead. And now, his very own sister who wanted nothing more than to protect him from his own ambition . . . Now, Marina, too, was . . .

Fausto shuddered involuntarily, collapsed to his knees, and buried his face in his palms.

12
TRO-VA

MARINA CLUNG TIGHTLY to the interwoven vines below the rocky lip, while below her, floating among the black muck of rotting vegetation, enormous crocodiles snapped angrily as they thrashed about the mire. They flung their fanged jaws wide and hissed in frustration, clearly enraged that what they had believed to be an imminent meal had eluded them.

Marina at last calmed her nerves. Never had she been trapped in such an unwinnable scenario as she had been only moments before. Her choices had been to either allow Sergeant Lago to make good his threat and kill her with a shot through her heart, or throw herself to the savage beasts that hungered for her flesh in the waters below the ledge. She had chosen the latter.

From his vantage point, the villainous Sergeant Lago would not be able to see Marina. After plunging from the ledge, she proceeded to kick her legs outward, the momentum causing her body to swing back toward a recess she had spied in the wall of the ravine. It was just big enough for her to crawl into and, with frantic haste borne of terror, she scurried into the space between the rocks and pulled on the tangle of vines so that they covered the opening.

Safely ensconsed in her hiding spot, she heard the hideous swamp creatures continue to lunge at one another in frustration. She reckoned Lago might crawl down after her if he believed she still lived, so a dramatic play was in order.

112

Marina began kicking at the rocks and mud at the opening of the crevasse, and within seconds a sizable chunk of stone and earth peeled away from the ravine wall. She screamed for help as her boot heels pressed against the loosened rocks, and with a final thrust of her legs, the chunks broke free and fell, splashing loudly into the muddy waters below. The giant crocodiles flung themselves immediately upon the fallen debris, Marina grew deathly silent, and within minutes she heard Lago's footsteps crunching through the jungle and away from the scene of her "death." Her ruse had worked!

She was alive, but her immediate problem remained unsolved. She was still lost and weaponless in a land overrun by monsters and dragons. With a determination forged by years of feelings of inadequacy to which she would never admit, Marina would survive. She would find her brother and expose the evils of the Spanish soldiers and their dastardly scheme. She would not fail.

When Marina was sure enough time had lapsed to allow Sergeant Lago to march far enough into the jungle that she could safely extract herself from her hiding place, she went to work. She had no idea whether the monstrous lizards of the swamp could climb, so exposing herself too soon without a clear means of escape could endanger her further. Through the leafy curtain of vines concealing the alcove, Marina peered down upon the group of predators, which had settled into basking in the brilliant sunlight at the base of the cliff face.

As quietly as she could, she began pushing against other mossy rocks and dislodging them with her boots. After collecting several large specimens, she pushed aside the leafy screen before her. One after another, the rocks splashed dully into the thick black ooze over a dozen yards past the lounging terrors. What followed was a cacophony of splashes as the beasts turned as one and charged through the muck with frightening speed away from the cliff face and toward the disturbance that had drawn their attention. Marina latched on to the distraction and quickly climbed from her hiding spot, over the lip of the ledge, and up the steep slope down which she had slid.

The young Caproni took stock of herself and her clothing. She had a few cuts and scrapes here and there, but these were minor. The bandage around her left arm was still secure, but she had lost her rapier, and her makeshift club and canteen. Which reminded her: She was frightfully thirsty. She looked to the jungle and listened to the panoply of sound wafting from within. In some odd way, the drone of insects, the chirps of birds, and the occasional growls of far-off animals of unknown species were almost comforting to her. It was an odd thing to think, she considered, about a place that had been trying to kill her since she first got here. She brushed her hands together and trudged back into the verdure.

Marina assumed the swamp water was undrinkable but concluded that it had to be fed there by one or more streams. Back at her family's estate in Palermo, the far end of the Caproni property was host to a small stream that wound across the field behind the lemon grove. After excessive rainfalls, the stream would swell past its banks in some spots, creating muddy ponds ripe for playful, childhood adventures. Perhaps that also applied to true swamps. And so she continued her trek, keeping the odorous quagmire within sight, hoping to discover a source of flowing water feeding into it.

After a short time, her attention was caught by something glistening in the distance and barely visible through the leaves surrounding her. Cautiously, she proceeded toward the white sparkles and pushed through a thick grouping of berry bushes. Marina was overcome with relief. She had found a robust river flowing down a rocky hill that terminated in a wide, thundering waterfall that emptied into a large reservoir of fresh water a dozen feet below. Thankfully, the pooled water did not appear to host the crocodilian monsters she had earlier encountered. She descended to the pool and knelt at its edge, drinking of the sweet, fresh water. It tasted glorious, as it did

not carry the lingering flavor of oak like the water drawn from
the casks aboard the *Redenzione.*

Refreshed at last, Marina sat quietly and took stock of her
surroundings. The trees and bushes that lined the jungle pond
were alive with activity. Small birds hopped among the branches, as did the odd feathered and flying lizards of Caprona that
she had already come to accept. Thankfully, she had not seen
a creature larger than any of the ship's cats in quite some time.
It was a brief respite, but in that time she allowed herself just
a few moments of tranquility to absorb the natural wonders
of the strange new land. But just as quickly, her thoughts
returned to her immediate peril, and the gut-wrenching fear
for her brother's well-being.

Still seated at the edge of the pool, she jumped with a start
as a barely perceptible snort came from her right, snapping
her from her repose. Instinctively, Marina prepared to lash
out and fight for her life until she saw the small creature that
curiously sniffed the air only a yard from her elbow. It was
one of the diminutive horses her party had seen among the
tall grass earlier in the day. Marina froze, not wanting to startle
the curious little animal.

Now at close range, she could better absorb its features,
down to the little lashes around its dewy black eyes. The coat
of the tiny horse was beautiful; its dark crème base was mottled
with splashes of white, while those highlights became stripes
at its rear and receded down its hind legs. The animal eyed
her and continued to tip its nose upward, and perhaps satisfied
that Marina was not a threat, it inched closer to her and sniffed
her booted legs, upon which she sat. She could not resist the
allure of the animal, so with a slow and fluid motion, Marina
held out her hand to the miniature horse. It took several deep
sniffs of her palm, then whinnied in a playful timbre. Sensing
no danger from the human, the tiny mammal turned and
proceeded to the edge of the pond, where it dipped its rounded
snout into the water to drink.

What incredible wonders this land hosted. It was all so

new, so mysterious, and so deadly. The most unsettling aspect of Caprona was there was no way to foretell what wonders or dangers might appear next and without warning.

A loud splash resounded from the base of the waterfall, startling both Marina and the tiny horse, which bolted into the shadows of the jungle. Upon investigation, Marina beheld a body floating in the water—a *person*!—half-dead and floundering weakly. He must have been in the river above, and then flung mercilessly over the waterfall. She wished to rush to the man's aid, but reaching him would require that she enter the water, and who knew what might lurk below the pool's surface. There were several smooth, flat-topped boulders in the pool; perhaps she could jump from one to the next to reach the man before he drowned. She only had seconds to act. The man appeared naked, the length of his dark hair confirming that it was neither Fausto nor any of the men aboard the *Pegaso II*.

He was a native of Caprona!

There was no time to think. Marina proceeded exactly as she had envisioned, jumping from one rocky platform to the next, finally leaping into the pool at the man's side, against her better judgment. The water was relatively shallow. With all her strength, she lifted his chest upward to prevent him from drowning and guided him toward the smooth granite ledge that formed the closest shore. The man had just enough strength to grip the rocks but was too weak from his ordeal to pull himself up and onto the ledge that ringed the far edge of the pool, a couple feet above the water's surface. It was only moments after Marina had climbed from the water and taken hold of his arms to pull him to safety that she noticed one of the boulders move. Inexplicably, it was coming toward them.

Earlier in the day, Marina had noted how the large animal that had them trapped behind the fallen tree resembled a turtle. But the water-bound creature that now approached was a true turtle. The thing was massive, the size of an ox, its mossy gray shell assuming the demeanor of a tiny island when seen from a distance. The reptile's brilliant yellow eyes focused on its target as it inched closer to the nearly drowned man, its massive beak held wide.

Marina tugged at the man's arms, but he was much too heavy for her to pull from the water and to safety. The enormous turtle bore down on him, now only a few feet away from clamping the mighty jaws upon a leg and dragging him into deeper water to feed upon his flesh. Marina rushed from the pond edge to the foliage behind her and, within seconds, emerged with a hefty tree branch. Wielding the limb like a club, she brought it down hard on the top of the beast's head, just as it was about to seize the man. Again and again, the limb crashed upon the cranium of the turtle until at last it retracted its head toward its shell, turned, and slid back toward the center of the pond.

To Marina's relief, the stranger was beginning to recover his wits, and with her help, he managed to climb from the water to lie face down on the shore.

With the danger now passed, Marina examined the being she had fished from the pond. He was nearly naked, wearing only an animal skin over the front and back of his pelvis and crude sandals on his feet, and the tightness of his muscles and skin indicated that he must be young, nearly her own age. The man rolled onto his back and inhaled deeply, then exhaled with equal relishment. He was fortunate to be alive.

At social gatherings over her twenty-seven years, Marina had encountered innumerable men, some of whose physical features quite intrigued her. But never before upon meeting a man had butterflies flit about her stomach as they now did, nor had her heart raced as when she looked upon the face of the man who smiled back at her. He was indeed young, but the indomitable set of his jaw and muscular sculpt of his chest and arms spoke of a man who had been chiseled to the peak of human perfection by a lifetime of rigorous activity. His eyes were dark and clear, accentuated by dark brows, all in stark contrast to his straight white teeth. He held up a strong hand and placed it gently against Marina's cheek, while speaking words that must have been a heartfelt "thank you," were she able to decipher them.

One grouping of syllables stood out to her, as the inflection of his voice rose to indicate a question. *"Cos-ju-lo?"* he asked, but the utterance's meaning was lost to the newcomer to Caprona.

Marina had an innate penchant for languages, which she employed while assisting her father with the family business. Although she was not fluent in any tongue other than her own, she was quite adept at pantomime and generally had a knack for quickly picking up foreign nouns and verbs. That talent made her an invaluable asset to her father's business, as she often helped smooth negotiations with import and export partners of foreign countries bordering the Mediterranean Sea. Now, she would need to employ that same keen linguistic skill to communicate with the native islander.

"Marina," she said, tapping her chest.

She recognized the glimmer of understanding in the young man's dark eyes. "Tro-va," he responded, touching his own chest. The road to full understanding would be long, but at least they were now on a first-name basis, a tiny milestone that meant far more to Marina than she would have expected.

But as was Caprona's wont, the brief respite from adventure was quickly supplanted by numbing fear.

The enormous creature did not announce itself with a terrifying roar; rather, it pushed forth from the palms surrounding the water hole and stood swaying upon two massive hind legs. The monster was similar in build to the hunter Marina had witnessed attacking the shelled giant earlier in the day, but unlike that creature, the head of this one had a long crocodilian snout with a mouthful of sharp, white teeth that must have numbered in the hundreds. The beast's leathery hide was a pale purple, with brilliant yellow bull's-eye markings down the length of its back and tail, and also speckling its head and snout. With a mouth like that, this creature needed no camouflage. The enormous weight of the body and tail was gracefully balanced upon the central fulcrum of the great hind legs, its head and forepaws held low to the ground. Curiously, a row of long, narrow spikes rose nearly a dozen feet into the air from its vertebrae and flowed down the length of its back from neck to pelvis. Between the spikes ran a pale yellow webbing of skin decorated with horizontal stripes of brilliant violet. Why nature had deemed the savage beast should possess such an extravagant physical feature, Marina could not begin to guess.

The three-fingered hands rhythmically clawed at the air in anticipation of its next meal. *"Rava,"* came Tro-va's whispered identification. He crouched and spread his arms protectively before Marina, who stood stock-still behind the young native.

With one terrifying sweep of its neck, the giant reptile swung its head toward Marina and Tro-va, its black eyes trapping them in its focus. The mouth remained tightly clamped shut, its nostrils flaring as it exhaled in great puffs like the engine of a locomotive. Tro-va yelled a warning to Marina and turned to run, grabbing her by the arm and pulling her with him. He must have sensed an imminent attack. Just as he yelled, the rava lunged in their direction, a single footstep of the beast covering a span of twenty feet. Within seconds, it would be upon them, but thanks to Tro-va's quick instincts, they were already moving before the rava took its first step in pursuit.

Marina's mind was a jumble of panicked thoughts, but as Tro-va pulled her toward the jungle, she resisted his lead. "This way!" she shouted, pointing toward the waterfall.

Seeing the wisdom of the woman's suggestion—and now seeing why she had made it—Tro-va followed Marina as she bounded across the rocks toward a hollowed-out recess behind the waterfall.

The ground vibrated from the massive footfalls of the savage rava, but before it could reach either of its intended prey, they leaped through the drenching waters. Once past the falls, they found themselves in a natural amphitheater, roughly circular in shape and thirty feet in diameter. Tro-va cautiously watched the thundering curtain of water, but Marina's firm tug on his arm pulled him from his scrutiny. She pointed to a break in the rock behind them and urged Tro-va to follow her. Against the wall of water, the shadow of the rava lingered and darkened, and ever so slowly, the long, toothy snout of the titan penetrated the veil by a full twelve feet, its nostrils flaring as it attempted to sniff out the humans. Marina and the young native rushed to the dark passage through the rock wall, which was just wide enough for them to slip through.

They found themselves in a cavernous chamber whose floor was composed of multiple descending layers of limestone that culminated in a pool of water at its base, presumably underground overflow from the freshwater pond on the other side of the rock barrier at which they stood. At the back of the chamber, Marina noted breaks in the ceiling that permitted beams of light to illuminate the cavern.

The river water was quite cold and Marina was drenched to the skin, but it could very well have been her brush with death that caused her to shiver. Tro-va began speaking and pointing about the room, but Marina had not the faintest idea what he was saying. All she could do was politely smile at him, which made him stop in midspeech. He stood quietly for several uncomfortable seconds and examined her from head to toe, as if perplexed. Just as Tro-va's lack of clothing had aroused Marina's curiosity, Tro-va must have been similarly fascinated by her overabundance of coverings in Caprona's hot clime.

He gently ran a hand down her bare arm, then stopped to linger on the bandage. She explained as best she could that she had been injured but was none the worse for wear. Tro-va peeked at the wounds under the silk covering and smiled in agreement.

They stood nearly eye to eye as Tro-va was only slightly

taller than her own height, and try as she might, she could not help but be fascinated by his lingering gaze. Marina could tell that he did not look upon her lasciviously; rather, his attitude was more akin to wonder, as if he had never seen a woman of her like. She determined he could not be enamored of her; there were men on Caprona, so must there be women, and if the females were anywhere near as beautiful as the tribesman who stood before her, surely there was nothing about her that he had never beheld.

He raised his hand above her breast and rubbed the silk of her collar between his fingers.

"All right, my friend," she said, blushing. "Let's find something else to do, shall we?" She took a step backward and pressed her soft hand against his chest, lightly pushing him away from her. Tro-va laughed and smiled in response, putting to rest any fear she might have about his intentions.

With a thunderous crash, the fang-encrusted nose of the rava thrust between the rocks behind them. How the beast had moved so silently was beyond Marina's grasp, but the enormous reptile had not been repelled by the waterfall; it was now beneath it and attempting to push its way into the cavern in which they had retreated.

Tro-va moved like lightning. He snatched the tree limb club that Marina still held and brought it down on the nose of the snorting beast, which now hissed in anger. Again and again, he hit the thing, but the monster continued to push forward against the wall. Chips of rock around the perimeter of the ingress began to fall to the floor, which spurred Marina into action.

With her own lightning move, Marina pulled the bone knife from the sheath that hung around the hips of the islander and plunged it into the nose of the encroaching giant. Dark red blood splattered against the rock as she withdrew the knife, but one strike would not suffice for Marina. Every horror she had so far experienced since setting foot upon Caprona had been boiling below the surface of her temperament, and now she unleashed a savage fury she did not know she possessed upon the snout of the monster. Repeatedly, she plunged the knife into the beast's thick hide, chopping at it until blood drenched her arm to the elbow. Tro-va had not ceased his defensive strikes with the club, and together they beat the creature until it could stand no more. With a high-pitched shriek, the rava withdrew its nose and crashed back through the waterfall to find easier prey somewhere in the jungle.

Soaked to the skin, her clothing torn and strands of dark hair hanging before her blood-splattered face, Marina looked every bit the savage.

Tro-va smiled approvingly. He held up one finger and curiously traced an invisible isosceles triangle in the air before Marina. "Cos-ju-lo," he declared with an affirmative nod.

Marina knew not what the repeated phrase meant, but she graciously accepted it as a compliment.

13
MYSTERY OF THE TRIBES

I N THE RELATIVE SAFETY OF THE CENOTE, Marina returned Tro-va's knife to him and washed the blood from her hands and face. She and the strapping young native then spent the next few hours conversing as best they could. The tribesman made a valiant effort to learn a few basic words of Italian; however, it was easier for Marina to absorb and comprehend the much simpler language of Tro-va. Naturally, it would take time to learn alternate words for things she already knew, but she found it surprisingly easy to memorize the names of things she was only now encountering. Marina and Tro-va found pantomime immensely helpful in relaying information, and though Marina tried her best to comprehend all he attempted to convey to her, much of it left her perplexed.

The native islander explained he was of a tribe called Galu, which he had only recently joined. Previously, he had been counted among the number of another tribe called the Krolus, the "bow people." Earlier in the day, his hunting party had encountered a stranger. In some form of ritual performance that would prove his loyalty to the tribe, Tro-va was commanded to kill the stranger. He fulfilled the duty, but in the process he lost his balance and fell from a cliff into a river that carried him far from the land of the Galus. He was certain they were now in the realm of a tribe called Band-lus, or "spear people." That, in itself, was an incredibly dangerous predicament for them both, as the Band-lus would likely kill them if they were to be captured.

Marina attempted to express to Tro-va that she had come from far away, but he scoffed at the suggestion. He was adamant that there was nothing outside the walls of Caspak, the native term for the land, and that Marina was a Galu. There was nothing else she could be. There was another tribe "one step above the Galus," as he curiously stated, but Marina was not a Wieroo. When she asked why she could not be a Wieroo, a grave expression settled over Tro-va's face. The Wieroo, he explained, had wings like the *jo-oo*, the flying lizards of the trees, or the mighty *ko-oo* that terrorized the land from high in the sky. Marina knew the latter must be the "dragon" that had downed the *Pegaso II* and carried Santos Ignacio to his death. But what could Tro-va's statement about winged people possibly mean? She found the very concept ludicrous, but it was best not to challenge the beliefs of what she recognized as a primitive society.

Something was nagging at her subconscious, a question that Marina had to ask. She needed more information about the man Tro-va had killed, even if she trembled at the thought of what he might tell her. Tro-va explained that the man had hair like Marina's, curly and dark. She pressed the tribesman about the color of his clothing, and after determining that the Caspakian word for white is "cos-vu," Tro-va revealed that the "skins" the man wore were cos-vu, just as was Marina's blouse.

All at once, her world came crashing down around her. Fausto was dead, and the handsome warrior now seated with her, alone and in a cave, had murdered him. Finally, she had been broken, and tears began to roll over the curves of her cheeks.

Tro-va stood and began nervously pacing as Marina wept. When he could stand it no longer, he spoke. "Ma-ree-na!" he called out in anguish. What followed was a sheepish confession that he had not killed the man he had fought. Something inside of him prevented him from delivering the killing blow. Not only was his hesitance a disgraceful act in the eyes of his fellow tribesmen, but the truth of the matter was that the stranger had overpowered him and thrown him from the cliff.

Tro-va hung his head in embarrassment, but Marina could not have been happier. She leaped to her feet and embraced the young warrior, and with soft touches and firm hugs she assured him that everything was all right and that she respected him for his strength. She had just witnessed a typical display of a man trying to impress a woman. Although the fabricated story contained the erroneous report of the murder of her brother, she was touched by Tro-va's eventual truthfulness and even more so by his compassion.

The sunlight streaming into the cavern from above had dimmed, now replaced by moonlight. This had been the most eventful and emotionally taxing day in Marina's life, and it had left her exhausted. Tro-va suggested that they sleep and in the morning they would leave together. He was relatively certain that he knew the location of the plain where Marina could reunite with her people, and the Galu village in which he resided was not far past that. She hesitated, but only for a moment; closing her eyes and drifting off in that most dangerous world could be the death of her, but with the earnest young native at her side, well . . . she would just have to see how the night went and cross her fingers that it would pass uneventfully.

Marina awoke to a distant symphony of chirping birds. She lay contented upon the rock in a warm patch of morning light, but she bolted upright when the blue haze of sleep dissipated and she remembered just where she was. Throughout the night she had been abruptly roused from slumber by the roar of unseen giants, but she had quickly fallen back to sleep, knowing that she and Tro-va were safe within the underground sanctum. That the young warrior was close to her registered in her mind not concern but comfort, which was an unusual reaction considering the quite vulnerable position into which she had been thrust and how very little she knew of the man.

Tro-va smiled and handed a large fruit to Marina. While she slept, he had climbed the rock wall to one of the holes in the cavern ceiling, and from the surrounding jungle, he had retrieved something to appease their hunger. Marina was famished, having eaten nothing since the previous morning, but as she examined the bright orange husk of the fruit, she was unsure what to do with it. The outer shell of the thing was as hard as a rock.

The tribesman watched patiently as Marina looked at the fruit from all angles, but at length, she handed it back to Tro-va with a shrug of defeat. For a moment, Tro-va furrowed his brow, but then he began to pound the offering against the rock they sat upon. With the shell now cracked, he broke off a chunk and handed it to Marina. Clinging to the piece of shell was a thick layer of melon-like meat, but she watched and waited until Tro-va ate a piece of his own before replicating his motions.

"You say you are not a Galu, that you are not of Caspak," he said; at least, that was an approximation of his statement as Marina understood it. She smiled at him innocently and nodded. "I am beginning to believe you," he chided her.

After finishing the refreshing morning meal, Tro-va led Marina up the narrow path he had used to reach the ceiling of the cavern, and the pair climbed out into the blazing sunlight. They found themselves a dozen yards from the river that had swept Tro-va into Marina's life and, after fashioning spears from the available resources, they were prepared to embark on their journey.

The spears quite intrigued Marina, as the plant stalk from which they had constructed them was very similar to bamboo, if not bamboo itself. In her estimation, shafts of the sturdy, hollow wood could effectively repair the damaged hull of the

Pegaso II, and from that point on she would try to recall in as great of detail as possible the location of the grove.

Throughout the remainder of the morning and well past noon, the pair made their way across the landscape of Caprona, which Marina now preferred to call Caspak. The river was hours behind them, and though following it was the surest way for Tro-va to trace the trail back to the Galus, that course would be fraught with danger as they would encounter a proliferation of animal life along the river's banks. But that was beside the point; his focus was not on himself or his personal well-being, but the return of Marina to her people somewhere amid the "Sea of Grass," as Tro-va called it.

Marina was torn about the direction of their travel. It pained her to move away from the jungles where Fausto had hopefully survived the night—if he had somehow escaped the Galus—but aimless wandering in search of her lost brother might result in nothing more than her death. She did not want to leave Fausto behind, but finding the wreck of the *Pegaso II* would reunite her with Leonardo Ricci and the sailors Puccini and Alamanni, if the Spaniards had not carried out their extermination plan on them. For all she knew, Fausto had made his way back to the sky cutter, and together they might overcome the threats from both Caspak and the soldiers of the Spanish Empire.

As Marina became more accustomed to her surroundings, she could not shake the sparks of wonderment that danced about her senses with each discovery of Caspak's majestic natural treasures. The colors that splashed the interior landscape of the continent were more vibrant than any she had ever beheld on Sicily; even the sky appeared more crystalline blue. The water was purer, the very air itself more invigorating. If not for the predatory carnivorous reptiles that terrorized its face and filled its skies, Caspak could be considered a paradise on Earth.

The dank smell of standing water and rotting vegetation

indicated to Marina and Tro-va that they were nearing another swamp. Rather than trudge through the muck, they scaled a rocky rise that skirted the acacia trees ringing the wetlands. The promontory flowed unbroken as if molded from a single gigantic rock, its surface rough and riddled with holes. Marina recognized the mile-long crag as cooled lava; in the distant past, it had erupted forth along a lengthy crack in the earth and solidified into a prominent ridge of volcanic rock. When they reached its peak far above the level of the jungle canopy, Marina turned in a circle to absorb the visual splendor of Caspak. Tro-va watched her soak in the wonders of the land, and he smiled to himself as if pleased to see the young woman so enraptured by her surroundings.

Behind her were several miles of untamed jungle that gradually assimilated into a great pine forest, itself spanning several miles while rising to higher, mountainous elevations and terminating at Caspak's barrier cliffs that reached for the clouds in the sky above. To her left and right, steaming jungles rife with life sprawled into the distance, while before her, beyond the swamps, jungles, and plains, she gazed down upon the sparkling shoreline of the grand interior sea, the body of water that dominated the heart of the remarkable continent.

As Marina surveyed her surroundings, something exceedingly large began moving within the swamp's thickly packed acacias near where they stood. A large section of tree canopy shook, sending a flock of winged creatures into the air in all directions, disturbed by the ambulation of the unseen creature.

With a slow, fluid motion, something rose above the uppermost leaves of the swamp trees. At first, Marina thought it to be some gigantic snake, but as the blue-gray form rose, it unfurled itself to reveal that it was the serpentine neck of an immense animal. Compared to the size and length of the appendage, the head situated upon its terminus was rather small, with a short snout and small black eyes. It was barely distinguishable as a head until its elevated end dipped toward the canopy and plucked an enormous mouthful of leaves from the treetops. Marina could now see its body between the tree trunks of the jungle swamp. The animal was similar in form to an elephant, but the titan's measure must have equaled that of the *Redenzione*. Tro-va casually explained that the animal was a doma and was not to be feared.

"Bellissima," she whispered.

Like a dutiful schoolboy, Tro-va repeated the word as best he could.

Marina's eyes sparkled, so overcome was she by the romanticism of the entire adventure. Impulsively, she wrapped her arms around the handsome warrior. She was thankful for him and thankful to be alive, and all the trivial inconveniences of Sicilian life she had previously believed to hold overwhelming relevance for her now meant absolutely nothing.

Before, she had merely been existing. Now, she was *living*.

The wanderers carefully made their way up the jagged flow. Upon reaching a crest, Tro-va held out a hand to prevent Marina's passage. Thirty feet ahead, a family of reptiles had crawled to the top of the lava bed and lay basking in the rays of the midafternoon sun.

Like everything Marina had seen on Caspak, the creatures were at once fearsome and oddly beautiful. The five olive-hued animals were at least twenty feet in length, with long, tapered tails and plump cylindrical bodies supported by short, but stout legs. Typical of predatory meat eaters, they were equipped with powerful jaws lined with sharp fangs. Their predominant feature was a large membranous dorsal fin that extended from their short, thick necks to halfway down the length of their tails. To Marina's eyes, the fins recalled the sails of schooners that docked at the port of Palermo. Not only were the fins ostentatious in design, but the brilliant yellow along their outermost edge faded to a deep orange where it met their bodies, ensuring that none within the jungle could dismiss the "sailbacks."

"Are they bad?" Marina asked.

"Very bad," Tro-va assured her in a hushed tone. The lizards had not yet seen them, as their eyes were closed and they appeared to have been lulled to sleep by the sunlight. "Come," Tro-va said, taking Marina's hand, and the two stealthily descended the steep incline of the flow to the jungle below. Their blocked passage would necessitate enduring whatever threats were hidden in the verdure until they had passed the slumbering beasts.

The fauna of Caspak was less than subtle in announcing its presence, and even when a creature lay in wait for prey, its sheer size often belied its best efforts to conceal itself. Humans, however, were another story. With higher intelligence comes greater deviousness, and that thought caused Marina some anxiety. As they made their way through the jungle's underpinnings, she questioned Tro-va further about the tribes of Caspak. Unfortunately, his explanation left her more perplexed than ever.

Tro-va stopped at a patch of soft earth and drew a circle with a stick. It was a map of Caspak. He sketched a mass within the circle to indicate the continent's immense central lake. He dragged the end of the stick clockwise around the circumference of the lake in one hemisphere of the continent. At specific intervals, he poked the stick into the ground and named a tribe, beginning with Alu. Next, he spoke, "Bo-lu, Sto-lu, Band-lu, Kro-lu, Galu," designating the territory of each tribe. Then, moving counterclockwise, he repeated the information around the other hemisphere of the island, showing a mirror image of the tribal lands on both sides of the central lake.

"What about the Wieroos?" Marina asked.

Tro-va drew a small island in the lake and jabbed the stick into it. "Here are the Wieroos," he said with contempt.

Marina asked Tro-va why he had left the Kro-lu tribe to join the Galus. She was still trying to grasp his language, and even with the help of pantomime, it was difficult for her to comprehend the full meaning of his words. It was entirely possible that her understanding of Tro-va's explanations was inaccurate, due to her misconstruing his statements, so she was cautious not to put too much faith in her assumptions.

Tro-va explained that he began life as an Alu, as do all the people of Caspak. Over time, Caspakians left their tribes to join other "higher" tribes as he described them, culminating in their acceptance by the Galu tribe. It was unclear to Marina why the societal progression was necessary or what precipitated it, but she accepted his explanation. Tro-va called himself *cor-sva-jo*, which was interpreted by Marina as meaning "up from the beginning." She knew not why the appellation held such importance to him, but being cor-sva-jo meant much more than she could appreciate at that time. Soon enough, she would learn the shocking truth behind the phrase.

14
IN ENEMY HANDS

SOMEHOW, CAPTAIN FAUSTO CAPRONI had survived the night.

That morning, he listlessly trudged through Caprona's seemingly endless jungle, his conscience flooded with guilt and numbing heartbreak. Marina was gone, and though he had not found her body, he had watched as the giant lizard devoured poor Trimboli. The beast left behind not a trace of the man's existence. In the blink of an eye, an entire lifetime was erased.

Now, Marina had likely encountered the same fate. The very thought sickened him.

He no longer cared how loudly his boots crunched over the ground cover. If Caprona had decreed his fate, better he face it defiantly, rather than sneak about like a mouse until the teeth of some ungodly trap slammed down upon his neck. A boiling anger seethed within him; anger with the capricious whims of fate; anger with Sergeant Lago, who had deserted Fausto and his crew; anger with himself.

If one might ask those who knew him—or even Fausto himself—they would tell you he had always been a young man in search of his place in the world, but most notably, he was a man in search of himself. By family tradition, Fausto had been molded into a ship's captain, for it was all the Caproni men had ever known. Regardless of his fitness to command or even his desire to pursue a career on the high seas, becoming a seaman was what was expected of him.

He knew nothing else, and without the temerity to strike out on his own and carve a future as he saw fit, he buckled and allowed the unwavering hand of expectation to dictate the direction of his life.

He only did what he was told.

And now look what had happened.

But was that entirely true? Was none of it his fault? Even Fausto must admit that his fate was partially a result of his actions. Was it not his idea to embark on this insane quest? It was. That being said, no one on God's green earth could have anticipated the horrors that the lost continent contained within its barrier cliffs. He had been driven to embark on the voyage to dispel the slanderous lies told about his family and quash the insults of bullies, plain and simple. His actions had been driven by ego. Still, he could not have foreseen the threat to his crew posed by Caprona.

Fausto had walked for what seemed like hours, but he had yet to find his way back to the plain of dense green stalks and the wreck of the *Pegaso II*. He changed course multiple times, determining that he must be traveling in the direction opposite his intended destination. He was lost.

Neither had he encountered the soldiers Lago and Ortega, nor Collazo, who had fled with Marina. Perhaps they were all dead. Perhaps everyone who had stayed behind with the sky cutter had been devoured by the beasts of Caprona. Perhaps he was the only one left alive. With no way of returning to the waiting *Redenzione*, and no means of signaling the crew of the galleon to inform them of his plight, the odds that he would ever return to Palermo were grim.

Maybe that was for the best. It would be a fitting punishment for the sins he had committed by dragging so many innocent lives into the hell that was Caprona.

Well past midday, Fausto had resigned himself to the truth: He was still no closer to finding his destination than at any other point in the past twenty-four hours. His wandering had carried him from the jungle to a meadow where he found fruit-bearing trees. He ignored Leonardo Ricci's stern warning and indulged in several crisp pink fruits. Fausto was hungry and had to eat to maintain his strength; to his delight, the fruits resembled an outsized variation of orchard apples as he enjoyed back home, and were just as delicious.

Throughout his journey, Fausto crossed several sparkling creeks that provided water to soothe his parched throat. Along his search, he encountered multiple species of wildlife, both reptilian and mammalian, but his sword ensured that none ventured too close to him. Had he a flint and been able to spark a fire, he might have killed any one of the creatures and cooked its flesh, at least the ones most closely resembling animals he recognized. Meanwhile, he would have to sustain himself on fruit.

Fausto wearily trudged onward and proceeded across an expanse of low, rolling hills. Herds of deer, elk, and other animals unknown to him scattered at his approach, which suited him just fine. As exhausted as he was, the last thing he needed was an encounter with a pack of angry herd animals when he had nowhere safe to run.

As he progressed farther and farther from the jungle, Fausto began to realize just how alone he was. In the middle of a field. On an uncharted continent. Predators could be lying in wait, watching him that very moment . . . and he would never know it until he unwittingly stumbled upon them and was torn to shreds in mere seconds. He looked all about him at the grandeur of Caprona. It certainly would be a beautiful place to die.

Then, he heard it, the unmistakable sound of human voices. Immediately, he crouched where he stood and began scanning the horizon in all directions. Because of the roll of the hills in the region, the authors of the guttural gibberish could have been anywhere around him. The voices rose to angry shouts directly behind him and he spun to face the approach of ten armed tribesmen, trotting in his direction. There was nowhere for him to run, as an arrow could easily pierce his back from a great distance.

As the natives drew nearer, Fausto noted that spears, rather than bows, seemed to be the weapon of choice of the men. But something about their faces, strides, and speech was unlike those of the warriors he had faced the previous day. These men were more bestial, with an abundance of bodily hair, their facial features bringing to mind descriptions he had heard from sailors of the hairy, humanlike creatures rumored to inhabit the jungles of central Africa. Their clothing consisted of snakeskin breechcloths, and they wore ornamentation that reflected the sunlight, as did the tribe he had earlier encountered.

These men stooped, almost animal-like, as they walked. Their eyes blazed with rage, their intentions self-evident by their conspicuous display of stone-shod spears, knives, and axes gripped in white-knuckled fists.

Within seconds the nimble warriors were upon him, circling Fausto and shouting. He had already drawn his sword, slashing it about in the warm-up exercises taught to him by Santos Ignacio. He hoped that his display would cause his attackers to think twice, if they could comprehend the danger of a rapier.

But the ape-men did not recognize the sword as a weapon. One charged forward, bearing a stone hatchet above his head.

Fausto Caproni was a man who had lost everything and was struggling for control of his very soul. The self-awareness of his despondency fueled his response to the attack, which was most unfortunate for the tribesman. Fausto was a young man with absolutely nothing to lose.

Before the savage islander was within striking distance of Fausto, the length of the young captain's rapier cut short the distance between them. There was a flash of silver and the attacker flinched in shock as an incision bisected the width of his hirsute chest.

The others of the tribe howled with surprise and anger as

their fellow turned to face them, blood streaming down his abdomen from the grievous wound across his breast. Fausto's slash had cut deeply. The man (at least, he closely resembled a man) fell to his knees, holding his palms to the wound, disbelief written upon his countenance.

Fausto sneered and his eyes blazed. "Who wants to be next?" he growled.

But the tribesmen had spent a lifetime defending themselves from the giants of Caprona, and fearless in their own right, they attacked Fausto en masse. Fausto's sword struck one, then another, but two more, then four, took the places of their stricken brothers. The howling islanders were overwhelming him, their filthy hands clawing and tearing, their rock- and bone-carven weapons slashing at him from every direction.

He could not let it end like this.

Fausto transformed into a fury born of desperation. He thrust backward, driving the pommel at the hilt of his sword into the chest of a man behind him, then jabbed the rapier forward to pierce the abdomen of another attacker preparing to stab him in the face. The sword slashed left, across the cheek of a third attacker, while he kicked outward, digging the heel of his right boot into the groin of a hatchet-wielding tribesman. Another kick forward knocked a bleeding attacker to his back. There came a flurry of slashes, right, left, right again, his body spinning to confront the furious assailants before and behind him. Fausto's sword had drawn blood from each of them, but none of the raiders had, as yet, been mortally wounded.

Fausto's ears rang as something heavy struck the back of his head. A shower of sparks glittered before his eyes, and then a curtain of blackness enveloped his senses.

They're going to kill me, and cook me, and eat me. The morbid consideration was the first fearful thought that shot through Fausto's mind upon awakening. Several hours must have passed while he was unconscious, as all around him was black. It was now nighttime. But no, it was still day, as he could see a portal of sunlight several yards away from where he lay on a stony floor. He was within a cave, with a sturdy cross-hatching of tree limbs barring his escape. The back of his head sorely ached, but he was glad to be alive.

His shirt had been torn to shreds, but thankfully, he still retained his pants and boots. As he expected, his sword was not upon his person. For reasons unknown, the tribesmen had not killed him. Instead, they had imprisoned him for some purpose he could not fathom. Fausto shuddered at the thought of just what that purpose might be.

Around him on the cave floor were strewn bits of animal fur and bones, along with human filth that indicated he was not the first captive to occupy the primitive prison. His head pained him from being struck, but he rose and crept to the door to determine his location. As he drew closer, he spied the back of a tribal guard at one side of the door. Around the man's waist looped Fausto's belt, from which hung his sword.

The bamboo door was simple in design, just a series of . . . But wait! *Bamboo!* It was just what Fausto needed to repair the damage to the hull of the sky cutter. The ill-fated expedition aimed to secure three items; Fausto had succeeded in two of the tasks: the discovery of fresh water and bamboo. Now all he needed to find were trees that secreted rubber beneath their bark to repair the hole in the rear balloon of the *Pegaso II.* Then, they might all escape . . .

Well, not all of them. He took a deep breath. He must push forward, despite Marina's loss.

Through the bars of his cell, his eyes fell upon a sight that gave him pause. He had anticipated neither the societal nor physical composition of the small village before him.

The tribespeople were far from nomadic wanderers; here, in a narrow canyon, a permanent village had been constructed. Many caves yawned from the ravine walls, some at ground level as was his, while others were much higher in elevation and accessible by crude bamboo ladders. The canyon floor had been cleared of vegetation, and dozens of thatch-roof huts of varying shapes and sizes had been constructed by the villagers.

Among the domiciles and in a central clearing, male and female tribal members busied themselves with mundane chores. The females shared the same odd facial structures as their male counterparts and were dressed similarly in the barest of coverings. Nowhere among the goings-on, however, were any children to be seen. Some tribespeople used crude stone tools to tan hides and fashion jewelry, while others, regardless of gender, roasted animal meat on spits over communal fire pits or prepared fruits and vegetables for consumption by the tribe.

Fausto could not help but observe that despite the villagers' initial antagonism toward him, they now seemed quite at peace. Their culture recalled reports of the native tribes of Alta California, the far-off land only recently forfeited to Mexican rule after the crumbling of the efforts of the Spanish Empire and the Franciscan missions to colonize the sprawling region on the west coast of North America.

It took no stretch of the imagination to conclude that the people of Caprona would share a common suffering with the indigenous tribes of Alta California if the warning of Sergeant Ortega were to come to pass.

Still, the tribe might want to kill and eat Fausto, so he needed to find a means of escape.

Flight through the door barring the entrance would only place him in the lap of the village proper, so he explored the cave for some alternate escape route. In the sparse light afforded him, Fausto examined the cave walls. There he found chalk drawings of animals and people; one or more of the cave's previous inhabitants fancied themselves artists, or perhaps they were leaving behind crude last wills and testaments. He ran his hands over the walls searching for loose rocks or anything to indicate a concealed connecting tunnel.

As his hands ran over the smooth stone, the texture changed against his palm. He crouched to look at the wall from a different angle. Several wide veins of quartz revealed themselves in the dim light. It was not the quartz that attracted his interest, but rather the darker bands of ore that interwove with them in parallel stripes. When aligned with the sunlight beaming in from the cave entrance, flecks within the dark bands sparkled with a life of their own. The mineral veins ran across the entire length of the rock wall.

But the dark ore was not just any mineral. He recognized it for what it was: *gold*.

There was untold wealth to be extracted from Caprona by those who claimed the land as their own.

Fausto pondered that thought long and hard before moving to continue his search for a means of escape, but the unintelligible conversation heard outside the bamboo gate told him his time had run out. From where he stood, he could see a number of weapons-bearing tribesmen huddling before the cave entrance, preparing to remove the barrier. Surely it meant his inevitable demise at their hands. But he would not meet his end cowering in the corner of a dark cave.

With only his bare hands to defend himself, Fausto rushed from the darkness toward the bamboo bars to meet his jailers head-on. Before the tribesmen could remove the barrier, screams of panic and angry shouts resounded throughout the village. The enemies at the gate all turned away from Fausto, and in the midst of the men, the young sea captain spied the source of the villagers' tumult.

The massive furred invader roared as it stood upright on its hind legs, nearly fifteen feet in height. Fausto had seen illustrations of bears in books, but he never imagined the animals could be as enormous and fierce as the one that had wandered into the center of the village. The bear's great fangs glistened behind fluttering black lips, its angry bellow ripped from the very core of a nightmare. Massive paws embedded with curved, ebon claws raked the air as the creature announced its intent in no uncertain terms.

Fausto looked on, fascinated in horror, as the beast dropped to all fours and began padding through the village's communal center. The tribespeople scattered in all directions; they had faced foes of this type on multiple occasions and knew that running, rather than fighting, was their best chance for survival. As the horrifying monster strode intently in the direction of the cave in which he was being held, Fausto realized that he was likely trapped in what the giant bear might consider an enticing den.

The guard and several others remained before the bamboo door, their eyes on the black beast that now stalked them. They shouted among themselves as if formulating a strategy. Fausto knew he only had seconds to act. His hand shot through the bamboo bars and gripped the handle of his rapier, hanging from the hip of the guard. Just as the burly islander realized the prisoner had stolen his weapon, the roar of the beast became deafening; the enormous bear was charging, at top speed, directly toward the cave!

The other warriors scattered, but the guard stood frozen in fear. Fausto leaped from the bars of his prison as the full weight of the monster smashed against the guard, splintering the bamboo barrier at his back. The man screamed in terror as the bear continued its charge, lifting him from the ground and carrying him to the back of the cave. With a sickening crunch, the guard slammed against the wall, his ribs shattering.

Fausto leaped through the fractured remnants of the bamboo gate. Spear-wielding warriors rushed toward the cave to confront the monstrous bear, and their attention being otherwise occupied, Fausto was all but ignored in the mayhem. He ran but altered his course abruptly to pass by one of the abandoned cooking fires. Within seconds, his sword firmly in one hand and a spit skewering some form of cooked animal flesh in the other, Fausto disappeared into the jungle. Behind him, the shouts, screams, and death cries diminished as his boots carried him farther and farther from the besieged encampment.

15
THE SECRET OF LIFE

MARINA AWOKE TO BIRDS SINGING and Tro-va again offering her fruit. She was relieved that another night had passed without incident, relatively speaking. Late the prior evening, the two wanderers had been forced to improvise their route when they encountered another group of sailbacks on their nightly hunt. At Tro-va's urging, he and Marina had taken to the trees. Her initial reservations about her ability to climb were soon put to rest; she capably followed her companion's lead and kept an equal pace with him as they navigated the jungle canopy and eluded their hunters.

Night had quickly approached, and soon Tro-va had identified a den abandoned by a former mammalian resident, tucked away inside a large tangle of briar bushes. They had slept among the bushes, where Marina now happily indulged in the juicy, peach-hued pomes foraged by the handsome young warrior.

He smiled at her as they ate in silence, and she smiled back. Before she realized what she was saying, the words had already left her lips. "Tro-va, do you have a mate?" she asked, in the closest approximation to his language she could render.

The look on his face indicated he had understood her question. She could see great loss in his dark brown eyes. Almost immediately, she regretted her inquiry.

"I had a mate, but she has now gone to Luata," he said, drawing a triangle in the air with one finger. Luata, as Marina understood it, was the deity of the people of Caspak.

Marina comfortingly placed a hand on his knee but immediately began chastising herself. *I should not have asked such a personal question. What was I thinking? Why in the world did I even do it?*

Tro-va seemed at peace with his past and spoke freely. Again referring to the odd explanation he had given her the day before, Tro-va explained that there was one named Roo-ko who had come up from the beginning with him. Not long ago and before they could ascend together to the Galu tribe, Roo-ko had fallen to one of Caspak's predators, a fierce beast called a goza. Throughout his explanation, Marina's mind dwelled on the great loss he must have suffered from the death of Roo-ko. Whether it was a wise move, she leaned forward, wrapped her arms around him, and held him close.

"I'm sorry," she said in her native tongue. He could not understand, yet he fully understood.

The pair walked for hours under Caspak's blazing sun, stopping occasionally to quench their thirst. The path Tro-va believed would lead back to the Sea of Grass was not straight, as they must circumvent various areas he knew to be rife with predators and hostile tribes. They were still in the region of the Band-lus and would need to proceed with extreme caution, as the tribes of Caspak were intolerant of those who lay before and after them in the societal structure of the savage land. Sometimes, if a lost tribesman strayed into the wrong territory, he would be driven away by a rival tribe; at other times, the response was much more deadly. As a rule, they would avoid contact with all Caspakians until Marina could be returned to her people.

At midday, they strode from the thick jungle growth that skirted what Tro-va called the Plain of Fire. It was an arid expanse littered with the skeletons of innumerable giant beasts. Even at the periphery of the plain, Marina could feel the heat radiate from the large area of parched, cracked ground. Why the Plain of Fire was so hot would remain a mystery to her, but its name certainly lived up to its reputation. Even birds and Caspak's other airborne creatures shied from flight over the wide, dead expanse.

The young warrior bade Marina to remain where she was in the shade of the jungle perimeter. She obeyed but was unsure why he had made the request. Tro-va then bolted onto the Plain of Fire toward the nearest animal skeleton, fifty feet from the trees. After examining it and finding it unsuitable, he gingerly trotted on to the next corpse. On his third attempt, as Marina watched intently, he found what he was looking for in a specimen that still retained patches of desiccated hide.

The tribesman hastily ripped a piece of fur from the mummified animal, then pulled free one of the scapulas. As a parting gesture, he brought his foot down several times on the skull of what had once been a monstrous tiger of the kind that had attacked the Spaniards at the wreck of the sky cutter. Tro-va gathered a handful of teeth knocked loose from the sun-bleached mandible and returned to Marina, but why he had made the short trek was unknown.

He bade her to follow him into the jungle. There, he sat and worked with the items he had retrieved from the scorched plain. With the tiger pelt, he fashioned a pouch with a drawstring of green vine. In this, he deposited the teeth for some later use and tied the pouch to the hip of his loincloth. He then took the scapula and carefully chipped away pieces along its edges with a small rock. The industrious warrior wrapped pelt scraps around one end to form a grip and bound the handle with more green vines. It was a primitive dagger, which he handed to Marina with pride. She graciously accepted the gift of the weapon, and they continued into the jungle.

Sometime later, the pair stopped to rest in a glade that appeared free from predators. Marina found the natural composition of the little clearing quite charming. Here, they discovered a freshwater creek that trickled down the face of flat granite promontories, stacked one upon the other in the form of a wide natural staircase that stretched across the width of the glade. Each granite tier was blanketed by rich, green moss and hosted small bushes bearing wild berries of red and dark purple. Tro-va instructed Marina to eat only the darker berries, as the red ones were not yet ripe.

As Marina squatted near the flowing water to wash her hands of berry juice, she noted several miniature horses—*eccas*, as they were known on Caspak—grazing among the trees. She watched as three of the animals left the safety of the jungle and wandered toward the flowing water, and surprisingly, toward her. Tro-va sat on one of the higher granite "stairs" twenty feet behind her. She slowly turned her head and smiled widely at him but did not speak, for fear of frightening the little mammals. She widened her eyes as if to say to Tro-va, "Do you see this? How exciting!" He smiled back at her but in a hesitant sort of way that indicated he could not believe what he was seeing.

The nearest ecca skittishly approached Marina, sniffed the air, and then walked up to her open hand. Tro-va watched in awe as Marina scratched the chest of the tiny animal with one finger and gently withdrew her hand. The ecca stepped forward and nudged her hand with its snout until she resumed petting it, ultimately running her hand over the length of its back. That was one step too far; the little horse whinnied and galloped back to the others of its meager herd. With Marina sitting only a few yards away, the eccas drank their fill from the stream, then disappeared into the jungle brush.

Marina stood and dried her hands on her pants. She giggled to herself, enchanted by the pleasant encounter with the ecca. When she turned to face Tro-va, however, he had a look of suspicion on his face.

"Ma-ree-na," he asked bluntly, "what is your tribe?"

She pointed upward into the distance. "Have you ever been to the top of the mountains?"

"I have."

"You have seen the water beyond Caspak?" she asked.

"I have," he replied.

"My people live in another land, like Caspak, far across the water."

Tro-va shook his head. He could not comprehend such a thing. He thought for a moment, then looked directly into her eyes. "You are Cos-ju-lo, are you not?"

"Explain to me, Trova," she responded gently, "what is Cos-ju-lo? I honestly do not know the meaning of the phrase."

Again, he was perplexed. "How can you not know?"

"You must believe me," Marina urged. "I am not of Caspak. I know nothing of your tribes. I am a stranger here. Please . . . explain it to me," she implored.

Tro-va sat on a patch of soft, low-lying grass and Marina joined him. He tried his best to educate her on the ways of the land, and though Marina struggled with the language barrier, she was fairly certain she understood much of what he said, fantastic as it was. As Tro-va talked, she realized she must suspend all disbelief; Caspak was a unique world, so perhaps what he said was true. That his words were more than primitive tribal lore seemed impossible, but she had never expected to encounter giant flying lizards or horses she could tuck under one arm. Marina listened intently.

Trova explained that all life on Caspak, even that of its people, begins with eggs. Those born from eggs are cor-sva-jos; they have come up from the beginning. At a specific interval, an Alu—the first form of man—will grow and change, and become a Bo-lu. Marina did not understand the concept, so Tro-va led Marina to the bushes. There, he found small insect eggs on the underside of a leaf. From another plant, he plucked a caterpillar.

He pointed to the leaf. "*Ata* (egg)," then holding up the caterpillar, he said, "Alu." He then motioned toward a butterfly, lounging upon the mossy ground near them. "Bo-lu," he said, then inferred through hand motions that the process continued up to Galus, tapping his chest to indicate he was a representative of the latter.

It was inconceivable. If Tro-va were to be believed, the

tribespeople of Caspak were born from eggs, after which, over time, they not only became members of successively higher-ranking tribes, but they physically evolved throughout the transitions. Marina knew this could not be so, that a human being could not change forms over the course of the individual's life as did an insect, but she allowed Tro-va to continue as if she were agreeable to the concept.

"All come from eggs, up from the beginning," he added, "except the *cos-ata-lu*, the no-egg man, and the *cos-ata-lo*, the no-egg woman." He explained that only under unique conditions could a male and a female conceive a child not from an egg but from mating. Both parents must be cos-ata-lu and cos-ata-lo for that reproduction method to succeed. And cos-ata-los and cos-ata-lus were apparently both quite rare and quite valuable to some on Caspak.

"Valuable to whom?" she asked.

The young tribesman squirmed before he delved into a horrifying topic. "The Wieroos," he said. "The Wieroos can breed only with cos-ata-los, who are either stolen by them or offered to the Wieroos as sacrifices to stay their wrath upon the tribes. The cos-ata-los are flown to the island of Oo-oh, which lies in Caspak's central lake. They are never seen again."

Marina was appalled but still had questions.

"What of the Cos-ju-lo?" she asked. "You have called me that several times. What does that mean?"

A mien of reverence washed over Tro-va's face. "The Cos-ju-los are cos-ata-lo women of the Galus who have broken with the tribe. They are savage, fearless fighters and live as wanderers across Caspak."

"Why did they leave the Galus?" Marina asked.

There was an air of respect in Tro-va's voice. "They would not submit to being offered as sacrifices. They refused to be taken by the Wieroos. That is an affront to the Galus, the Wieroos, and Luata. It is said that the Cos-ju-los can tame the beasts in the jungles, and the plains, and the skies. Even the

Wieroos fear them. You understand . . . 'cos-ju-lo' means '*no stop woman*,'" he said in Marina's native language.

Marina smiled to herself. "The unstoppable women," she said profoundly, flattered that the handsome young tribesman considered her worthy of the mantle of Cos-ju-lo.

16
FRIEND OR FOE?

THE SETTING SUN HUNG just above the rim of Caprona's great barrier cliffs, bathing the jungle in amber hues. Fausto reckoned that two more hours of sunlight remained before the ebon abyss of night would plunge the primeval glade into darkness. After sundown thousands of miles away, flickering tavern oil lamps along the walk of Palermo's port enticed nighttime revelers and suggested carefree adventures that could be had in exchange for a few wisely spent coins. In the jungles of Caprona, utter darkness ruled the night, save for the glow of fireflies and the occasional glint of moonlight on fangs.

Another night, lost and alone, was not a comforting prospect for the young captain.

After escaping from the native village, Fausto made his way east, as best he could tell. Then again, how could he be sure which way anything was? Did north, south, east, and west mean the same thing on Caprona as in the civilized world? The island confounded magnetic compasses, after all. But no; Caprona had no hold over the rotation of the Earth around the sun, at least not that he was aware. The next morning he would continue moving toward the brilliant orb in the dawn sky. He hoped to reach the great interior sea, and from there he might work his way back to the wreck of the *Pegaso II*, if he had correctly remembered the topography he had viewed from the air.

Reuniting with the Spaniards would be another matter

altogether. The warning of Sergeant Ortega still rang in his memory. If he made it back to the sky cutter—no, *when* he made it back—he would be a fool if he did not have his sword in hand.

In the waning daylight, Fausto thought it best to find a safe place to bed down. He descended the incline of a ravine to find a narrow canyon strewn with boulders that had toppled from the walls above, leaving behind crevices large enough to accommodate a human. One of the small caves would provide adequate protection until the morning, when he would continue his arduous search for the sky cutter.

With his sword drawn, Fausto cautiously inspected several cave openings but found them all too small to accept his frame. Above him, he spied an opening larger than the others, at least eight feet in diameter and ten feet from the canyon floor. It appeared ideal for his needs, and he easily scaled the wall and peered inside the opening.

Had he not flung himself backward, the gigantic pincer that thrust toward him from the darkness would surely have taken off his head. Fausto hit the canyon floor heavily and awkwardly, but by good fortune missed landing on any rocks. His eyes darted to the cave opening above him and the terrifying nemesis that crawled forth.

It was a scorpion, like those found creeping among the sands of Egypt, but the nightmarish creature that skittered down the wall on eight legs was nearly six feet long. Its color was sickly white, with a dark blue carapace, the deadly barb at the end of its upcurved tail waving above its back. The thing's foreclaws repeatedly snapped in succession, and within seconds the creature was on the canyon floor and darting toward Fausto.

He leaped to his feet and drew his sword; there would be no running from this creature. It was much too fast. He would have to stand his ground, much to his horror.

The hideous beast's first instinct was to attempt to reach Fausto with its massive pincers. Fausto struck with his sword to the right, then to the left, furiously beating back the chitinous claws, but neither pincer reaching for him was damaged by his steel. The monstrous arachnid was covered by a tough, rigid shell that a sword could not pierce. The beast lunged again, but the agile young captain deflected the snapping appendage thanks to the training drilled into him by Santos Ignacio.

Fausto quickly realized that the back-and-forth could continue all night until he dropped from exhaustion; in terms of defeating his opponent, his sword strikes were futile. His attacker must have made the same assessment, for now it craned its barbed tail backward in preparation for impaling its prey. Fausto saw the move, and just as the poison stinger thrust toward him, he took a wild swing with his sword.

The giant arachnid shuddered in mute agony as the amputated tip of its tail thudded to the ground. With one strike, Fausto had denied the creature its most potent offensive weapon. But it still had its deadly pincers.

Like lightning, the gigantic scorpion lashed out, a pincer tightly snapping around Fausto's left leg, just above his ankle. Before he could react, the other pincer thrust forward and clamped down on his sword arm like a vise. Fausto screamed in pain. What was left of the creature's tail waved in the air hideously and thrust repeatedly against Fausto's chest. Deprived of the poison barb, the normally deadly attacks did nothing more than stain his shredded shirt with the creature's dark blood.

But Santos Ignacio had taught Fausto well. Though his right arm was subdued in the crushing grip of the monster, his left arm was free. Now Fausto understood why Señor Santos had trained him to fence equally well with both hands.

Fighting through the pain, Fausto took the sword in his left hand and drove it straight into the face of the nightmare creature. The blade found a soft spot and sank deeply. Immediately, it released its grip on him and convulsed for several seconds before the tail dropped lifelessly to the ground.

Fausto leaped away from the dead attacker and inspected his arm and leg. Both were cut and red with blood, but thankfully the wounds appeared to be superficial. He wiped the edge of his rapier on his pants leg and returned it to its sheath.

Just then, a voice rang out behind him. "Don't move, Captain Caproni."

At the top of the small canyon, a Spanish soldier—Sergeant Garza—stood with his rifle aimed and ready to fire. He was one of the men who had remained behind at the wreck of the sky cutter with Colonel Valdez.

"It's all right," Fausto shouted. "I killed it."

Garza laughed. "That's not where I'm aiming."

Fausto's heart skipped a beat and he shut his eyes tightly as the shot rang out. With a look of utter shock on his face, Sergeant Garza fell to the floor of the canyon like a ragdoll, a musket ball embedded in his spine.

"You can trust me, Captain Caproni," came the voice from the dusk shadows. Fausto's savior stepped into the light. It was Sergeant Ortega. "Do you need any assistance?" he asked politely.

Fausto beamed at the Spanish soldier. "A simple explanation would suffice, Sergeant," he replied. Complete and utter relief overwhelmed him, a feeling he had not experienced in days. The sensation was fleeting, however, when he recalled the fate of Marina and the bloody scrap of cloth he had found. He would never, ever get past her loss.

Captain Caproni and Sergeant Ortega abandoned the small canyon, fearing it might host more gigantic scorpions. As night descended upon Caprona, the two men hauled the body of Sergeant Garza up into the jungle and buried it in the soft earth, then climbed a tree with wide, thick horizontal branches on which they could sit in relative safety. At the suggestion of Ortega, Fausto was now in possession of the dead soldier's halberd, rapier, musket balls, gunpowder and wadding, and rifle. Fausto had only minimal experience with firearms, but the additional weapons shored up his confidence.

"Where do I begin," Ortega asked himself.

"Do you know what happened to Marina?" It was difficult for Fausto to ask the question, but he needed to know.

"When we ran from the fallen tree, we all took different paths," Ortega recalled. "I have not seen your sister or the sailor Collazo since. I tried to find Sergeant Lago, but could not, and he never returned to the sky cutter."

"You made it back!" Fausto noted. "Is everyone there safe? How is Signore Ricci?"

Ortega nodded. "He is in good health, although not in good spirits. He's very concerned about you and Marina. But yes, by sheer luck I found the sky cutter the following morning after I last saw you. There is a stream nearby, so we have water. Colonel Valdez and Garza managed to kill a deer, so they have food."

"That's good," Fausto responded. "But I have questions . . ."

Ortega cut him off in midsentence. "Captain, I have answers for you."

Fausto crossed his arms. "Go on."

"Plainly, Colonel Valdez plans to kill all of you and claim Caprona for Spain. As for those on board the *Redenzione*, they will either be paid for their silence, or murdered."

"Valdez will have to find a way back to the ship to do that," Fausto stated tersely.

"There is a plan for that, too," Ortega replied. "Signore Ricci suggested if there is no way to repair the torn balloon, a basket could be constructed to hang below the undamaged balloon. It would not hold many of us, but several trips could ferry us all back to the ship. The undamaged balloon has since deflated, but Signore Ricci is certain there are enough iron filings and acid to reinflate it. But . . ." He paused, crestfallen. "Signore Ricci doesn't know that not a single Sicilian will return to the *Redenzione*. Including him."

Fausto fumed at the nefarious plot. "Why are you back here, then? And why did you kill Garza?"

"I am a man of honor. I serve God and country faithfully," Ortega proclaimed with unmistakable pride. "But the plan of Colonel Valdez," he spat, "that is the work of the devil. The reason I am here is that the Colonel must have absolute proof that you and your countrymen are dead. Garza and I were dispatched to either kill you or confirm your death. And to ensure Marina and your sailors also do not return." Ortega's tone grew overtly sarcastic. "But out here, in this savage land, Valdez will never know what happened if his lapdogs do not return, will he?"

"Thank you, my friend," Fausto responded. He then asked if Queen Regent Maria Christina had devised the scheme. Ortega assured the captain that Valdez had boasted that he alone concocted the plan and expected a substantial reward—to be shared with his soldiers, he said—upon his return to Spain.

"Valdez has even prepared a new name for Caprona," Ortega revealed. "He plans to call this place *Nueva España*."

"Over my dead body," Fausto growled. "I've encountered men like Valdez before. He wants to kill us so he can steal Caprona for himself. I know his type. His soldiers are sadly mistaken if they think they will be rewarded for doing his dirty work."

Fausto thoughtfully considered all that he had heard. "Let me get everything straight, so we know where all the pawns are in this game. Valdez is on the sky cutter, with Sergeants Montes and Alonso. Sergeant Lago is missing, and you are with me. Also on the sky cutter are Leonardo Ricci, and my sailors, Puccini and Alamani. They are all still alive?" Ortega confirmed the sailors remained unharmed. "Good," Fausto said. "Of my crew out here, there is me and maybe Collazo. One of those terrible lizards killed Trimboli. And my sister . . ."

After Fausto recounted that he had found Marina's torn and bloody sleeve and her handprints on the tree, Ortega stiffened officially and placed a hand on Fausto's shoulder. "You must have faith, Captain. I've seen firsthand that your sister is a woman not to be trifled with, am I right? I will make it my duty to do everything I can to find her."

Fausto smiled, and for the first time in days a spark of hope filled his heart.

Another note of vital importance stirred in his memory, and Fausto proceeded to inform Ortega of the primitive native islanders he had encountered. The Spaniard said his country-men had not seen any people on Caprona, but Fausto's revela-tion made the soldier uneasy.

"This is what I most feared," Ortega admitted, sighing heavily. He paused and collected himself, while Fausto waited, nervously anticipating what the soldier might share next. It was not good news at all. "Have you noticed anything unusual about the health of Sergeant Lago?"

Fausto immediately knew to what Ortega referred. "Coughing." And then the gravity of the situation struck him. "What does he have, Ortega?"

"I suspect scarlet fever," the soldier said, "but he insists he's fine, that it's nothing. I know better, though. I told you and Marina I had served my country in Alta California. I was assigned to a monastery garrison and was there for two years. During that time, I saw things I cannot forget, crimes against the native peoples whose souls the Franciscan monks were trying to save, or so they said. Whippings. Torture. Murder. All in the name of God." Ortega looked wistfully at the treetops. "But what could I do? I was one soldier, sickened by what I saw as all those around me proclaimed it to be salva-tion while doing nothing to stop it. I cannot let that happen again. I cannot sit by and watch innocent people become enslaved. And now what? Look at this land and its beauty. Isolated from conquerors and the evils of the outside world. What do you think scarlet fever would do to the people here, just as smallpox did to the tribes of North America?"

Fausto was silent as various threads of thought began to

intertwine in his mind. He quickly drew to a conclusion. "Somewhere out there, Lago is roaming free, ready to spread whatever illness he has. So we stop him by whatever means necessary, yes?"

Ortega nodded in agreement and added a supposition. "Then, let's say we stop Colonel Valdez's plan and Caprona is claimed and colonized by the Kingdom of the Two Sicilies. My question is, Captain," he said with dead seriousness, "will your countrymen treat the tribes of Caprona with the same benevolence and compassion as would mine?"

The sarcastic edge to Ortega's question could not outweigh its dire importance. For Captain Fausto Caproni, the answer was all too apparent.

The two men slept among the branches that night, each taking turns on watch, and in the morning they set out to find Marina and Collazo, if they still lived. They had no way of knowing, at that time, that Collazo had been murdered by the detestable Sergeant Lago, who was also unaccounted for somewhere in the wilds of Caprona. Of all Colonel Valdez's men, Lago was the most despicable, and Ortega deeply disliked the man. Practically everyone on board the *Redenzione* reciprocated the sentiment.

Sergeant Ortega had made a careful mental account of the path he and Garza had taken from the sky cutter to where they had found Fausto. He reasoned that it would be simple enough to retrace his voyage back to the downed airship should he and Fausto fail in their search. The young captain had asked for a detailed explanation of the route, and being convinced that he had memorized it, Fausto implored Ortega to return to the *Pegaso II*, thanking him for all he had done to help. Ortega refused to depart. He would assist Fausto until the bitter end, should things come to that.

The sun had only just risen, its warming rays chasing off the shadows of the night across the lush interior of the lost continent. The usual early morning mist hung over the jungles of Caspak, and flying creatures of all shapes and sizes abounded in the skies and trees, some soaring gracefully to heights that seemed to surpass that of the lofty barrier cliffs. Tro-va was already busying himself with some task when Marina awoke in the small cave they had secured within a jungle swamp. Her surroundings resembled where she had plunged from the ledge to escape Sergeant Lago, but here there were no gigantic crocodiles to torment them. At least, not presently.

"Good morning," Marina said, stretching her arms over her head and yawning contentedly. Tro-va was seated at the entrance to the cave. As she crawled to him on her hands and knees to avoid the low ceiling of the hovel, he finished whatever he was doing with the tiger teeth he had recovered from the Plain of Fire and returned them to the pelt bag at his hip. He smiled at her, and she smiled back. *This is beginning to become a pleasant routine*, she thought.

After eating fruit they had collected the night before, the pair set out across the bog. Tro-va was certain of the location of the great Sea of Grass; once they passed through the swamp they would encounter a forest, and beyond that lay lowlands that adjoined the huge meadow where lay the *Pegaso II*. On multiple occasions, Marina had tried to explain the principle behind the flying ship, but Tro-va would have none of it. The primitive nature of his intelligence was mildly frustrating, but it held a certain charm, Marina thought.

The swamp was thick with insects and trees, and not entirely free of hungry predators that would occasionally spring at them or snap at their feet as they traversed the bog on raised tree roots or elevated patches of deep saw grass. At least here they would not encounter any of the heavier of Caspak's monstrous lizards, who shied away from the swamp for fear of sinking into the muck and becoming trapped.

However, of constant concern was Tro-va's warning that the path they followed crossed very near the boundary of the land of the Sto-lus, or hatchet men. Currently, they were in the territory of the Band-lus, or spear men, which was no less dangerous. Although she wanted to avoid further obstacles at all costs, Marina secretly desired to see the other humans of whom Tro-va spoke; she was quite intrigued by his description of the physical metamorphosis he claimed his people experienced when ascending from one tribe to the next. But if they were also as savage as he described, it was probably for the best that they proceeded on their journey in relative solitude.

Marina's wish was not to be.

17
THE SWAMP OF DEATH

THE DENSITY OF THE TREES within the jungle marsh began to thin as Marina and Trova scaled a muddy bank to a raised plateau blanketed with a sward of verdant grass. Although the ground was still quite soft, the odorous muck through which they had trodden was behind them. The foul odor of the air was reminiscent of the canals of Venice, where she had visited once as a child, but this was exponentially more pungent. Wildflowers dotted the mossy jungle floor and runners wove across the ground, leading to thick, netlike curtains of vines that hung from the overhead acacia branches. Marina longed for the sword she had lost; it would make cutting a path through the jungle much easier, but she would have to settle for using the bone knife Tro-va had fashioned for her.

The beauty of the large dragonflies that proliferated in the surrounding air momentarily distracted Marina. Some of the insects were nearly two feet in length. Fortunately, they were uninterested in the travelers and had not once molested them as they trudged through the swamp. In the scintillating rays of light that penetrated the thick canopy overhead, the transparent wings of the dragonflies sparkled with iridescence. Caspak was a land of terrifying monsters, but also one of breathtaking beauty.

Tro-va touched Marina's shoulder as she watched the insects hovering around them. She did not turn to face him; instead, she smiled to herself. His warm hand upon her skin was like a balm on her soul. Tro-va was so unlike the ruffians and boors of Palermo whom she had spent her entire life trying to avoid. None of them understood her; none were equipped with the innate ability to listen rather than dictate, to treat her as an equal rather than a possession. Somehow, this young primitive islander was all she had searched for in a man and more, and it did not even seem like he had to try to please her. It is very simply who he was.

Tro-va's hand tightened on her shoulder, and she realized that his touch was not an expression of tenderness but a warning of danger. She snapped from her romantic daydream and realized that all around them human figures lurked among the trees facing the swamp. Marina and Tro-va were surrounded.

"Band-lu?" she whispered.

"No. Sto-lu," he replied in a dire tone.

Marina had been curious about the other natives of Caspak; now, she wished she had never longed to meet them. As the watchers stalked forth from the twisted vines, she could behold their every detail, as shocking as they were. Tro-va's prior description placed this tribe three steps distant from his own tribe, the Galus, with Kro-lus and Band-lus between them in descending order.

As difficult as it was to accept, the evidence that Tro-va's words had been sincere stood before her: The members of the other tribes truly were of a wholly different form from that of Tro-va. Those who now stood before her were men, but their odd features suggested the vague semblance of apes. All were naked, their bodies—arms, shoulders, backs, and torsos—covered in short hair. Had they stood upright, their height would have equaled that of Tro-va, but these beings stood stooped, their arms dangling before them mere inches from the ground. They wore no ornamentation, each man equipped with a crude stone axe. Their faces were their most striking feature, with glassy, close-set eyes, exaggerated cheekbones and brows, and facial hair that flowed from their jaws, down their necks, and merged with the hair covering their barrel chests. They were at once a fascinating and terrifying sight.

The Sto-lus pressed forward, weapons in clenched fists, their full attention on Marina. Some emitted crude, guttural noises while raising their arms into the air in some form of primitive intimidation technique meant to assert their dominance. The behavior unsettled Marina, but Tro-va stood firmly and met their advance without a flinch. Throughout the display, they shouted; it was the same language spoken by Tro-va, so Marina recognized a few words, but most of it was delivered too rapidly for her to process. One thing was obvious, however: They were greatly interested in her. Not only did they frequently point to Marina as they shouted, but she heard the suffix "lo" repeated multiple times. It was the Caspakian word for "woman."

The largest of the Sto-lus, apparently the leader of the band, met Tro-va face-to-face with arms raised and fury written on his features. They exchanged angry words for several minutes, ending in a stalemate. Marina suspected the worst; the Sto-lu leader wanted her for his own and Tro-va refused that demand. It was then she realized Tro-va was indicating she was his mate. Could any other conclusion be reached to explain his stalwart rebuff of the Sto-lu?

The standoff seemed to last forever, and at length, all verbal communication abruptly ceased. The Sto-lu swayed back and forth on his bowed legs and glared at Tro-va. At last, the hirsute enemy lifted his weapon arm and held high his axe.

Tro-va immediately lunged forward like a jungle cat, thrusting his muscled shoulder into the midsection of his apelike opponent. The sudden impact forced the air from the lungs of the Sto-lu. Moving like quicksilver, Tro-va intertwined the fingers of his hands and drove both elbows into his enemy's back. The ape-man dropped his axe and screamed in pain, the outburst echoing through the trees as he fell to his hands and knees.

Although gasping for air, the Sto-lu was a resilient fighter.

He quickly hooked an arm around the knees of Tro-va and pushed forward, knocking the young Galu onto his back. Their bloodlust fueled by the violence, the gibbering and shrieking Sto-lu onlookers encircled the combatants. The Sto-lu was now on top of Tro-va and pounded him with his fists, but Marina's companion would not relent. Tro-va blocked the attacker's blows with his forearms, and through the frantic pounding, he managed to slip a hand through the flailing arms of his opponent and raked his fingers across his eyes.

The Sto-lu fell back and screamed in rage, holding his hands to his face. As the chorus of bloodcurdling shrieks rose around him, Tro-va's hand found the discarded stone axe. Marina watched with a mix of pride and revulsion as Tro-va raised the weapon above the head of the writhing Sto-lu leader.

Before he could deliver the death blow, the axe was ripped from Tro-va's hands. He spun to find another Sto-lu behind him, nearly as mighty as the one he now fought, gripping the axe and screaming. The ape-man thrust downward, and buried the crude rock blade in the head of his leader, shattering his skull and killing him instantly.

Tro-va jumped away from the corpse and stared at the hatchet, dripping with gore. He then looked to Marina, who had backed toward the edge of the grassy plateau that over-looked the swamp. In the blink of an eye, Tro-va dashed toward Marina and roughly pushed her from the ledge. Her scream of confusion—laced with a healthy dose of anger—resounded from the jungle canopy as she ungracefully plunged into the algae-laced water ten feet below.

"Ortega! Did you hear that?" Fausto Caproni shouted to his traveling companion. The two men were just crossing over from a pasture to swampier territory, and both froze in their tracks.

"I did!" Ortega replied. "A woman's scream! Do you think . . . ?"

"It was!" Fausto boomed. "Marina!"

Without hesitation, the two men plunged into the swamp, running as they never had before.

Tro-va was in an unwinnable situation since he faced enemies for whom honor held no value. Each would kill the other to win the prize of the strange Galu woman who now splashed about in the muddy water. One Sto-lu would fall and another would take his place in an unending cycle until only one of the ape-men remained standing.

Marina understood that Tro-va had not pushed her into the swamp with malice. Earlier he had explained that he still held dim recollections of his time among the Sto-lus and that the tribespeople had a great fear of the black mud beneath the dark waters of the swamp. That was the reason Tro-va had pushed her from the ledge; it was his best effort to protect her while he dealt with the Sto-lu warriors and perhaps met his death at their hands. At least Marina had been allowed an opportunity to escape.

"Run, Ma-ree-na!" he shouted in his native tongue.

Marina was in a panic and wanted to tell him she would not leave him, that he meant more to her than she had realized, but she knew none of the Caspakian words for the emotions that now surged through her. She sloshed through the turbid water, intending to climb the embankment and stand beside Tro-va as he engaged their enemies. Her only weapon was the bone knife, but she would use it to its full devastating potential.

As Tro-va grappled with the second Sto-lu warrior and Marina fought against the sucking pull of the mud beneath her boots, neither of them saw the hulking figure that crept from behind the swamp trees and silently made its way through the foul water toward Marina.

Savage, hairy hands bearing cracked and filthy fingernails gripped Marina by her shoulders and ripped her away from the embankment. It was a Caspakian man, more physically primitive than a Galu, but not as apish as the Sto-lus. This must have been a Band-lu, of whom Tro-va had warned. His body reeked, as did his hot breath, and he held Marina close as she kicked and pounded him with her fists. In anger, the Band-lu threw her into the mire and held her head beneath the surface for several seconds to break her resistance.

She held her breath and kept her eyes tightly shut as his hands gripped her throat. White sparks glistened before the blackness; she was losing consciousness and would surely drown within seconds. But Marina Caproni would never surrender without a fight.

The Band-lu shrieked in pain, causing Tro-va and the Sto-lus to cease their skirmish and look to the swamp. There, a Band-lu warrior stood, desperately trying to contain the intestines that spilled out from the great gash across his lower stomach. His blood mixed with the muddy water, and as he fell dead, another figure broke the surface of the muck. Marina rose and gasped and filled her lungs with precious, life-giving air. In her white-knuckled fist, she tightly gripped her knife.

Enraged that a Band-lu had invaded their territory, the Sto-lus threw savage shouts to the sky. Where walked one Band-lu, there would certainly be more. They were right. Marina spun to find six more spear-bearing Band-lu warriors tightening a circle around her as they trudged through the waist-deep quagmire.

Distracted by Marina's plight, Tro-va was overcome by the Sto-lus, who held his arms tightly behind him, their stone hatchets primed to hack him to pieces.

It was as if time—and the jungle itself—stood still as a shrill wail split the air. The sound rose in volume and pitch, to be joined by another, then another. The sounds merged into a harmonized chorus that was both beauteous and ominous in its composition. All save Marina moved not a muscle, for they seemed to know what the sounds signified.

Thirty feet behind and to the right of the furious Sto-lus, an enormous head thrust through the heavy curtain of vines and leaves. It was another of Caspak's monstrous lizards, unlike

any Marina had yet seen. The head was like that of a hippo-
potamus but three times the size, its leathery skin colored
maroon and mottled with tan and yellow splotches. Its nose
drew to a point and terminated in a massive, bony beak. Three
horns adorned the head; the smallest rose vertically from the
top of the snout just behind the beak, the two others at least
eight feet in length jutting forward over the small, black eyes.
From the upper curve of its neck rose a bony frill that encircled
the head from one side of its jaw to the other.

The creature was breathtaking to behold, but it had not
come alone. Behind and to the left of the Sto-lus, another
monstrous head crashed through the vine curtain. This goliath
was lime green and yellow, but rather than possessing the two
forward-facing horns of the other beast, this creature's horns
extended forth from the perimeter of its bony neck frill. Both
beasts roared, joining the crescendo of the higher-pitched
wails that accompanied their arrival.

The distraction was all Tro-va needed to twist from the
grips of the startled Sto-lus. He pulled free and ran, leaped
from the grassy promontory into the black muck of the swamp,
and sloshed to Marina's side.

The Sto-lus were torn between screaming in apelike grunts
over the loss of their captive and shouting in fear of the two
titans that stomped through the underbrush and vines. The
mighty creatures shook the boles of the trees as their massive
forms pushed past them.

Marina's eyes grew wide with wonder as the beasts were
fully revealed. Both were twice the length of a horse with tails
matching that length. They marched on four muscled legs
with bodies the circumference of the largest of elephants. Yet,
nothing about the behemoths could compare to the awe-
inspiring grandeur of their riders, for on the back of each
monster rode a woman.

Marina looked to Tro-va for an explanation. He looked
into her dark brown eyes and mouthed a word she had heard
several times from his lips: "Cos-ju-los."

The women astride the behemoths were both strikingly beautiful. From their heads flowed long dark hair adorned with colorful feathers. They were nearly nude, wearing only what appeared to Marina to be snakeskin bibs over their breasts, backs, and pelvises, and fur boots that protected their legs to just below their knees. Both carried multiple weapons, and it was readily apparent they were prepared for battle. Their arsenal included clubs, stone axes, spears, bows, and ropes, representing the weapons of each of Caspak's tribes. In addition, each Cos-ju-lo was equipped with a shield enrobed by tough animal hides, in the center of which was painted a single triangle, the representation of Luata, as Tro-va had explained to Marina. Above their breasts depended necklaces of sharp, white animal teeth.

The most stunning feature of the women was their faces, painted with a bright blue slash that ran directly down the center, from their foreheads to chins and between their dark, intense eyes.

These were the Cos-ju-los. The unstoppable women.

18

UNSTOPPABLE

THE REMAINING STO-LU WARRIORS, seven in all, bellowed in rage at the two Cos-ju-lo women and their enormous mounts. The ear-piercing wail had stopped, having been generated by the women through the use of speckled conch shells they had blown into, which now hung at their hips by thin leather straps.

Tro-va came under attack by one of the Band-lu warriors, who thrust a spear toward his back. The tribesman attempted to leap to one side to avoid the spear thrust, but the pull of the swamp bed held him fast, affording him minimal movement. To his good fortune, the environment also hindered the mobility of the attacker. The Band-lu's deadly strike missed Tro-va's flank by inches. The latter pushed forward through the muck and lunged at the Band-lu, plunging the two combatants into the foul black water.

Marina's heart urged her to rush to Tro-va's aid, but the other Band-lu warriors had encircled her. "Get away from me!" she shouted in her native tongue, not caring that the tribesmen would not understand her. The knife held tightly in her fist would surely better convey her warning. If only she had a club or sword, something to keep her attackers at a distance.

In a fleeting instant, during the intangible flood of possibilities that rush through one's mind in a moment of crisis, she recalled her confrontation with Sergeant Lago in the hold of the *Redenzione* months before. Marina slipped her knife beneath the belt at her waist and sprang into action. Not anticipating an attack, the Band-lu nearest her was taken by surprise. Just as she had done to Lago, Marina targeted the right arm of her opponent. She applied all of her strength, and with a simple twist of his forearm away from his body, the warrior's elbow painfully dislocated. He screamed out in shock. In the blink of an eye, his spear was now in Marina's hands. The blunt end of the weapon crashed against his jaw, knocking him from his feet and into the murky water.

The Sto-lu warriors had by now recovered from their confusion and as a group had determined their greatest enemy in the melee: the Cos-ju-los. After shouting among themselves, the ape-men quickly formed an attack plan and charged toward the massive animals on which the women rode.

Before their stone hatchets could sink into the leathery hides of the mounts, the jungle foliage around the beasts burst outward. Five additional Cos-ju-los leaped through the air toward the Sto-lus. They did not carry shields, as their focus was attack, not defense. Before the booted feet of the charging Cos-ju-los even touched the ground, two of the seven Sto-lus had been dropped, both nearly decapitated by the blades of the warrior women.

In the swamp, Tro-va burst to the surface of the water and pulled the Band-lu warrior from the muck by his neck. With mighty swings, his fist smashed against the jaw of his foe again and again until the Band-lu lost consciousness. The body splashed into the muck. One of the fallen warrior's companions rushed to his aid and dragged the limp form away from Tro-va.

Marina was now holding two other Band-lus at bay with the spear she had requisitioned from them. Although their original intent appeared to have been her abduction, Marina's attackers now seemed hell-bent on her death. She used her spear to strike away the thrusts of the Band-lus, but she was facing two of them at once. The slightest miscalculation would result in a stone blade plunged through her torso.

Tro-va burst in from Marina's right, tackling one of her

tormentors. The unrelenting fist strikes upon the Band-lu was a display of savagery that took her breath away. Never had she seen a man so driven, so consumed by primal bloodlust, yet at the same time his actions were measured in a way she could not hope to describe. He fought like a wild beast, yet retained the intelligent composure of a civilized man.

While her male counterpart was engaged, Marina now faced three opponents, as two additional Band-lus rushed to join in either her capture or her death. Like a born warrior, Marina struck like a viper with the spear, stabbed one of her attackers in the thigh, then ripped the spear tip from his leg to block an attack from her left. In a move of amazing grace, she instinctually leaned backward as another spear was thrust at her; had she moved a fraction of a second slower, the stone spearhead would have penetrated her breast. His attack having failed, the islander pushed backward through the murky water to stand seven feet from her, the demeanor of his cruel face daring her to come after him. Marina was not one to let a taunt go unchallenged.

She lashed out at the tribesman, holding the spear near its end to extend her deadly reach. He must have considered himself safe from harm, but Marina's scythe-like swing of the spear bridged the distance between them. The stone tip destroyed his throat as it ripped beneath his chin, sending a shower of rich, red blood into the dark water.

Marina was a whirlwind of motion, as was the handsome man who fought at her side. The attacker whose leg she punctured had fled, leaving only one assailant in her proximity. Enraged by her resilience, the warrior howled as he attacked, bringing his spear down again and again like a club. Marina lifted her spear and blocked the blows, then spun out of the path of his next strike. The spear smacked harmlessly against the water.

The Band-lu growled, hunched over like an animal, incensed beyond comprehension or logic. Because of this, he was easily outsmarted. As he spun to face his elusive prey, Marina threw a handful of black slime into his face, which she had dredged from the floor of the swamp. The tactic was disorienting enough for him to pause, and that was the only opening she needed. She raised her boot from the water and kicked, driving her heel into his stomach. The temporarily blinded savage buckled over, and with three quick jabs her spears pierced his chest and both shoulders. The bloody strikes were not deadly and would surely send the message that should he wish to live, he had better retreat. He would not back down, however.

Tro-va crouched in the muddy water to avoid the swinging spear of the Band-lu he fought, then lunged at the ape-man. He gripped the savage warrior around the waist and lifted him, straining his thews to their limits. Tro-va hefted the warrior over his head and flung him against the bleeding Band-lu that engaged Marina behind him. It was an unlucky turn of events for the Band-lu, as he fell against the raised spear of the other tribesman. The sharpened stone spearhead pierced the flesh of the man Tro-va had thrown, impaling him just below his sternum. The warrior's weight and the momentum of his fall caused the blade to travel upward into his chest beneath his ribs. He choked on his own blood and fell dead into the water.

Above them, the Sto-lus were no match for the Cos-ju-lo warriors. One by one, the Sto-lus fell beneath the stone weapons of their female foes until only one of the men remained alive. Seeing his fellow tribesmen lying bloody and torn on the earth around him, he dashed for the jungle and disappeared into the brush.

Tro-va rushed to Marina's side. The bleeding Band-lu warrior who had challenged her reconsidered his options and moved away through the swamp to join the other tribesmen, all of whom eyed the couple warily.

"Are you hurt?" Marina asked of Tro-va.

His warm smile eased her fears and she placed a hand upon his muscled chest, a gesture of appreciation for what he had done for her.

She looked to the high ground of the promontory. At its edge and overlooking the swamp stood the two great beasts. Their riders and the five Cos-ju-los on the ground stood silently and proudly, as if in contemplation of some great riddle. Marina could only guess what they were thinking, but one thing was certain: All eyes were upon her.

"Will the Cos-ju-los harm us?" she asked Tro-va.

He shrugged, for he honestly did not know. Then, things got worse.

The gigantic mounts of the Cos-ju-los sniffed the air and snorted, and using the thick gray nails of their forelegs, they threw mounds of soft earth to their rear. In the eyes of Marina, they were behaving just as bulls do when enraged and preparing to charge. The Cos-ju-los, alarmed by the behavior of the beasts, raised their weapons and tensed into battle-ready stances. Something was about to happen, something bad.

Marina and Tro-va turned, hearing movement from the swamp trees behind them. At least two dozen Band-lu warriors were wading through the algae-covered morass toward them. The Band-lus they had fought must have been advance scouts for a much larger hunting party, now drawn to the scene by the sounds of battle and the cries of the wounded.

The two young wanderers were trapped, waist-deep in the swamp; before them stalked bloodthirsty male savages in the count of two score, and behind them stood a small band of female warriors whose intent was just as mysterious as the Caspakian legend that surrounded them.

"What do we do?" Marina asked Tro-va, squeezing his hand with her own.

He looked at her calmly. "We do as Luata commands," was his resolute response.

Marina whispered, "What does Luata command?"

"Luata commands," he said with a smile, "that we live until we die."

The doctrine of the god of the Caspakians did not soothe her soul, but it was quite sensible. She squeezed Tro-va's hand one final time, then raised her spear before her. At Tro-va's side, Marina would live until she died.

The horrifying shouts of the Band-lus filled the air as they crept increasingly closer to Marina and Tro-va. His dark eyes met hers, then he looked down at the animal skin pouch at his side. From it, he pulled a tangle of pearly tiger teeth strung together with a thin strip of leather. This he placed over her head to rest upon her bosom. In secret, Tro-va had fashioned a necklace that was the symbolic ornamentation of the Cos-ju-los.

Marina's eyes welled with tears, not for fear of dying or due to the cumulation of the horrors she had endured over the past several days. No. Hers were tears of joy, and her heart sang.

Tro-va slid his knife from his loincloth and held it at the ready.

The Cos-ju-lo warrior astride the three-horned brute raised her spear directly over her head, but she did not speak. Marina assumed that due to the abundance of feathers in her hair, she must have been the leader of the warrior women. The face of the wild-maned tribeswoman showed not a trace of emotion, and then she spoke. It was a command of some kind. Her warriors, assembled before her, all raised their bows in unison, plucked arrows from the quivers on their backs, and notched them with dizzying speed.

Again, the Cos-ju-lo leader shouted. As one, the female warriors unleashed a wave of arrows in Marina's direction. She instinctively closed her eyes, anticipating the dreadful sting of death. To her amazement, the wooden shafts whizzed past her and her Galu companion and embedded themselves in the chests of the foremost line of Band-lus.

The screams of the wounded and dying intermingled with the war cries of the Band-lus, and the blood-chilling cacophony resounded throughout the swamp. The furious savages charged forward, and Marina and Tro-va steeled themselves for the end.

Several Band-lus were now only twenty paces from Marina and Tro-va, and another volley of arrows rained down upon the attackers. Warriors behind the wounded sloshed forward and roughly pushed the bleeding ape-men aside, intent on reaching the two nearest enemies and rending them to pieces.

The leader of the Cos-ju-los raised the conch to her lips and blew into the shell. The sound reverberated through the air like a call from the heavens. Upon hearing the sound, the two great beasts tensed and charged toward the precipice of the embankment, followed by the five warrior women on the ground. The muscular legs of the Cos-ju-los pumped furiously as they ran. All five women slung their bows over their shoulders, drew knives and hatchets, and leaped from the edge of the elevated patch of land. Their momentum carried them over the heads of Marina and Tro-va, and they splashed gracefully into the swamp, weapons at the ready.

Not to be outdone, the duo of horned titans also charged off the short precipice into the swamp. Unlike their human counterparts, they did not so much as leap as they slid, their great weight collapsing the ledge upon which they had trodden. Into the marsh they splashed, their mighty legs churning up the mud as they bore down on the Band-lus. Marina and Tro-va leaped headfirst away from the leviathans as they barreled past in a shower of mud and fetid swamp water, the beasts driven on by their riders.

Within the swampy arena ensued a battle that Marina could never have imagined even in her wildest nightmares. All about her rang the bellows of the Band-lus as their superior numbers were slowly whittled down by the furious attack of the Cos-ju-los. The warrior women threw themselves upon their foes fearlessly and enwrapped them with their arms and legs as they stabbed, slashed, and bit them in a display of frightening savagery.

The giant beasts stomped through the mud in circles, their bellows intensifying the din of battle. Upon their backs, their riders methodically placed arrows through the hearts of any

Band-lus who managed to get remotely close to Marina. As she traded blows with a muck-covered tribesman, Marina could not help but notice that their saviors kept a particularly close eye on her; it was as if they had joined the battle expressly to defend her.

Tro-va, his arm around the neck of one Band-lu, kicked his legs into the air, swung himself around to the ape-man's back, and kicked in the teeth of another attacker who had rushed forward in an attempt to drive his spear through Marina. His arm still around the neck of the warrior, Tro-va landed on his feet in the water and lifted the man into the air, flinging him backward over his head and shoulders. A sickening crack indicated that the savage Band-lu's neck had been broken, and he sank into the mud.

Behind Marina, a particularly large savage succeeded in running his dagger across the back of one of the female fighters. As she fell forward in pain, he rushed toward Marina, bloody knife in hand. Just then, the three-horned monster reared back on its hind legs and crashed down upon the Band-lu warrior, grinding him into the muddy floor of the swamp. The maroon giant abruptly turned and its tail struck Tro-va, knocking him away from Marina. He had not been harmed, but the wind had been knocked out of the brave warrior's lungs by the strike and he gasped for air, momentarily stunned.

Tro-va's temporary disabling had given a nearby Band-lu warrior an opening. He charged at Marina and was nearly upon her before she knew it. She could do nothing but wait for the cold edge of the stone axe to end her life.

19
THE PENDULUM

THE SLAVERING MONSTER—for that is how Marina viewed the Band-lu—screamed with rage and charged through the waist-deep swamp water toward her. His axe was held high, ready to cleave her skull. She was helpless.

Marina flinched as two loud cracks split the air.

The savage attacker was knocked backward off his feet as blood and flesh erupted from twin holes in his chest. With a loud splash, the hairy back of the Band-lu slapped against the water. His unseeing eyes were wide as water filled his gaping mouth, and he sank below the surface in a swirl of blood and algae.

"Marina!" Fausto screamed in joy.

The two loud explosions had stopped all present in their tracks, and all the combatants spun toward the source of the shout. Captain Fausto Caproni and Sergeant Ortega stood atop the promontory, with the islanders surrounding Marina in their musket sights. Residual smoke from their spent gunpowder charges wafted from the priming pans of their weapons and dissipated in the cloying atmosphere of the swamp.

"Run, Marina!" her brother shouted, as Ortega reloaded his rifle. "We'll hold them off!"

Confusion was written on Fausto's face when Marina shouted back, "No! These are friends!"

The surviving Band-lu had fled, leaving only Marina, Tro-va, and the band of warrior women and their frightening steeds on the submerged battleground. The Cos-ju-los, perpetually ready for battle, fought against the thick mud that pulled at their feet. They were heading for the newest threats, Fausto and Ortega, and nothing would stop them.

"Don't shoot," Fausto told the Spaniard by his side. "I have no idea what's playing out before us, but I trust my sister's instincts.

"No!" Marina again shouted in the tongue of the Cos-ju-lo warriors who intended to confront the two strange enemies. The women's faces were stone, resolute devotion to duty etched into them. They would not yield. They would not surrender. They were unstoppable.

"What? . . . what did she just say? What language was that?" Fausto asked Ortega. The soldier shook his head and shrugged.

Marina turned her head to her brother. "I'm all right, Fausto! Don't hurt them! They're protecting me!" She spun to Tro-va and explained her relation to the man on the promontory, but the islander seemed confused. In the heat of the moment, the words spilled forth from Marina's mouth were in her native language, none of which the Galu man grasped.

The leader of the Cos-ju-los had watched the entire interaction with calculated detachment. She analyzed Marina from afar and spoke to the woman warrior astride the spike-collared beast. Together, they discussed the young woman before them, who stood in the muck, her strange clothing shredded and soiled, and a spear in her hands. At length, the leader pointed to the necklace around Marina's neck, and the women nodded in agreement. It was decided.

The Cos-ju-lo again raised the conch to her lips, and with three short melodic bursts, the large sea shell delivered her decree. Instantly, the ground warriors stopped advancing toward the Europeans and lowered their weapons.

Marina waded to the side of the tri-horned beast and thanked the tribeswoman mounted on its back. The woman lightly tapped against the side of her reptilian steed and the great maroon beast lowered itself into the mud. The tribal leader extended the blunt end of her spear to Marina, indicating that she should climb onto the back of the enormous beast with her, and the young Sicilian complied. Marina was relatively certain she could trust the warriors who had saved her and Tro-va, but she would still exercise caution.

She smiled and innocently waved to Fausto, as a child riding a carnival carousel might wave to her parent as she was carried past them. She knew not what else to do, for she had no idea what she was doing or why. But there she sat, upon the back of a massive animal unlike anything else that walked the Earth, behind a primitive warrior woman wearing only scraps of snake hide to conceal her nakedness.

Marina ran her hand over the leathery skin of the mount. It was cool to the touch, and she could feel the animal's chest expand below her as it inhaled great gulps of air. What an extraordinary beast it was, and here she was, mounted upon its back, as if she were born to ride such a fantastic creature!

The leader turned and spoke to Marina in a pleasant, soothing manner, but the meaning of her words was lost to the Sicilian. Marina's conversations with Tro-va were built upon her understanding of some basic Caspakian nouns and verbs, but her grasp of his language was rudimentary at best. The warrior chief must have assumed that Marina was a Galu, as her words flowed at a rate much too rapid for Marina to comprehend.

The Cos-ju-lo chief again blew through the conch and Marina anxiously awaited the explanation of the signal's meaning. The two large beasts and the five warrior women on the ground turned their backs to Tro-va and the strange men on the promontory and began slowly trudging through the dark water toward the jungle beyond.

Tro-va watched sadly as the group plodded away from him. The women did not even acknowledge his presence, as if he were beneath their notice. But worse, the Cos-ju-los were departing and taking Marina with them.

"Marina! Who are those women?" Fausto called out with great concern.

Marina shouted back, "They are the Cos-ju-los. I think . . . I think they're friends."

"Well, where are you going?" he yelled across the brackish water.

"I have no idea!" she shot back.

Adrenaline still surged through her, an aftereffect of the life-and-death struggle she had just endured. Marina was relieved that the fighting was over, and to establish a peaceful rapport with the Cos-ju-los, she had accepted the offer to mount the huge creature. But now, as the animal moved toward the jungle, Marina questioned the wisdom of her impulsive act. Were the outcast tribe of women kidnapping her? She had no way of knowing and began to regret climbing onto the back of the tri-horned creature.

Sergeant Ortega whispered out of the side of his mouth to Fausto. "What do you suggest, Captain?"

A dozen scenarios raced through the head of Fausto Caproni, but all led to the same conclusion. "Marina is alive. That's the most important thing," he said, relief in his voice. "I know my sister. No one ever gets the better of her, and it seems she has a more secure grasp of local customs than we do," he admitted. "I've never known anyone as hardheaded as Marina, but she's no fool. If she needed help, she would say so."

"Then . . . what?" Ortega said nervously.

"We wait and see," Fausto replied.

In the swamp below him, Tro-va stood sorrowfully, his arms hanging limp at his sides. An air of utter dejection shrouded the handsome young warrior as he watched Marina's departure, and Fausto's eyes narrowed as he speculated on what might have prompted the primitive man's sadness.

As the tri-horned beast swayed on through the marsh and neared the curtain of twisted vines at the periphery of the water, Marina nervously looked over her shoulder. Tro-va's face said all she needed to know.

She threw her legs to one side of the belly of the titanic steed and slid down its leather hide to the muddy water below. It was quite possible she would be immediately apprehended by the tribeswomen, but she had to take the risk and try to escape while she had an opportunity. Another chance might not come for her.

The Cos-ju-los turned and watched Marina splash into the mire. The leader looked upon Tro-va, then again to Marina, and with a smile and a laugh, she turned and did not look back again. The two giant creatures and their Cos-ju-lo mistresses disappeared into the tangle of the jungle.

Marina waded through the swamp past the bodies of the dead and rejoined Tro-va. She took his strong hand in hers and was unsure what to say, as she was confused about the underlying motivation for what had transpired.

"Tro-va . . . What did they want?" she asked in his language, or at least in the closest approximation of that language.

The tribesman smiled. "I told you, Ma-ree-na. You are a Cos-ju-lo," he said proudly, tapping the necklace draped upon her breast. Marina considered the statement a moment, and then all became clear.

The Cos-ju-los, the second most-feared tribe on Caspak after the Wieroos, recognized Marina as one of their own and offered her admission into their mysterious sisterhood. The enormity of the honor brought tears to her eyes.

A lifetime of memories rushed through her mind, along with innumerable instances when her desires were dismissed. Since the days of her childhood, regardless of the frivolous nature of her requests, so often she was told, "No." "Can I take fencing lessons like Fausto?" *"No."* "Can I be a sailor like Fausto?" *"No."* "Can I go to the tavern with Fausto?" *"No."* And why? Because she was a girl; because she was a young woman. Her parents meant well, as do all parents, and they dutifully adhered to raising their daughter by the code of conduct dictated by societal norms, regardless of how it impacted the growing heart of their daughter. "Some things are not for girls," she was told.

Marina had watched her friends mature and drift into prearranged nuptials, bearing children to men they barely knew. Even Maria Christina, now Queen Regent of the Spanish Empire, let herself be led by what was dictated by her father and the world. For as long as she could remember, a fire burned within Marina's heart, a desire to break free from the cruel and oppressive weight imposed upon her simply because of her femininity.

Here, far from the hand of civilized men; here in a land that time forgot; here she had found, at last, that she was not alone. The darkness of self-doubt cleared. She knew she had just as much right to choose her destiny as did Fausto. Here, on Caspak, she was accepted for who she was, not for how well she kept her simple and justifiably human desires to herself.

"Get up here!" Fausto yelled excitedly to Marina, extending a hand to help her climb the crumbled section of the promontory. He hugged her as if he would never let go.

Marina giggled and tapped Fausto on the top of his head, then scowled in mock disapproval. "You lost your expensive new hat, didn't you?" she teased.

Fausto laughed heartily at the jest and they both hugged again, so relieved were they to see one another still alive.

"Signora," Ortega said warily, as Tro-va scaled the embankment as effortlessly as a monkey climbs a tree. The soldier and Fausto tensed, prepared for anything as the mud-covered Galu stood upright before them at the side of Marina.

"It's all right," she assured them. "This is Tro-va. He is my . . . friend."

Tro-va stiffened, as did Fausto, for they both recognized one another from their unfortunate encounter days ago that had flung the young warrior from the cliff and into the river. Tro-va leaned forward in preparation to leap at Fausto, but Marina held him back.

"Fausto! Tro-va told me he had fought a strange man," she said. "That was you, wasn't it?"

"He attacked me! I had no choice," Fausto replied in his defense. "Tell him . . . tell him I'm sorry!"

Marina calmed Tro-va and explained Fausto's relation to her by using the tribesman's earlier description of cos-ata-los/cos-ata-lus, or Caspakians who are not born from eggs. She drew stick figures in the dirt to assist in her explanation, and satisfied with what he had heard, Tro-va smiled and patted Fausto on the shoulder.

The young captain seemed pleased that there would be no further fisticuffs or bloodshed. He also appeared to be most impressed with Marina, as she engaged in effortless conversation with the primitive warrior, speaking in his native language as best she could. She also caught her brother watching her with a sly look in his eyes as she and Tro-va exchanged bashful smiles during the course of their banter.

At last, Fausto ran his hand through his black curls. "I think we both have stories to tell," he said with a chuckle.

The members of the little party talked for what seemed almost an hour, Marina and Fausto telling of their adventures while they ate fruit gathered by Tro-va and refreshed themselves with sparkling water from a nearby stream. Sergeant Ortega joined the conversation to reveal his own story, along with the abhorrent plan of Colonel Valdez and Ortega's refusal to follow that plan to its conclusion.

"I know you're going to say, 'I told you so,'" Fausto chided Marina, "but yes, you told me so."

Marina did not want Fausto to shoulder too much of the blame. "No one could have known, Fausto," she assured him.

"Perhaps not," he replied, "but the signs were all there. I accept that. What has come to pass cannot be changed, but this is no longer some stupid squabble over land. It's much more than that. Not a single one of us has a right to be here, and I'll be damned if I will allow Caprona—no, *Caspak*—to be colonized."

Marina was taken aback by the decisive nature of Fausto's pronouncement. What they had endured over the last few days, and the personal losses they had both suffered, had forged each of them into someone they had not been before, but dearly needed to be. During their trials, in a manner unique to each of them, Fausto and Marina Caproni had matured in ways they could not have anticipated.

As a group, it was decided that they would seek out the wreck of the *Pegaso II*, but only Ortega would return to the ship. Fausto, Marina, and Tro-va would stay hidden and watch for Ortega's signal. The Spanish soldier planned to covertly warn Leonardo Ricci, Puccini, and Alamanni of Colonel Valdez's intentions. If presented with the opportunity, they would disarm the Colonel, along with Alonso and Montes, the two soldiers still upon the ship. Sergeant Ortega was unsure if his two fellow soldiers were truly committed to the plot of Valdez, but he could not risk warning them of his intention to mutiny.

When all were ready, the explorers plunged into the jungle, led by Ortega and Tro-va, who each knew the path to the "Sea of Grass." The tribesman was quite enamored of the halberd he carried, given to him by Fausto. It was a weapon unlike any he had ever seen, Tro-va told Marina. He admired its polished sheen that reflected the sun's rays, but he seemed even more impressed by its incredibly sharp cutting edge. The Caspakian warrior had mastered the construction of bone knives, axes, and spear tips, but nothing he had ever made could cleave through jungle vines like the halberd.

They walked for the remainder of the day, clearing the jungle before them, and by nightfall had reached the midpoint of the forest that stretched along one edge of the lowlands and the crash site of the sky cutter. Tro-va's assistance during their travel was invaluable. He led the travelers around natural pitfalls that Caspak was all too ready to subject them to and helped them avoid dangerous plants and animals alike.

After careful consideration by Tro-va, a large abandoned animal warren dug into a precipitous forest hillside was selected for an overnight campsite. Within, they gathered around a fire ignited by the flint from Ortega's kit, which Tro-va found quite fascinating. In the dimly lit hovel, they dined on roasted rabbit, and the brother and sister continued to catch up with one another on their experiences in the strange, primitive world. The party members took turns guarding the entrance as the others slept, and as the sun's morning rays began to pry through the thickly wooded region, they embarked on their final day of voyage—at least, they hoped that would be the case.

After walking for less than half an hour, Tro-va raised a hand and looked about them, listening intently.

"What is it?" Marina asked.

He did not answer and kept listening.

Then they all heard the sound. It was a cough. Their initial reactions were to look at one another, but none had made the noise. Tro-va spun, as there was movement behind them.

Standing between two great tree boles on a slight rise was Sergeant Lago, his musket barrel trained on the group. He coughed and cleared his throat. "None of you move. Drop your weapons or I take off the girl's head," he croaked harshly.

Marina knew Tro-va's first instinct would be to defend her, but she whispered, "No," to him. The tribesman could not possibly understand the deadly nature of the stick pointed in their direction, so she did her best to calm him. His eyes were ablaze with bloodlust, but he complied with her request.

"Sergeant Lago," Fausto said with an air of authority. "I'm so glad we've found you. We feared that you had . . ."

"Shut your mouth, little boy," Lago hissed.

Fausto continued to press ahead as if he were ignorant of the subversive plot of the Spaniards. "Lower your weapon,

Sergeant. You seem confused. You are safe with us," he suggested gently.

Lago was standing twenty feet from the party, but even at that distance, all could see that he was sweating profusely, and his neck, face, and hands were covered with a rash of red blotches. He was bent forward as if weary with fatigue and an occasional sway rocked him back and forth like a seedling in a shifting breeze. It was readily apparent that the Spaniard was quite ill.

"Good work, Lago," Ortega beamed. The Spaniard strode away from the others to join Sergeant Lago on the rise.

Fausto's knuckles were white, wrapped around the musket held at his waist. "You lying bastard," he hurled with venom at Ortega. The soldier only smiled.

"They had me outnumbered," Ortega explained to his countryman. "I figured that if I led them back to the ship, we could deal with them all in one nice, tidy execution."

"Smart," Lago wheezed, "but no longer necessary. There are two of us now. We'll fulfill our duty right here."

Sergeant Ortega laughed and raised his musket. "And a man of honor always fulfills his duty, isn't that right, Captain Caproni?"

Fausto simmered with rage, but there was nothing he could do. He, Marina, and Tro-va were about to die, ushered into the great beyond amid a chorus of chirping jungle birds.

20
THE MEADOW

AFTER EVERYTHING WE'VE BEEN THROUGH, *this is how it's going to end?*

The thought reverberated through Marina's mind as she stared mutely at the musket barrels pointed at them. The Spaniards intended to kill her and Fausto, but knowing the disposition of Sergeant Lago, he would surely murder Tro-va as well, just for good measure.

Sergeant Ortega held his musket aloft by the side of Lago, his countryman, his fellow soldier-at-arms. How could she have been so wrong about the Spaniard? Marina cursed herself for blindly trusting Ortega's sincerity, even if it was counter to his duty to obey the orders of his commanding officer, Colonel Valdez.

It was now a question of time. The first pair of shots would instantly kill two of them. Considering the time it took to reload a musket rifle, the surviving member of the trio might escape before either Lago or Ortega could fire again; still, she knew she would be the first to fall to a musket ball.

Lago hated her . . . but why? She knew the answer. She had committed the unforgivable act of standing her ground in the *Redenzione's* hold when the vile soldier sought to kill her cat, Sovrano. Simply put, she had told him, "No." That was all it took for him to wish her dead.

"I'm sorry, Marina," Fausto said weakly, keeping his eyes on the rifle.

He had nothing to apologize for, Marina thought. Here, on

the lost island continent of Caspak, she reached the epiphany that had daunted her for her entire life. With the precious last few seconds of her existence ticking away, she would at least die knowing that she was right all along, that every woman should be free to pursue her destiny, to follow her heart wherever it may lead. If that meant forging a path of independence counter to the dictates of European society, then so be it. Marina Caproni was a woman of the modern world and the Cos-ju-los were a primitive tribe that resided in a land of monsters, but they were kindred spirits. They were all unstoppable women. She cherished that inner peace and would carry it to the meeting with her maker, whether that divinity was God or Luata.

Fausto glared at Sergeant Ortega, the soldier's musket held parallel to Lago's. Ortega met Fausto's gaze . . . and winked.

Nearly faster than the eye could follow, Ortega swung his musket barrel to his right, lifting the end of Lago's rifle just as his shot rang out. Within the haze of sulfurous smoke, Ortega dropped his musket, spun Lago to face him, and thrust the blade of his dagger up through the lower jaw of the nefarious soldier. With utter contempt, he pushed the corpse away from him and it fell to the ground with a sickening thud.

The others stood in shock at what they had just witnessed, their hearts beating wildly in their chests. Ortega stood upon the hillock between the two giant boles, wiped his knife on his pants leg before returning it to its sheath, and took his rifle in both hands.

"Now. Let's find the sky cutter and take care of Colonel Valdez, shall we?" he cheerfully called out.

Before he could descend from the leaf-covered rise to join his new allies, Sergeant Ortega was lifted into the air. He screamed out in abject terror. Around his midsection, pearl-white teeth penetrated his uniform and punctured the flesh of his torso. Ortega was being crushed in the jaws of a massive beast that had crept upon him and had been hidden from the view of the others by the hillock upon which the Spaniard stood.

"It is a rota!" Tro-va shouted in alarm as he instinctively reached for Marina. "Do not move!" he frantically warned.

For the past few seconds, however, Fausto had been in motion that he could barely recollect. Upon seeing Ortega's hideous plight, his instincts took hold. He retrieved a cartridge from the supply purse of Sergeant Garza, tore off the end with his teeth, poured a small amount of gunpowder into the rifle's priming pan, and was now using the ramrod to jam the cartridge to the bottom of the musket barrel. A trained soldier of the Kingdom of the Two Sicilies would have been impressed by the fluidity of Fausto's actions. Within seconds, he had the barrel trained on the horror that rose before them.

The enormous brute was another of the two-legged variety of giants. This variation of predator was not nearly as large as others of its type but was no less deadly. Stooped forward, the rota was just over the height of a man, but as it lifted the helpless Ortega from the ground in its powerful jaws, it rose nearly twenty feet in the air. The thing bore a short bony horn on its nose, with a triangular horn situated over each of its serpent-like eyes. Its leathery tan hide was adorned with stripes that were the shade of deep red blood.

Gravely injured by the teeth that held him fast between the attacker's jaws, Ortega fought valiantly, pounding at the rota with his fists. Marina choked in revulsion as blood poured down Ortega's chin from his mouth, his teeth now stained a hideous red.

Fausto's gunshot rang out, the musket ball embedding in the soft chest tissue of the beast, but he might as well have saved his ammunition. The terrible lizard did not flinch and continued to hurl Ortega through the air in its jaws. As if annoyed by the struggles of its prey, the rota swung its head rapidly from side to side, shaking Ortega like he was weightless and slinging his blood against the surrounding trees.

In seconds, it was over. Sergeant Ortega moved no more

and hung limply from the bloody jaws of his killer. The rota dropped the mangled corpse to the ground, nudged it several times to ensure its prey was dead, then clamped its jaws around the soldier's torso and carried the body into the jungle.

Marina trembled after witnessing the sickeningly violent attack and looked to Fausto for his reaction. He, too, was stunned by the savagery they had just beheld.

She turned to Tro-va, who did not display the same emotions as she and Fausto. The revolting scene that had just played out before them was the way of Caspak, to which the tribesman was well enured. His eyes were not upon the departing beast but rather on the strange weapon that Fausto still held in firing position. Tro-va reached out a hand in tentative amazement. He touched the barrel of the musket, then quickly withdrew his hand.

"It might make a lot of noise, but don't be too impressed," Fausto said, sadly. "It didn't do a damn thing to that monster."

Tro-va motioned for Marina and Fausto to be silent and began to lead them into the forest, but the young captain resisted. "Wait," he said. "I have to do something first."

"What?" Marina asked.

Fausto looked to the hillock, between the two huge trees upon it and the body of Sergeant Lago at its summit. "I need to bury Lago and bury him deep," Fausto proposed.

"Why?" Marina asked. "Let the animals pick him to pieces."

Fausto explained why that would be the worst of scenarios. "You saw his face, his hands. He was sick. I'm fairly certain it's scarlet fever, maybe even something worse. I don't know if there are diseases like that on Caspak, but if there aren't . . . Imagine what something like that would do to the people here."

Marina's eyes fell upon the handsome warrior by her side before turning back to Fausto with a glint of grim determination. "You're right," she said. "I'll help you."

Tro-va kept vigilant watch over the surrounding area as Marina and Fausto went about their task. They dug into the loamy earth with knives and cut through the impossible tangle of underground roots. They scooped large handfuls of dirt and rocks from the pit, which they deposited in a large pile beside the grave. The endeavor was a curiosity to Tro-va, who glanced at the siblings occasionally with a look of confusion. Marina assumed that Caspakians did not bury their dead. Even if the practice of interring corpses was not a part of the societal or religious practices of the various tribes, the number of enormous predators that roamed the land would never allow for solemn and protracted funerals, anyhow. If one died on Caspak, a scavenger would be along soon enough to pick the bones clean.

At last, the grave was fully excavated. Exercising great caution, Fausto and Marina used their feet to push the body into the hole; to protect themselves, they would not touch the corpse with their hands, and all of the dead soldier's armaments and belongings would be buried with him. Neither of them could risk contracting whatever disease Lago had carried. The pit was filled and they resumed their trek through the forest, leaving behind the unmarked grave of the despicable military man.

The sun was now high overhead, its unrelenting rays nudging upward the temperature of Caspak's humid air. Marina, Fausto, and Tro-va stepped forth from the jungle. Before them was a half-mile-wide expanse of low-lying, rolling hills covered with deep grass and sprinkled with vast patches of white, yellow, and purple flowers. Rocky walls on both sides of the party formed a canyon of sorts, the tops lined with forests of deep green. Roughly a mile away at the foot of the plain of descending hillocks, the grass changed in hue to a lighter green.

Tro-va pointed to the lighter-colored ground cover. "The Sea of Grass," he explained to Marina.

After several days lost in the savage wilds of Caspak, the Capronis were nearly returned to the wreck of the *Pegaso II*. What they would find upon their arrival was a mystery, and the minds of Fausto and Marina were filled with uncertainty. The encampment was manned by three heavily armed Spaniards and three Sicilians, one of whom was the elderly astronomer. Leonardo Ricci was not physically equipped to partake in a fight, should it come to that. They would need a plan, but there was still a long way to walk.

"Well, let's get started," Fausto said, trying to sound positive in the face of the inevitable confrontation.

Tro-va placed a hand on Fausto's arm to stop him, then explained to Marina the aspects of the land that they must heed. Fausto watched as Tro-va motioned to the grass and cliffs that hedged the meadow while he spoke to Marina in the language of Caspak. The young Galu man then pointed to the dark gray boulders that had fallen from the heights and now rested in the valley of grass and flowers. Marina absorbed all her companion had to say, and responded in his language, along with the hand motions and pantomime that she and Tro-va had developed as a unique form of communication shared exclusively between the two.

His sister impressed Fausto immensely. Marina arched an eyebrow when she saw him smiling.

"What?" she asked her brother.

"Look at you," Fausto replied. "It's like you're a different person. In a good way. Not that you were a bad person before, not at all. What I mean to say is . . . I don't know what I mean to say."

"Well, that's obvious," she laughed. "But why don't you try?"

Fausto thought for a moment. "You and I always had a certain balance between us. We both know that. You're the smart one, I'm the impulsive one. You've always been—how shall I say it?—very driven. Focused. Even, to be honest, short-tempered."

"Mm-hmm," Marina replied, unsure where his words were leading.

Fausto continued hastily, to avert any misinterpretation of

his intent. "Look, I know how difficult things are for you, and I'm sorry you have to deal with everyone expecting you to be what you're not. We're a lot alike in that respect. Look at what we've been through here. Look at what you've accomplished with Tro-va. Somehow, you've done what no one else could. You've made a friend here, and more than just one. That's special. I guess what I'm trying to say is I'm proud of you," he said with a smile, "and to hell with what the rest of Palermo expects of you."

Marina hugged her brother. "All of that you just said? The same goes for me about you. I'm proud of you, little brother."

The three travelers strode forth and began their gradual descent down the rolling hills of the canyon.

Traveling by foot through the meadow was much less arduous than fighting through jungle undergrowth or slogging through swamps. The grass grew knee deep, the flowers that adorned its shoots attracting pollinators of all shapes and sizes, including ordinary honey bees identical to the breed found among the lemon blossoms of Palermo. The valley—indeed, all of Caspak—was of such primal, pristine beauty that it would leave an indelible impression upon the memories of Fausto and Marina. Here, no boat whistles screeched above the serene sounds of nature; no shouts of dockhands rang out as they labored to fill the coffers of industrialist traders; no coal furnaces belching smoke and draping the verdant landscape in a shroud of soot. Here, on Caspak, nature reigned supreme, unspoiled by the greed, corruption, and aspiration of military conquest subscribed to by modern men. How quickly that all could change, Fausto thought, if the outside world were to intrude upon the sanctity of the lost continent.

The trio descended into a rocky ravine within the canyon, carved out by the passage of a small stream. There, they drank, and Marina removed the bandage from her arm to inspect the wounds she had received while fleeing through the jungle days before. She washed the cuts, which were healing nicely. The drying of the abrasions would benefit from exposure to fresh air, so she balled the unnecessary bandage and motioned to toss the material into the tall grass. She caught herself and tucked the soiled and bloody blouse sleeve under her belt rather than discarding it. The scrap of material, manufactured in a Sicilian textile mill, would be an affront to the reverence of the natural landscape.

"Look at that!" Fausto said, pointing downstream. A small herd of diminutive, striped horses was crossing the shallow river atop rocks that had long ago dislodged from the canyon walls and rolled into the water.

"Oh, they're so cute," Marina observed. "They're eccas."

"Eccas," Fausto repeated, then laughed. "I don't even know what they are, and you're on a first-name basis with them. I wonder if you're more at home here than in Palermo."

Fausto's comment was uttered in jest but his notion gave the siblings pause. Marina glanced at Tro-va, then back to her brother. "I wonder that, too," she said with a smile.

When the small herd completed its crossing and disappeared into the tall grass, the travelers continued their journey to the Sea of Grass, which lay just beyond a collection of boulders at the lowermost point of the canyon. The dark gray chunks of stone were much larger than they looked from a distance; some were larger than a house, Marina reckoned.

Before moving among the giant stones, Tro-va gave instructions to Marina, which she relayed to Fausto. He warned that animals could often be found sleeping in the shadows cast by the enormous rocks, and so they would need to proceed with caution.

After passing between the first several boulders, Tro-va's warning was borne out.

The resting places of the giant stones were such that the wayfarers could easily walk between them; some were nearly thirty feet distant from the next. Because of this, they felt reasonably comfortable that they could outrun or outmaneuver the giant oxen that bellowed in surprise when they rounded one of the boulders.

Like everything on Caspak, the animals were at least double the size of their Mediterranean counterparts. The fur of the powerfully muscled mammals was shaggy and a shade of deep crimson, and rising upward from the end of their snouts grew a bony protuberance that looked to Marina like a slingshot. Upon seeing the humans, the largest of the three immediately took a defensive stance, kicking great clumps of grass into the air with its hind legs.

Tro-va took charge of the situation and led Fausto and Marina to the nearest boulder, behind which they hid. Once out of sight of the oxen, the bellowing ceased. The three travelers proceeded to dart from boulder to boulder, keeping out of sight, until they were well past the angry animals. Not everything on Caspak wanted to eat you, Marina considered, but some of its denizens would kill you simply because you disturbed them. Here there were very few second chances.

Three hundred feet away, the Sea of Grass beckoned. Only a few more boulders lay between the voyagers and the lowest portion of the canyon. Before them stretched a vast plain of green, the same plain onto which the *Pegaso II* had made its disastrous descent.

Above the tops of the stalks, a most shocking sight was now revealed.

"Fausto!" Marina shouted. "The balloon!"

Swaying lazily in the breeze a half mile from where they stood bobbed the undamaged balloon of the *Pegaso II*, now fully inflated.

"Oh, no," Fausto moaned. "This is very, very bad."

"What do you mean? We've found the ship!" Marina replied.

"No, it's not good," Fausto explained. "The balloon shouldn't be inflated. If I'm calculating correctly, we would have only enough iron filings and acid for one more successful, full infla-tion. Sergeant Ortega said the undamaged balloon had deflated, which means that if they've inflated it again to full capacity, they intend to take flight. They must have followed Leonardo's plan of constructing a gondola to carry them back to the ship."

Marina felt her heart pounding in her chest. "They're abandoning us . . ."

Two loud cracks rang out from across the sea of green and reached the ears of the travelers.

"Gunshots!" Fausto exclaimed. "What's happening?"

Louder than the musket fire that had echoed from the canyon walls around them came a terrifying roar that froze the blood in their veins. It was one of Caspak's giants, the creature Tro-va called a goza, and was the same breed of two-legged beast that had terrorized the exploratory party days ago as they hid behind the downed tree.

It was also the same breed of monster that had killed Tro-va's beloved Roo-ko.

The taloned feet of the massive titan carried it from behind the walls that framed the entrance to the canyon, and it came to a stop at the center of the egress to the vast Sea of Grass. Their escape was now blocked by one of the fiercest creatures to roam the face of Caspak.

21
BATTLE TO THE DEATH

THE PRIMAL LEVIATHAN BENT FORWARD on the fulcrum where its massive leg bones met the sockets of its pelvis as it shrieked a warning at the tiny humans who stood vulnerable before it. Saliva dripped from its gaping jaws, its full arsenal of deadly fangs on display. Unlike the hides of the hunting pack of gozas that had previously tormented them, the skin of this creature was a dark blue, fading to a cream color on the underside of its neck, belly, and tail. An irregular pattern of white blotches ran the length of its back, from the tip of its counter-balancing tail to the fierce maw of glistening teeth.

Marina, Tro-va, and Fausto had nowhere to hide within the canyon. Enormous boulders that had fallen from the sides of the cliffs surrounded them. Other stones had also rolled and come to rest at the mouth of the wide gully in some distant past, but none of the rocks offered an opening for concealment either within or beneath them. All they could do was run, but to where? If they fled back up the ravine, they would encounter the enormous oxen that had been none too accepting of their presence. In terms of flight, they were out of options.

"Do not move!" Tro-va warned. Marina had learned that motion incensed the larger of Caspak's carnivores to attack their prey. However, if one stood stationary, the animals could become distracted by other disturbances around them and leave their initial target unmolested.

Marina sighed heavily, and then looked from Tro-va to Fausto. The two men returned her gaze. An incredible heaviness hung in the air that could not be denied or ignored, a palpable aura exuding from the young Sicilian woman. Before them stood an enormous predatory beast, its growls rattling deeply in its throat, and though the immediate threat should have spurred them to action, instead, they paused to acknowledge whatever weighed so heavily upon Marina.

"What is it?" Fausto whispered. A bead of sweat rolled down his cheek, but he did not wipe away the tickling droplet. The slightest movement might cause the giant to lunge upon them.

Marina's voice was filled with emotion, but more so, exhaustion. "I'm so tired, Fausto," she said. "It never ends here. Never." The days of constant flight, the lack of sleep, and the scarcity of any sustenance besides foraged food had finally caught up to her. The past week had been one life-or-death encounter after another, and all at once, any lingering stores of vitality drained from Marina's spirit. The woman who had fought so hard her entire life now felt beaten by the oppressive forces of Caspak.

Marina's sudden reversal of confidence surprised even her. Never had she allowed Fausto to see her in such a state. She had been his rock, his eternal guide, and she winced knowing that her tenacity was crumbling before her brother's eyes.

A sudden disturbance rose from the stalks behind the huge reptilian sentinel. A small group of eccas scurried about, engaged in some manner of tiny horse squabble, oblivious to the predator that loomed only a few yards from them. The monstrous lizard turned its head to watch the tiny creatures as they whinnied, bucked, and darted back into the field. Tro-va was right; the giant could become easily distracted.

Quietly, Fausto tried to shore up his sister's spirits. "Marina, you can do this," he said, with calming assurance. "I've followed your lead all my life. I look up to you as the person I want to be. You always know what's best. You're always right. And you never give up."

Marina's gaze was fixed on the great blue beast that stood motionless as if confused by the stillness of its intended quarry. "We're never going to get out of here alive, Fausto," she whispered. Marina was glad that Tro-va could not understand her words in that most fragile of moments.

"No," her brother said firmly. "I will not let you do this, Marina. You've always told me what to do, what to say, how to act. Now it's my turn." He looked at her sternly. "If Tro-va and I are going to get out of this alive, we're going to need you. We can't do it without you. And don't forget, four cats are waiting for you on the *Redenzione*. What does Giovanni Pellegrino know about taking care of cats, anyhow?"

Fausto had struck upon just the right words, and Marina felt a wave of calm wash over her. Fausto was right. Regardless of her mental and physical exhaustion, regardless of how hungry and terrified she was, giving up now would be akin to cowardice. Was she not a Cos-ju-lo, an unstoppable woman? Others believed that she was and Marina knew it to be true in her heart.

Marina smiled and nodded at her brother. "This is the one and only time you'll ever speak to me that way, do you hear?"

"I'm not crazy," he said, laughing. "From here on out, we never say never, agreed?"

A loud, rough exhale akin to a hiss filled the air. Although the three had been quite still, the adventurers remained tempting targets for the azure-skinned beast that swayed anxiously on its great hind legs. Marina wished for any of Caspak's creatures to dart or fly near; anything to again distract the goza would suffice, but nothing broke the beast's gaze.

"Should we use the muskets?" Marina whispered nervously.

"No," Fausto replied, an odd hint of cold acceptance in his voice. "They take too long to load and musket balls are worthless against that skin."

"Then what?" Marina asked, her eyes wide.

Fausto stepped toward the beast that towered at least fifteen feet above them. He reached to his hip and withdrew his sword, slashed a complex and untraceable pattern in the air before him, and then settled into a traditional fencer's stance. "We give this monster a taste of Sicilian steel," he said.

Marina stepped forward to stand beside her brother and drew the sword once owned by Garza, given to her by Fausto. The goza roared in contempt of the defiant humans.

"Scream all you want," Marina sneered. "You're facing the Capronis now, you bastard."

The great beast bellowed again to announce its attack. To Marina's surprise, the goza sprang, rather than trod, covering the distance of twenty feet with a single leap. They met the creature valiantly, their blades flashing in slash after slash. The thing had lowered its head to snatch either of them with its jaws, but the goza recoiled instantly with several bloody gashes now carved into its nose and the forward-facing edges of its mouth.

The fang-filled maw snapped shut just inches from Fausto as he leaped backward. In a flash, he lunged, sinking the end of his rapier several inches into the leathery blue flesh of the enraged animal's nose. As Fausto fell back, Marina pushed forward and leaped upward, cutting across the underside of the goza's neck as it lifted its head away from Fausto. The creature stood upright upon the dim realization that the humans were causing it pain.

In whatever passed for reasoning in the brain of the goza, it chose an alternative course of attack. The giant spun, bringing its massive tail into play.

"Watch out!" Fausto yelled, and he and Marina fell to the ground as the tail whipped over them.

The goza paused as if unsure its attack was effective, giving Marina time to react. She was back on her feet in a flash. Marina slashed downward with her sword and severed two feet of length from the tip of the whipping appendage.

The beast roared in anger and pain as Fausto, following

Marina's lead, began hacking at its bloodied tail. Again, the monster spun to face them and, in doing so, its tail knocked Fausto against one boulder only a few feet behind him. The impact of his back against the surface of the enormous stone forced the air from his lungs, and as the stars cleared from his vision, the creature's open maw rushed toward him.

He spun on his feet, rolling horizontally against the rock face. With only a split-second to spare, he avoided the attack. The jaws of the creature slammed shut, but it was upon the unyielding rock that they closed, not upon the fleshy prey as the goza had intended. Several huge fangs splintered, their sharp points falling from the mouth of the beast.

Seeing her brother's precarious situation, Marina pushed her attack and leaped toward the rear of the roaring creature. Near its mighty legs, she was out of the goza's range of vision. She made slash after slash upon one leg, just above its black-taloned toes, then sank the end of her rapier deep into the calf muscle. The monster raised its injured leg from the ground and attempted to stomp on her, but Marina bravely rushed under the beast and past the other leg to safety.

Distracted by Marina's attack on one leg gave Fausto an opening. As Marina dashed from the creature, Fausto plunged toward it and rained several strikes upon the uninjured leg. The monster was now stomping wildly and bleeding profusely from the multiple injuries it had sustained, but it would not yield. Instead, it crouched, and then sprang into the air and spun wildly to face Marina. The mighty leg muscles of the goza coiled as it prepared to give chase.

"Marina! Run! Get behind a boulder!" Fausto screamed. But there were no huge rocks before her, nothing but the wide open expanse of the Sea of Grass. There, she would find nowhere to hide. Marina turned to face the predator and stared into its blazing yellow eyes.

Tro-va acted without hesitation. The tribesman had climbed one of the great boulders and now charged toward its edge. With arms outstretched, Tro-va flew through the air twenty feet above the ground to land heavily on the back of the enraged goza. The selfless act caused the beast to falter in its pursuit of Marina. Tro-va quickly wrapped his legs around the shoulders of the roaring killing machine and tucked his legs under its arms.

"Tro-va!" Marina screamed. "No!"

But there would be no stopping the muscular Galu. As the goza bucked and spun to try to dislodge the small creature upon its back, Tro-va held high the Spanish halberd given to him by Fausto. Both of his strong hands gripped the long handle of the weapon, and with a mighty slash he embedded the axe blade into the spine of the goza, just below its skull.

Tro-va ripped the blade from the bloody flesh of the beast, held it high, and chopped again at the neck of the shrieking creature. The goza spun, changed course repeatedly, teetered on its gruesomely injured legs. As Marina and Fausto watched in amazement and horror, the handsome tribesman hacked at the beast again and again, his face and bare chest showered with gore. The thrashing of the goza slowed and a shiver rippled through its great frame before it crashed to the ground, its head nearly severed from its body. After several more pained inhalations, the goza's labored breathing ceased altogether.

Marina exuberantly embraced the bloodied warrior, who had risked all to save her life. Despite the language barrier, Fausto managed to convey his thanks to Tro-va, although the young Galu graciously dismissed his heroics as ordinary behavior.

They had prevailed, together, as a team. But none of the trio could be sure what they would encounter once they crossed the Sea of Grass, what they would find at the crash site of the *Pegaso II*, or if they could arrive before the balloon's departure and avoid being forever stranded on the savage lost continent of Caspak.

Marina and Fausto also wondered aloud why they had

heard two musket shots ring out just before the attack by the goza.

The three dashed from the carcass of the vanquished predator and plunged into the Sea of Grass. Within seconds, the maze of stalks wholly enveloped them. How much fleeting time remained before the balloon was cut free and soared into the crystal blue sky was a mystery.

22
RACE AGAINST TIME

SEVERAL DAYS OF CONTINUOUS FLIGHT and terror had taken its toll on the weary muscles of Marina and Fausto. At home in Palermo, rarely, if ever, had they the need to run, nor did either of them have to exert themselves physically in their day-to-day routines on the Mediterranean island. Such were their rather pampered lifestyles. But here, on Caspak, both had stretched their endurance to their limits, and their legs ached as they raced through the tall stalks of the Sea of Grass. To complain would be a waste of breath, and they dared not rest for more than a few moments; doing so might cost them their only chance to escape the accursed horrors of the primeval lost continent.

Tro-va pressed forward at top speed with seeming effortlessness and had to halt himself each time the Caproni siblings stopped momentarily to catch their breaths. To say that they ran is an overstatement, as their passage through the field was slow going. The stalks that rose above the heights of their heads did not yield passively, and efforts to cut through the hardy vegetable matter would only have slowed them even more. Thus, they pushed their way through the resistant growth, just as did the animals in the field. To their good fortune, they had yet to encounter any of those animals, particularly the enormous saber-toothed cats they had seen days before. During momentary rest breaks, Fausto would stretch to look above the stalks, to verify they were traveling in the right direction, and to ensure that the huge hydrogen-filled balloon remained grounded. After spanning half the distance to the wreck of the *Pegaso II*, Fausto was relieved to see the white silk envelope still tethered to the ground.

It was during one of their stops that Tro-va noticed something peculiar. Fausto and Marina warily raised their loaded muskets as Tro-va crept away from them into the stalks. He called to Marina, and she and Fausto rushed to his side. Before them was a path of crushed growths, a tangent that led both toward the sky cutter and away from it.

"An animal path?" Marina asked Tro-va in his language.

"No," he responded, crouching to the ground. "Look here." He ran his hand over the clearly delineated boot tracks. "Your Galus?" he asked.

Fausto furrowed his brow and looked down the path leading away from the *Pegaso II*. Something had caught his eye. "Wait here," he said as he began down the trail, his rifle held ready. Neither Marina nor Tro-va obeyed Fausto's request to stay behind.

Twenty feet from where they had intersected the path, the trail ended. There they found the bodies of the Sicilian sailors, Puccini and Alamanni, each with a bullet in his back. Fausto examined the corpses with disgust and remorse. "They're still warm," he reported.

"The two musket shots we heard," Marina said. "The Spaniards murdered these men." Then another uncomfortable thought crossed her mind. "Fausto, do you think Signore Ricci . . ."

"No," her brother interjected with confidence. "No, I'm sure he's all right. He's the only one among them with any scientific knowledge. At least, I hope so. Valdez will need him to safely operate the venting ropes of the balloon to get them back to the *Redenzione*."

Marina scowled. "You're probably right," she said unconvincingly.

Suddenly, Tro-va held out his hand to hush the Capronis.

Marina's eyes widened, as she had come to unconditionally heed the warnings of the handsome warrior. Since he had ascended from the primitive Alu tribe to the dawn of civilized man exhibited in the Galus, he must have survived innumerable threats in his lifetime. Marina found it heartbreaking that such a pure soul had lost his mate to the savage land they inhabited, and she resolved that they would not similarly fall victim to Caspak's brutal whims. That was all the more reason to heed the words he uttered next.

"We must run," he whispered.

Tro-va took Marina's hand and the two began to trot down the trail toward the sky cutter. "Fausto!" Marina urged her brother, but a captain must know the colors of his enemy. Before following them, Fausto had raised his head above the level of the grass in an attempt to glimpse that which had prompted Tro-va to issue his warning.

Only a few hundred feet from where Fausto stood, a gigantic fin rose and fell above the tops of the pale emerald stalks. It was not unlike the dorsal fin of a shark, cleaving the water of the Mediterranean. Closer scrutiny revealed to Fausto that the fin was constructed of multiple long spikes, at least twelve feet in length and enwrapped by a webbing of pale yellow skin and slashed with stripes of brilliant violet.

Based on its movement, whatever beast it was that boasted the extravagant fin was either foraging or hunting.

Fausto's boots crunched over the trampled stalks as he followed quickly down the path behind Marina and Tro-va.

It was cold comfort that after several more minutes of travel, the voyagers could no longer see the huge fin of the rava behind them. With luck, it had changed course and was now in the jungle, but Fausto and Marina could not discount the possibility that the thing had only crouched lower to the ground and was crawling in its pursuit of them. Either way, they had to keep moving, and after another twenty minutes of dashing stealthily through the stalks, they were now only three hundred feet from the sky cutter.

As they ran, the three crouched low to remain concealed from view, but now, exercising great caution, Fausto rose to get a better view of the damaged craft.

"What do you see?" Marina whispered anxiously.

Fausto ducked back down. "It's just as Ortega said," he replied. "There's a bamboo basket beneath the balloon, like a gondola, with one of the vats in the center. Looks like it might hold three or four people at the most."

"Who's there? Do you see Signore Ricci?" Marina asked.

"Yes, Ricci is there, alive," Fausto revealed. "Along with Colonel Valdez, Alonso, and Montes."

Marina noticed Fausto watching Tro-va closely. The islander was keeping a close eye on the tall stalks around them, but periodically he would divert his attention to look fondly upon Marina. At these times, Fausto smiled to himself.

Marina knew well why her brother grinned, but his demeanor changed swiftly as harsh reality settled upon him.

"We might only have minutes," Fausto said sternly, "so we need to make a plan quickly." He looked again at Tro-va. "Marina," he asked gently, "what are your feelings about our friend here, if I may ask?"

Every minute of the past few days had been an unending flood of emotion and adrenaline, and throughout, Marina had little time to contemplate anything other than her minute-to-minute fight for survival. Fausto had asked a pointed question. What were her feelings, and did they even matter now that she and her brother were within reach of escaping Caspak?

"Let me put it another way," Fausto said, noting Marina's conflicted emotions. "If we can overpower the Spaniards and seize the balloon, should we take Tro-va with us to the *Redenzione*?"

Marina felt her heart drop into the pit of her stomach as she looked into the dark eyes of the tribesman, who smiled innocently back at her. He was beautiful, unlike any man she had ever met, and that he was nearly naked at all times had not ceased to give her butterflies in her stomach. He was sensitive and clever, and not once during their time together had he made a single ungentlemanly gesture toward her. He had risked his life for her and had now traveled far from his tribe to ensure her safety, even to the forfeiture of his own. Now, they were only a few hundred feet away from the balloon, the white gossamer silk glowing under the sun as it swayed in the warm breeze. Marina knew a decision must be made.

"I don't know, Fausto," Marina instead replied. "Maybe we should just let destiny follow its course."

"Yes, but . . ."

"Fausto, I don't know, all right?" Marina's retort was adamant. Emotionally, she could not discuss the matter further. "What do we do about Valdez and the soldiers when we get aboard the sky cutter?" she asked, directing the conversation to its most vital aspect.

Her brother could not deny that a discussion of Tro-va's fate was pointless if the Spaniards murdered the three of them. "For Valdez's plan to succeed, we must all die. Chances are they'll shoot us as soon as they see us. To our advantage, we know that all the other soldiers are dead, but Valdez has no idea how many of us are still alive. They also don't know," Fausto added as he tipped his head toward Tro-va, "that we have one hell of a warrior on our side."

"What do we do, then?" Marina asked.

"You're not going to like it, but I have to do what I have to do," Fausto announced with surety. "I must go to the sky cutter. Alone. You and Tro-va stay hidden and . . ." he paused, "come to my rescue if things get rough?"

"That's not much of a plan, Fausto." Marina lifted her musket. "What if . . ."

The young sea captain stopped his sister in midsentence. "What if we just shoot them from here? One stray spark and the balloon could explode. We can't risk it. There's no other way. I'll go to the sky cutter and either negotiate a deal or do as much damage to them as I can. You and Tro-va will just need to stay hidden and take whatever steps you feel are necessary."

Marina's voice was an amalgam of anger, frustration, and fear. "But they'll kill you, Fausto. You know that."

"I know, Marina," he said firmly. "But what else are little brothers for except to protect big sisters?"

Marina shook her head in faux patronization. "We'll be old and gray and you still won't understand that I can take care of myself." Marina punched her brother in the shoulder.

"Will we?" Fausto asked grimly.

They smiled at one another, and Marina brushed away a tear. How or if Fausto's plan would proceed became irrelevant when, suddenly, guttural growls began rattling through the stalks around them.

Tro-va put a hand on Marina's arm and she and Fausto fell silent. The enormous jungle cats had found them. Not one of the magnificent killing machines was visible, but it was clear the beasts had surrounded them.

Fausto and Marina raised their muskets, knowing full well that firing shots would alert the Spaniards aboard the wreck of the *Pegaso II*, but they could not just sit and wait for the predators to tear them to shreds. Tro-va rose, the halberd in his strong fists. He would not go down without a fight. The gurgling rumble of the growls intensified as Marina, Fausto, and Tro-va scanned the surrounding stalks for the first sign of an attacker.

But an attack upon them was not to be. From somewhere across the vast Sea of Grass came loud wails that rose in volume, then abruptly ceased. Again the sounds rang out, three to four distinct notes that seemed to come from all directions.

"Listen!" Marina gasped. "The growls stopped!" Not only had the raspy exhales of the hidden beasts ceased, but she could hear the great hulks crashing through the stalks away from the surrounded party.

The loud wails had surely reached the ears of the Spaniards, and now it became inevitable that the soldiers would spot

Fausto and Marina hidden in the surrounding stalks. The Capronis raised their heads, no longer concerned about concealing themselves. To their astonishment, they observed trails of waving stalks moving away from them across the field as the vicious tigers darted in multiple directions toward the sources of the mysterious sounds.

Marina ducked down and joyously gripped the arm of Tro-va. "The Cos-ju-los!" she exclaimed. Tro-va smiled and nodded in the affirmative. When Marina turned to share the good news with Fausto, she found her brother had disappeared.

Her heart sank, for she knew what that meant. He was heading toward the sky cutter, and he had gone alone.

23
THE GRAND ILLUSION

OLONEL VALDEZ SCANNED the densely packed plain of tall stalks surrounding the wreck of the *Pegaso II*. Receding from the vessel in several directions were trails left by the feral beasts that had killed Sergeant Molina following the ship's crash. The men could not see the tigers, but they knew what creatures lurked in the dense vegetation that encircled them.

Leonardo Ricci stood nervously beside the basket beneath the enormous white balloon. At the center of the gondola was mounted one of the glass-lined vats. In the vessel, iron filings dissolved in an acid bath while noxious vapor rose into the silk envelope overhead. The incensed soldiers stomped about the slanted deck of the disabled ship, their rifles aimed down at the impenetrable verdure surrounding them. Although the crew of the sky cutter had cleared the vegetation in a thirty-foot circle around the ship and torches mounted on bamboo poles burned to ward off Caprona's immense predators, the actions of the Spaniards laid bare the fear manifested in each of them. Ricci observed them warily.

"There's a big one," Colonel Valdez reported to the two soldiers, who then joined him at the fore of the craft. A quarter mile from the sky cutter, the huge fin was slowly cleaving through the stalks with no discernible intent. "Keep a close watch," he ordered the men. "If whatever that is wanders in this direction, inform me immediately." Valdez noted Ricci's suspicious glare and joined the astronomer beneath the balloon.

"Did you spot what made those horrendous noises?" Ricci asked.

Valdez ignored the elderly man's query. "The balloon looks full to me, or at least full enough to carry the four of us over those peaks. I understand your hesitance to depart, Signore, but we must face facts: Captain Caproni and his crew are dead. Is there anything further to be done before we depart?"

The Spanish colonel spun as a youthful voice called out behind him.

"I knew I could count on you to find a way out of this, Signore," Fausto said cheerily as he climbed from the hatch to the sky cutter's hull. His shirt and pants were in tatters and cuts and scratches covered his exposed skin, but the ship's captain strode toward Valdez as if nothing noteworthy had occurred during his absence. Fausto gripped his primed and loaded musket in his hands.

The wrinkles at the outer edges of Leonardo Ricci's eyes gathered as a wide smile stretched across his face. "My dedication to duty to the Capronis has never wavered. Welcome aboard, Captain!" Ricci beamed. Beside him, Valdez straightened his uniform and pretended to test the fit of his gloves.

Moments before, Fausto had watched from within the stalks, waiting for just the right time. It had come when the Spaniards gathered at the fore of the sky cutter to watch the mysterious fin. While their backs were turned, Fausto had dashed from his hiding place and crawled through the rupture of the hull of the *Pegaso II*. He had regretted not saying good-bye to Marina, but had he announced his pending departure he knew the words might never come, such was the persuasiveness of every one of his sister's arguments. At that point, as he had faced the enemy, he knew there would be no backing down. Fausto's mind had flashed to poor Santos Ignacio, carried off to his death, and in honor of the memory of his mentor, young Captain Caproni had resolved that he would succeed or die trying.

With the appearance of Fausto on the deck of the ship, Sergeants Alonso and Montes had turned to face him, their rifles at the ready and awaiting orders of their colonel. Fausto's impromptu strategy had been to feign ignorance, stall for time, and hope for a negotiation with Valdez. But now, in the heat of the moment, his instincts took over. Words began to flow forth from his mouth and a plan began to form as if of its own volition.

Fausto remained near the hatch leading belowdecks, knowing that any advancement toward Valdez would be met with musket fire from the soldiers under his charge. "Is the balloon ready to fly?" Fausto called to Leonardo Ricci. He did not know precisely why he had said what he did, but that is what he blurted in a straightforward, commanding tone.

Leonardo responded with casual aloofness. "Ready to cast off, Captain." The astronomer was familiar with Fausto's ways, having known the young Caproni since he first came into the world, and Leonardo played along with the captain's bluff without missing a beat. "Just as you commanded," the elder added.

Valdez raised an eyebrow and narrowed his eyes. "What do you mean, as *he* commanded?" The pronouncement of the old astronomer was just what was needed to knock Valdez off his mental footing.

"This was our plan all along, Colonel," Leonardo replied. "We just didn't tell you." By the look on his face, Valdez was now completely flustered and confused.

Fausto took immediate advantage of Valdez's unease and rolled the dice of fate by lowering his musket. Doing so was an immense risk, but he must play the charade until its end. "Colonel Valdez, I regret to inform you that your men, Sergeant Lago and Sergeant Garza, are both dead. Sergeant Ortega has joined my men, Trimboli and Colazzo. My sister Marina is also alive, as are Puccini and Alamanni, who survived your assassination attempt only this morning. All are armed and have the sky cutter surrounded, with muskets pointed at you and your soldiers at this very moment. I would suggest you lower your weapons." Nearly all of what he had said was a fabrication, but Fausto was out of options.

"He lies, Colonel!" sputtered Montes. "They were dead! Puccini and Alamanni . . ."

"Shut up, you idiot!" Valdez spat with venom before growing quiet. After a moment of thought he resumed his stoic demeanor in the face of the threat made against him and his men. "Captain Caproni, I have no idea what you're talking about. What do you mean, 'Sergeant Ortega has joined your men?' All I can assume by your words is that you have in mind some fiendish plot to break the covenants of your contract with the Queen Regent by eliminating us, thereby leaving no Spanish witnesses to the discovery of Caprona. Already you have murdered two of my men. So tell me, Captain . . . Am I correct in my assessment?"

Fausto laughed, not only in bravado but also because Valdez had fallen for his impromptu lie. "Tell your men to lower their weapons, Colonel, and we will talk like civilized men." Fausto's smile belied the undercurrent of deadly intent in his glare.

The eyes of Valdez cut sharply to the gently rippling Sea of Grass before locking on Alonso and Montes. "Do as the captain requests," he instructed his soldiers without a shred of concern in his voice. He turned back to Fausto. "Now. Your intent, Captain?"

Fausto relaxed his stance, but still kept a firm grip on his musket as he walked up the slanting deck to stand before the Spanish officer. "First, Colonel . . . Yes, Ortega has joined my men. He informed us of *your* intent to kill *us*, thereby allowing Spain to claim this land. Being a man of moral character, Ortega did what was right. Second, my men did not kill Lago and Garza. Sergeant Ortega did."

Sergeant Alonso could not contain himself. "It's as I told you, Colonel! I told you Ortega could not be trusted!"

"Silence!" the commander shouted, then turned his

attention back to Fausto. "Have you any other accusations, Captain Caproni?"

Fausto looked to the sky in a dramatic fashion and rolled his eyes as if he were considering the question. All of it was for show and an expression of sarcasm. "No, I think that's it," he replied curtly. "Ah. Wait," he added, "there is one other thing. This continent cannot be claimed by the Kingdom of the Two Sicilies *or* by Spain. You see, it's already been claimed by the tribes who reside here. And the name of this land is not Caprona," Fausto said with veneration. "It's *Caspak*."

The young captain exchanged a glance with Leonardo Ricci, but neither man smiled or made any overt gesture to insinuate that Fausto was being anything other than truthful. At the ship's rail, Montes and Alonso anxiously watched the stalks, their firearms slung over their backs at the order of Valdez. The colonel did not bear a musket, but such was the way of commanders, Fausto reasoned. How often had he heard tales of military generals not firing a single shot during a conflict as those they commanded died by the hundreds while defending their leader and progressing the cause of colonialism? Valdez was such a man, and in his heart, Fausto despised everything about the Spanish officer.

"Well, then," Valdez said with a sigh of resignation, and then resumed his commanding tone. "I understand you, Captain, and you understand me. If you call off your men in hiding, I assure you, we will comply with your wishes. As you know, the gondola will support the weight of four men. How many are you, again, Captain Caproni?"

Valdez must have intended to fluster Fausto with his abrupt mathematical question, but the young captain spat out an answer forthwith. "Five of us are here on deck and six are in the grass awaiting my orders. That's eleven. We will increase the number of passengers to five. One of us, either Signore Ricci or myself, must travel back and forth to pilot the balloon, which means we can ferry all of us to the *Redenzione* in three trips."

"Very well," Valdez said. "I admit, I am none too comfortable knowing that my men and I are still within reach of your assassins' musket balls. Would you kindly call them off, Captain?"

Until that point, Fausto's fabrication had given him the upper hand over the Spaniards. Now Fausto's proposal to move forward would require that he call his men back to the ship—men who, in truth, did not exist. Only Marina and Tro-va lay hidden within the stalks. Fausto's mind raced for an answer. If the three Spaniards made the first foray to the ship with either Fausto or Leonardo acting as the balloon's navigator, the soldiers could easily overpower the pilot during the flight, reach the *Redenzione*, and never return. But how could Fausto produce sailors who had all died? He knew the second that Valdez suspected a subterfuge, the muskets of Alonso and Montes would blast him into oblivion.

Fausto could think of only one recourse: to continue lying. He walked to the ship's taffrail, cupped a hand to his mouth, and shouted.

In her hiding place amid the tall stalks, Marina bolted upright when she heard the voice of her brother call out: *"Remain in your positions, men, and wait for further orders!"*

"Oh, Fausto," she said aloud, "what in the *world* are you doing?"

Captain Caproni strolled the perimeter of the sky cutter's deck and repeated his call to his nonexistent compatriots. "Colonel Valdez," he addressed the Spaniard, "I will consult with Signore Ricci and let you know how we will proceed. In the meantime, relax, enjoy the beautiful day, and don't make any sudden moves." Having made his pronouncement, Fausto fearlessly strode to the side of Leonardo Ricci, where he engaged the elderly astronomer in hushed conversation.

Leonardo's arm was now in a sling, having been injured during the crash of the *Pegaso II* as Marina had suspected, but he assured Fausto that he could operate the balloon's venting ropes with ease. The older man quickly summarized the events of the past few days and explained that he was in generally good health and spirits.

After only Sergeant Ortega of the exploratory party had returned to the sky cutter, he and Garza volunteered to strike out again to determine the whereabouts of the missing soldiers and crew. They also did not return. Puccini and Alamanni were suspicious that something was amiss, but both agreed to accompany Alonso and Montes on a rescue mission that morning. Shortly after they left the ship, musket fire rang out and only the Spaniards returned. It was then that Leonardo had fully understood the insidious plot of Colonel Valdez, and it also explained why he had received exceptional treatment by the Spaniards: They needed the elderly astronomer to operate the balloon that would return them to the *Redenzione.*

Leonardo had refused to agree to the colonel's insistence that Fausto must be dead. Over the past two days, Leonardo had surreptitiously vented hydrogen from the balloon even as it was filling to delay the launch of the escape vessel. Deep down, something told him Fausto had not succumbed to the horrors of the lost continent, and the elder was overjoyed the young captain had survived.

"What are your orders, Captain Caproni?" Leonardo asked. "I assume you will recall all of the men from the field? We can depart on the first trip back to the *Redenzione* immediately."

Fausto's mein was most dour. "Signore, they are all dead, either killed by the Spaniards or by the beasts of Caspak."

"But Marina . . . ?" Leonardo's voice wavered as it caught in his throat.

Fausto put a hand on the shoulder of his elder and smiled. "Marina is just fine. She's out there right now, hiding, accompanied by a . . . well . . ." He searched for the right words. "There are people here. We found people. They are primitive, but one of them is with her now. She's in good hands."

"Is that so?" Leonardo replied with a canny grin.

"But understand, we are at a great disadvantage," Fausto said. "We have no army. Just Marina and the tribesman, and you and me. Our only hope is to convince the Spaniards to surrender their weapons."

"And once we are all back on the *Redenzione*?"

"They will be treated as are all mutineers. They'll be kept in chains."

"You, Captain Fausto Caproni," Leonardo declared, "are about to become a very famous man."

"No," Fausto said firmly. Leonardo cocked an eyebrow at the unexpected pronouncement. "No, Signore, we will burn your maps and forget we ever came across this land. As outlined in my contractual agreement with the Queen Regent of Spain, we will continue our voyage. But *never* will we ever return to Caspak, nor will we ever speak of it again."

"But Valdez and his men were here," the astronomer objected. "The crew and the soldiers aboard the *Redenzione*, all know what we found. How can such a thing be kept secret?"

"Look what happened to my grandfather, Signore," he reminded Leonardo. "No one believed him, either." Fausto grinned. "And he had a far better reputation than I do, to be honest."

"No offense," Leonardo said, "but point well taken, my son."

Fausto laughed. "That might work on the crew, but you're right. The Spaniards. How can we possibly silence them?"

A great rush of air tossed Fausto's hair, and as he looked to the bamboo deck, a wide shadow swept across the sky cutter, over the inflated balloon, and then glided like a phantom across the field of verdant stalks. The men on deck searched the sky around the ship for the creature that threw the shadow, but there was one person on board that the sudden incursion did not distract.

When Fausto turned his attention away from the sky,

he found Sergeant Alonso kneeling before the taffrail at the far edge of the deck. In the man's hands was his musket, which he pointed not at the clouds, but at Fausto, who stood beside Leonardo Ricci and the vat of acid. Before Fausto could utter a word, Alonso aimed the barrel of his weapon and fired.

24

Battle Aboard the Sky Cutter

VEN AS SERGEANT ALONSO pulled the trigger of his musket, Fausto had leaped into motion on the far side of the ship's deck. Alonso's musket flint struck the frizzen, creating sparks to ignite the gunpowder in the weapon's pan, but in that brief moment before the ball was expelled from the barrel, Fausto raised his own musket and pulled the trigger. He had acted instinctually, his mind and body reacting in a single fluid motion beyond the ability of his intellect to comprehend.

A duo of explosive blasts rang out; two clouds of acrid smoke billowed from weapons. The bamboo taffrail to Alonso's right exploded as Fausto's musket shot struck the wood, sending a shower of splinters into the air. Fausto's mind was awash with a torrent of adrenalized thoughts, one of which was, *Have I been hit?* But he felt no searing pain, no splash of warm blood against the inside of his shirt. *Alonso's shot missed!*

But even as Fausto inwardly rejoiced that luck had favored him, a force harder than a musket ball struck him: the sight of Leonardo Ricci, standing to his right, gripping his chest, as dark red blood streamed between his bony fingers. Without a word, the astronomer fell against the vat, slid down its side to the deck of the sky cutter, and breathed no more.

Whether Alonso's rifle shot was intentionally aimed at the defenseless astronomer or not, a red haze of fury fell before Fausto's eyes and every nerve in his body screamed in an electric wave of mania. He threw down his musket and flew across the deck, his hands balled into fists, his knuckles white. With the might of a charging bull, Fausto slammed into Alonso as the soldier fumbled with the ramrod of his musket. In the sickening collision of bodies, Fausto's skull impacted the Spanish soldier's eye socket, shattering the man's upper cheekbone. Before Alonso could comprehend what had happened, his musket was ripped from his hands. In a flash, the shoulder stock of the weapon smashed into his breastbone, knocking him backward over the taffrail and to the ground fifteen feet below.

A stab of panic ran the length of Fausto's spine as he realized that his attack on Alonso had left him vulnerable to the blades and muskets of Valdez and Montes. It was then that a shot rang out, but the rifle fire was not directed at him. Rather, Montes had fired at an enormous dragon, as Marina called the beasts, that now hovered over the ship. The musket ball had either missed the creature or had passed harmlessly through one of its leathery wings. The legs of the creature pumped rhythmically in the air, the taloned toes curling in strike after strike as it attempted to snatch either of the Spaniards from the ship's deck.

A sudden dual explosive roar startled Marina and Tro-va. For the latter, it must have sounded like an unanticipated roll of thunder. But Marina knew exactly what was the source of the blasts: It was musket fire. Fausto had run afoul of the Spaniards and was now in deep trouble.

"We must go!" Marina cried to her warrior companion, who was all too willing to follow her direction. Cautiously, she stood and peered above the stalks only to see the body of a Spanish soldier hurtle over the taffrail of the sky cutter and plunge to the ground. Compounding the frantic situation, a gigantic blue ko-oo hovered above the downed airship, avoiding the halberd thrusts of Colonel Valdez and Sergeant Montes.

That meant it was Sergeant Alonso who had fallen from the sky cutter, but Marina had no idea whether he was injured, nor could she see Fausto engaged in the melee. Perhaps her brother was safe. But perhaps not. She must know.

Suddenly, there came a sound.

Thoom. Thoom. Thoom.

It was rhythmic and heavy, and with each resonance, Marina felt a tremor beneath her feet.

She turned and peered over the stalks behind them, her heart leaping to her throat. Not three hundred feet from where they stood rose and fell the hideous yellow fin of the rava that prowled the Sea of Grass. It was moving. And it was rushing in their direction!

Fausto watched with mixed emotions as the Spaniards fought against the advances of the flying predator. The airborne creature shrieked in frustration, unable to sink its claws into either of the tiny beings who opposed it. Colonel Valdez had ordered the deaths of the Sicilians, it was true, but Fausto knew he could never live with himself if he sat idle while another man—even an enemy—was murdered before his eyes by one of Caspak's bloodthirsty beasts.

The creature ceased flapping its wings just as Valdez took a vicious swing with his halberd, dipping swiftly downward and wrapping its claws around the end of the colonel's weapon. The flapping resumed, and as Valdez stubbornly clung to the bladed shaft, the massive dragon lifted him from the deck of the sky cutter like a hawk snatching a mouse from a hayfield.

Before the military commander could be lifted more than a few feet, the flying terror shrieked as a musket ball tore a chunk from its shoulder. The mighty talons released their hold on the halberd, and Valdez landed hard on his feet below the hovering beast.

Within seconds, a second shot rang out from Fausto's

musket, the iron ball piercing the monster's wing. Valdez turned and looked to Fausto, but spoke not a word. His life had been saved by the man he had sworn to kill.

Marina and Tro-va plunged through the stubborn stalks toward the sky cutter, not knowing how close on their heels was the rava, though its thunderous footfalls still shook the ground beneath them. At last, they reached the perimeter of the clearing that circled the base of the airship.

Without a word, Marina pointed to the damaged portion of the hull that opened into the interior of the sky cutter. Alonso, who had fallen to the ground, was nowhere in sight; he must have scuttled into the ship by way of the damaged hull.

After Marina had taken only a few steps beyond the edge of the verdant sward, something struck her from the side and threw her brutally to the ground. As she struggled to regain her senses, she found the full weight of Sergeant Alonso pressing down upon her. He grabbed her roughly by the shoulders and rolled her over to face him, his steely blade pressed against her throat.

Marina looked into the eyes of the Spaniard and laughed. A look of confusion crossed his face.

"Don't you know you're about to die?" he hissed.

"That's what's funny," she said. "I don't think I am."

In a flash, the arm of Sergeant Alonso was pulled from Marina, upward over his head, then forcibly thrust to the left across his back, dislocating it from his shoulder with a gut-churning crack. Whatever pain the soldier felt was brief, as Tro-va swiftly threw him upon his back and thrust his bone knife upward under the rib cage and into the heart. Marina looked up into the vengeful eyes of the primal warrior, which softened as they lowered and met her gaze.

There was no time to celebrate their victory, however. Behind them, a gigantic toothy snout pushed forth from the greenery. The skin of the monster was pale violet and adorned with yellow bull's-eyes, and its nostrils flared with each great inhale. Across the tip of its long crocodilian snout were barely healed cuts and punctures. Marina gulped hard. It was the same rava she and Tro-va had fought when it pursued them beneath the waterfall days before. If the Caspakian creature could hold a grudge, they were in big trouble indeed.

A mighty roar of rage announced the beast's attack, but the rava's intended victims had already slipped through the cracks of the odd construction before it and disappeared into the darkness within.

Hearing the bellow of the monstrous intruder, Fausto rushed to the port side of the sky cutter. As he reached the taffrail, the rava lowered its massive tail and reared up to its full height, its soulless eyes focused on the meaty morsel that stood before him. Fausto no longer held the musket, as he had used the last ball in his supply pouch to save the life of Valdez and had no further use for the weapon. He drew his sword and prepared for the beast's lunge.

The reptilian predator's nostrils flared and emitted great bursts of air. It had picked up the scent of something more interesting than the man who stood before it. The head of the monster bobbed from side to side as it sniffed the air, then turned upward. Above the sky cutter, the ko-oo still hovered, beating its wings to maintain its position as it re-considered its attack in the aftermath of the damage inflicted upon it by its intended prey. This was a fatal miscalculation, however, for the rava had now smelled the blood that trickled from the flying creature's multiple wounds.

With astounding speed, the rava made three bounding leaps: two that carried it around the stern of the *Pegaso II* and a third that launched it into the air. The jaws of the nightmarish beast clamped shut upon the body of the ko-oo and ripped it from the air, dozens of razor-point fangs embedding in the flesh of the screeching flier. Among the green stalks, the raza began thrusting its snout upward as it shredded flesh and bone until its victim lay dead in the blood-splattered Sea of Grass. There, the rava feasted, only a dozen yards from the sky cutter and the balloon that might carry its human survivors to freedom.

As the primal spectacle played out before him, Fausto was relieved that two immediate threats had countered one another; the flying creature was killed and its hunter would hopefully be distracted by its gory feast. Now, only the opposition of the Spaniards remained. But before he could turn to face his human adversaries, he felt a sharp pain in his shoulder blade. He knew instantly that the tip of a pointed sword blade was pressing into his back.

"Well, Captain Caproni," Colonel Valdez flippantly announced, "I'll admit, you're an excellent liar, but it's time we draw the curtain on your charade." Fausto turned slowly to face Valdez, the end of the commander's sword still inches from his chest. "I would have expected your loyal sailors to have rushed to your aid by now. Either they are cowards or you are here alone. I think it's the latter. Perhaps you're the only one left alive."

Beside Valdez, Montes stood impassively, his musket barrel trained on the face of the man who had led them to the incredible continent. "Give the word, Colonel, and I'll take his head off," the soldier hissed.

"Not necessary, Sergeant," Valdez said. "I'm more than capable of handling this boy."

Fausto kept a stiff upper lip, feigning as much arrogance as he could muster. "You can't kill me, Valdez," he said. "With Signore Ricci murdered, I'm the only one who can operate the balloon. I'm your only hope for escape."

Valdez scoffed at the suggestion. "Not so, Captain. I think we can easily figure out how to fly a simple balloon. No. You will die here, and the *Redenzione* will become mine. Should any of your sailors resist the change in command, they'll either be shot or thrown into the brine." He grinned. "Both, actually."

A plethora of actions and likely repercussions flashed through Fausto's mind, but none seemed particularly weighted in his favor. He could not let his ship and crew fall into the hands of the Spaniards. And what of Marina? He could not die without knowing what fate lay in store for her. At last, he arrived at the only possible solution.

To his surprise, Valdez had also come to an identical decision. The soldier took a step back. "You may raise your sword, Captain. As a man of honor, I will allow you the notion that you might best me, steel against steel." The Spaniard laughed. "You will not prevail, of course, but I'm not entirely cruel. I'll let you die thinking you had a chance against me."

Fausto knew that he must now dredge forth every last shred of training imparted to him during his fencing lessons with Santos Ignacio if he had any hope of overcoming his foe. He fell back into a traditional *en garde* posture, his sword raised and his left hand uplifted beside his head.

"Let's have at it, then," Fausto quipped.

Valdez tested Fausto's reflexes, quickly tapping his blade against the young captain's steel. Fausto reciprocated the gesture; as Señor Santos had taught, the formality of the maneuver allowed time for one to calm the mind and formulate a plan of attack. The unrelenting sun of Caspak gleamed along the top edges of their swords.

Fausto's hope of striking first was dashed as Valdez initiated his attack. The slash was easily parried by a right from Fausto, who rotated his hand to circle into a leftward swing. Their blades encircled one another in several quick loops, and then each man took a sharp step back to disengage.

Again, Valdez pushed forward with a thrust, parried by Fausto. Although his eyes were focused on his opponent's blade, Fausto kept a subconscious awareness of the bamboo beneath his feet. The surface was uneven, even a bit slippery;

unsure footing could cause a fighter to falter, giving his opponent the opening for a deadly strike. Valdez advanced again with his blade, but a spin to the left allowed Fausto to avoid the lunge. He followed with three quick *ripostes*, each parried by the military man.

The adrenaline surging through Fausto bolstered his ego and his tongue. "You thought I'd be easy prey, didn't you?" he said, striking down another of Valdez's swipes.

The taunt only seemed to anger the Spaniard, which was made evident by several rapid—if undisciplined—thrusts, each deflected by Fausto's flashing blade. The young captain pressed forward, feigned left, then cleverly struck right. Valdez barely had time to deflect the blow, but a frantic swing met with success.

The sound of steel striking steel in rapid succession rang across the bamboo deck of the sky cutter. Loyal to his commander's order, Sergeant Montes stood by silently, but he would come to the aid of Valdez should the man call out. Fausto kept the soldier in his peripheral vision, aware that at any moment, the unscrupulous colonel could cast off his honor and order a musket ball to be shot through his heart. The eyes of Sergeant Montes remained on his commanding officer, and thus he was oblivious to the hatch leading to the sky cutter's lower deck slowly opening twenty paces behind him.

"Stop at once and drop your weapons!" Marina shouted in rage. She stood before the open hatch, Tro-va at her side, and she looked down the barrel of her musket, aimed at the head of Sergeant Montes. "Do as I say or I'll shoot!"

If Fausto broke his concentration for even a fraction of a second it could prove fatal, a sentiment surely shared by Valdez. Neither relented from his attack against the other, and their battle continued in a ballet of strikes, lunges, and parries.

"Sir! Your order?" Montes called out, his rifle now focused on the young Sicilian woman.

"Kill her!" Valdez screamed, not daring to take his eyes off the valiant ship's captain.

Marina only had seconds to act. She had one shot, but there were two adversaries. Tro-va was at her side, the halberd in one hand and his bone knife in the other. Even if Tro-va attacked, Montes would cut him down before he took two steps.

Three melodic bursts of sound filled the air, a triplet of notes that rose in pitch and volume, then abruptly ceased. Montes looked away from his gun sight, unsure what had just fallen upon his ears. But Marina knew, as did Tro-va. To the ship's port side, the tall stalks swayed as something rushed across the ground, heading straight for the sky cutter.

Marina turned, as a clattering of the bamboo at the other side of the ship drew her attention. Over the crude taffrail the leader of the Cos-ju-los deftly climbed, just ten feet from the startled Sergeant Montes. The woman was a fluid blur of motion, of colorful feathers and snakeskins, of tanned flesh painted on a muscular physique; she was a majestic warrior who moved more like a ballerina than a barbarian. The Cos-ju-lo leaped to the deck running, never breaking stride, and bolted across the midsection of the sky cutter. As she did, she blew through the conch, then threw the large shell toward Marina before bounding for the far taffrail. Montes attempted to follow the strange woman across the deck, but before he could even close upon her, the warrior launched herself fearlessly into the air and disappeared into the stalks twenty feet from the ship.

For only a moment were Marina and Tro-va perplexed by the bizarre action of the Cos-ju-lo. Then a guttural roar that rang out chilled them all to the bone. At the side of the ship where Montes had stood, an enormous tiger bearing impossibly long upper fangs leaped to the deck of the *Pegaso II*. The bamboo beneath its taloned claws creaked in distress as the monster unleashed another mighty roar, its upper lips curling over the ivory canines that depended well past its lower jaw.

In a flash of tawny fur and gleaming tusks, the giant cat bounded across the deck with lightning speed, snatched the screaming Sergeant Montes between its hideous jaws, and leaped from the opposite taffrail. From somewhere in the broad expanse of vibrant green stalks, the blood-choked shrieks of the soldier rose into the air, then abruptly halted.

In defense of Marina, the Cos-ju-lo leader had used the conch to lure the nightmarish tiger to the enemy's camp, where it would find easy prey that would be powerless against it. It was not conventional, modern warfare. It was how the warrior women of Caspak dealt with enemies.

Marina snatched the conch from the deck and slung it over her shoulder by the carrying strap. She was not sure what compelled her to do so, but piece by piece she was looking less like a Sicilian debutante and more like a resident of the primitive world.

The Capronis' only remaining enemy was Colonel Valdez. Fausto's sword battle with the villainous commander was still at a fever pitch. Neither combatant had slowed his pace, but Fausto was beginning to feel the early signs of fatigue in his right arm. Even as Valdez would push an advantage, Fausto would counter and reverse his advancement. Forward and back they moved across the deck, each evenly matched and fighting with equal measures of offense and defense.

Throughout the protracted sparring, Fausto had noticed a pattern to the fighting style of Colonel Valdez. The older military man was an adept swordsman, to be sure, but everything about his moves indicated an adherence to regimentation. It was as if his fencing skills were honed only in training exercises and not on the battlefield, where conventionality is crushed within seconds, or so Santos Ignacio had often lectured Fausto. Valdez fought by the book and there might lie a disadvantage Fausto could exploit.

How one plucks an idea from the aether is not known. How brilliant concepts coalesce within the mind without critical contemplation remains a mystery. All Fausto knew was that at that moment, as he parried attack after attack, as his right arm began to feel as heavy as lead, his mind drifted to his first meeting with Sovrano, one of the alley cats taken in by Marina at the family estate in Palermo.

Marina had introduced Fausto to the large orange cat that she cradled in her arms. He was a big fellow with a pleasant enough face, and he looked absolutely at ease and purred contentedly in Marina's embrace. Everything changed when Fausto held out his arms and Marina attempted to hand the burly tomcat to him. In a flash, the animal whipped himself into a twisting, hissing tornado of slashing claws. He spun in the air, repeatedly evading Fausto's grip, then dropped to the marble floor and scampered away as if nothing had happened.

Santos Ignacio was a very wise man and Sovrano was a very wise cat. The battle being waged was one in which Colonel Valdez had set the rules, but the conflict was stacked against Fausto, as he and Valdez did not fight for the same goal. The military man was fighting to humiliate his foe, but the young sea captain was fighting for his life. With no common objective, there were no common guidelines of conduct, nor would there be a sense of sportsmanship or even moral decorum between them.

Fausto realized that it was time to fight like Sovrano.

The young Caproni lunged forward, his blade intentionally missing the left flank of Valdez. The Spaniard fell for the feint and parried, bringing his sword arm across his front. That is when Fausto struck. Rather than deliver another forward strike with his blade, Fausto lowered his shoulder and charged. Valdez was unprepared for such an unsportsmanlike attack and the impact threw him against the taffrail of the sky cutter. Before the colonel could draw another breath, Fausto struck again. He delivered a blow with his fist across the Spaniard's face and Valdez folded forward in pain, only to receive Fausto's knee to his ribs.

Fausto was a blur of furious motion. At such close range, a sword was useless. He dropped it to the bamboo deck and relentlessly pounded his dazed opponent; a punch to the chest; a strike to the ear; an elbow driven between Valdez's shoulder blades. Gripping the back of the soldier's coat, Fausto pulled him from his teetering stance and swung him in a circle, sending Valdez tumbling across the unyielding bamboo flooring. Bloodied and disoriented, the Spaniard came to a rest beside the gondola and the lifeless body of Leonardo Ricci.

Marina had stood in silent admiration of Fausto's unleashed savagery, but as she watched Valdez tumble to a stop, her heart dropped. She had not yet noticed the body of Signore Ricci. The eternal gaze of regret carved into the bone-white face of the sweet old man etched itself forever in her memory. A flame of unbridled hate engulfed Marina and burned to her core.

"Kill him, Fausto!" she screamed in rage.

Fausto heard his sister's passionate outburst, but already was he rushing toward the downed officer. Bloodied and battered, Valdez had only a moment to gather his wits before Fausto was upon him again, but it was long enough for him to spy a halberd of one of his soldiers propped against the nearest bulwark. The Spaniard abandoned his rapier and scrambled away from the gondola to snatch the weapon from its resting place.

Before Valdez had an opportunity to swing the deadly weapon, Fausto lunged. Desperate instinct took over and Valdez managed to twist, avoiding the full weight of Fausto's body as it slammed against him. Valdez must have known that his death was imminent and began slashing with the halberd—left, right, left—barely missing Fausto with each swing. But the counterattack was enough to place the young captain on the defensive. Fausto found himself backstepping continuously as the axe smashed into the bamboo at his feet again and again.

Valdez pressed his advantage and took a wild horizontal swing with the weapon. Had Fausto not reacted as quickly as he did, the razor edge would have gutted him, rather than only carve a superficial wound across his bare chest.

The follow-through of Valdez's frenzied swing did far more damage than the cut to Fausto's breast. The halberd struck the rickety bamboo gondola, shattering one full side of the hastily constructed conveyance. Two of the four ropes that reached skyward to the netting holding fast the balloon now flapped in the Caspakian breeze. Even worse, the damage to the basket had resulted in the untethering of two of the four lines that held the balloon to the deck of the sky cutter and prevented it from ascending into the sky.

Even from where Marina stood, she could hear the sickly cracking of the two remaining tether lines, pulled taut by the great balloon's upward pull. The orientation of the hydrogen-filled envelope shifted awkwardly, tilting to one side as it began to slip loose from the wide netting that stabilized it. Within seconds, the Capronis' sole means of escape from the savage land would depart without them.

25
THE ULTIMATE SACRIFICE

S O ENGROSSED WAS FAUSTO by his duel with Colonel Valdez that he was unaware of the disastrous turn of events about to befall them all. With two of its retention ropes dangling freely, the balloon began to rise and roll beneath the webbing that contained it, and the bamboo gondola lifted from the deck of the *Pegaso II*.

Fausto dove away from the taffrail as Valdez's halberd cleaved through the bamboo construct, missing him by only inches. Fausto would likely have remained on his feet had he not been standing on an irregular surface tilted at a thirty-degree angle. But a slight miscalculation upset his balance, and he crashed to the deck.

"You delay the inevitable, you fool!" Valdez barked. Another overhead swing came down at Fausto, but he rolled away just in time to avoid the death blow.

Fausto continued his roll and gracefully leaped to his feet. He was now functioning on sheer adrenaline and took in great gulps of air whenever possible. His entire body was covered in sweat and every limb ached, but he would not relent. As he crouched, preparing to dodge the next swing of the razor-sharp halberd, he was elated to observe Valdez angrily pulling on the handle of the weapon to free it from the bamboo stalks that had been lashed together to compose the ship's deck. In a stroke of providence, the Spanish colonel's last attack had driven the halberd blade cleanly between two rods of bamboo where it now remained solidly wedged.

230

Fausto immediately capitalized on the unforeseen delay by charging at the distracted officer. He dove through the air, hitting his foe full-force. The impact tore the colonel's grip from the halberd, which remained embedded in the deck, and the two men crashed against the slanted bamboo surface. The tilt of the deck caused them to roll away from the fore of the ship where the gondola was secured.

As he slid, Fausto glanced toward the escape vessel. To his utter dismay, he found the bamboo basket was *not* secured. Only two ropes held it—and the balloon above it—to the deck. The other two ropes had been cut free, one held by Marina and the other by Tro-va, who were both fighting valiantly to pull downward on the restraints and prevent the balloon from escaping.

"Pull, Tro-va, *pull!*" Marina yelled as panic began to overtake her. She was not shouting in the language of Caspak, but she knew Tro-va was clever enough to interpret the meaning of her directions. They pulled with all their might, but the enormous balloon seemed intent on escaping, lifting them from the deck by a foot or two each time it bobbed in the air.

Marina thought they might reel in enough rope to secure the balloon to the deck, but tying the restraints to the mooring cleats would be a challenging endeavor at best. They would be fighting against the pull of a fully inflated balloon, and even worse, one cleat was missing after being ripped clean from the bamboo during Valdez's attack.

Fausto and Valdez rose wearily to their feet at the lowest end of the damaged sky cutter and began swinging at one another with abandon. Punch after punch landed on each of the men, and both were now bloodied, bruised, and exhausted. Fausto watched as Marina, desperately fighting with the rope, was pulled into the air, only for her feet to land once again upon the deck after Tro-va heaved with all of his might on the restraining rope in his grip. Fausto knew he only had seconds to act.

Gritting his teeth, he balled his fist and swung with every ounce of vitality remaining within him. The punch smashed into the face of Valdez. For a moment, the colonel stood there swaying, his eyes rolled up into his head and blood streaming from his nose. Then, with his mouth agape, he at last collapsed into a heap at the base of the aft bulwark.

Marina was again lifted from the deck, but the weight and muscles of the stone age warrior pulling against the other rope was sufficient to impede the balloon's upward momentum, and her feet again touched down.

"Fausto!" she yelled, unable to see her brother. "We can't hold the balloon!"

From the deck of the sky cutter came a cracking sound as another of the cleats was pulled from the bamboo flooring by one of the two remaining restraining ropes. Marina ducked as the metal fixture flung past her head. Now, with only one rope left to prevent the escape of the huge balloon, Marina and Tro-va were lifted into the air.

Marina screamed, "Fausto! Hurry!"

Before she could complete her warning, she began to descend, and the scrambling feet of Marina and Tro-va again made contact with the deck. She did not know why they had not soared into the sky until she looked to her right. There, Fausto gripped the third loose restraining rope, crouching in the feeble hope that doing so might somehow increase his weight.

"We can't hold it!" Marina yelled, but the explanation was unnecessary. The Sea of Grass swayed as a sudden draft of hot wind caused the top fringes of the sturdy plants to ripple toward the ship. The gust pushed the balloon sideways several feet, with Marina, Tro-va, and Fausto in tow. The single rope still fastened to the ship's deck whined in protest.

"Wrap your rope around you!" Fausto shouted. "We can do it without the gondola! Trust me, we can!"

Marina did as her brother instructed while Tro-va watched

in sad fascination. After checking the security of the knotted rope around her waist, she reluctantly looked into the eyes of the young warrior.

It was then that time seemed to stop around her. There were no visions of nightmarish creatures chasing her through the forest, no recollections of teeth ripping flesh, no remembrances of the deaths she had witnessed over the past week.

For Marina, all of the fear and stomach-churning dread that for days had lived within her was drained from her consciousness into the vacuum of nothingness. Every affectivity that had dominated her every waking minute on Caspak drifted away like a feather upon the wind, allowing but two burning emotions to rush to the fore of her awareness.

One of those emotions was heartache.

She looked deeply into Tro-va's dark eyes and knew what must be. To take Tro-va with them, to the *Redenzione*, to Palermo; to thrust this simple, caring individual into a world he could not comprehend would be the height of selfishness. She knew, within her breaking heart, that it could not be. She hoped that within him, he would understand.

Marina thrust herself toward the startled warrior and wrapped her arms around him, crushing her breast against his. Tro-va did the same, and all sound around her dissolved, leaving only the wild beating of her heart. She wished Tro-va's strong arms around her did not feel so good, but she could not deny the stirrings within her ushered forth by his touch. The cultured "Rose of Palermo" and the handsome warrior were both overcome by the moment, overcome by the inevitable that each had hoped would never be.

"I have to go back to my Galus," she said tearfully, then pressed her lips against his. They were only locked in their embrace for fleeting seconds but to Marina, it felt like a lifetime. As they kissed, she was awash in the euphoria of what could have been, and the bittersweetness of knowing those dreams would never be realized.

Fausto was silent as his sister and the warrior hesitantly

parted, still holding the hands of one another. Using the sword he had grabbed from the collection of weapons that slid to the rear of the ship during his battle with Valdez, he continued sawing at the last remaining rope that held the balloon to the sky cutter. With a snap, the hemp was severed, and the balloon began a slow rise into the air, the two passengers dangling precariously from the ropes beneath. As the balloon ascended, Marina's heart sank as Tro-va's hand slipped from her grasp.

"Ma-ree-na!" Tro-va shouted with great alarm from below. He pointed desperately toward the lowest end of the wreck.

Colonel Valdez stood shakily, peering down the barrel of one of his soldiers' discarded muskets. The weapon was not pointed at Marina or Fausto but at the glowing white balloon creeping in ascent. At such close range, with such a large target, Valdez could not possibly miss. Swept up in the madness of combat, the Spaniard was ready to doom them all to the prison of the fortress primeval.

Marina looked at Tro-va on the deck below them. The balloon was now at least thirty feet in the air and rising steadily. A fall from that height might kill her and Fausto if the balloon were to be punctured; if by chance it exploded, any hope of their survival was nil. She grasped for a plan, some last-ditch flash of genius that would save them. Equally exasperated, Fausto turned his head to Marina, and she knew from his expression that he was befuddled by what he saw.

As she clung to the rope with one hand, her other held the conch shell to her lips. She blew through it in short bursts, the hollow, shrill sounds filling the air and resounding across the Sea of Grass.

Marina anxiously scanned the green expanse, knowing that in less than a single pounding heartbeat Colonel Valdez would be staring into the face of death.

With massive force, the gigantic rear claw of the rava slammed down upon the deck of the sky cutter, shattering the fragile bamboo. Valdez was thrown backward as the ship's balance shifted when the full weight of the rava split the vessel in two. Valdez tumbled over the taffrail and to the cleared earth below. Somehow, he had kept hold of the musket.

"What did you just do?" Fausto shouted to Marina. "You called that thing . . ."

Marina smiled, her eyes wide with astonishment, for even she was surprised her impulsive act would have such shocking results. She shrugged. "Did I do that?" she said modestly.

Valdez leaped toward the stalks as the enraged rava flung its head in his direction. The grimace of the monster was nightmarish, its face and teeth smeared with the dark blood of the ko-oo on which it had gorged itself. The powerful hind legs of the giant crushed the bamboo beneath its immense bulk as it slowly trod forward in pursuit of the colonel. In what could only have been called futility, Valdez fired the musket at the huge predator, but the beast did not flinch. Instead, it flung wide its jaws and issued a thunderous bellow, then lunged forward.

From the ascending balloon, Marina and Fausto watched as Colonel Valdez was lifted from the ground, only his kicking legs visible beyond the knifelike fangs of the rava. The beast tipped its nose skyward, throwing the soldier into the air end over end, then snapped down upon him again, cleaving his body neatly in two, his bloody lower torso hitting the ground at the feet of the terrible lizard.

At their ever-increasing altitude, the wind was now whipping past the ears of Marina and Fausto. Both Capronis clung to the ropes as the landscape below them continued to recede.

"Do you see Tro-va?" Fausto shouted hopefully.

Marina scanned the field far below them as Fausto ensured that the venting lines were securely in their closed positions. "He jumped from the sky cutter when the rava attacked," she yelled. "I don't see him now. He disappeared into the stalks."

Fausto responded with assurance. "He'll be fine."

"I know," Marina said sadly. "And so will I." The tone with which she spoke was not exactly convincing.

Now hundreds of feet in the air, the balloon easily cleared the tall trees of the jungles and forests, the unusual but—for Caspak—natural outward-flowing air currents carrying them over the higher mountainous regions and toward the towering barrier cliffs that ringed the lost continent. Fortune smiled upon them; the prevailing wind was pushing them westward toward the waiting *Redenzione* on the other side of the sheer granite cliffs of Caspak.

Only five hundred more feet, then three hundred feet, then one hundred to go before the balloon cleared the wall behind which Marina and Fausto had nearly lost their lives, and where Santos Ignacio, Leonardo Ricci, and the rest of the crew of the *Pegaso II* would sleep for eternity.

"For Caspak's sake," Fausto said as the balloon passed the barrier wall, "we'll treat this as a dream that never really happened. We forget it all and never speak of it to anyone. But most of all . . ." He paused his thought. His next pronouncement would pain his sister, but Marina knew Fausto must say it, for both their sakes. "We must never return," he concluded.

Marina averted her eyes to look down at the oceanic expanse below them. "No, we must not," she said sadly.

Marina gazed one last time at the majestic splendor of the primitive world of Caspak; its mountains, valleys, and jungles; its vast plains and deserts; its immense central lake. All paled in comparison to one man who walked that primal landscape, one who had touched her heart. He was a man she would never see again.

He was a man with whom she had fallen in love.

EPILOGUE

ONE YEAR HAD PASSED since the balloon carrying the exhausted and desperate Caproni siblings splashed down into the icy waters of the South Pacific, just a mile north of where the *Redenzione* had kept vigilant watch for them over the preceding week. Even now, the horrors they had encountered in the interior of Caspak gave Marina nightmares. Fausto also admitted that gigantic reptiles occasionally haunted his dreams, where they chased him through primordial jungles. Bad dreams were a small price to pay for escaping with their lives.

The remainder of the voyage was an interesting undertaking. First, Fausto and Marina had to concoct a sound explanation for what had transpired during the flight of the *Pegaso II*. The crew and the remaining pair of Spanish soldiers who had stayed behind on the ship were told the *Pegaso II* had been swept far inland by high-altitude gale-force winds and had crashed on the flat, rocky surface of the dead continent of rock. All, save the Capronis, had unfortunately perished in the disaster. Fausto and Marina fictitiously recounted several days spent dragging one silk envelope, a vat, and the acid and iron filings the many miles back to the plateau's edge. There, they said, they had reinflated the balloon and embarked on their return voyage to the *Redenzione*. Marina had carefully hidden the tigers-tooth necklace given to her by Tro-va and explained that she had brought the conch with her from Palermo for good luck. That she possessed the beautiful shell was irrelevant to their story, and no one aboard the ship questioned her.

The *Redenzione* sailed from Caprona, but without Quartermaster Santos Ignacio and the astronomer Leonardo Ricci to guide him, Fausto had to assume the seabound duties of both of his dear, lost friends. He completely immersed himself in the additional responsibilities and performed those tasks admirably. Marina beamed with pride at the accomplishments of her brother. Fausto was now every bit the sea captain, as was his father, and his father before that.

Of utmost concern to Fausto was his contract with Queen Regent Maria Christina. After his infectiously optimistic pitch to the Spanish Court that previous spring, he did not want to return to Madrid empty-handed, so the voyage had continued as proposed. For the duration of the route, the two Spanish soldiers on board had expressed not a hint that they knew of Colonel Valdez's nefarious plot, but if they did, they wisely kept it to themselves.

As for the story of the strange continent they had encountered, Fausto had to employ several methods of discouragement among the crew. Sailors being sailors, unfounded rumors were easily disseminated among them. While it could not be denied that the ship had moored for a week beside a great rocky island, and Fausto had proclaimed it the lost continent of Caprona, it was easy enough to plant the seeds of doubt among the crew about what they had discovered at sea. As the ship sailed over the next several months, rumors circulated among the crew that the island was not the fabled Caprona, and the *Redenzione* had been thrown far off course and merely landed upon one of the many desolate rocky islands in the Antarctic Ocean. Fausto's approach with the Spanish soldiers was more direct; he warned them that should they speak a word of the strange land—or his embarrassing navigational mistake—he would reveal to all the true intentions of the Spaniards. He did not have to say another word, nor did they.

The *Redenzione* anchored at every known port of call

throughout the East Indies, if only for appearance's sake. With Marina at his side, Fausto pursued impressive negotiations with the leaders of thirteen existing Dutch colonial settlements at multiple ports, opening the door to future trade importation agreements with Spain.

After nearly nine months at sea, the *Redenzione* cruised into port at Valencia and the Capronis were granted an immediate audience before the Queen Regent. Although saddened by the loss of Colonel Valdez and his men, Maria Christina was heartened by the financial potential of the tentative deals with the Dutch and fulfilled her part of the bargain that she had struck with Fausto. Within the hour, three chests of silver *reales* were dispatched by royal courier and delivered to the cautiously guarded hold of the *Redenzione*. As it goes at the end of every oceanic expedition, the weary sailors were overwhelmed with joy when they returned to their home port and were paid for their diligent efforts and loyalty during the voyage.

That was one year ago.

Warm morning sunlight shone down on Palermo as Marina guided the horse-drawn wagon down the dirt path that terminated at the dockside quay. Before her, the waters of the Mediterranean lapped at the hull of the majestic *Redenzione*, the ship she had now come to love. After unloading the wagon of its burden of wooden crates full of lemons, she carried the wicker basket containing her four feline friends to the ship's gangway and released them. Sovrano and his three companions scampered into familiar surroundings in the hold, just as they had before each of the many voyages of the *Redenzione* over the past year. The grand old ship—and by extension, Captain Fausto Caproni—had made quite a name for itself in the last twelve months, embarking on one lucrative trade voyage after another around the Mediterranean.

Marina and Fausto had become quite busy with the burgeoning family shipping business. Although they spoke not a breath of their previous adventure to anyone, the remembrances of Caspak lingered around them like an unseen specter. For Marina, thoughts of what might have been haunted her every day and every night.

"Good morning!" Fausto called to Marina as he descended the ladder from the quarterdeck. He skipped the last few wooden stairs, jumped playfully to the deck, and gave his sister a comforting hug.

Marina looked at him with a mock scowl. "Another new uniform, I see," she said, brushing her hand over the shoulder of his bright olive waistcoat. "And a matching hat. Please try not to lose that one." Fausto chortled. "How much did all this cost?" she added suspiciously.

"We can afford it now, Marina."

His sister gave a spirited shove to his shoulder and said, "Don't let the family treasures go to your head, Your Excellency," but she was grinning. "You know, I've had a lot of fun on these trips, but I confess . . . I've gotten a bit bored with the same old ports around the Mediterranean."

Fausto laughed. "I know what you mean. I guess you can't wait for tomorrow morning," he said knowingly.

"It can't get here soon enough," she replied with a smile.

The siblings looked skyward. There, among the rigging of the *Redenzione*, the sailors worked ropes and pulleys to lower the large bamboo construction to the ship's deck. It appeared to be some manner of schooner with four round metallic vats firmly strapped to its topside.

"Are you all packed?" Fausto asked his sister.

Marina pulled the tiger's tooth necklace from under her blouse to lay over her chest and lifted the conch shell that hung from a leather strap around her shoulder. "I think I have everything."

"You know," Fausto said, smiling at the new sky cutter lying across the deck of the grand ship *Redenzione*, "we said we'd never go back."

"That's true," Marina said wistfully, "but if Caspak taught me anything, it's to never say 'never.'"

EDGAR RICE BURROUGHS UNIVERSE™

WeiRD WORLDS™

VOYAGE INTO TERROR

Transcribed and Retold by Mike Wolfer

BASED ON CAPTAIN CONOVER'S REPORTS
ARCHIVED AT THE OFFICES OF
EDGAR RICE BURROUGHS, INC.,
TARZANA, CALIFORNIA

ERB
INC.

PROLOGUE

MY NAME IS DOUGLAS WARREN CONOVER. When I'm on the clock, they call me Captain Conover, and in certain circles, I'm "Crash" Conover, which suits me just fine. Back in the Roaring Twenties, the nickname "Crash" made me a slightly better-than-average draw at barnstorming exhibitions across the United States. Yes, sir, people came from miles around to see the daring aerial exploits of "Crash" Conover, hoping I'd live up to my name and spread myself and my Curtiss JN-4D across the county fairgrounds in little bloody flaming bits. To the disappointment of spectators at my every performance, I never crashed. Not once. I'm too good a pilot. That's not bragging; I'm just that good.

For as long as I can remember, I've been fascinated by aviation. Soaring above the clouds has been my life's ambition. When I was a kid growing up in San Francisco, I was fascinated by newsreels of the aerial exploits of the U.S. Army's 103rd Aero Squadron operating out of France during World War I. Dreams of joining their heroic ranks filled my youthful head, but the armistice of November 11, 1918, ended World War I before I was old enough to be eligible for enlistment. My family wasn't exactly made of money, so without the free ride offered by the military, my dream of scraping together enough dough to pay for flying lessons and one day buying an aircraft of my own remained just that: a dream.

Over the course of the next year, I worked a string of un-remarkable odd jobs while I read and learned everything I could about aviation. If I couldn't fly, the least I could do was memorize all there was to know about airplanes, right down to each model's bolts, washers, and nuts. In 1920, I finally hit pay-dirt: I secured a job on the runway maintenance crew at the new Marina Air Field, which amounted to little more than the daily clearing of the unpaved landing strip of weeds and rocks. It was menial work, but at least I was right there to thrill to the takeoffs and landings of the JL-6 postal airplanes. In short order, through diligence and a lot of pleading, I was quickly promoted to a job in the hangar as an assistant mechanic. But I didn't stop there, and thanks to what was considered "on-the-job training," within a year I could tear apart and rebuild a JL-6 and pilot one as well.

Let me tell you, flying was everything I imagined it would be, and at seventeen, I knew what I'd be doing for the rest of my life. Upon achieving my dream, however, I soon realized that making mundane coast-to-coast flights to deliver the U.S. mail wasn't the action I craved.

That's when I fell in with a Southern California barnstorming troupe, most of whom had flown daring missions over Europe during World War I. Their stories were thrilling, full of excitement, adventure, and romance, which was exactly what I was looking for. Over the next five years, I soaked in every bit of knowledge I could from the greatest pilots to ever soar the skies, real seat-of-the-pants guys who were more than eager to pass the torch to the next generation of daredevil aeronauts. In exhibitions across the country and flying a spare JN-4D on loan from the troupe, I performed loops, rolls, stall turns, the whole shebang, and I was darned good at all of it. There was no doubt about it: Flying was what I was born to do.

Even as my fame and reputation soared, it all came crashing down when the traveling circuses were disbanded due to the Air Commerce Act, instituted by Congress in 1926. It took a couple years for the act to be enforced, so I kept flying as long as I could. When I touched down on the airstrip after my farewell performance in Santa Monica in the fall of 1928, things took a spin I did not see coming. One casual conversation with a show attendee would change my life forever.

I wasn't even out of the pilot's seat of my "Jenny" when a dapper gent, about my same age, and wearing a pinstripe suit excitedly approached my plane. He introduced himself as Jason Gridley and wanted to give me a tip on a job opportunity he thought would surely intrigue a now-unemployed pilot. He scribbled down the telephone number of a guy looking for a test pilot with a cast-iron disposition. Gridley certainly had me pegged.

The next morning, I called the number and spoke to a fellow named Bowen J. Tyler, Jr. It turned out Tyler was the head of Tyler Shipyards and Aeronautics, right there in Santa Monica, where a new airship was being designed and constructed under Gridley's direction. The codesigner of the ship was another fellow, an explorer named Erich von Harben who had discovered and mined a metal from Central Africa's Wiramwazi Mountains that's lighter than steel and a heck of a lot stronger, the metal used to construct the odd ship.

It was the second such vacuum airship to be made using the strange metal, the first being named the O-220, which had been built in Germany and modeled after a traditional zeppelin. The new aircraft was something else altogether. It's called the *Favonia*, the flying ship I am now captaining.

I explained all of that to explain all of this: I don't expect you to believe the accounts compiled in this ever-growing journal. Heck, I hardly believe them and I lived through them.

Barely.

The point I want to make is I'm a regular, everyday practical guy, not some daydreaming writer type prone to fanciful exaggeration. I tell it like it is because there's no other way to tell it. With that in mind, the journals of the crew of the *Favonia* will raise eyebrows, and it's quite likely you'll either think we're pulling your leg or we're all nuts. But that's okay by me;

I know what I've seen, and my crew will back me up on every bit of it, God bless 'em.

About my crew: I can honestly say that the members of the *Favonia* expeditions are the finest individuals it has ever been my pleasure to know. That includes the one who's not even from Earth. Yeah, you heard me right. But more on him later.

Because of the fantastic nature of our travels, I have instructed the crew members of every one of our flights to document our adventures in their own words to corroborate what we saw. At the insistence of Jason Gridley, copies of all of our accounts are turned over to Edgar Rice Burroughs, Inc., and are locked away in a safe in their offices. Gridley assured me that what we have witnessed is vital to science and the world. If anyone is qualified to become the guardian of that knowledge, it is the estate of the famed novelist.

What will become of our reports is anyone's guess. They might never again see the light of day. Or, as in the cases of Lord Greystoke, John Carter, and even Jason Gridley and Erich von Harben, the accounts of the crew of the *Favonia* might be collated, rewritten, and released to the public in the form of science-fiction novels by authors unknown, since Mr. Burroughs himself passed away back in 1950. If these tales are one day published, I fully expect our accounts to be fancified and the events exaggerated, because that's what writers and editors do. I'm also certain that much—if not all—of my salty language will be tossed right out the window. But I guarantee that whatever embellishments are made to our reports, no amount of crazy imagination can surpass what we saw with our own eyes. They say that truth is stranger than fiction. It's also much more terrifying.

If someone somewhere is reading this, you can go two ways with it. You can believe these tales—and even Captain Douglas Conover—are just figments of a writer's imagination. Or you can believe what you're reading are the actual accounts of actual events, witnessed by actual people. The choice is yours. But remember this: One day in the future the world will be advanced enough to accept and understand the fantastic realities of the dark horrors that infest our universe, just sitting out there in the blackness waiting for us, and in some cases, coming for us. And when that day arrives, you might look back on the chronicles of the *Favonia*, and you'll kick yourself for having had the incredible truth right before your eyes the whole time. That, of course, depends on whether these are undeniable facts or merely pulp fantasy.

I know for a fact which it is. What you think depends on how open you are to embracing the unbelievable.

Signed,
Captain Douglas W. Conover

The FAVONIA

DESIGNERS: ERICH VON HARBEN & JASON GRIDLEY
VESSEL CONSTRUCTED AT TYLER SHIPYARDS AND AERONAUTICS,
SANTA MONICA, CALIFORNIA, U.S.A.

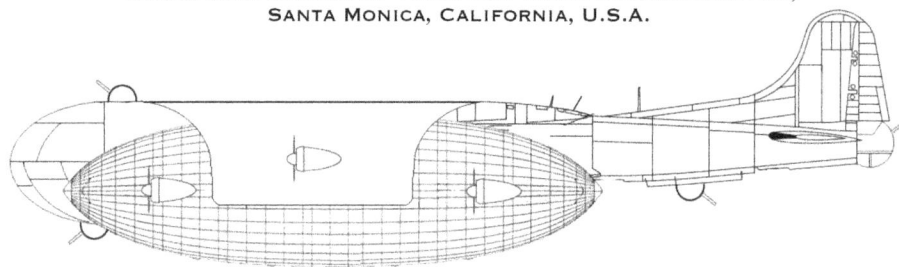

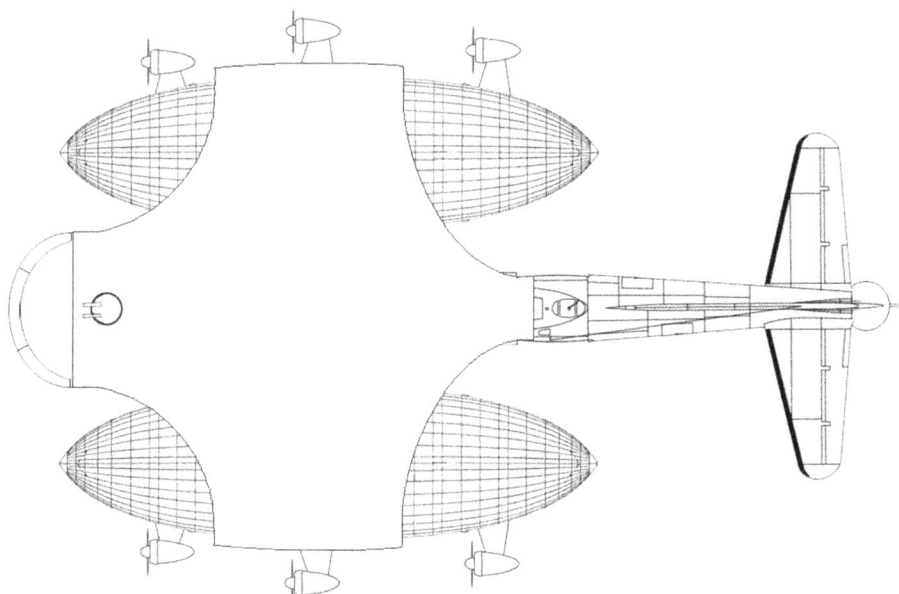

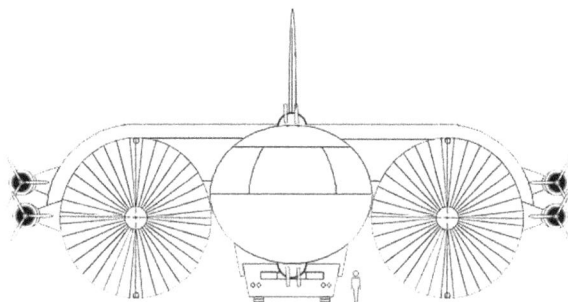

LENGTH: 158 FEET
WIDTH: 98 FEET
FUSELAGE HEIGHT: 38.5 FEET
HEIGHT OF TAIL: 47.5 FEET

The FAVONIA

Cargo Crawler

Autonomous all-terrain exploratory vehicle

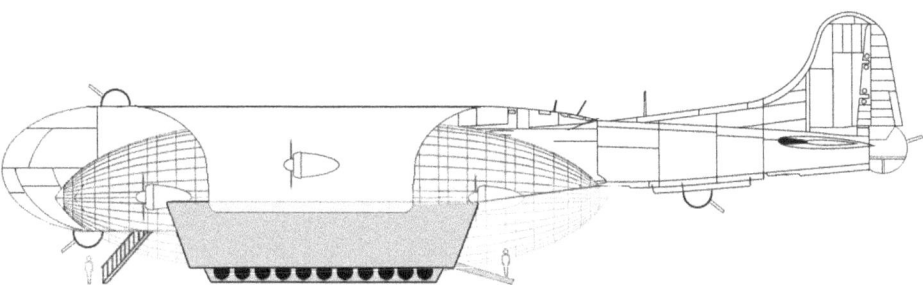

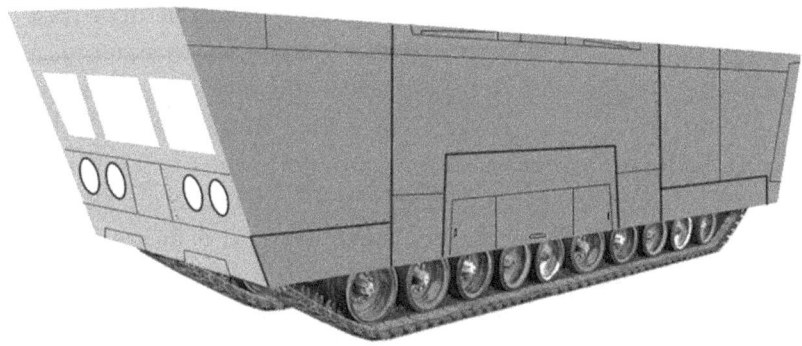

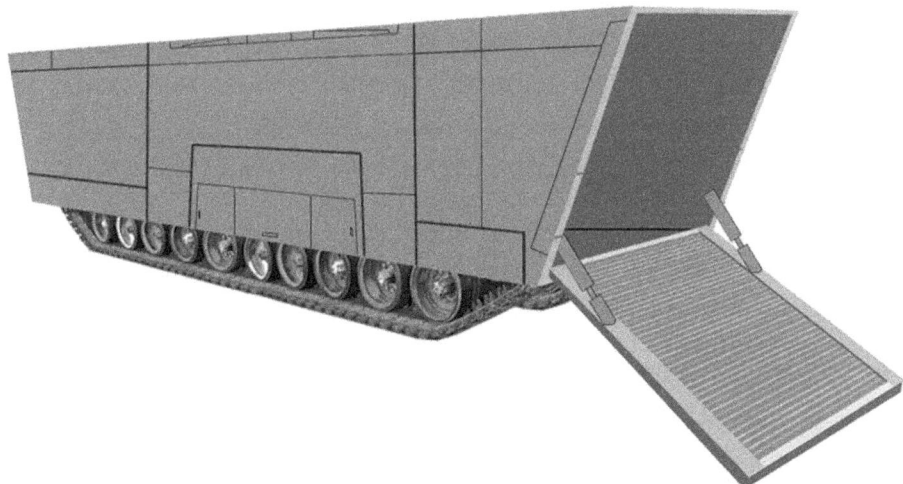

Length: 52 feet
Width: 16 feet
Total height: 15 feet
Cargo hold height: 12.5 feet

1
FLIGHT OF THE *FAVONIA*

CAPTAIN DOUGLAS CONOVER drew in a deep breath of contentment as he looked to the rising sun that had burned off the morning fog hours ago, and now rose high in the clear skies of Santa Monica. Those assembled on the tarmac of Tyler Shipyards and Aeronautics were grateful for the canvas tarp above their heads. Beneath the sun shade, the captain and crew gathered around two wooden picnic tables draped by cheery red-and-white checkered cloths. The smell of charcoal briquettes and lighter fluid wafted through the air, an inimitable scent that immediately conjured recollections of carefree summers past. There was plenty to eat, an assortment of cold macaroni and potato salads, boiled corn on the cob, and an ice chest filled with bottles of Coca-Cola. Tafari, the most recent addition to the *Favonia*'s small command team, cleared away several bowls to make room for the tray of barbecued kosher beef franks Captain Douglas Conover served to his fellow crew members, his friends.

"Dig in, men," Conover said, before adding, "and lady." Vivian Ouellet, seated next to her husband, smiled at the captain and tipped her head in acceptance of his cordial recognition of her.

Jerry Ouellet patted his wife's knee under the table. "I'm so excited for you, my dear. I don't even know if I can eat."

Vivian kissed his bearded cheek. "The day you're too nervous to eat is the day I fly to the moon," she laughed.

The Canadian mathematician smiled and looked behind him toward the open hangar doors one hundred yards to the east. "From what I understand, a trip to the moon would not be beyond statistical probability."

Jerry Ouellet was not far from the mark. None of the crew members gathered at the picnic to celebrate the pending embarkment of the vacuum airship *Favonia* had the slightest idea where the voyage the following morning would lead them. The *Favonia* loomed over the crew as they spent the next hour doing their best to clear the tables of everything edible. Who knew when they would next be able to enjoy such a relaxed afternoon? That thought alone—along with the unspoken fear that they might never enjoy *another* afternoon—instilled an undertone of nervousness into the entire celebratory gathering.

Tafari was the youngest member of the *Favonia's* team and began his attachment as a security soldier. Gagare, Tafari's father, had served alongside Security Chief Waranji in Africa at the right hand of John Clayton—the legendary Tarzan—and on the security team on the *Favonia*. Twenty-two years after a heroic sacrifice that led to Gagare's death in the prehistoric land of Pellucidar, Waranji's elite team in Santa Monica inducted Tafari into their group. Tafari was determined to follow in his revered father's footsteps. On the young warrior's first mission aboard the *Favonia* in 1952, he displayed an acute propensity for understanding the ship's advanced electronics and was soon after promoted to assistant avionics mechanic. Still, the young Waziri wore two hats and continued his duties on the security team under the command of Waranji. Tafari felt his acceptance of a safer job placement would betray Waranji and his five brothers-in-arms; thus, he was adamant that he continue his service among them. Even at the informal afternoon gathering, Tafari spent much of his time with his fellow warriors, laughing, joking, and enjoying the odd American delicacies served up by the head grill cook, Captain Conover. Tafari was a long way from his native Africa, but he was adjusting to American culture and customs.

One of Tafari's closest American friends was Aito Sato, the navigation and communications specialist aboard the *Favonia*. Aito was Nisei, an American-born Japanese man, whose parents had become naturalized United States citizens in 1907, with Aito arriving the following year to the proud new parents. In 1925, he enrolled at the University of Southern California, where after only one semester his exceptional electronics aptitude caught the attention of local industrialist Bowen J. Tyler, Jr. Upon graduation, Aito was offered a position at Tyler Shipyards and Aeronautics in Santa Monica to work on a top-secret project known only as "The *Favonia*," headed by young genius inventor Jason Gridley.

After the Japanese bombing of Pearl Harbor in 1941, thirty-three-year-old Aito, and his parents and younger sister living in Fresno, were forcibly removed from their homes. The Satos—along with all Americans of Japanese extraction—were considered potential espionage agents and the family was cruelly reunited in May 1942 at the Fresno internment camp, whitewashed with the gentler title of "assembly center." Conover and Tyler did everything in their power to prevent the family's unjust incarceration. Their efforts were for naught against the might of the United States government at wartime. The Sato family languished in the camp for four months before its closure, after which they were transferred to the Jerome facility in Denson, Arkansas, before being uprooted, yet again, and shipped off to the assembly center in Rivers, Arizona. There they remained until the camp's closure in November 1945. For nearly four years, the Sato family had endured the humiliation and uncertainty of their imprisonment, but never did they surrender their pride.

Despite being warned not to return to California by fellow detainees and even government officials, the Sato family did just that and resettled in Fresno. The streets of their old hometown no longer seemed familiar, as snide insults from passersby on sidewalks and suspicious glares from store windows barely concealed the townspeople's hatred of them. Aito fared better than his family, as he resumed his duties at Tyler Shipyards and Aeronautics, reuniting with Douglas Conover after the captain's daring and patriotic exploits as a U.S. Air Force pilot during World War II. Although Aito rarely admitted it, he was deeply hurt by the bigotry heaped upon him and his family due to their ancestry, but none in the Sato family would be broken and all walked with heads held high.

"Are you nervous about the voyage?" Tafari asked Aito as they stood together at the end of one of the picnic tables.

Aito took a swig from his bottle of soda and contemplated his friend's question. "I'm excited about what we might find and where we might go, but nervous?" He grinned. "You bet I am. After that trip last year, I'd be a fool not to be nervous," he added with a laugh.

At the mention of the past excursion, both men turned their heads toward a fellow crew member who sat quietly, contemplating a hot dog as if he had never seen one before. The truth was, he had not.

Brahk Zahla lifted his paper plate to eye level and examined the charred tube of meat nestled within the bread envelope. Displeased but much too polite to make a show of it, he shook his head only slightly and placed the plate back on the table.

"You gonna eat that?" Nathan "Weino" Weinberg asked. The team's chief avionics mechanic reached for the plate before the unearthly being could answer.

"I have learned much about Earth," Brahk admitted, "but contrary to my best efforts I still cannot bring myself to eat some of the delicacies of your people." He winced as he watched Nathan happily take a bite of the hot dog, then another. "Why you Earth beings destroy your food by carbonizing its outer skin before consuming it is beyond my understanding."

Over the past year since Brahk Zahla joined the crew of the *Favonia*, the Rolodon Xinnar (the words denoting his tribe and species) had diligently studied the English language and by now did not need the small electronic translation device his people regularly wore in their ears on his home planet of Odon. Tafari and Aito might have faced difficulties assimilating into California life, but their plight was nothing compared to that of a being from outer space. Notwithstanding Brahk's odd facial configuration, his pale moss-green skin was a dead giveaway that he was not of this Earth.

The crew's first meeting with Brahk Zahla had nearly cost all of them their lives. Jane Porter, Director of Archaeological and Zoological Field Studies at the Robeson Museum of Natural History in Baltimore, had requested the services of Captain Conover and the *Favonia* in late February 1952. The assignment was simple: Transport three recently revived prehistoric megafauna to Pellucidar, a savage land resembling their home from eons past. The *Favonia* was equipped with a "skeleton key" device created by young quantum physicist Victory Harben that would allow the ship to traverse the mysterious field permeating the space-time continuum that lay between our realm and that of Jasoom, an alternate-dimension Earth whose hollow core was host to the fantastic world of Pellucidar. However, delivering the woolly mammoth and two smilodons to the prehistoric land where they would thrive was fraught with unexpected danger.

As the *Favonia* passed through the dimensional passage opened by the Gridley Wave skeleton key, an unknown anomaly caused the ship to travel not to Jasoom, but to a strange world elsewhere in the adjoining universe. On the planet later identified as Odon, Captain Conover and Aito found they could not reopen the sealed "doorway" to return to Earth, and the entire crew soon became embroiled in a conflict between two warring factions, the Rolodon Xinnars and the Valodon Xinnars. They did not know who was fighting, or why, or if they should even choose sides. Just as a fleet of Rolodon airships decimated the evil Valodons in a massive bombing run, the *Favonia* lifted off, and it was only through the assistance of Tafari that Aito unscrambled the fouled Gridley Wave skeleton key, enabling the Earthlings to escape to their home planet.

With them traveled Brahk Zahla, a Rolodon Xinnar scientist who had seen enough of war and strife, and longed to explore the wonders of the universe. The physical characteristics of Rolodons were not far removed from those of humans; Captain Conover had noted that perhaps the Xinnar species *was* human, just a different make and model from that found on Earth, as it were. Although Brahk's hair was dark green, he had two arms, two legs, and the same skeletal and muscular frame as an average human male. That was where the similarities ended. The bony beak-like covering over his nose, the two triangular plate-like protrusions that extended down from his cheeks on each side of his mouth, and his large, glassy green eyes devoid of irises were the features that unavoidably denoted his alien heritage. However, most of the crew quickly grew to overlook the striking physical characteristics of the athletically built alien scientist and accepted him as one of their own. How could they not? Based on the wide array of backgrounds the crew encompassed, they were a hearty mix of cultures and ethnicities, and the being from another world fit in swimmingly.

Nathan wiped his mouth with the back of his hand after downing a Coca-Cola. He called over to Conover. "Hey, Cap . . . You gonna break out the hard stuff at this shindig?"

Conover shook his head like a teacher disappointed by a student on a school playground. "Oh, no. I'm not letting this get out of hand. Not again." He tossed his cooking apron to the brash mechanic from Flatbush, Brooklyn. "Front and center, Weino. You're up on the grill."

"Aye, aye, Captain," Nathan chimed. He took a few steps

toward where Brahk Zahla sat, then stopped and walked around the other side of the table and over to the grill.

Vivian watched Nathan's change of course and whispered to her husband. "You see?" she said cryptically. Conover was aware that all at the gathering knew of Nathan's unease with the team's alien crewman. Going out of his way to avoid even the most minimal contact with the Rolodon Xinnar was standard behavior for the New York native. Nathan donned the apron and snapped the barbecue tongs in the air a few times before flipping the hot dogs roasting over the coals.

"New round of dogs comin' right up," Nathan proclaimed.

Harmony among the members of his crew was always a paramount concern for Conover, so he was heartened when Waranji moved behind the seated green-skinned man and placed both hands on his shoulders in a show of friendship. "Foreign foods take some getting used to, do they not?" he laughed.

Brahk smiled and shook his head. "They do, but I find understanding the logic behind your planet's customs an even more daunting task. For example, I have learned of the unusual Earth concept of keeping dogs as companions," he went on, his deep voice tinged with confusion, "so I do not understand why you would eat them."

Vivian raised a hand to her mouth to stifle a giggle. The *Favonia*'s crew and Brahk Zahla still had much to learn about one another, at least those who cared to learn. Not one to hide his feelings, Nathan scoffed audibly at Brahk's misunderstanding of the composition of a hot dog.

Ever the vigilant captain, Conover knew his crew well, except for Vivian Ouellet, who had visited the Tyler facility in Santa Monica on only a handful of occasions, during her interview and security assessment period. Among the others, Waranji and Aito had the longest tenures aboard the *Favonia*, their service under Conover's command dating back to the ship's first extended flight in 1930. That mission met with unfortunate disaster in the land of Pellucidar. It was on that voyage that Tafari's father, Gagare, had lost his life while his son was still an infant.

"It's too bad you weren't on that mission to Pellucidar back in '30," Conover said to Nathan, keeping his voice low to prevent the others from hearing. "We sure could have used an A-1 grease monkey like you when the ship's tail had the structural failure."

Nathan muttered an unintelligible reply that hovered somewhere between a thank-you, self-deprecation, and flattery.

"We have a good team," Conover said. "When I was a kid, me and my older brother didn't see eye to eye on very much. We were always squabbling about something or other. You know how kids are." The captain wasn't looking for a conversation; he was delivering another of his gentle lectures. "One time when I was eight, my brother—Billy his name was—planned to go fishing and I wanted to tag along. Billy didn't want to be weighed down by an annoying little brother, but my parents made him take me with him. So we went. Had a good time. Until I splashed him with mud, and he hauled off and walloped me one, and knocked me on my keister in the same mud puddle. That was our relationship; I constantly annoyed him and he'd whack me one good." From the confused look on Nathan's face, it was obvious he had no idea where the story was going. Conover continued. "On our way home, me covered with mud, we had to cross the street car tracks. I rushed ahead, right in front of an oncoming street car. And my brother, who had earlier punched the daylights out of me, charged at me and pushed me out of the way. That son-of-a-gun saved my life. But he didn't make it," he said ominously.

Nathan's face paled. "Jeez, Cap, I didn't know . . ."

Conover laughed. "Oh, he was fine. Just got clipped by the car and ended up with a broken leg. Had a limp for the rest of his life from it. But that's what brothers do for one another, Weino." Conover looked purposefully in the direction of Brahk, who was grimacing after taking a gulp of the odd carbonated drink the others called Coke. "We've got a pretty good band of brothers right here." The point of his story made clear, Conover squinted up at the morning sun and said no more.

Nathan smirked, returning his attention to the roasting hot dogs. "I hear you, Captain," he said robotically. Conover made a mental note of Nathan's unconvincing response, gave him a reaffirming pat on the back, and rejoined the rest of the crew in their farewell gathering. With luck on their side, they would soon celebrate their welcome home.

The deep icy blue of the Arctic Ocean rippled as if in slow motion, its surface undulating as it had for millennia. The sun was now high overhead, casting the shadow of the *Favonia* upon the foam-flecked crests below. Following Conover's strict timetable, the ship was impeccably on schedule and would reach the coordinates of its target location within minutes.

Nothing gliding through the Earth's skies was anything like the *Favonia*. The massive flying vehicle resembled a military bomber, with a fuselage measuring one hundred and fifty-eight feet, roughly the length of a U.S. Air Force B-52. The forward third of the ship widened considerably to twice the width of the main cabin, with a wide horizontal window stretching across its front to provide a panoramic view to those in the auditorium-like bridge area. Beneath the wings and attached to the hull were two huge envelopes containing the vacuum tanks, one port, one starboard, each two-thirds of the ship's length. The *Favonia*'s wings curled downward around the envelopes, like a parent tightly hugging its children. Mounted along the lengths of each envelope were three twelve-hundred-horsepower turboprop engines, upgraded from radial engines after World War II. The propellers generated considerable thrust for directional maneuvering, leaving the ascension of the fantastic vehicle to the twin vacuum tanks. Those alone gave the *Favonia* its lift, allowing the ship to reach altitudes of up to twenty thousand feet as the propellers actuated its forward momentum and changed the vehicle's course, even rotating it in place as it hovered.

Without Harbenite, however, the fantastic ship could never have left the ground because of its weight, nor could the vacuum tanks have withstood the exterior atmospheric pressure without collapsing. The ultra-strong, extremely lightweight metal of which it was constructed was the *Favonia*'s great secret, one that Erich von Harben could have exploited for personal gain, but never did he reveal the existence of the exceedingly rare metal to the public or the manufacturing community. The very thought of enemy nations filling the Earth's skies with nearly indestructible fighter planes—not to mention the metal's scarcity—ensured that Harbenite's use was relegated to inventions designed by Jason Gridley and Erich von Harben, whose wife was the namesake of the majestic airship *Favonia*.

At the fore of the ship, Vivian, Waranji, and Tafari drank in the splendor of the vast Arctic Ocean. They stood before the transparent Harbenite shield that wrapped around the nose of the *Favonia* and curved to either side of them like a great warped drive-in movie screen. Twenty feet behind them rose a dais-like platform, atop which Captain Conover and Aito sat at the ship's twin pilot seats, surrounded by banks of dials, gauges, radar screens, and controls. Brahk Zahla stood diligently behind them, absorbing their every word, memorizing every flipped switch, every knob adjustment. His fascination with earthly mechanisms was boundless.

"It's so beautiful," Vivian remarked, transfixed by the undulation of the waves below them. "How many times have you made this kind of trip, Waranji?" she asked the tall warrior dressed in his uniform of khaki shorts and shirt.

"I stopped counting after the first ten or so voyages," Waranji admitted. Vivian looked at him, perplexed by his answer.

260 WEIRD WORLDS: VOYAGE INTO TERROR

He explained. "My life has been quite full. I have divided my time between my duties in Santa Monica; spending time with my people, the Waziri tribe in East Africa; and extended periods in Pellucidar. Because of this, I have developed a unique view of life. Most of us fixate on numbers. Increments. Minutes, hours, days, years. As a result of my time in Pellucidar, I focus on the totality of my experience, rather than how many events make up that experience. Abner Perry calls it 'salient wisdom.'" Vivian's look of confusion urged Waranji to explain further. "You see, time passes strangely in Pellucidar, much slower than on the surface, on Earth."

"Yes, Captain Conover mentioned that to me," Vivian said. "The eternal daylight would account for that, or at least for a distortion of the human perception of the passage of time."

Waranji's smirk was in no way condescending. "It is far more than just perception. How old would you say I am?"

Vivian looked him up and down, pursed her lips, and answered. "I'd say maybe thirty?"

"I am fifty-three years old."

"You look great for your age," Vivian replied, surprised by his admission.

Waranji smiled, then turned toward the cockpit platform. "What about Aito?"

She thought for a moment. "No more than twenty-five?" she guessed.

"Aito Sato is forty-five years old."

Vivian absorbed what he had said and reshaped it into a statement that made no sense to her, even as she spoke it. "Spending time in Pellucidar impacts the aging process."

Waranji looked out at the vast blue under the midday sun. "Abner Perry and Jason Gridley have both tried to explain it to me. I'm afraid I am more adept with a rifle or a bow than advanced scientific principles." He glanced at Vivian, a bit forlornly. "I have spent what seemed like one month in Pellucidar, only to return to find my friends and family have aged years. And so," he concluded, "I will maximize every moment that I draw breath to give meaning to that which has no true meaning: time."

Vivian looked out at the waves, thoughtfully absorbing Waranji's message. Suddenly, her mind became awash in panic. "My husband, Jerry," she said, as realization dawned on her. "When we return, what if . . ."

Tafari respectfully interjected a comforting thought. "But we are not traveling to Pellucidar, Dr. Ouellet," he reminded her.

She nodded, then looked into Waranji's dark eyes. "Let's hope that wherever we end up, one day does not equal one hundred years on Earth." Vivian Ouellet sighed but would not let her imagination run wild. When she signed on to Conover's team, she had known the journey held great risk. Despite that, her husband Jerry had encouraged her to join the expedition. Now, she thought back to last night, to how they had held each other for hours without speaking. His strength was all the encouragement Vivian needed to dispel any last-minute hesitation and now here she was, aboard the *Favonia*, flying into the unknown. She straightened her posture and her boot heels clicked on the polished flooring as she strode to the piloting platform.

"Okay, Captain," Aito said eagerly as he leaned forward toward one of the radar screens before him. "Dead ahead, two thousand feet." Vivian and Brahk Zahla both inched closer to the pilots' seats behind which they were standing. Both were equally excited about the mysteries their journey would soon unveil to the crew.

"Let me put it into park," Conover said casually as he cut the power to all but Starboard Engine One. Through the assistance of the tail rudder, the *Favonia* slowly turned to port from its present course. As the airship banked, power to the propeller was reduced to decrease its rotation speed, and by the time the *Favonia* made a full circle, all forward momentum had ceased. The great gray vessel hovered silently at seven hundred and fifty feet above the icy waters.

Vivian strained to identify the target for which they had searched. "I don't see anything," she said in vexation.

"You won't, Doctor," Aito responded. "But trust me." He tapped the blue blip on the screen to his left. "It's right in front of us."

"What's next, Captain Conover?" Vivian asked. "The new girl on the team could use a refresher." Although she had been fully briefed on every aspect of the mission, she had absorbed the information in only two short weeks. Her years of study as a botanist had taught her that it was one thing to read about a process in a manual, whereas performing that process in the wild could be an altogether different experience.

Conover removed his ubiquitous captain's hat, smoothed his wild light brown hair, and secured his cap on his head. "The first thing we do is send out a probe. Aito? You want to embellish on that?"

"Sure, Captain," Aito said. "The process is a bit complicated, but I'll keep it simple. Hanging out there in the air in front of us is what you might call a doorway, or more accurately, a liminal field. It's a weak point, of sorts, between our dimension—Victory Harben would call it our *angle*— and . . . others. In our past travels to Pellucidar, we always locked onto Gridley Wave radio transmissions from the city of Sari, and followed those as we passed through the field. Like following a trail of breadcrumbs. But a year ago, quite by accident, we discovered that other natural emanations— what the Barsoomians call planetary and solar rays—radiate from parts unknown throughout our universe. Jason Gridley and I devised a means to upgrade the *Favonia*'s apparatus to detect not only Gridley Wave transmissions, but also the emanations of planetary and solar rays. If our onboard device locks onto one of those natural emanations as we go through the liminal field, we'll travel not to Pellucidar, but to the source of the planetary or solar ray, wherever that may be. That's how we found ourselves on Brahk's home planet of Odon, albeit quite by accident that time."

Vivian tipped her head to acknowledge that she understood. "What about the 'skeleton key,' as you call it?"

"That's also something new," Conover replied. "As you're well aware, only a handful of people on Earth know about Pellucidar and we keep it a closely guarded secret. It's a very fragile world just ripe for plundering if the wrong people stumble upon the passageway to their front door. So Victory Harben and Jason Gridley worked out a means to lock down the field, and only we have the skeleton key doohickey to open it. That's pretty much how that works, right, Aito?"

"Pretty much." Aito turned so his captain could not see his face and shot a furtive grin at Vivian.

The botanist picked up the conversation from where Conover had left it. "If I remember correctly, the probe will approach the field, lock onto a planetary or solar ray—or even a Gridley Wave, if one is being transmitted—and then pass through to . . . wherever."

"Right," Aito affirmed, "and it will gather atmospheric samples for Brahk and me to analyze. The probe also contains two cameras that will take photographs, which Tafari will develop and print."

"If we didn't use the probe," Conover said, "we could find ourselves five miles underwater in some ocean somewhere, or in the middle of an erupting volcano. I don't think the *Favonia*'s insurance covers that." With that, the captain stood, pressed a headset to one ear, and held down a button on the pilots' console. "Weino, you reading me?"

"Loud and clear, Captain."

"You might have guessed we're at the coordinates," Conover told him. "Go ahead and send out a bug."

In a cramped avionics compartment on the underside curve of the *Favonia*'s nose, Nathan went to work. With practiced precision, he placed the basketball-sized device on the feeding tray that extended from an opened circular hatch on the ship's hull. He tested the connections of the insulated wire bundle attached to the underside of the metal sphere. All was secure. With the flick of a switch, the tray retracted within the fuselage wall. He closed the hatch, careful to ensure that the long black cord was within the cutout notch on the bottom edge of the door, and spun the lock shut. After retrieving a handheld control module, Nathan spun his chair to face the small port window and toggled the device's power switch to the "on" position.

On the exterior of the *Favonia*'s nose, a circular hatch slid open and the feeding tray rolled out. On it sat the silver globe. With the flick of another switch, Nathan activated the propellers on the top and rear of the globe and the strange gyrocopter lifted from the tray and floated away from the ship, trailing the black cord bundle behind it.

From the windscreen of the command center, Tafari and Waranji watched the device move away from the ship. Because of the two round camera lenses mounted on the front of the probe, Conover had dubbed the devices "bugs," as they reminded him of fat, metal insects.

"The bug's away, Captain," Nathan's voice crackled over the ship's intercom. Vivian and Brahk joined the two Waziri warriors at the transparent Harbenite windscreen, the innovation of mechanical-engineering whiz Stanley Moritz. As one, the members of the group held their breaths in anticipation.

Nathan toggled the twin sticks on the handheld remote-control unit, its wires feeding through the umbilical cord attached to the underside of the "bug." The probe ventured farther from the ship and into the frigid winds of the Arctic region. The bug veered left and right, ascending and descending, ever searching. Vivian's eyes widened as, inexplicably, the probe vanished into thin air, yet the black tether trailing behind it was still visible, leading outward from the ship and into complete nothingness.

Nathan's staticky voice echoed through the cabin. "Found it!" he announced, although all could see that the probe had stumbled through the invisible weak spot between the angles. Now that the weak point in the field had been located, Nathan reversed the probe's course and it reappeared as its propeller carried it back into the *Favonia*'s realm.

On the bridge, Aito had donned his headset and was acutely focused on a glowing blue screen on his console. At the center of the screen danced a jumble of skittering, jittering white lines, all fused into a violently swirling tumbleweed of electricity. He adjusted several slider knobs beside the screen, the effect of which caused the lines to separate into individual waveforms. Each line represented a different emanation identified by the probe. In the lower forward cabin, Nathan's eyes were on an identical display.

Conover anxiously watched over Aito's shoulder. "Now it's just a matter of picking one," he mused. "Which one's the Gridley Wave emanating from Sari?"

"This one," Aito responded, pointing to the strongest waveform at the bottom of the display.

"My lucky number's always been three, so let's go with the third one from the top."

In his flight journal, Aito logged the parameters of the emanation picked by Conover and relayed the message to Nathan. The mechanic wrote notes in his journal, adjusted the dials on the remote control unit, and transmitted the information through the long black wire bundle to the hovering "bug." The spherical gyrocopter proceeded again until it disappeared through the invisible veil.

On the command deck, Vivian, Waranji, Tafari, and Brahk now stood anxiously behind the chairs of Captain Conover and Aito. After only a few minutes, Nathan's voice again crackled over the speaker. "Bug recaptured successfully, Captain!"

Nathan rushed the recovered probe to the *Favonia*'s lab. Aito and Brahk immediately began analyzing the collected atmospheric samples using scientific principles and apparatus that commingled Earth and Xinnar technology. In the adjoining darkroom, Tafari developed the two rolls of color film, printed contact sheets, and then enlarged several prints that were hung briefly and fed into the dryer. Together, the four men reported to Captain Conover and the others on the command deck, who had been waiting anxiously for the past hour.

"Will you look at that!" Nathan exclaimed as the crew looked upon the photographs spread before them. "Ain't that somethin'!" he added in his thick Brooklyn accent.

The photographs revealed an alien vista, seen from the perspective of the probe's twin cameras. It was a smooth, perfectly flat plain of vivid pink, woven with patches that ran to nearly orange. The horizon was demarked by a cerulean belt that rose into the air before dissipating, indicating a planetary atmosphere, and above that sparkled a galaxy of twinkling stars lying in the vast arms of a purple-and-green celestial nebula.

Conover spoke quietly as the others tried to digest what they were seeing. "The atmosphere readings?"

Aito opened his journal and dictated what he and Brahk had deduced. He explained that the planetoid's atmosphere was primarily composed of carbon dioxide, followed by nitrogen, and only eight percent oxygen. The collected sample contained water vapor, also visible as condensation on the camera lenses of the "bug." Finally, the Xinnarian equivalent of a torsion balance, constructed by Brahk and installed within the probe, indicated the planetoid's gravity was roughly one-third that of Earth.

Captain Conover slapped his hands against his knees and turned to address those behind him. "Okay, crew. It's briefing time."

2
THROUGH THE ANGLES

ONOVER HAD COMPLETE CONFIDENCE in his crew, but
his years of experience as a ship's captain had taught him
that a good, stern, preparatory lecture never hurt. While
each team member had duties preordained and was quite
efficient in fulfilling them individually, he reasoned that all
would benefit from a detailed overview of the entire mission;
each cog had its specific function, but all must work in unison
to achieve the greater objective. If any of them already knew
some of the details and found them boring, that individual
would just have to grin and bear it.

Aito maintained surveillance of the ship's controls while
the rest of the crew sat attentively in the jump seats installed
around the bottom perimeter of the control platform. Before
them, Captain Conover stood passively, his hands behind his
back, as he reiterated the specifics of the mission.

"Okay, folks, here's the rundown." Conover knew his casual
demeanor was in direct contrast to the fantastic thrill that
surged through all present, emotions barely kept in check by
a healthy dose of fear of the unknown. "A year ago, this ship
did the incredible. It traveled to another world, completely
by accident. Today, we're doing it again, but this time with
specific intent. We've located the liminal field, identified the
signals coming through, and tuned in to one of them. The
bug we sent through shows a relatively benign environment.
The atmosphere isn't breathable, but the renovations we've
done to the *Favonia* will keep it airtight and pressurized.

267

If—and I stress, if—we take a walk, we'll need to break out the bumblebee suits."

"Each of you has your assignment. Tafari, our resident photographer, will take photos of the entire sky and the stars and constellations so that we may pinpoint the planetoid's location when we get back. If the surface is determined to be safe, Vivian will collect any possible soil and plant samples for later examination. In addition to being a botanist, Mrs. Ouellet has a medical degree, just in case . . ." Conover paused. "Well, she'll handle any cuts or scrapes if it comes to that. But do me a favor: Let's try to not have any accidents." The crew chuckled nervously.

"If we do go outside the ship, Mr. Weinberg will set up a Gridley Wave beacon, which is our way of marking the planetoid to either lead us back at some time in the future or warn us to stay very far away. Our security—our *only* security—is Waranji and Tafari. I might make most of the decisions on this ship, but no matter what I say, Waranji overrules me when it comes to safety." All in the room looked to the security chief and nodded in appreciation and recognition of his stature. Before embarking from Santa Monica, Conover had conferred with Waranji and together they decided the five-man security team would stay behind on this first mission to test the *Favonia*'s new apparatus. Waranji explained he would not expose his men to the unnameable threats they might encounter on this initial exploratory jaunt, even if facing danger was their job. Conover had heartily agreed. The security team would accompany the crew on subsequent missions, but for this first test of the *Favonia*'s new capabilities and navigational equipment, it was best to mitigate any possible losses. And so Waranji had ordered his men to remain in California, with only Tafari and him making the trip.

"One other note about security," Conover continued. "What we encountered on Odon, being caught in a battle between two warring humanoid peoples . . . that was probably a fluke. If the laws of probability hold any weight, it's unlikely that we'll again encounter intelligent life, or any life, for that matter. But just in case, you've all had your training on the .50 calibers, and Waranji will determine if they're used. Remember: We're on a scientific mission, a peaceful mission, and no matter what we find, we should make our best effort not to upset the locals, no matter what they are. Unless"—he smiled at Waranji—"our security chief says so. Got it?"

All present nodded and replied in the affirmative.

Conover pulled a silver flask from a pocket of his leather bomber jacket and twisted off the cap. He held it up, toasting his crew. "Safe travels to the brave souls who are the heart of the *Favonia*." With that, he took a swig. In succession, each of the crew took a sip and passed the flask onward. Brahk Zahla abstained from tasting the Earthly intoxicant, and the flask ended its journey in the hands of Vivian.

She sniffed the contents, smiled at the others, and said, "Here's to leaving 1953 . . . and returning to 1953." Knowing the whiskey was harsh, Conover was impressed that Vivian's reaction to her sip indicated that she had tasted stronger in her life. She handed the flask to the captain with a smile, seemingly unfazed by the gulp she had taken of its contents.

"What do you say?" Conover spread his arms wide. "Shall we pay a visit to Mystery Planet Number One?" The crew's response was unanimous, and the sounds of safety belts clicking in place resounded in the cavernous compartment as Conover trotted up the metal steps of the dais to join Aito at the controls. He could see nothing but blue sky and sunshine ahead of the *Favonia*.

"Brahk Zahla, I have a question," Vivian said to her green-skinned companion, who was seated next to her.

"Yes, Dr. Vivian Ouellet?"

"Let's not be so formal. Please, call me Vivian," she said gently. There was an innocent naivete about Brahk, Vivian thought, but the depth of his scientific focus quickly affirmed his value to the team. His large, green eyes reminded her of a cuddly cartoon character, but anecdotes of his prowess as a warrior shared by Waranji told her not to underestimate Brahk due to his casual demeanor.

"And you can call me Brahk," he replied, smiling. "What is your question?"

She narrowed her eyes a bit. "Just how big is the liminal field we will pass through? This is an awfully large vessel, after all."

Brahk briefly put his index fingers on each side of the beak-like covering over his nose and touched his thumbs together below his chin. This was a Rolodon cultural trait that signified the speaker was about to make a factual statement based on scientific evidence. "From the information I have collated, the 'doorway' is not a doorway, as we know it. It has no dimensions of height, width, or depth."

"I see." It was a confounding concept. "But continue, please."

He smiled. "Think of the substance you call oil when it is poured upon water. The structural integrity of the oil pool fluctuates, depending on the turbulence of the water's surface. In this metaphor, the thinning of the dimensional wall between realms is represented by the oil, and the matter within each realm is the water, two pools of ever-shifting water, one butting against the other. Thus, if the liminal field were visible, it would have no definite form, or size, for that matter; it would be unstable due to the shifting of the two planes of cohesive matter upon which it adheres."

"Still, how can the field accommodate the entire ship?" she asked.

"When we walk through a doorway from one room to another," he explained, "our physical form appears not to change. However, on a subatomic level, many changes *do* occur, based on such things as room temperature, air pressure, and the like. But outwardly, on a macrolevel, it would appear as if our physical form does not change. In the case of inter-angular travel, it is much the same in principle, although quite more complicated. A resonance between the angles—that is, the dimensions—occurs. The molecular structure of the entire ship, and everything and everyone within, is realigned with the spacetime continuum of the new angle. The energy of which you or I or this ship is composed is not so much transported through space and time as it is, to use another metaphor, retuned on a quantum-vibrational level. Once any part of an object on this side touches the field, the molecular structure of that part will begin to vibrate at the same frequency. As the rest of the object moves within the field, it too becomes tuned to the new frequency, until at last the entire object loses its former frequency and gains the new one. At that point, the object has passed from one angle—that is, dimension—into the other."

"I see," Vivian said, although she was still processing the information she had just heard. She looked to Tafari, strapped into the seat at her right. "Do *you* see?" the botanist asked quizzically. Tafari grimaced and shrugged.

"I just take photographs, ma'am," he said, holding up the Brownie camera hanging from a strap around his neck. The young man's warm smile put Vivian's uncertainty about the voyage at ease, but nothing could put to rest her lingering guilt about leaving her husband behind. She knew the latter would eat at her until they were reunited. Hopefully, that would occur in only a few short and scientifically profound days.

All eyes were fixed on the enormous windscreen, and from their expressions Conover knew the members of the crew were consumed by the anticipation of what they were about to experience.

"Signal locked?" Conover asked aloud.

"Signal locked, sir," Aito called out.

"Pressurize fuselage."

"Yes, sir," Aito responded. He proceeded to toggle a row of switches, pressing a corresponding button after each one was thrown. With each pair of actions, a loud but brief metallic click reached their ears from various unknown locations within the fuselage of the ship, followed by several seconds of what sounded like the hissing of air. The entire din lasted only a few seconds. "Pressurization complete," Aito reported.

"All ahead, one-quarter speed, Mr. Sato," Captain Conover decreed in a commanding tone.

Aito laughed at the overly dramatic proclamation.

Conover also laughed and looked at Aito sheepishly. "I saw that in a movie," he admitted. "In any case, take us in slow and get ready to tingle, everyone."

Vivian snapped her head toward Tafari. "What did he just say?" she asked with alarm.

Outside the ship, the propellers roared to life. The *Favonia* began to glide forward toward the nothingness ahead of them.

And just like that, the vacuum airship *Favonia* and its crew went from hovering over the Arctic Ocean to gliding over the surface of an alien planet. Captain Conover watched the crew as they surely felt the fleeting sensation he had just experienced. The odd tingle coalesced at the base of his skull and rushed through his body as if taking a lightning-quick tour of his entire nervous system, ending in his fingertips and toes. But as quickly as the sensation manifested, it had disappeared. Vivian, along with the others in the jump seats, immediately unbuckled themselves and rushed toward the transparent Harbenite windscreen to view the wonders that no Earthling—or Xinnarian—eyes had ever beheld.

While on Earth, the *Favonia* had been cruising at an altitude of seven-hundred and fifty feet. According to the altimeter, they were now at just under eighteen thousand feet—nearly four miles—from the planetoid's surface, the high elevation providing the opportunity for a thorough examination of the terrain.

The planetoid's distance from the nearest sun was considerable, its surface in somber shadows reminiscent of twilight on Earth. The colors of the alien world were more vibrant than Conover had expected. Below, the landscape was oddly smooth. There appeared to be no mountains, valleys, bodies of water, or regions of vegetation, just irregular deviations in the pink-and-orange mélange of sand or dirt, or whatever comprised the orb's outer crust. Conover had made immediate adjustments to the vacuum tanks that held the *Favonia* aloft to maintain the craft's stability under the altered gravitational pull, and he gradually decreased the ship's altitude as it continued its slow glide miles above the surface.

While Tafari photographed the surface and the stars above the planetoid, Vivian consulted with Brahk. "Are you familiar with any of the star patterns or constellations?"

The green orbs that dominated his face scanned the heavens. "Nothing is recognizable to me from what I know of the night skies of Odon and Earth. Not that the stars we see are necessarily *not* familiar to us. We could simply be viewing them from an angle unnatural to our previous observation, and thus we are seeing known stars in unfamiliar alignments."

"Good point," Tafari said. He glanced down into his Brownie's viewfinder. "Just look at that." The shutter snapped several times, capturing the vibrantly illuminated purple-and-green nebula that hung like a phantom against the blackness of outer space.

"Those photos would make you famous," Vivian said with measured assurance, "if we were allowed to tell the world about just what we're seeing . . ." She turned toward the command dais and continued. "Which is *incredible!*" she exclaimed with a playful laugh. Vivian seemed not to care if her outburst was emotional or unprofessional. In truth, it did not matter; all on board were reveling in unbridled scientific euphoria. Her candid enthusiasm had swept over the others and they cheered and hugged as if their team had just won the Rose Bowl.

At the controls on the command dais, Conover smiled at Aito, who was trying very hard to maintain his composure. "Let's take her down for a closer look, huh?" The captain adjusted the vacuum controls and the *Favonia*'s snail-like descent toward the planetoid's surface increased.

Aito cautiously monitored the gauge on the frequency receiver unit. The waveform denoted that the signal emanating from the planetoid was unusually intense. "Captain, I have a concern."

"Whatcha got?"

Aito tapped his finger on the screen. "The planetary ray coming from the world below us. It's through the roof." He pointed to an electric numerical readout that gauged the wave's intensity. "We usually see wave strength in the ten to fifteen range, but it's now seventy-three and rising."

"And rising?" Conover repeated.

Aito nodded. "The more we descend, the stronger it gets."

Conover had an immediate follow-up question. "Where do we top out?"

"Anything over one-fifty-two will likely burn out the receiver," Aito warned. "Eighty-eight. Ninety-two, one fourteen," he counted ever upward.

"Okay, shut it down," Conover ordered. "We made it here, so it's no longer necessary, correct?"

Aito nodded and flipped a row of switches. The waveform screen went black. Both men looked at one another and silently breathed a sigh of relief.

The *Favonia* glided ever lower toward the planetoid's surface, revealing more discernible features. The vessel was now at an altitude of three hundred feet. What the observers had first assumed to be sand or dirt was neither, nor did it appear to be rock. The terrain was devoid of vegetation and the pink-and-orange surface was smooth, with only slight topographical modeling. It stretched before the hovering ship in an unbroken sheet, as if polished by the planetoid's travel through space. As there were no detectable weather patterns, it was unlikely wind had smoothed the ground; perhaps storms had ravaged the surface eons ago, but now all indications were that it was a dead world devoid of atmospheric turbulence.

Minutes before, after the *Favonia* first breached the barrier and its passengers came to terms with the reality that they had traveled to another world, Nathan Weinberg darted from the control dais. He passed through the bulkhead separating the control room from the living quarters and jogged down the port corridor to the next bulkhead. After spinning the central locking mechanism and pulling open the Harbenite door, he closed it behind him and bolted down the central passage of the cargo hold that stretched the length of the craft's tail. Odd orange light filled the passage, reflecting upward from the ground below the ship after passing through the round viewing portals along the *Favonia*'s tail. Each window that he passed tempted Nathan to stop and stare in wonder at the alien landscape, but duty called and he would not be distracted. He made his way past the stacks of supply crates secured against the fuselage walls, and at the rear of the craft he flung open the last bulkhead and entered the tail gunner's chamber.

The room was round, fifteen feet in diameter, and jutted from the rear of the tail inside a transparent Harbenite bubble. The focal point of the chamber was the central gunner's seat behind the massive twin Browning .50 caliber guns, their barrels extending through sealed apertures in the transparent bubble. The defensive weapon was mounted on a swiveling hydraulic platform attached to the transparent bubble itself, with the entire apparatus and its encasing sphere capable of one hundred eighty-degree movement, both horizontally and vertically. During the *Favonia*'s first excursion to Pellucidar in 1930, Erich von Harben's sister Gretchen had been present in this very chamber, then a simple observatory room, when a flying prehistoric reptile shattered the glass bubble and pulled her from the craft. Gretchen von Harben was fortunate to have survived the attack. Upon the eventual return of the *Favonia* to Santa Monica, Jason Gridley redesigned the aft observation deck, transforming it into a tail gunner's room, fortified by a transparent Harbenite sphere. The *Favonia* already hosted gunners' rooms above and below the nose of the craft, with a third beneath the midsection of the tail. Jason Gridley had reasoned one more gun would not harm the ship's visual aesthetic one bit.

But Nathan was not in the room to man the gun. He shimmied between the platform and the glass, flipped the trigger on the specially designed sixteen-millimeter movie camera, and then bolted from the room. On his return trip to the fore of the ship, he performed an identical task in the underside tail gunner's room and the gunner's chamber on the *Favonia*'s topside. If anything worthy of filming occurred on the voyage, the cameras would capture it from as many angles as possible, their shutters opening and closing once per second before advancing the film to the next frame.

Nathan descended the ladder to his final stop, the gunner's bubble on the underside of the ship's nose. Through the bubble's transparent flooring, he could see the brilliantly colored ground a few hundred feet below the ship. He reached down between the footrests of the upholstered leather gunner's seat and activated the last film camera, then realized . . . had he just caught the barest glimpse of something odd on the ground below before he had diverted his attention to the camera? He quickly leaned away from the chair to peer down through the Harbenite bubble. Yes, he had seen *something*, but he was uncertain exactly what it had been. Scattered across the landscape were odd black forms, some in large clusters, others solitary. Every one of the things was identical, in the shape of an "X." The *Favonia* was very low to the ground now, perhaps only a hundred feet from the surface. Nathan leaned closer to the glass. Were the black marks a sign of intelligent life, some kind of message to be seen from the air? He lay on his stomach in the gunner's sphere to get a better look. If only he had binoculars. To his disappointment, the ship passed the dark shapes before he could identify them. But there were more ahead, and he refocused his eyes in preparation.

The *Favonia* passed over another field of odd black shapes, sprinkled haphazardly like spilled pepper on a picnic tablecloth. He was glad the camera was clicking away behind him. Maybe later analysis of the film would— But wait! One of the shapes moved! It had clearly moved. Then another. And yet another— all seemingly reacting to the shadow of the *Favonia* falling upon them. Whatever the Xs were, they were alive.

Before his eyes, the appendages of one of the human-sized ebon shapes peeled upward from the ground, the entire thing rippled, and it propelled into the air. Nathan yelled in shock and fell away from the glass as the creature adhered to the transparent Harbenite bubble with a sickening smack. It was an animal of some kind, its four arms secreting a clear viscous substance that allowed it to stick to the chamber's spherical shield. The creature was hideous, like nothing Nathan had ever seen. Pressed against the glass was a hideous mouth full of sharp gnashing teeth that dominated the center of its X-shaped body. It was apparent that the beast was hungry.

And worse, its companions were taking note and following the course of the first. As the *Favonia* flew over them, dozens of the creatures launched into the air, most missing the ship but some passing above and beyond Nathan's field of vision. If or where they were attaching themselves to the *Favonia*, he could not tell.

Captain Conover started as Nathan's voice shrieked over the intercom. "Captain! We're under attack!" Waranji rushed to the front windscreen of the ship.

"You see anything?" Conover shouted.

"Nothing, Captain," Waranji replied stoically.

Conover pressed the intercom button. "What do you see, Weino?"

After a few tense seconds, Nathan responded. "They're . . . They're jumping up from the ground!"

"Who's jumping up from the ground?" Conover replied with confusion. He was unsure if he had heard Nathan correctly.

"Some kind of creatures," the mechanic replied. "I don't know what they are, but they're jumping into the air, attaching to the ship!"

"Waranji?" Conover asked again of his security chief.

"Still nothing, Captain," Waranji replied. "Tafari! Come with me!" he commanded. The two warriors rushed from the chamber and disappeared through the bulkhead doorway.

Conover could not be sure just what Nathan had seen, but out of an abundance of caution, he cut the ship's engines and increased the buoyancy of the twin dirigibles. Slowly, the *Favonia* ascended as it glided over the alien landscape.

Vivian approached the command dais. "Do you know what it is, Captain?" she asked nervously.

"Not yet, but if it's dinosaurs, we know what to do."

"And if it's not?" the botanist asked.

"We'll let Waranji make that call." He had hoped his smile would allay her fears, but he knew the uncertainty in his voice betrayed him.

Waranji's mind was awash with contingencies as he and Tafari rushed toward the nose gunner's compartment just as Nathan clambered past the top rung of the access ladder. "Did you see them?" Nathan shouted.

The security chief descended the ladder into the gunner's sphere to assess the situation. Within seconds, he climbed free of the hatch and straightened his uniform.

"What is it, sir?" Tafari asked anxiously.

"Come with me," Waranji commanded, and the two Waziri trotted toward the ship's living quarters, which adjoined the science lab and weapons room.

Within minutes, Captain Conover and Brahk Zahla joined the security chief and his assistant in the weapons room.

Nathan was still shaken by the attack of the odd creatures outside the ship, but had calmed considerably. The three observers watched as Waranji and Tafari completed their wardrobe change, both men now wearing formfitting black polyester mylar suits. Although the suits could be pressurized like high-altitude pilots' coverings, that capability would not be necessary based on the ship's readings of the planetoid's environment. All external apparatus, such as the helmet collars, utility belts, shoulder harnesses, and boots were bright yellow, a color scheme that led Conover to dub them "bumblebee suits." On their backs they wore twin oxygen tanks whose flexible polyurethane hoses attached to the round, clear helmets the men held in their arms.

Tafari flexed his gloved fingers to test his maneuverability. "This is much more comfortable than it looks," he observed happily.

Waranji knew that Conover's eternal smile disguised the Captain's unease. "I wish we could have gotten in more practice with those things," Conover lamented.

"We will be fine, Captain," Waranji assured him as he tugged upward on Tafari's helmet ring to certify the suit's proper fit across the younger man's shoulders.

Tafari continued to marvel at his protective outfit, bending his knees and twisting at the waist. "You would think the interior protective plates would make it heavy, but thanks to being made of Harbenite, it's light as a feather."

"What's your plan, Waranji?" Conover inquired.

The security chief outlined his intentions. As the *Favonia* hovered, he and Tafari would exit the ship through the maintenance hatch on the top side of the aft fuselage. They would walk the ship's exterior, with security tethers ensuring their safety should either of them slip. In that fashion, they would clear the *Favonia* of its uninvited passengers.

"And how do you intend to change their minds about hitching a ride with us?" Conover asked.

Waranji turned to the table behind him and lifted an

odd rifle. "With these," he said confidently. Brahk Zahla smiled, as the rifles were an invention of his, based on Xinnarian weapons technology.

"Good thinking," Conover said. "We don't know if they're intelligent, so that makes sense."

Nathan still seemed unnerved. "In my book, the only good alien is a . . ." He halted his sentence as Waranji's glare drilled holes into him. All but Nathan turned to look consolingly at their alien companion. Brahk, however, appeared unfazed by the intended insult and simply smiled and shrugged.

"Well, let's get on with it," Conover commanded. "Be sure to keep your communications transmitters open once you have those fishbowls on," he said, referring to the helmets. Upon hearing their captain's go-ahead, the two Waziri quickly completed their preparations and made their way with haste to the maintenance hatch in the tail of the *Favonia*, the strange rifles slung over their shoulders.

The heavy boot soles of the two men clanked against the Harbenite hull of the *Favonia* with each step they took. The sky above was dark but clear, and not so much as a breeze caressed them as they stood perched upon the top curve of the airship's fuselage. Both men firmly gripped their tethers as they began their hunt for the creatures that had attached themselves to the ship.

"Up ahead," Waranji warned over his suit-to-suit intercom. He counted five black starfish-like creatures lying flush against the fuselage, at the summit of the wings' downward curve over the enormous dual vacuum-tank envelopes mounted on the vessel's sides. Cautiously, they approached the things, but the creatures seemed oblivious to their presence. To Waranji, it looked as if they had climbed to the top of the ship to absorb whatever warmth they could from the dim sunlight. Waranji looked at Tafari and nodded; he would take the first shot.

The rifle Waranji held was unusual in design. The weapon began life as an M1 Thompson machine gun, but after Brahk

Zahla applied Xinnarian scientific principles to its design and function, it became something different altogether. While the stock and barrel remained unchanged, a second barrel was mounted atop the first. It, too, was hollow, but through its interior ran wires attached to a thick glass globe the size of a baseball at its terminus. The other end of the top tube fed into an oval metallic contrivance above the trigger that hosted two glass bulbs: one unlit and blue, the other blinking and bright yellow.

Waranji was now only twenty feet from the nearest creature. He raised the rifle, took aim, and fired. The projectile hit the dark shape in the central mass of its body, between two of its four legs. It was not a bullet that hit the thing, but rather a dart, which pierced the ebon flesh and stuck tight. Within two seconds, a blue bulb on the end of the dart illuminated. Waranji looked at the metal egg shape on his rifle and as the yellow light ceased blinking, the blue bulb flashed to life. He pulled back on the secondary trigger installed by Brahk.

A bolt of electrical energy arced through the air between the weapon's glass globe and the dart. The effect on the creature was immediate. Just as it had leaped from the ground to the *Favonia*, the black thing now sprang into the air, away from the ship, and plummeted to the ground far below. As Waranji watched, the creature skittered away across the landscape.

Tafari stepped to Waranji's side and repeated his superior's actions. The younger man's dart hit true, and a second creature flung itself from the ship after being hit by the lightning-like discharge of the weapon.

"More humane than killing them," Waranji reassured himself aloud. He knew that no matter what kind of being one was, electric jolts like those must hurt. The creatures might be malevolent or they could be intelligent and their intentions innocent. If the latter was the case, such an attack was outright savagery. Either way, the integrity of the ship had to be preserved.

"I'll take the one on the right," Tafari declared. Waranji raised his weapon and looked down the sight at the creature on the left.

Before either warrior could fire, the entire ship rocked, then dipped sharply to starboard. Around them, the air seemed to come alive as a huge gust knocked them from their feet. Tafari scrambled on his hands and knees. He released the tether and dug his fingers around a raised Harbenite plate into which a large running light was installed. Waranji did not fare as well. His attempt to maintain his footing worked against him; because he rose to his feet again, the ship's tilt caused him to lean backward at a forty-five-degree angle.

Waranji fell into open space toward the surface two hundred feet below, his tether trailing above him.

3
DEADLY DESCENT

WHAT THE HELL WAS THAT?" Conover shouted as he adjusted the dials that controlled the vacuum tanks' equilibrium. But as abruptly as the cyclone wind had appeared, it ceased, and the ship's balance stabilized. Then it dawned on him. "Waranji!" he yelled into his headset.

His rapid heartbeat calmed when the voice of his longtime friend crackled over the intercom. "I am here, Captain," Waranji announced.

"Is he all right?" Vivian asked with great alarm as she climbed the steps to the command dais, two at a time.

"Waranji," Conover spoke into his headset, "what's your status? Dr. Ouellet is having kittens up here." He shot Vivian a patented Conover smirk and she smiled and rolled her eyes in mock disapproval.

In response to Conover's question came Tafari's voice. "Captain Conover, Waranji has fallen from the ship, but he is still attached to the safety tether. I am trying to pull him up, but he is too heavy!"

"Great Scott!" Conover exclaimed, distracted momentarily by Brahk Zahla's rushed departure from the command chamber. But he had no time to wonder about the Odonian's actions; his friend's life depended on him. "Waranji. I'm going to descend so you can reach the ground."

"Captain," Waranji replied, "no matter what, please do not do that."

Conover cursed, suddenly understanding.

283

Below his friend, the odd ebon creatures lay in wait.

Waranji swung like a pendulum more than a hundred feet from the ground. The black starfish-like creatures had taken notice of his plight and had launched themselves into the air. One after another, the terrifying beasts zoomed upward, the teeth in the centers of their bodies ready to latch hold of his dangling legs. All fell short by at least twenty feet, but they were getting successively closer.

Tafari maintained his grip on the metal cord, then turned suddenly as the three remaining creatures on top of the ship leaped toward him. There was nothing he could do; his weapon was slung over his back.

Swinging helplessly below, Waranji heard three distinct pops, followed by a sustained discharge of an electric current. Three black X-shaped bodies fell past him, trailing wisps of smoke. "Tafari!" he yelled. "Are you all right?"

Just then, something heavy smashed against Waranji's legs. One creature had reached him! Like an octopus, all four appendages wrapped around his lower extremities. The grip was crushing. Waranji had both hands free, but because the tether was hooked to the front of his belt to avoid becoming entangled in the oxygen tanks on his back, he was facing skyward and unable to reach down to pry the ravenous animal from his legs. If not for the Harbenite plates sewn into the interior lining of the bumblebee suit, the creature would surely have been feasting on his flesh.

He turned his head toward the surface. The ebon nightmares continued to catapult themselves into the air like popping corn kernels. A second beast reached sufficient altitude and latched onto its brother, still trying desperately to bite through Waranji's suit. Then another found success, attaching itself to the second creature.

"Tafari!" shouted Waranji as he looked skyward. But it was not his fellow tribesman who flung himself into the air, arms spread, as he leaped from the top of the ship.

Inside the transparent helmet of the bumblebee suit was the face of Brahk Zahla.

Like a natural-born aerialist performing in an earthly circus or a cliff diver in Acapulco, Brahk plummeted downward toward Waranji in a graceful arc. His great leap from the top of the ship carried him away from the vessel and far past Waranji, who by now could bend and pound with his fists against the muscular arms of the predator clinging to him. Below the beast, the two other monsters maintained their hold on the first, battling one another to climb past the creature with the death grip on Waranji's legs. Brahk's tether grew taut, and the resulting pendulum swing of his body carried him past the legs of Waranji. The Odonian lashed out with one hand as he passed, and bright blue internal fluid spurted from a severed arm of the beast gripping Waranji. His swing brought him back again, and another appendage was severed, this time from the middle creature. Before Brahk could make his third pass, Waranji was able to kick one leg free of the injured killer's grip and smashed downward, knocking it and the two monsters who clung to it toward the pink-and-orange ground below.

As a precautionary measure, Conover had increased the altitude of the *Favonia*, and both spacesuit-clad beings were safe from the terrors below them. As Brahk's swing began to slow, Waranji called to him. "Thank you, my friend! But how did you injure them?"

Brahk grinned from inside the glass bubble. "Sometimes, the simplest of technologies is best." He held up his hand to display the kitchen knife he used against the ebon menaces.

Above, Tafari had been joined by Nathan, now wearing a protective suit of his own, and together they began reeling in Waranji's tether with the help of a winch Nathan had hastily positioned just inside the maintenance hatch. Waranji assisted their effort by climbing the rope as they hauled him upward. He looked to his side to gauge the status of Brahk's safety. To the security chief's amazement, the Rolodon Xinnar was climbing his tether as easily as a spider would skitter up a strand of silk. Once atop the ship, Tafari returned Brahk's weapon, which he had discarded in favor of using a simple knife to rescue Waranji.

At last, Waranji again stood atop the ship and caught his breath. "Thank you, all of you," he said to his fellow crewmen.

"There is no need for thanks, sir." Tafari smiled. "Brothers defend brothers."

Brahk also smiled. "Indeed, we do."

Nathan cringed visibly within his helmet. "Brothers? Give me a break. You're not even human." Although Brahk was completely dismissive of the insult, the mechanic's comment steamed Waranji.

The security chief exchanged an uncomfortable look with Nathan. "With all of our lives at stake, our focus must remain on our mission," he stated coldly. "But at its conclusion, you and I will have words." The four men collected their weapons, reeled in the tethers, and sealed the maintenance hatch behind them.

When adrenaline levels had all settled down, Conover stood on the control dais before his crew to conduct a reassessment of their mission. Aito remained at the ship's controls while Waranji, Tafari, Nathan, Vivian, and Brahk listened intently.

"Here's what I'm thinking," the captain began. "The objective of this mission is to make contact with an alien world, mark it, document its characteristics, and collect inorganic—and if possible, organic—samples for study. We're not here to make friends, or enemies, for that matter. This is just a reconnaissance flight, a fact-finding mission, and it would be in our best interests to do everything we can *not* to get involved with whatever or whoever might live here."

Nathan posed a question. "Captain, should we have captured one of those creatures out there? I'd think the science boys back home would have a field day with that."

Conover's response was immediate. "No. That's my point. One, we don't know if they're intelligent. We could be kidnapping someone's mother. Two, we don't know what kind of diseases an alien life form might carry and we don't want to be transporting anything deadly back to Earth. And three—not to jangle any nerves—we're already risking our lives just by being here. I'm not about to jeopardize your lives any further than they already have been by chasing down monsters."

"Captain," Tafari interjected respectfully, "Vivian's task is to collect soil and plant samples. Could a plant not also carry a disease?"

Vivian responded with both modesty and self-assurance. "It's a good question, Tafari, and I had the same concern. I've brought along specially designed collection tubes for any samples I acquire, and they'll remain sealed until our return to Santa Monica where they'll be analyzed under the most stringent of protective measures. The captain is right, we cannot afford to take any risks."

Conover adjusted his cap. "Okay. We're here, Aito has collected a ton of readings, Tafari has gotten a slew of photos of the stars overhead. Next on the agenda is to find a safe place to land, and if one can be found, some of you will go out, do what needs to be done, get back here, and we sail back home." All those assembled nodded in agreement.

The *Favonia* continued its slow trek through the skies of the alien planetoid, maintaining an altitude high enough to avoid the X-shaped creatures that seemed to be everywhere on the surface. At times, the crew noted the minor undulation of the pink-and-orange landscape below, and only once was the *Favonia* again subjected to the sudden turbulence in the planetoid's atmosphere. Aito maintained an unwavering course, which would assist them in relocating the interangular rift when they chose to depart for home.

"Holy cats," Conover whispered, "will you look at that."

Ahead of the ship, a yellow glow filled the air, emanating from the ground and dissipating into the upper atmosphere. As the *Favonia* drew closer, the source of the glow came into view: an enormous hole several miles across punctured the surface to allow the release of a dim yellow light from somewhere below the planetoid's outer crust. Conover's first instinct was to avoid the luminescent ray, but the tantalizing prospect of what might lie below the surface was too much to ignore. The crew gathered at the front windscreen. As the airship passed beyond the lip of the sheer-walled crater, the sight that met their eyes astounded them. The chasm was nearly round and fell to a depth of at least two miles. Far below, the expansive cavern floor radiated a phosphorescent glow. Astonishing tower-like formations joined the upper and lower subcutaneous crust of the planetoid, visible at the bottom of the crater.

"What in the world kind of topography is that?" Vivian pondered. The rest of the observers were at a loss for words.

Conover turned to Aito, who was already looking toward the captain in anticipation of a command. Conover smiled. "I'm gonna cut the engines and take us down a bit. This is too weird to pass up without at least taking a look." Aito nodded in agreement.

All three port engines chugged to a halt while the trio of starboard propellers continued their spin, driving the *Favonia* into a graceful turn to port. Conover cut the power to the three running engines while decreasing the buoyancy of the vacuum tanks, causing the ship to undertake a slow spiraling descent into the great glowing pit.

Behind the windscreen, Tafari and Waranji watched as the lip demarcating the surface of the planetoid grew more and more distant as the *Favonia* continued its descent. When viewed from above, the pink-and-orange formations that rose from the bottom of the crater appeared to be composed of rock, but upon closer inspection, they looked nothing like rock. The surfaces of the towers were smooth and riddled with holes that passed completely through them, some tunnels hundreds of feet in diameter. On all sides of the pit rose the constructs, and as the crew peered anxiously beyond them, they could see miles of glowing caverns and hundreds more of the towering pillars that seemed to support the planetoid's outer crust.

"Looks like Swiss cheese," Nathan commented.

Vivian focused intently on the constructs. "Or coral? They're almost . . . membranous, like plant matter. There is nothing like this on Earth." She laughed at herself and the obviousness of her statement.

"Does anyone see any of those creatures out there?" Conover called out. The response was negative. "Good. Since this is the only place we've found clear of those things, I'm going to set us down. We'll get the beacon set up and Dr. Ouellet can gather her samples, Tafari can grab some photos, and we'll be on our way."

As light as a feather, the *Favonia* made contact with the crater bottom. No dust flew, no rocks tumbled. From Waranji's perspective at the front windscreen, the ground beneath the ship was as clean as an operating room floor. After so many hours of flight, several crew members breathed a sigh of relief to be on solid ground at last.

On the underside of the *Favonia* and nestled between its two massive vacuum tank envelopes sat a rectangular vehicle, pragmatically named the Cargo Crawler. The Crawler resembled a large shoebox, the length of whose top side exceeded that of the bottom. Tank wheels and treads lined its lower sides, and its flat front end hosted a wide rectangular window and four large headlights. The rear of the vehicle—similar to an earthly tractor trailer—opened outward like a drawbridge and served as a loading ramp. The measurements of the Cargo Crawler were fifty-two feet in length, sixteen feet in width, and fifteen feet in height, large enough to transport the megafauna relocated to Pellucidar on the *Favonia*'s imperiled 1930 flight to the inner world. Now, the large cavernous warehouse-on-wheels would be used as the base of operations for excursions beyond the ship. On this mission, the Cargo Crawler would not be disengaged from its mother vessel, as the crew had no intention of venturing far from their landing location.

Waranji assisted Nathan in wheeling the trolley containing the planetoid-marking beacon down the lowered loading ramp. Both men—along with Vivian, Tafari, and Brahk—were outfitted in bumblebee suits. Waranji's suit was new, as the fabric of the one he had previously worn was incinerated after he removed it, a precautionary measure since it had been covered by the viscous slime secreted by the creature that had attacked him earlier. At the bottom of the ramp, Waranji looked into the Cargo Crawler, where Brahk, Vivian, and Tafari talked excitedly among themselves. Assured of privacy, he turned to address Nathan. He got the mechanic's attention, then tapped his helmet to indicate he wanted to speak to Nathan privately. Both men turned off their suit-to-suit intercoms so the others would not hear them.

"What's up, Chief?" Nathan asked, speaking loudly enough to be heard through the transparent bubble encasing his head.

Waranji's demeanor grew stern. "I want to discuss your feelings about Brahk Zahla," he said bluntly.

Nathan rolled his eyes disrespectfully. "There's really nothing to discuss. You know how I feel."

"Yes, everyone knows how you feel, Nathan," Waranji replied. "Everyone on the *Favonia* knows how you feel about Brahk. Including Brahk."

Nathan snapped back, "Well, good. I'm glad. Any other questions, Chief?" he asked snidely.

Not a muscle flinched in Waranji's face. "Yes. Why do you hate Brahk Zahla so?"

"I don't hate him," Nathan responded flippantly. "I just don't trust him. And next you're gonna ask why I don't trust him. It's because he's an alien. He's been tagging along with us for a year, but we don't know a damn thing about him."

Waranji cut him off. "That is not true. It is only *you* who knows nothing about him. Because you've never cared to learn."

"There's nothing to learn," Nathan retorted stubbornly. "The guy's from outer space, Waranji, from another world! How can we trust him?"

The security chief was quiet for a moment before finally speaking. "You are from Brooklyn. I am from Africa. Are you and I not from two different worlds, in a sense? We are, but you know me well enough to talk to me with disrespect . . . I apologize. I meant to say candor."

Nathan was beginning to sweat in his bumblebee suit. "The guy's skin is green, for God's sake."

"And yours is pink, and mine is brown, but we all have red blood flowing through our veins."

Nathan scoffed, "Do we really know that?"

"Dr. Schlessinger in Santa Monica confirmed that Brahk's blood is scarcely different from ours," Waranji said matter-of-factly.

The hot-headed mechanic was not ready to let go of his argument. "You saw him, Waranji, just a couple of hours ago. You saw him climb that rope like some kinda inhuman freak. It's not natural."

Again, Waranji was quiet as he composed his thoughts. "There was another man who looked at his fellows and viewed them as 'inhuman.' Just nine years ago, Captain Conover returned from war in Europe. He risked his life in a P-51 Mustang at the Battle of the Bulge to defend those people who were labeled inhuman and unnatural. I think you know who those people were, Nathan Weinberg. And you know why Captain Conover—and I—will fight so everyone can live free from tyranny," he paused, "and bigotry."

Nathan was speechless.

Waranji never broke eye contact with the mechanic and tapped the button on his helmet collar to reactivate the intercom. "Captain, this is Waranji. Nathan is ready to position the beacon."

Conover's voice came through the team's helmet speakers. "Great. Keep me posted on what you find out there."

"Yes, sir," Waranji responded, maintaining his glare at Nathan even as he turned to walk up the loading platform and into the bay of the Cargo Crawler.

Aito more or less agreed with Vivian's prior assessment that the beacon was an unremarkable device. It consisted of little more than a metal cylinder casing the circumference of a basketball containing the apparatus to emit a Gridley Wave signal of a specific frequency.

Now that the beacon was in place on the surface, Nathan radioed Conover that it was ready for testing. Aito reminded the captain that upon their arrival the ship's transceiver had been switched off, as they feared the planetoid's strong signal emission would burn out the delicate apparatus. A consensus was reached that the planetoid's rays might not be as strong now that they were underground but just to be safe the ship's transceiver would be switched on for only a few seconds, just long enough to capture the beacon's signal to ensure it was properly functioning. And so, the apparatus was activated.

Immediately upon throwing the switch, Aito's eyes grew wide, and he hastily shut down the device. The meter that measured the strength of incoming signals shot to one hundred and sixty units, exceeding the transceiver's danger threshold of one hundred fifty-two. Aito looked at Conover and saw his own failed attempt to hide his panic reflected back at him. The device emitted no odd sounds or the scent of smoking transistors, nor was there anything to indicate the planetoid's overpowering emissions had fried the transceiver. It was a success; the device had captured the beacon's waveform, which was now displayed on the Gridley Wave console screen. But the question remained: What was the source of the strange world's emission?

Outside the ship, Vivian examined the planetoid's glowing inner surface as she walked toward an area of rounded mounds.

Each was almond-shaped and roughly two hundred yards in length, some reaching nearly fifty feet in height. The mounds were tightly woven together, butting one against the other. They stretched into the distance in multiple directions, to the feet of the towering pink-and-orange columns that rose two miles toward the planetoid's outer crust. Tafari, carrying one of the rifles of Brahk's design, followed closely behind Vivian.

She looked down, as she did quite often, to marvel at the yellow glow of the surface upon which they trod. Like the columns, it too was smooth. She bent to run her hand over it, then held it in place for several seconds. "I can barely feel it through my glove, but it's there." She looked back at Tafari. "The ground is exuding warmth."

"What does that mean?" he asked.

"I don't know," she said. "At least, according to the ship's detectors, it's not radioactive. If it were, we wouldn't be having this conversation." She smiled curtly, then stood to resume her walk.

They were now two hundred yards from the *Favonia*, which waited patiently behind them. Over one shoulder, Vivian carried a utility bag containing her tools and collection vials, but there had yet to be a use for the containers. There was no vegetation and no rocks, not even any dust present on the slightly spongy ground. The planetoid's composition was baffling. And it was so quiet. Deathly quiet.

Tafari jumped as Waranji's voice echoed in their helmets. "Everything all right, Tafari?" he asked with concern.

"Waranji," Vivian responded. "I'm not having much luck out here. There's simply nothing to collect. I'm going to try scraping a sample from the ground to at least say we recovered something. We'll return to the ship shortly."

Vivian glanced up at the top of the loading ramp of the Cargo Crawler, where Waranji was cautiously watching his charges. At the foot of the ship, Nathan was inspecting the *Favonia*'s landing gear tires to ensure they were not sinking into the soft ground, while Brahk paced about aimlessly as if cataloging every fantastic sight in his mind.

Vivian now crouched and used a trowel with a serrated edge to attempt the collection of a sample from the ground. Rather than break through the surface, the tool's edge stretched it as if the ground were rubber. When she released the pressure on the tool, the section she had pulled shrank back into place. "This is unprecedented," she said to herself.

"Dr. Ouellet," Tafari said behind her.

"What do you think this is, Tafari? It's not dirt, it's not rock."

"Dr. Ouellet!" Tafari repeated in a more commanding tone.

The clouds from on-the-spot scientific theorizing cleared when Tafari shouted her name a third time. She realized it was a warning and stood nervously, looking all about her. "What is it? What's wrong?"

Tafari had his weapon raised. It was aimed right past her. His eyes were locked on something behind Vivian. She did not want to look but she had to. Slowly she turned.

It was the mounds, the gigantic almond shapes beyond the clear plain on which the *Favonia* had landed. They were moving.

From the tone of Tafari's voice, he had gathered his composure. "What's causing that? An earthquake, maybe?" Vivian replied that she did not know. "I should probably be taking photographs of this," he said sarcastically as he continued to stare down the barrel of his weapon. The Brownie camera hung from its strap across the front of his bumblebee suit.

Vivian's steps carried her slowly backward as she kept her eyes on the undulating mounds. "Maybe we should . . ."

"I agree," Tafari said quickly. Together, they began a gingerly, backward march toward the sanctuary of the *Favonia*, which now seemed so very far from them.

Waranji's keen eyes must have detected something amiss

about the movements of the two explorers in the distance, for he called out, "Tafari, is everything all right out there?"

Vivian and Tafari now faced the ship and had increased their pace to a trot, craning their necks to watch the odd movement of the ground behind them. "I'm not sure," Tafari said. "The ground is moving."

Nathan jolted upright from behind one of the *Favonia*'s wheels. "What did he say?"

The security chief sprang into action. "Waranji to Conover! Do you see anything unusual from where you are?" He unslung his modified rifle and leaped to the ground from the top of the loading ramp.

Captain Conover's voice rang over the intercom system within the bumblebee suits. "We heard through the headsets, something about the ground moving? Aito's at the front window now . . . hold on. He says he sees it. Get everyone inside, pronto!"

Vivian and Tafari's rushed pace had become frantic, both now taking great strides. As they took anxious glances behind them, the pair drew too close to one another and Tafari's foot came down upon Vivian's boot heel, causing them both to crash to the spongy pink-and-orange ground.

"I'm sorry!" he yelled, but Vivian was not listening. She pointed behind them in silence.

Something was crawling upward between two of the oval mounds. Something black. It was a leg, like a spider's leg, followed by another, and another. They clawed at the air as the creature pulled itself free from the crevice formed by the juncture of two of the closest mounds. Within seconds, it was within full view of the panicked explorers.

The ebon horror stood on six legs, its body at least the size of a horse. In fact, it somewhat resembled a seahorse, with a long tail curled into a spiral and a craned neck supporting a head that looked like all mouth and nothing more. No eyes were visible, but the teeth . . . they were horrifying and black, just like the rest of it. It must have sensed prey, for the six segmented legs that sprouted from its sides began to carry it across the mottled plain toward Vivian and Tafari.

The explorers pulled each other to their feet and began a mad dash toward the *Favonia*.

Waranji was running in their direction at top speed, his weapon in his steely grip. He had already formulated a backup plan. "Nathan! Man the nose turret! Brahk! You take the belly turret!"

Before he had gotten fifty feet from the *Favonia*, Waranji's flight was halted. He leaped to one side as something thrust upward from the ground. It was long and black, like a tentacle from Hell. It rose twenty feet into the air and whipped wildly, its front side covered by chitinous plates and thousands of short, clawed legs reminiscent of a millipede's. What appeared to be a single, bulbous sickly white eye peered from the terminus of its hideous body. As Waranji scrambled to his feet, he noticed that the eye—if that is what it was—was ringed by a corona of dancing blue arcs of electricity.

Following Waranji's command, Nathan rushed toward the metal boarding stairs at the nose of the *Favonia* by which they had originally disembarked. As he neared Brahk, however, the green-skinned man stood tensed, not at all prepared to follow the mechanic.

"Do you not hear it?" Brahk cautioned at the top of his voice.

"Come on!" Nathan yelled. "The chief ordered you to—"

The ground erupted as three ghastly black tentacles burst forth and whipped the air around the two crewmen.

Across the plain, Tafari and Vivian were now trapped. Behind them charged the gigantic seahorse/spider monster, while ahead towering black tentacles had encircled Waranji, who had been rushing to their rescue.

"Go!" Tafari screamed to Vivian as he dropped to one knee and aimed his weapon behind him. A pop resounded as he pulled the forward trigger. A horrendous shriek erupted from the nightmare beast. The end of the dart embedded in its neck glowed bright blue. The blinking yellow light on the ovoid capsule on Tafari's gun dimmed. The blue bulb flashed to life. He curled his finger around the rear trigger and fired. Instantaneously, an arc of electricity spanned the thirty feet between Tafari and their hunter. It knocked the beast backward off its six spindly legs and caused it to thrash on its back, the legs curled inward toward its midsection while it spasmed and shrieked wildly.

"Come on!" Vivian yelled, pulling Tafari to his feet.

Each roll Waranji took only put him in close proximity to another of the thrashing black tentacles. They lashed out at him, giving him no time to aim his rifle. He knew it was only a matter of time before one of the creatures reached him. One of the things began to stiffen, catching his attention; it stopped its whipping motion and shuddered. Suddenly, the dancing electrical sparks around its central eye coalesced into a single bolt of lightning that shot from the white orb and raked the ground, headed right toward him. Waranji leaped as the bolt passed, missing him by only one foot.

To his right, a second snakelike creature stiffened, the electricity around its central eye growing in intensity. Waranji raised his weapon, took aim, and fired, but not at the immediate threat. Instead, he had targeted the tentacle behind him, which blocked his path to the *Favonia*. The dart sank into the writhing body of the ebon creature behind him just as the monster before him released a bolt of lightning. Waranji ducked down in place and cringed as the vicious bolt flew over him and slammed into the chest of the beast behind him. The electrode dart of Brahk Zahla's invention had attracted the lightning bolt! The midsection of the creature exploded, bisecting it sickeningly. Whatever was left of the creature retracted back into the hole from which it had burst.

Before the severed top of the thing hit the ground, Waranji

was already aiming his rifle at another of the creatures. He fired. Spun in a circle. Aimed at another and fired again. Spun and fired, five times in all. The creatures that encircled him—all embedded with darts—stiffened, ready to unleash their final assault.

Waranji threw himself to the ground and lay as flat as he could. Above him, the eyes of the monsters released arcs of lightning, and in a crisscrossing web of electrical mayhem, they killed one another in one glorious burst of light.

Tafari and Vivian reached Waranji just as Conover's voice boomed over their helmet receivers. "What the hell is going on out there? Waranji!"

The two explorers streaked past Waranji, not even slowing an iota. He ran to catch up with them as they bolted toward the waiting *Favonia*. "We will be aboard shortly, Captain," he said in a casual tone, as if to belie the direness of the situation. "I would prepare to lift off immediately."

But Nathan knew the fight was not over yet. The ship was surrounded by the writhing black horrors. As Waranji, Tafari, and Vivian drew closer to the *Favonia*, the avionics mechanic ran to the front of the craft in an attempt to reach the sharply ascending steps into the nose of the ship. Brahk followed close behind. The tentacles, however, were blocking their escape, and unable to reach the ladder, the two men sought refuge behind the forward landing gear.

Nathan watched anxiously as Waranji hesitated to follow the others up the ramp of the Cargo Crawler. "Chief!" the mechanic shouted inside his helmet. "You can't save us all! Get them inside!"

Nathan could only imagine Waranji's scowl as the security chief cried out. "Into the Cargo Crawler! Quickly!" Vivian and Tafari bolted up the Harbenite ramp, successfully avoiding several writhing tentacle creatures as they ran.

With his eyes on the nearest of their threatening foes, Nathan did not see the ebon terror rip upward through the rubbery ground behind him and Brahk until it was too late. The creature unleashed a bolt of lightning from its hideous eye. It raked the ground and struck the huge landing gear tires. The attack caused no damage to the vulcanized wheels, but it forced Nathan and Brahk to leap in opposite directions, separating them. The sound of the hydraulic system raising the door ramp at the rear of the Crawler rang through the air.

"Get in the Crawler! Help protect the others!" Nathan shouted to Brahk. The green-skinned Xinnarian hesitated. "Just go!" the Brooklyn native commanded. "I'll cover you!"

In that instant, with death looming over him and only seconds to act, time stopped for Nathan. Had he just said what he had said? If truth be told, Nathan was repulsed by Brahk, and though he would never admit it, he was terrified of the alien being. Perhaps that was because Brahk was different. Nathan's childhood was idyllic within the secure bubble of the borough of Brooklyn and in the comforting embrace of his own people. There he was free to tinker with his machines and silly inventions, while also happily laboring in his father's automobile repair garage. How many times had he overheard someone say, "That kid is a genius," in reference to whatever quirky gadget he had cobbled together from spare auto parts? Nathan had heard it enough throughout his childhood and teen years to let it sink in. And stick. As he got older and ventured beyond Brooklyn, beyond his own neighborhood, he found that he was the target of hate, simply because of his religious and ethnic background. The more they pushed, the more he pushed back, and very quickly, Nathan developed a thick skin and abrasive personality. In his mind, it was a survival tactic, plain and simple. And now, among his new family aboard the *Favonia*, he was still respected but no longer the "genius." Brahk, with his superior scientific knowledge, had assumed that role. An alien. An outsider. Just as Nathan had been when he left Brooklyn . . .

It's been both jealously and bigotry all along, he realized, *just as Waranji had said.* In that instant, Nathan cursed himself for every word of hate and dissent he had ever uttered against the well-meaning alien, Brahk Zahla, who only wanted to share his knowledge with others.

Moments before, Waranji had hit the button on the control panel for the Cargo Crawler's loading ramp door. The hydraulic system groaned as the massive door continued its slow, upward swing.

Suddenly, a black-and-yellow figure leaped onto the rising ramp. Waranji raised his rifle, but there was no need; it was Brahk Zahla.

"Is everyone safe?" Brahk shouted to Waranji, Vivian, and Tafari. They assured him that was the case. Brahk nodded, and as the door reached a 45-degree angle to the ground, he leaped not into the Cargo Crawler but outward onto the alien landscape. Without a sound, he disappeared.

Waranji shouted into his microphone. "Brahk! Where are you going?" There was no response. Other matters jolted the trio into action as one of the black tentacles snaked around the rear of the Crawler and entered the bay. Immediately it discharged a blue-white bolt of lightning that ricocheted around the interior walls of the vehicle. Fortunately, the attack did not hit any human marks. In unison, Waranji and Tafari raised their weapons and fired. Two electrode darts struck the flailing beast. Twin bolts of electricity then leaped from the warriors' guns and struck the thrashing creature. The ramp door groaned against the obstruction created by the thing's body when, at last, it severed the beast in half and hissed into its locked position. The three crew members looked at the dead section of the black thing lying on the floor of the Cargo Crawler as the automatic interior lights flashed on overhead.

"Well, Dr. Ouellet," Tafari sighed with relief, "there's the sample you were searching for."

*   *   *

Outside the ship, Nathan faced an impossible conundrum. Moments before he had assured Brahk's escape but now found himself hopelessly trapped. The stygian creatures swayed through the air in search of him as he hid behind the enormous forward wheels of the *Favonia*. At seemingly random intervals, the beasts unleashed electrical bolts, which were now beginning to strike the Harbenite hull of the ship. If they could not find smaller prey, they would attack the larger target en masse. Nathan took a deep breath and stepped out from behind the wheels. He could not let the creatures damage the *Favonia*, as it would doom them all. He raised his rifle. He would shoot, and keep shooting until he fell. But as his weapon released a deadly bolt at one of the monsters, another creature was struck by a second bolt. Then another.

Brahk Zahla rushed past the front of the Cargo Crawler, vicious bolts of electricity leaping from his rifle.

For only a moment was Nathan stunned by his unexpected rescuer. Then he joined Brahk and together they forged a path past the nightmare creatures and scrambled up the metal steps leading to the nose of the *Favonia*.

As they climbed the steps, Nathan asked, "Why did you come back for me?"

Brahk looked up at him with a smile. "I have dedicated my life to acquiring knowledge," he said. "I will preserve and protect it at all costs. Thus, I can let no ill befall you, for as the others assured me, only you can explain the divine secret of Earth's revered kosher beef frank."

Nathan's laugh echoed through the compartment as he slammed and locked the hatch behind them.

In the command center, Conover was working with Aito to prepare for departure, all too aware of the electrical barrage his ship was enduring.

"We're being hit right and left, but I'm not detecting any damage," Aito shouted.

"Not yet, anyhow," Conover replied darkly. "Is everyone on board?" he asked into his headset and all responded that they were safe. He proceeded to ease up on the sticks to increase the buoyancy of the vacuum tanks, and the *Favonia* began to rise. Outside, vicious bolts continued to strike the ship.

"Come on, baby, get us out of here," he whispered.

Inside the Cargo Crawler, Waranji watched as Tafari and Vivian ascended the ladder to the roof hatch that provided access to the fuselage of the *Favonia*. All three flinched as a muffled roar echoed through the vehicle. It was coming from outside.

Waranji knew the sounds in an instant. "The gun turrets!" he shouted excitedly.

Nathan's voice shot over their interior suit speakers. "Keep goin', Captain!" he shouted. "Brahk and I are on those things!"

The twin .50 caliber Brownings of the forward and tail turrets barked death at the black beasts attacking the rising ship. The blazing projectiles rained down on the creatures and cut them to ribbons, but as some fell, others burst forth from the ground to join the fray. In the forward turret, Nathan spoke with assurance into his headset. "Keep it up until we're clear, Brahk! You're doin' great!"

Nathan grinned to himself as he continued depressing the guns' triggers, shell casings tinking to the floor all around him as the Brownings showered carnage upon the attackers. Many of the bullets fired by the two gunners missed their marks and drilled into the spongy ground below. This had a most unexpected effect.

Nathan squinted past the waving black stalks to the pink-and-orange ground from which they had sprung. It *was* moving, almost as if in response to the bullets penetrating the surface. Vibrating. *Quivering.* He stopped firing for a moment to catch his breath and clear his head. The ground could not be moving, as Vivian and Tafari had earlier stated. But it was moving—as if an earthquake were shaking the entire floor of the enormous pit. The *Favonia* rose higher past the reach of the black creatures' electrical attacks, and Nathan and his companion in the aft turret ceased firing. The ground vibrated even more powerfully as entire sections hundreds of feet in diameter shifted and contracted toward the almond-shaped mounds. Then those began to move, rising upward as if something beneath the surface was trying to free itself. A split formed across the middle of the elevating, bumpy plain. The chasm widened and separated into two halves, which slowly lowered away from each other.

As the *Favonia* approached the lip of the miles-wide pit, Nathan had his clearest view yet of the seismic activity occurring hundreds of feet below, as did the sixteen-millimeter film camera installed in the belly of his turret.

The two sides of the raised plain had fallen away from the chasm, now revealing the enormous form beneath. A gigantic white globe, at least a half mile in diameter, lay exposed. A vibrant purple ring along its top hemisphere glistened in the yellow phosphorescence and a smaller orb of obsidian black lay at the center of the purple ring.

Nathan choked as he spoke into his helmet's headset.

"My God," he stuttered in shock. "It's an eye."

In the science room at the center of the ship, Vivian stepped from behind the partition. Her four companions had by then also removed their bumblebee suits and donned their normal attire. She knew they were as anxious as she was to get to the command center and witness the *Favonia*'s transit back through the interangular rift, four miles above the planetoid. After they stored the bumblebee suits in vacuum-sealed containment vessels for later decontamination, the crew members hastened down the port hallway leading to the front of the ship.

A voice rang over the intercom system. "Aito to crew: We've reached the location of the field if you want to watch our departure from the planetoid."

"It's not a planetoid," Nathan said to himself, his voice cracking slightly.

Vivian did not slow her pace, but turned to look incredulously at Nathan. "What did you just say?"

"Nothing," he said. "You'll see when we get the film from the ship's cameras developed."

Vivian increased her pace to catch up with the rest of the crew. "Gentlemen, I want to thank all of you for what you did out there." She glanced behind her and smiled cordially. "You too, Nathan."

The man shrugged. Clearly, there was something else on his mind, something strangely haunting. Vivian determined that whatever was bothering him would have to wait.

As she and her companions entered the command auditorium through the bulkhead door, they found Conover and Aito engaged in an intense conversation on the pilots' platform. Suddenly, Conover barked out, "All engines maximum! Everyone find a seat and buckle up!"

Something was wrong.

Vivian fought against the ship's sudden acceleration and secured her safety belt just as the tingling wave overtook them all. They had passed through the barrier between realms. But the looks on the faces of Conover and Aito were even more disquieting than the urgency of their departure called for.

Captain Conover cut the power to the six external prop engines as the crew looked across the wide chamber to the windscreen. Vivian unbuckled her harness and silently moved to the window, followed by Brahk, Tafari, Waranji, and Nathan.

Before the *Favonia* lay not the expanse of the Arctic Ocean, as Vivian had expected, but something else.

A thick and unbroken layer of ominous dark clouds painted the ceiling of the vista. Below stretched a secondary patchwork expanse of stratus clouds, their shapes morphing as high-altitude winds moved them about. There was no sunlight, as the heavy cloud cover prevented not even a single ray from reaching the fog-shrouded forests below. A strange glow illuminated the underside of the billowing vapor, but there appeared to be no visible source of the pale light shining upward from beneath the clouds. Most of the trees appeared normal, except for their brilliant leaf shades of violet, heliotrope, and lavender. However, the boles of some were immense, with a circumference of several city blocks. The trees' upper branches and canopies rose for miles and broke through the lowest cloud layer to reach even higher into the dark sky above.

"That's not Earth!" Vivian cried with alarm. She turned. "Captain Conover! We're not on Earth!"

Conover was fuming. "Damn it, not again!" In frustration, he hit his fist against the metal console.

"Captain, what happened?" Vivian demanded.

Aito stood as the others joined Vivian. The dismay on their faces read as a silent demand for an explanation. The navigation and communications specialist seemed determined to offer them a good one. "All of you know how we had to shut down the Gridley Wave transceiver because of the intensity of the waves coming from the planetoid," he said. "Obviously, we had to turn on the device to use the 'skeleton key' to return to Earth. Which we did, but something went wrong. I can only assume that the strength of those planetary waves might have had an adverse effect on the transmitter-receiver. I'll know more when I take it apart, but until then . . ."

"Until then," Conover interrupted, "we need to remain calm. We'll figure this out and we'll get home."

Vivian, standing beside Nathan, heard the man muttering to himself. "They weren't planetary waves," he murmured. "They were brain waves."

She opened her mouth to respond to the avionics mechanic, but Conover held up a finger and clasped his hand over one ear of his headset. "Hold on . . ." He sat and began adjusting a few dials on the console. He looked up, listening intently, his eyes focused on nothing as if he were seeing beyond the crew into another world that was invisible to them.

"Captain," Aito asked nervously, "what is it?"

Conover's perennial smirk played across his lips. "It's a radio signal!"

"A Gridley Wave radio signal?" Aito asked excitedly. "But I shut it off . . ."

"No," Conover replied, as if in shock, "a *radio* radio signal." He toggled a switch to feed the incoming communication to the ship's public address system. A voice began to take form, extracted from the static, but it was in a language unintelligible to Vivian, and from their puzzled expressions to the others as well.

Conover took a deep breath and depressed the transmit button on the traditional radio transmitter. "This is Captain Douglas Conover of the United States airship *Favonia*. To whom have I the pleasure of speaking? Over."

The crew looked at one another in wide-eyed confusion as the phantom speaker tried to hide his exuberant laughter. He composed himself and replied in perfect English. "I am the Tanjong of Korva. But seeing as how you're from Earth, you can call me Carson Napier of California, over."

Conover raised his eyebrows at Vivian, and then turned to survey the other faces of the crew fixed upon him, taking in the array of emotions they displayed. "Nice to hear a friendly voice. You said we're from Earth. So we're not on Earth now, is what you're saying? Over."

There was a pause, then the voice crackled over the room's speakers. "Sorry, my friend, but you're on Amtor . . . or as we Earthmen call it, Venus."

About the Author

A professional writer and illustrator for over thirty years, MIKE WOLFER has been a key talent working on dozens of canonical Edgar Rice Burroughs Universe comic books, including Jane Porter, Victory Harben, Beyond the Farthest Star, Pellucidar, The Land That Time Forgot, The Monster Men, and The Moon Maid. He has also authored the ERB Universe novelettes "Victory Harben: Clash on Caspak" and "Beyond the Farthest Star: Rescue on Zandar." Best known for his Widow series, Wolfer is the creator of the Daughters of the Dark Oracle franchise, and has contributed to numerous comics series based on licensed properties.

EDGAR RICE BURROUGHS:
MASTER OF ADVENTURE

The creator of the immortal characters Tarzan of the Apes and John Carter of Mars, EDGAR RICE BURROUGHS is one of the world's most popular authors. Mr. Burroughs' timeless tales of heroes and heroines transport readers from the jungles of Africa and the dead sea bottoms of Barsoom to the miles-high forests of Amtor and the savage inner world of Pellucidar, and even to alien civilizations beyond the farthest star. Mr. Burroughs' books are estimated to have sold hundreds of millions of copies, and they have spawned 60 films and 250 television episodes.

About Edgar Rice Burroughs, Inc.

Founded in 1923 by Edgar Rice Burroughs, one of the first authors to incorporate himself, EDGAR RICE BURROUGHS, INC., holds numerous trademarks and the rights to all literary works of the author still protected by copyright, including stories of Tarzan of the Apes and John Carter of Mars. The company oversees authorized adaptations of his literary works in film, television, radio, publishing, theatrical stage productions, licensing, and merchandising. Edgar Rice Burroughs, Inc., continues to manage and license the vast archive of Mr. Burroughs' literary works, fictional characters, and corresponding artworks that has grown for over a century. The company is still owned by the Burroughs family and remains headquartered in Tarzana, California, the town named after the Tarzana Ranch Mr. Burroughs purchased there in 1919 that led to the town's future development.

In 2015, under the leadership of President James Sullos, the company relaunched its publishing division, which was founded by Mr. Burroughs in 1931. With the publication of new authorized editions of Mr. Burroughs' works and brand-new novels and stories by today's talented authors, the company continues its long tradition of bringing tales of wonder and imagination featuring the Master of Adventure's many iconic characters and exotic worlds to an eager reading public.

Visit **EdgarRiceBurroughs.com** for more information.

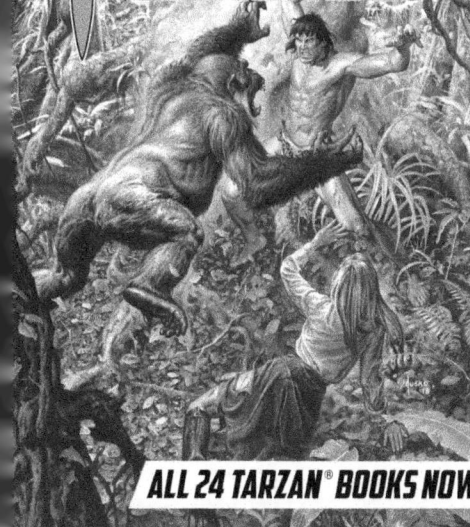

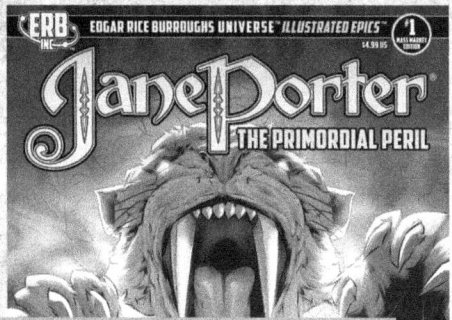

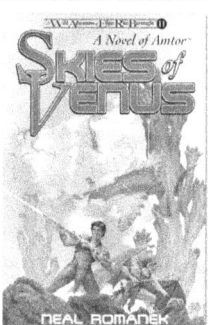

Edgar Rice Burroughs, Inc.

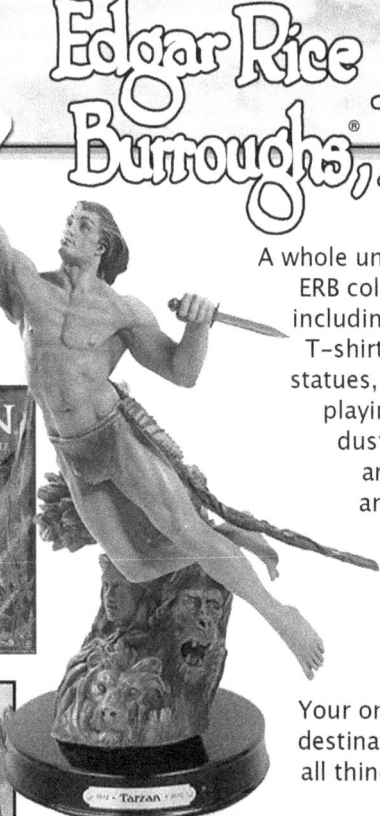

A whole universe of ERB collectibles, including books, T-shirts, DVDs, statues, puzzles, playing cards, dust jackets, art prints, and MORE!

Your one-stop destination for all things ERB!

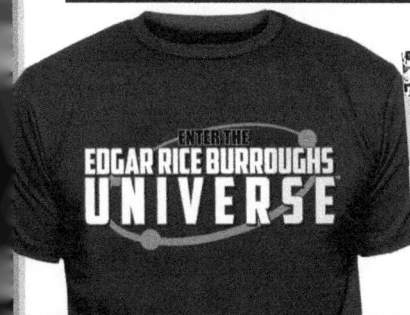

ERB INC.

VISIT US ONLINE AT ERBURROUGHS.COM

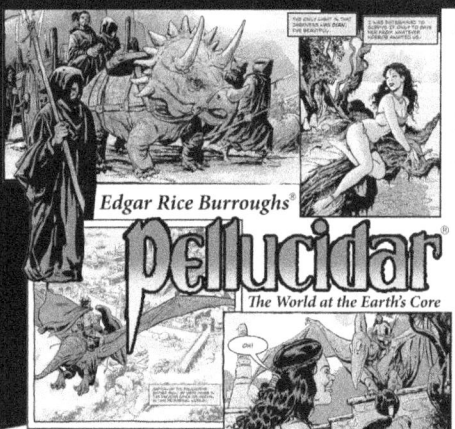

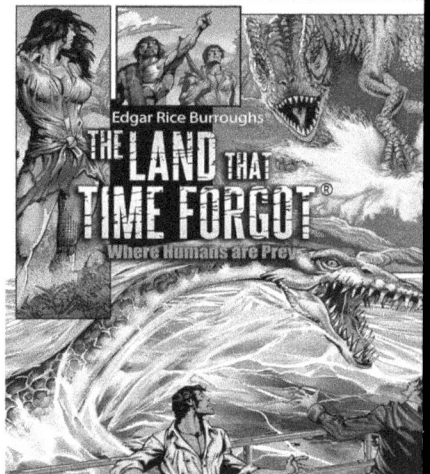

www.ingramcontent.com/pod-product-compliance
Ingram Content Group UK Ltd.
Pitfield, Milton Keynes, MK11 3LW, UK
UKHW040620130225
4576UKWH00015B/145

9 781945 462764